Her Last Breath

Bestselling author Linda Castillo has always known she wanted to be a writer and penned her first novel at the age of thirteen. She is the winner of numerous industry awards, including the Holt Medallion, the Golden Heart, the Daphne du Maurier and a nomination for the prestigious Rita. She lives in Texas with her husband, four loveable dogs, two barn cats, and two Appaloosa horses.

Also by Linda Castillo

Sworn to Silence

Pray for Silence

Breaking Silence

Gone Missing

Her Last Breath

LINDA CASTILLO

PAN BOOKS

First published 2013 by St Martin's Press, 175 Fifth Avenue, New York, N.Y. 10010

First published in the UK 2013 by Macmillan
This edition published 2014 by Pan Books
an imprint of Pan Macmillan, a division of Macmillan Publishers Limited
Pan Macmillan, 20 New Wharf Road, London N1 9RR
Basingstoke and Oxford
Associated companies throughout the world
www.panmacmillan.com

ISBN 978-1-4472-0216-5

This is a work of fiction. All of the characters, organizations, and events portrayed in
the novel are either products of the author's imagination or are used fictitiously.

1 3 5 7 9 8 6 4 2

A CIP catalogue record for this book is available from the British Library.

Typeset by Ellipsis Digital Limited, Glasgow
Printed and bound by CPI Group (UK) Ltd, Croydon, CR0 4YY

Visit www.panmacmillan.com to read more about all our books
and to buy them. You will also find features, author interviews and
news of any author events, and you can sign up for e-newsletters
so that you're always first to hear about our new releases.

This book is dedicated to all of the people
who've read and loved the books.

Acknowledgements

As is always the case when I complete a book, I have many people to thank for helping to make it happen. First and foremost, I wish to thank the usual suspects: The outstanding publishing professionals at Minotaur Books: Charles Spicer. Sally Richardson. Andrew Martin. Matthew Shear. Matthew Baldacci. Jeanne-Marie Hudson. Stephanie Davis. Sarah Melnyk. Hector DeJean. Kerry Nordling. April Osborn. David Rotstein. Thank you for your ideas, your endless hours of hard work, your support, and your undying enthusiasm for the Kate Burkholder series. I hope you know how much I appreciate each and every one of you.

I also wish to thank some of the behind-the-scenes folks who, in the course of my writing *Her Last Breath*, went above and beyond to broaden my knowledge of the Amish culture. Heartfelt thanks to Denise Campbell-Johnson with the Dover Public Library for sharing your knowledge of the Amish with me and especially for those two fun-filled days in Ohio's Amish Country. I appreciate your taking time out of your busy schedule to hang out and show me around.

Many thanks to Mark and Salome Oliver of Millersburg, Ohio, for inviting me into your home and offering me a glimpse of your lives. It was such a pleasure to sit and chat, and I very much appreciated the opportunity to drive your buggy. I hope you could tell by the smile on my face that I loved every minute!

Thank you to my other Amish friends in Millersburg, Ohio, for opening your home to me. I enjoyed our dinner and the tour of your beautiful farm.

I also wish to thank John and Janet Shafer of Killbuck, Ohio, for all of the research material you've shared with me over the years. Every story begins with an idea and you have supplied me with scores. In return, I can only hope to bring you many more hours of reading enjoyment.

Once again, I'd also like to shout out a huge thank-you to Chief Dan Light of the Arcanum Ohio Police Department, for his insights and ideas with regard to motor vehicle accidents. As always, any procedural errors are mine.

I'd like to thank my agent, Nancy Yost, for pulling off the impossible and making it look easy. You are the best of the best.

Many thanks to the Divas: Jennifer Archer, Anita Howard, Marcy McKay, and April Redmon.

Thank you to my author friends Jennifer Miller and Catherine Spangler for all the support over the years. What a journey it's been!

Finally, I'd like to thank my husband, Ernest, who has been by my side every step of the way. I love you.

The cruelest lies are often told in silence.

—Robert Louis Stevenson,
Virginibus Puerisque

Prologue

The clip-clop of the standardbred's shod hooves against asphalt echoed within the canopy of the trees. Paul Borntrager had purchased the four-year-old gelding at the horse auction in Millersburg six months ago – against his better judgment. His daughter, Norah, promptly named the animal Sampson – after the world's largest horse – because he was so big and strong. Fresh off the racetrack, Sampson had been a challenge at first, breaking his gait and spooking at cars and loose dogs. But after six months of training and a lot of miles, the horse turned out to be a good investment. Now, Sampson was one of the fastest trotters he'd ever owned and a pleasure to drive. Paul was glad he'd taken a chance on the animal.

The leather reins were solid, but soft in his hands. The jingle of the harness and the rhythmic creaking of the buggy lulled Paul into a state of quiet contemplation. The children had behaved well this afternoon, even though they had to wait more than an hour for their appointment at the clinic. They were silent now, but only because he'd stopped at the Dairy Dream and bought them ice cream cones. The instant they finished, he was certain the chatter and games would return. The thought made him smile. It had been a good day.

Dusk was fast approaching and the low clouds were spitting

drizzle. He hoped it rained; the drought had been tough on the crops over the summer. Clucking, giving the reins a sharp snap, he pushed Sampson into an extended trot. Though he'd added battery-powered taillights and affixed a reflective slow-moving-vehicle sign to the rear of the buggy, Paul didn't like being on the road after dark. The *Englischers* were always in a hurry and drove too fast. Half of the time they didn't pay attention where they were going, especially with all the cell phones and texting they did.

'Look, *Datt! Die sunn is am unnergeh!*'

Smiling at the voice of his four-year-old son, Paul glanced to his right. Through the blood-red foliage of the maples, elms, and black walnut trees that grew alongside the road, glowing pink fingers of the setting sun speared through deepening clouds. 'The Lord blessed us with another beautiful day, eh?'

'*Datt,* David won't botch with me,' came six-year-old Norah's voice from the rear of the buggy.

Botching was a clapping game their *mamm* had been teaching young Norah for the last few days. The girl had been pestering her older brother to play with her since. 'I think he must be busy eating his ice cream,' Paul offered.

'But he's finished.'

David, his oldest child at eight years of age, poked his head out from the interior of the buggy and looked up at him. 'Botching is for girls, *Datt.* Don't make me play with her.'

Paul glanced over his shoulder at his daughter. 'He has a point, Norah.'

She came up beside her brother and set her hand on his shoulder. Paul saw a sticky-looking patch of melted chocolate ice cream on her knuckles. 'I won't tell anyone,' she said with grave seriousness.

That made Paul laugh. Love for his children moved through him with such power his chest ached. Not for the first time that day, he thanked God for all of the blessings bestowed upon him.

'We're almost home,' he said. 'Why don't you sing one of the botching songs instead?' He posed the question absently; they were coming upon a blind intersection. He liked to be ready in case Sampson spooked.

Tightening his grip on the reins, Paul craned his head forward to check for oncoming traffic. The trees were too thick to see, but there was no telltale glow of headlights. He didn't hear an engine or the hiss of tires against the pavement. It was safe to proceed.

In the rear of the buggy, Norah began to sing *Pop Goes the Weasel*.

> *'All around the mulberry bush.*
> *The monkey chased the weasel.*
> *The monkey stopped to pull up his sock . . .'*

Paul could hear the children clapping now, and he knew Norah had persuaded her older brother to play. He smiled to himself; she was quite the little negotiator and strong willed, like her mother.

They were nearly to the intersection and wholly alone on the road. Clucking to Sampson to pick up the pace, Paul began to sing along with the children.

> *'All around the chicken coop,*
> *the possum chased the weasel.'*

The roar of an engine came out of nowhere, with the sudden violence of a jet falling from the sky. Paul caught a glimpse of the screaming black beast to his right. A knife slash of adrenaline streaked across his belly. A deep stab of fear. Too late, he hauled back on the reins, shouted, 'Whoa!'

The horse's steel shoes slid on the asphalt.

The impact jolted him violently. He heard the *crash!* of splintering fiberglass and wood. A hot streak of pain in his side. And then he was airborne. Around him, the buggy exploded into a hundred pieces. Paul thought he heard a child's cry and then the ground rushed up and slammed into him.

The next thing he knew he was on the ground with his face pressed against the earth. Dry grass scratching his cheek. The taste of blood in his mouth. The knowledge that he was badly injured trickling into his brain. But all he could think about was the children. Where were they? Why were they silent? He had to go to them, make sure they were all right.

Please, dear Lord, watch over my children.

He tried to move, groaning with the effort, but his body refused the command. Unable to move or speak, he listened for the children's voices, their cries, for any sign of life, but he heard only silence, the tinkle of rain against the asphalt, and the whisper of wind through the trees.

ONE

When it rains, it pours. Those words were one of my *mamm*'s favorite maxims when I was growing up. As a child, I didn't understand its true meaning, and I didn't spend much time trying to figure it out. In the eyes of the Amish girl I'd been, more was almost always a good thing. The world around me was a swiftly moving river, chock-full of white-water rapids and deep holes filled with secrets I couldn't fathom. I was ravenous to raft that river, anxious to dive into all of those dark crevices and unravel their closely guarded secrets. It wasn't until I entered my twenties that I realized there were times when that river overflowed its banks and a killing flood ensued.

My *mamm* is gone now and I haven't been Amish for fifteen years, but I often find myself using that old adage, particularly when it comes to police work and, oftentimes, my life.

I've been on duty since 3:00 P.M. and my police radio has been eerily quiet for a Friday, not only in Painters Mill proper, but the entirety of Holmes County. I made one stop and issued a speeding citation, mainly because it was a repeat offense and the eighteen-year-old driver is going to end up killing someone if he doesn't slow down. I've spent the last hour cruising the back-streets, trying not to dwell on anything too serious, namely a state law enforcement agent by the name of John Tomasetti and a relationship that's become a lot more complicated than I ever intended.

We met during the Slaughterhouse Murders investigation almost two years ago. It was a horrific case: A serial killer had staked his claim in Painters Mill, leaving a score of dead in his wake. Tomasetti, an agent with the Ohio Bureau of Identification and Investigation, was sent here to assist. The situation was made worse by my personal involvement in the case. They were the worst circumstances imaginable, especially for the start of a relationship, professional or otherwise. Somehow, what could have become a debacle of biblical proportion, grew into something fresh and good and completely unexpected. We're still trying to figure out how to define this bond we've created between us. I think he's doing a better job of it than I am.

That's the thing about relationships; no matter how hard you try to keep things simple, all of those gnarly complexities have a way of seeping into the mix. Tomasetti and I have arrived at a crossroads of sorts, and I sense change on the wind. Of course, change isn't always a negative. But it's rarely easy. The indecision can eat at you, especially when you've arrived at an important junction and you're not sure which way to go – and you know in your heart that each path will take you in a vastly different direction.

I'm not doing a very good job of keeping my troubles at bay, and I find myself falling back into another old habit I acquired from my days on patrol: wishing for a little chaos. A bar fight would do. Or maybe a domestic dispute. Sans serious injury, of course. I don't know what it says about me that I'd rather face off with a couple of pissed-off drunks than look too hard at the things going on in my own life.

I've just pulled into the parking lot of LaDonna's Diner for a BLT and a cup of dark roast to go when the voice of my second shift dispatcher cracks over the radio.

'Six two three.'

I pick up my mike. 'What do you have, Jodie?'

'Chief, I just took a nine one one from Andy Welbaum. He says there's a bad wreck on Delisle Road at CR 14.'

'Anyone hurt?' Dinner forgotten, I glance in my rearview mirror and make a U-turn in the gravel lot.

'There's a buggy involved. He says it's bad.'

'Get an ambulance out there. Notify Holmes County.' Cursing, I make a left on Main, hit my emergency lights and siren. The engine groans as I crank the speedometer up to fifty. 'I'm ten seventy-six.'

I'm doing sixty by the time I leave the corporation limit of Painters Mill. Within seconds, the radio lights up as the call goes out to the Holmes County sheriff's office. I make a left on Delisle Road, a twisty stretch of asphalt that cuts through thick woods. It's a scenic drive during the day, but treacherous as hell at night, especially with so many deer in the area.

County Road 14 intersects a mile down the road. The Explorer's engine groans as I crank the speedometer to seventy. Mailboxes and the black trunks of trees fly by outside my window. I crest a hill and spot the headlights of a single vehicle ahead. No ambulance or sheriff's cruiser yet; I'm first on scene.

I'm twenty yards from the intersection when I recognize Andy Welbaum's pickup truck. He lives a few miles from here. Probably coming home from work at the plant in Millersburg. The truck is parked at a haphazard angle on the shoulder, as if he came to an abrupt and unexpected stop. The headlights are trained on what looks like the shattered remains of a four-wheeled buggy. There's no horse in sight; either it ran home or it's down. Judging from the condition of the buggy, I'm betting on the latter.

'Shit.' I brake hard. My tires skid on the gravel shoulder. Leaving my emergency lights flashing, I hit my high beams for light and jam the Explorer into park. Quickly, I grab a couple of flares from the back, snatch up my Maglite, and then I'm out of the vehicle. Snapping open the flares, I scatter them on the road to alert oncoming traffic. Then I start toward the buggy.

My senses go into hyperalert as I approach, several details striking me at once. A sorrel horse lies on its side on the southwest corner of the intersection, still harnessed but unmoving. Thirty feet away, a badly damaged buggy has been flipped onto its side. It's been broken in half, but it's not a clean break. I see splintered wood, two missing wheels, and a ten-yard-wide swath of debris – pieces of fiberglass and wood scattered about. I take in other details, too. A child's shoe. A flat-brimmed hat lying amid brown grass and dried leaves . . .

My mind registers all of this in a fraction of a second, and I know it's going to be bad. Worse than bad. It will be a miracle if anyone survived.

I'm midway to the buggy when I spot the first casualty. It's a child, I realize, and everything grinds to a halt, as if someone threw a switch inside my head and the world winds down into slow motion.

'Fuck. *Fuck.*' I rush to the victim, drop to my knees. It's a little girl. Six or seven years old. She's wearing a blue dress. Her *kapp* is askew and soaked with blood and I think: *head injury.*

'Sweetheart.' The word comes out as a strangled whisper.

The child lies in a supine position with her arms splayed. Her pudgy hands are open and relaxed. Her face is so serene she might have been sleeping. But her skin is gray. Blue lips are open, revealing tiny baby teeth. Already her eyes are cloudy and unfocused. I see bare feet and I realize the force of the impact tore off her shoes.

Working on autopilot, I hit my lapel mike, put out the call for a 10-50F. A fatality accident. I stand, aware that my legs are shaking. My stomach seesaws, and I swallow something that tastes like vinegar. Around me, the night is so quiet I hear the ticking of the truck's engine a few yards away. Even the crickets and night birds have gone silent as if in reverence to the violence that transpired here scant minutes before.

Insects fly in the beams of the headlights. In the periphery of my thoughts, I'm aware of someone crying. I shine my beam in the direction of the sound, and spot Andy Welbaum sitting on the ground near the truck with his face in his hands, sobbing. His chest heaves, and sounds I barely recognize as human emanate from his mouth.

I call out to him. 'Andy, are you hurt?'

He looks up at me, as if wondering why I would ask him such a thing. 'No.'

'How many in the buggy? Did you check?' I'm on my feet and looking around for more passengers, when I spot another victim.

I don't hear Andy's response as I start toward the Amish man lying on the grassy shoulder. He's in a prone position with his head turned to one side. He's wearing a black coat and dark trousers. I try not to look at the ocean of blood that has soaked into the grass around him or the way his left leg is twisted with the foot pointing in the wrong direction. He's conscious and watches me approach with one eye.

I kneel at his side. 'Everything's going to be okay,' I tell him. 'You've been in an accident. I'm here to help you.'

His mouth opens. His lips quiver. His full beard tells me he's married, and I wonder if his wife is lying somewhere nearby.

I set my hand on his. Cold flesh beneath my fingertips. 'How many other people on board the buggy?'

'Three . . . children.'

Something inside me sinks. I don't want to find any more dead children. I pat his hand. 'Help is on the way.'

His gaze meets mine. 'Katie . . .'

The sound of my name coming from that bloody mouth shocks me. I know that voice. That face. Recognition impacts me solidly. It's been years, but there are some things – some people – you never forget. Paul Borntrager is one of them. 'Paul.' Even as I say his name, I steel myself against the emotional force of it.

He tries to speak, but ends up spitting blood. I see more on his teeth. But it's his eye that's so damn difficult to look at. One is gone completely; the other is cognizant and filled with pain. I know the person trapped inside that broken body. I know his wife. I know at least one of his kids is dead, and I'm terrified he'll see that awful truth in my face.

'Don't try to talk,' I tell him. 'I'm going to check the children.'

Tears fill his eye. I feel his stare burning into me as I rise and move away. Quickly, I sweep my beam along the ground, looking for victims. I'm aware of sirens in the distance and relief slips through me that help is on the way. I know it's a cowardly response, but I don't want to deal with this alone.

I think of Paul's wife, Mattie. A lifetime ago, she was my best friend. We haven't spoken in twenty years; she may be a stranger to me now, but I honestly don't think I could bear it if she died here tonight.

Mud sucks at my boots as I cross the ditch. On the other side, I spot a tiny figure curled against the massive trunk of a maple tree. A boy of about four years of age. He looks like a little doll, small and vulnerable and fragile. Hope jumps through me when I see steam rising into the cold night air. At first, I think it's vapor from his breath. But as I draw closer I realize with a burgeoning sense of horror that it's not a sign of life, but death. He's bled out and the steam is coming from the blood as it cools.

I go to him anyway, kneel at his side, and all I can think

when I look at his battered face is that this should never happen to a child. His eyes and mouth are open. A wound the size of my fist has peeled back the flesh on one side of his head.

Sickened, I close my eyes. 'Goddammit,' I choke as I get to my feet.

I stand there for a moment, surrounded by the dead and dying, overwhelmed, repulsed by the bloodshed, and filled with impotent anger because this kind of carnage shouldn't happen and yet it has, in my town, on my watch, and there's not a damn thing I can do to save any of them.

Trying hard to step back into myself and do my job, I run my beam around the scene. A breeze rattles the tree branches above me and a smattering of leaves float down. Fingers of fog rise within the thick underbrush and I find myself thinking of souls leaving bodies.

A whimper yanks me from my stasis. I spin, jerk my beam left. I see something tangled against the tumbling wire fence that runs along the tree line. Another child. I break into a run. From twenty feet away I see it's a boy. Eight or nine years old. Hope surges inside me when I hear him groan. It's a pitiful sound that echoes through me like the electric pain of a broken bone. But it's a good sound, too, because it tells me he's alive.

I drop to my knees at his side, set my flashlight on the ground beside me. The child is lying on his side with his left arm stretched over his head and twisted at a terrible angle. *Dislocated shoulder,* I think. Broken arm, maybe. Survivable, but I've worked enough accidents to know it's usually the injuries you can't see that end up being the worst.

One side of his face is visible. His eyes are open; I can see the curl of lashes against his cheek as he blinks. Flecks of blood cover his chin and throat and the front of his coat. There's blood on his face, but I don't know where it's coming from; I can't pinpoint the source.

Tentatively, I reach out and run my fingertips over the top of his hand, hoping the contact will comfort him. 'Honey, can you hear me?'

He moans. I hear his breaths rushing in and out between clenched teeth. He's breathing hard. Hyperventilating. His hand twitches beneath mine and he cries out.

'Don't try to move, sweetie,' I say. 'You were in an accident, but you're going to be okay.' As I speak, I try to put myself in his shoes, conjure words that will comfort him. 'My name's Katie. I'm here to help you. Your *datt*'s okay. And the doctor is coming. Just be still and try to relax for me, okay?'

His small body heaves. He chokes out a sound and flecks of blood spew from his mouth. I hear gurgling in his chest, and close my eyes tightly, fighting to stay calm. *Don't you dare take this one, too,* a little voice inside my head snaps.

The urge to gather him into my arms and pull him from the fence in which he's tangled is powerful. But I know better than to move an accident victim. If he sustained a head or spinal injury, moving him could cause even more damage. Or kill him.

The boy stares straight ahead, blinking. Still breathing hard. Chest rattling. He doesn't move, doesn't try to look at me. '. . . Sampson . . .' he whispers.

I don't know who that is; I'm not even sure I heard him right or if he's cognizant and knows what he's saying. It doesn't matter. I rub my thumb over the top of his hand. 'Shhh.' I lean close. 'Don't try to talk.'

He shifts slightly, turns his head. His eyes find mine. They're gray. *Like Mattie's,* I realize. In their depths I see fear and the kind of pain no child should ever have to bear. His lips tremble. Tears stream from his eyes. 'Hurts . . .'

'Everything's going to be okay.' I force a smile, but my lips feel like barbed wire.

A faint smile touches his mouth and then his expression

goes slack. Beneath my hand, I feel his body relax. His stare goes vacant.

'Hey.' I squeeze his hand, willing him not to slip away. 'Stay with me, buddy.'

He doesn't answer.

The sirens are closer now. I hear the rumble of the diesel engine as a fire truck arrives on scene. The hiss of tires against the wet pavement as more vehicles pull onto the shoulder. The shouts of the first responders as they disembark.

'Over here!' I yell. 'I've got an injured child!'

I stay with the boy until the first paramedic comes up behind me. 'We'll take it from here, Chief.'

He's about my age, with a crew cut and blue jacket inscribed with the Holmes County Rescue insignia. He looks competent and well trained, with a trauma kit slung over his shoulder and a cervical collar beneath his arm.

'He was conscious a minute ago,' I tell the paramedic.

'We'll take good care of him, Chief.'

Rising, I take a step back to get out of the way.

He kneels at the child's side. 'I need a backboard over here!' he shouts over his shoulder.

Close on his heels, a young firefighter snaps open a reflective thermal blanket and goes around to the other side of the boy. A third paramedic trots through the ditch with a bright yellow backboard in tow.

I leave them to their work and hit my lapel mike. 'Jodie, can you ten seventy-nine?' *Notify coroner.*

'Roger that.'

I glance over my shoulder to the place where I left Paul Borntrager. A firefighter kneels at his side, assessing him. I can't see the Amish man's face, but he's not moving.

Firefighters and paramedics swarm the area, treating the injured and looking for more victims. Any cop that has ever worked patrol knows that passengers who don't utilize safety belts – which is always the case with a buggy – can be ejected a long distance, especially if speed is a factor. When I was a rookie in Columbus, I worked an accident in which a semi truck went off the road and flipped end over end down a one-hundred-foot ravine. The driver, who'd been belted in, was seriously injured, but survived. His wife, who hadn't been wearing her safety belt, was ejected over two hundred feet. The officers on scene – me included – didn't find her for nearly twenty minutes. Afterward, the coroner told me that if we'd gotten to her sooner, she might have survived. Nobody ever talked about that accident again. But it stayed with me, and I never forgot the lesson it taught.

Wondering if Mattie was a passenger, I establish a mental grid of the scene. Starting at the point of impact, I walk the area, looking for casualties, working my way outward in all directions. I don't find any more victims.

When I'm finished, I drift back to where I left Paul, expecting to find him being loaded onto a litter. I'm shocked to see a blue tarp draped over his body, rain tapping against it, and I realize he's died.

I know better than to let this get to me. I haven't talked to Paul or Mattie in years. But I feel something ugly and unwieldy building inside me. Anger at the driver responsible. Grief because Paul is dead and Mattie must be told. The pain of knowing I'll probably be the one to do it.

'Oh, Mattie,' I whisper.

A lifetime ago, we were inseparable – more like sisters than friends. We shared first crushes, first 'singings,' and our first heartbreaks. Mattie was there for me during the summer of my fourteenth year when an Amish man named Daniel Lapp introduced me to violence. My life was irrevocably changed that day, but our friendship remained a constant. When I turned eighteen and made the decision to leave the Plain Life, Mattie was one of the few who supported me, even though she knew it would mean the end of our friendship.

We lost touch after I left Painters Mill. Our lives took different paths and never crossed again. I went on to complete my education and become a police officer. Mattie joined the church, married Paul, and started a family. For years, we've been little more than acquaintances, rarely sharing anything more than a wave on the street. But I never forgot those formative years, when summer lasted forever, the future held infinite promise – and we still believed in dreams.

Dreams that, for one of us, ended tonight.

I walk to Andy Welbaum's truck. It's an older Dodge with patches of rust on the hood. A crease on the rear quarter panel. Starting with the front bumper, I circle the vehicle, checking for damage. But there's nothing there. Only then do I realize this truck wasn't involved in the accident.

I find Andy leaning against the front bumper of a nearby Holmes County ambulance. Someone has given him a slicker. He's no longer crying, but he's shaking beneath the yellow vinyl.

He looks at me when I approach. He's about forty years old and balding, with circles the size of plums beneath hound dog eyes. 'That kid going to be okay?' he asks.

'I don't know.' The words come out sounding bitchy, and I take a moment to rein in my emotions. 'What happened?'

'I was coming home from work like I always do. Slowed down to turn onto the county road and saw all that busted-up wood and stuff scattered all over the place. I got out to see what happened . . .' Shaking his head, he looks down at his feet. 'Chief Burkholder, I swear to God I ain't never seen anything like that before in my life. All them kids. Damn.' He looks like he's going to start crying again. 'Poor family.'

'So your vehicle wasn't involved in the accident?'

'No, ma'am. It had already happened when I got here.'

'Did you witness it?'

'No.' He looks at me, grimaces. 'I think it musta just happened though. I swear to God the dust was still flying when I pulled up.'

'Did you see any other vehicles?'

'No.' He says the word with some heat. 'I suspect that sumbitch hightailed it.'

'What happened next?'

'I called nine one one. Then I went over to see if I could help any of them. I was a medic in the Army way back, you know.' He falls silent, looks down at the ground. 'There was nothing I could do.'

I nod, struggling to keep a handle on my outrage. I'm pissed because someone killed three people – two of whom were children – injured a third, and left the scene without bothering to render aid or even call for help.

I let out a sigh. 'I'm sorry I snapped at you.'

'I don't blame you. I don't see how you cops deal with stuff like this day in and day out. I hope you find the bastard that done it.'

'I'm going to need a statement from you. Can you hang around for a little while longer?'

'You bet. I'll stay as long as you need me.'

I turn away from him and start toward the road to see a Holmes County sheriff's department cruiser glide onto the shoulder, lights flashing. An ambulance pulls away, transporting the only survivor to the hospital. Later, the coroner's office will deal with the dead.

I step over a chunk of wood from the buggy. The black paint contrasts sharply against the pale yellow of the naked wood beneath. A few feet away, I see a little girl's shoe. Farther, a tattered afghan. Eyeglasses.

This is now a crime scene. Though the investigation will

likely fall under the jurisdiction of the Holmes County Sheriff's office, I'm going to do my utmost to stay involved. Rasmussen won't have a problem with it. Not only will my Amish background be a plus, but his department, like mine, works on a skeleton crew, and he'll appreciate all the help he can get.

Now that the injured boy has been transported, any evidence left behind will need to be preserved and documented. We'll need to bring in a generator and work lights. If the sheriff's department doesn't have a deputy trained in accident reconstruction, we'll request one from the State Highway Patrol.

I think of Mattie Borntrager, at home, waiting for her husband and children, and I realize I'll need to notify her as soon as possible.

I'm on my way to speak with the paramedics for an update on the condition of the injured boy when someone calls out my name. I turn to see my officer, Rupert 'Glock' Maddox, approaching me at a jog. 'I got here as quick as I could,' he says. 'What happened?'

I tell him what little I know. 'The driver skipped.'

'Shit.' He looks at the ambulance. 'Any survivors?'

'One,' I tell him. 'A little boy. Eight or nine years old.'

'He gonna make it?'

'I don't know.'

His eyes meet mine and a silent communication passes between us, a mutual agreement we arrive upon without uttering a word. When you're a cop in a small town, you become protective of the citizens you've been sworn to serve and protect, especially the innocent, the kids. When something like this happens, you take it personally. I've known Glock long enough to know that sentiment runs deep in him, too.

We start toward the intersection, trying to get a sense of what happened. Delisle Road runs in a north-south direction; County Road 14 runs east-west with a two-way stop. The speed limit is fifty-five miles per hour. The area is heavily wooded and hilly. If you're approaching the intersection from any direction, it's impossible to see oncoming traffic.

Glock speaks first. 'Looks like the buggy was southbound on Delisle Road.'

I nod in agreement. 'The second vehicle was running west on CR 14. Probably at a high rate of speed. Blew the stop sign. Broadsided the buggy.'

His eyes drift toward the intersection. 'Fucking T-boned them.'

'Didn't even pause to call nine one one.'

He grimaces. 'Probably alcohol related.'

'Most hit-and-runs are.'

Craning his neck, he eyeballs Andy Welbaum. 'He a witness?'

'First on scene. He's pretty shaken up.' I look past him at the place where the wrecked buggy lies on its side. 'Whatever hit that buggy is going to have a smashed up front end. I put out a BOLO for an unknown with damage.'

He looks out over the carnage. 'Did you know them, Chief?'

'A long time ago,' I tell him. 'I'm going to pick up the bishop and head over to their farm to notify next of kin. Do me a favor and get Welbaum's statement, will you?'

'You got it.'

I feel his eyes on me, but I don't meet his gaze. I don't want to share the mix of emotions inside me at the devastation that's been brought down on this Amish family. I don't want him to know the extent of the sadness I feel or my anger toward the perpetrator.

To my relief, he looks away, lets it go. 'I'd better get to work.' He taps his lapel mike. 'Call me if you need anything.'

I watch him walk away, then turn my attention back to the scene. I take in the wreckage of the buggy. The small pieces of the victims' lives that are strewn about like trash. And I wonder what kind of person could do something like this and not stop to render aid or call for help.

'You better hide good, you son of a bitch, because I'm coming for you.'

TWO

One of the most difficult responsibilities of being chief is noti-
fying next of kin when someone is killed. It's a duty I've carried
out several times in the course of my career. I want to believe
experience has somehow made me more compassionate or better
at softening that first devastating hammer blow of grief. But I
know this is one of those occasions when past experience doesn't
count for shit.

My headlights slice through the darkness as I speed down
the long gravel lane of Bishop Troyer's farm. There's no lantern
light in the windows. It's not yet 9:00 P.M., but they've probably
been asleep for hours. I park next to a ramshackle shed, grab my
Maglite, and take the sidewalk to the back door. I know the
bedrooms are upstairs, and the Troyers are getting up in years,
so I open the screen door and use the Maglite to knock.

Several minutes pass before I see movement inside. Then the
door swings open and the bishop thrusts a lantern at me. He
blinks at me owlishly. 'Katie Burkholder?'

I've known Bishop Troyer most of my life. When I was a
teenager, I thought he was a judgmental, mean-spirited bastard
who had it out for me because I was different – and different
isn't ever a good thing when you're Amish. No matter how
minor my offense, he never seemed to cut me any slack. More

than once he took a hard line when I broke the rules. Now that I'm older, I've come to see him as fair-minded and kind, traits he balances with unyielding convictions, especially when it comes to the rules set forth by the *Ordnung,* or the unwritten rules of the church district. We've butted heads a few times since I've been chief. He doesn't approve of my leaving the fold; he certainly doesn't appreciate my lifestyle or some of the choices I've made. But while he never hesitates to express his disapproval, I know if I ever found myself in crisis, he'd be the first in line to help me.

Tonight, it's Mattie Borntrager who's in crisis. She's going to need his faith and strength to get through the coming hours. I know he'll be there for her, too.

'*Was der schinner is letz?*' he asks in a wet-gravel voice. *What in the world is wrong?*

I stare at him for the span of several seconds, trying to put my thoughts in order and get the words out. We need to get over to the Borntrager farm stat and relay the news to Mattie before she finds out secondhand from someone else. I need to get back to the scene so I can get a jump on what promises to be a long and grueling investigation. Instead, I do the one thing I've never done in all of my years as a cop and burst into tears.

'*Katie?*'

I try to disguise that first telltale sob as a cough and noisily clear my throat. But the tears that follow betray me.

Shock flashes on the bishop's face, followed quickly by sharp concern. 'Come inside.'

I hold up my hand, angry with myself for breaking down at a time like this. I remind myself this isn't about me or my emotions, but a young mother whose world is about to be shattered. 'Paul Borntrager and two of his children were killed tonight,' I tell him.

'Paul?' He presses a hand against his chest, steps back as if pushed by some invisible force. 'The children? But how?'

Quickly, I tell him about the buggy accident. 'Mattie doesn't know yet, Bishop. I need to tell her. I thought it would be helpful if you were there.'

'Yes, of course.' He looks shaken as he glances down at the long flannel sleeping shirt he's wearing. 'I need to dress.' But he makes no move to leave. 'Which child survived?' he asks.

'A boy. The oldest child, I think.'

'David.' He nods. *Mein Gott.* Is he going to be all right?'

'I don't know. They took him to the hospital.' Mortified that I lost control of my emotions, I use the sleeve of my jacket to wipe away the tears.

Reaching out, he squeezes my arm. 'Katie, remember God always has a plan. It is not our place to question, but to accept.'

The words are intended to comfort me, but I wince. The tenet of acceptance is one of the belief systems I disagreed with most when I was Amish. Maybe because my own philosophy differs so profoundly. I refuse to accept the deaths of three innocent people as part of some big divine plan. I sure as hell don't plan on forgiving the son of a bitch responsible.

Ten minutes later, Bishop Troyer and I are in my Explorer, heading toward the Borntrager farm. Dread rides shotgun, a dark presence whose breath is like ice on the back of my neck.

Glock called while I was waiting for the bishop and informed me that one of Sheriff Rasmussen's deputies is a certified accident reconstructionist, which will be extremely beneficial in terms of resources. It will also allow us to restrict the investigation to two jurisdictions: the Holmes County Sheriff's Department and the Painters Mill PD. I'm not territorial when it comes to my job. If an outside agency offers the resources I need, I'll be the first in line to ask for help. But in all honesty, I'm relieved to keep this case in house because I don't want to share.

The Borntrager farm is located on a dirt road that dead ends at a heavily wooded area that backs up to the greenbelt along Painters Creek. Neither the bishop nor I speak as I turn onto the gravel lane and start toward the house. It's almost nine thirty now; Paul and the children should have been home hours ago. I suspect Mattie is out of her mind with worry.

I notice the yellow glow of lantern light in the kitchen as I make the turn and the rear of the house comes into view. I imagine Mattie inside, pacing from room to room, wondering where her family is and trying to decide if she should walk to the neighbor's house to use the phone. I hate it, but I'm about to make her worst nightmare a reality. . . .

My headlights wash over the falling-down wire fence of a chicken coop as I park. Disturbed by the light, two bantam hens flutter down from their roost, clucking their outrage.

'What are the names and ages of her children?' I don't look at the bishop as I shut down the engine.

'David is eight,' he tells me. 'Samuel was the youngest. About four years old, I think. Norah just turned six.'

Grabbing my Maglite, I swing open the door and slide from the Explorer. I'm in the process of going around the front end to open the door for the bishop to help him out when I hear the screen door slam. I look toward the house to see Mattie Borntrager rush down the steps, her dress swishing at her calves, a lantern thrust out in front of her.

'Hello?' she calls out. 'Paul? Is that you? Who's there?'

I start toward her, lower my beam. 'Mattie, it's Kate Burkholder and Bishop Troyer.'

'What? But why—' Her stride falters, and she stops a few feet away, her gaze going from me to the bishop and back to me.

'*Katie?*' Alarm resonates in her voice now. Even in the dim light from her lantern, I see the confusion on her features. 'I thought you were Paul,' she says. 'He took the children into town. They should have been home by now.'

She's fully clothed, wearing a print dress, a prayer *kapp*, and sneakers, and I realize she was probably about to leave, perhaps to use the phone.

When I say nothing, she freezes in place and eyes me with an odd mix of suspicion and fear. She's wondering why I'm here with the Amish bishop at this hour when her husband and children are missing. I'm aware of Troyer coming up beside me and in that moment, I'm unduly relieved he's here because I'm not sure I could do this on my own without going to pieces and making everything worse.

'Why are you here?' A sort of wild terror leaps into her eyes, and for an instant, I think she's going to throw down the lantern and run back to the house and lock the door. 'Where's Paul? *Where are my children?*'

'There's been an accident,' I say. 'I'm sorry, Mattie, but Paul and two of the children were killed. David survived.'

'What? *What?*' A sound that's part scream, part sob tears from her throat and echoes like the howl of some mortally wounded animal. 'No. That's not true. It can't be. They were just going to town. They'll be home soon.' Her gaze fastens onto the bishop, her eyes beseeching him to contradict me. 'I don't understand why she's saying these things.'

The old man reaches out to her, sets his hand on her shoulder. 'It is true, Mattie. They are with God now.'

'No!' She spins away from him, swinging the lantern so hard the mantle flickers inside the globe. 'God would not do that! He would not take them!'

'Sometimes God works in ways we do not understand,' the bishop says softly. 'We are Amish. We accept.'

'I do not accept that.' She steps back, but the old man goes with her, maintaining contact.

I reach for the lantern, ease it from her hand. 'David is in the hospital,' I tell her. 'He needs—'

Before I can finish, her knees buckle and hit the ground. I rush forward; the bishop reaches for her, too. But the grief-stricken woman crumples. Shaking us off, she leans forward, and curls into herself, her head hanging. *'Nooo!'* Her hands clench at the grass, pulling handfuls from the ground. *'Nooo!'*

I give her a moment and glance at the bishop. The resolve and strength on his ancient face bolsters me, and not for the first time, I understand why this man is the leader of the congregation. Even in the face of insurmountable tragedy, his faith is utterly unshakable.

The old man kneels next to Mattie and sets his hand on her shoulder. 'I know this is a heavy burden, my child, but David needs you.'

'David! Oh, my sweet, precious boy.' She chokes out the words as she straightens and wipes the tears from her cheeks. 'Where is he? Is he hurt? Please, I need to see him.'

I step forward and, gently, the bishop and I help her to her feet. She's unsteady and I'm afraid if I let go of her, she'll collapse again, so I maintain my grip. Her body shakes violently against mine and I wish there was some way I could stave off those tremors, absorb some of her pain, bear some of her burden.

'He's at the hospital,' I tell her. 'I'll take you.'

Silent tears stream from her eyes. She brushes at them with shaking hands, but the effort is ineffective against the deluge. Slowly, haltingly, we start toward the house. When we reach the steps, I move ahead and open the screen door. The bishop helps her inside. We shuffle through a small porch where an old-fashioned wringer washing machine watches our sad procession. We end up in the kitchen. A single lantern burns atop a large rectangular table with bench seats on two sides and a blue and white checkered tablecloth draped over its surface. I look at the table and I think of all the meals that will never again be shared.

While Bishop Troyer helps Mattie into a chair, I go to the sink and run tap water into a glass. Crossing to the table, I hand the water to Mattie. She's gone quiet and accepts the glass as if she's lapsed into a trance. She sips and then looks up at me. 'How is David? Is he all right?'

'I don't know,' I say honestly.

'I have to get to him.' She rises without finishing the water, then looks around the kitchen as if she's found herself in an unfamiliar place and doesn't know what to do next. 'If Paul were here, he would know what to do.'

I go to her side and gently take her arm. 'We're here,' I tell her. 'We'll help you.'

Bishop Troyer douses the lantern and we start toward the door.

Mattie, Bishop Troyer, and I arrive at the Emergency Room of Pomerene Hospital in Millersburg only to be told David was taken to surgery upon his arrival. Most hospitals won't perform any kind of surgery on a minor patient without parental consent unless it's a life or death situation. That the boy has already been taken into the operating room confirms his injuries are life threatening. I keep the thought to myself.

Mattie is barely able to hold it together as we take the elevator to the second floor. We garner a few curious stares as we make our way to the surgical waiting area. It never ceases to amaze me that there are people living in this part of Ohio who react as if they've never seen an Amish person.

It isn't until we're beneath the bright fluorescent lights of the surgical waiting room that I realize the stares aren't directed at the bishop, but at Mattie, and it has nothing to do with her Amishness. I've been so absorbed in the situation at hand, I hadn't noticed how strikingly beautiful she is.

Mattie was always pretty. When we were teenagers, her loveliness made her somewhat of a curiosity among our brethren. I remember the boys on *rumspringa* going to great lengths just to catch a glimpse of her. Mattie was demure enough to pretend she didn't notice. But she did, of course, and so did I. In contrast, I was a rather ordinary-looking girl. A long-limbed tomboy and a late bloomer to boot. I didn't begrudge Mattie her beauty; I wasn't jealous. But there was a part of me that secretly envied her. A part of me that wanted to be beautiful, too. I remember trying to mimic the way she laughed, the way she talked, even the way she wore her prayer *kapp,* with the ties hanging down her back just so. Generally speaking, the Amish have very little in terms of personal expression, especially when it comes to clothing. But where there's a will there's a way, especially if you're a teenage girl and determined to establish your identity; we found creative ways to express our individualism.

Even after bearing three children, her body is slender and willowy. Though she spends a good deal of time in the sun, her skin is flawless and pale with a hint of color at her checks. Her eyes are an unusual shade of gray and fringed with thick, sooty lashes. All without the benefit of cosmetics.

She doesn't go to the gym or get her hair colored at some fancy salon. Her clothes are homemade, and she buys her shoes at the Walmart in Millersburg. But when Mattie Borntrager walks into a room, people stop what they're doing to look at her. It's as if a light shines from within her. A light that cannot be doused even by insurmountable grief.

I buy two coffees at the vending machine and take them to Mattie and the bishop, who are sitting on the sofa in the waiting room. A television mounted on the wall is tuned to a sitcom I've never watched and turned up too loud, but neither seems to notice.

'I'll see what I can find out,' I tell them.

At the nurse's station, I'm told David is listed in critical condition. He was taken to surgery after his blood pressure dropped. The physician believed he was bleeding internally – from an organ or perhaps a blood vessel that had been damaged – and went in to repair it.

Back in the waiting room, I relay the news to Mattie. Closing her eyes, she leans forward, bows her head, her elbows on her knees. It isn't until I notice her lips moving that I realize she's praying. When you're Amish, grief is a private affair. Generally speaking, they are stoic; their faith bolsters them in the face of life's trials. But they are also human and some emotions are too powerful to be contained, even by something as intrinsic as faith.

Speaking in Pennsylvania Dutch, Mattie asks if this could be some kind of misunderstanding. If the *Englischers* had somehow gotten their information wrong. She asks if perhaps God made a mistake. I don't respond, and the bishop doesn't look at me as he assures her God doesn't make mistakes and that it's not her place to question Him, but to accept His will.

Bishop Troyer knows how I feel about the tenet of acceptance. When I was Amish and fate was unjust, I raged against it. I still do; it's the way I'm wired. My inability to accept without question was one of many reasons I didn't fit in. Mattie's life stands in sharp contrast to my own. We may have been raised Amish, but we've lived in different worlds most of our lives. In light of what happened tonight, I wouldn't blame her if she railed against the unfairness of fate or cursed God for allowing it to happen. Of course, she doesn't do either of those things.

I didn't reveal to her that the accident was a hit-and-run. She deserves to know, and I'll fill her in once I have more information, hopefully before word gets around town – or the rumors start flying. But I don't see any point in adding to her misery tonight, especially when I have so few details.

By the time I'm ready to leave the hospital, Mattie has fallen silent. She sits quietly next to Bishop Troyer, her head bowed, staring at the floor, gripping a tissue as if it's her lifeline to the world. I leave her like that.

As I walk through the doors of the Emergency entrance and head toward my Explorer, the weight of my connection to Mattie presses down on me with an almost physical force. I know all too well that when you're a cop, any personal connection to a case is almost always a bad thing. Emotions cloud perceptions and judgments and have no place in police work. But as chief in a small town where everyone knows everyone, I don't have the luxury of passing the buck to someone else.

And even as I vow not to let my past friendship with Mattie affect my job, I know I'm vulnerable to my own loyalties and a past I've never been able to escape.

THREE

The house wasn't anything special. In fact, it was probably one of the most unspectacular pieces of real estate John Tomasetti had ever laid eyes on. His Realtor had referred to it as a 'Victorian fixer-upper, heavy on the fixer-upper.' He didn't look very amused when Tomasetti had countered with 'a broken down piece of shit, heavy on the shit.'

The house, tumbling-down barn, and storm-damaged silo were located at the end of a quarter-mile-long gravel track. Set on six acres crowded with mature hardwood trees and a half-acre pond that had purportedly been stocked with catfish and bass, the three-bedroom farmhouse had just turned one hundred years old. It had looked peaceful and quaint in the brochure. All semblance of drive-up appeal ended the instant he saw the place up close and personal.

The house looked as if it had earned each of those one hundred birthdays the hard way, weathering blizzards and hailstorms and blazing sun without the benefit of maintenance. The paint had long since weathered to gray and the siding had rotted completely through in places. Tomasetti was pretty sure those were yellow jackets swarming out of that two-inch gap near the foundation. The rest of the exterior, including the eaves and trim, would need to be scraped, sanded, primed, and painted – all of which wasn't cheap.

At one time the windows had been adorned with slatted wood shutters. All but two lay in pieces on the ground, forgotten and left to rot in the knee-high weeds. The remaining shutters hung from rusty hinges at cockeyed angles, creaking in the breeze and giving the house the unbalanced appearance of a listing ship. The wrap-around porch had once been a focal point, but the wood planks sagged now, so that the house seemed to grin when you came up the lane. Not the dazzling smile of some proud patriarch looking out over his domain, but the lopsided, toothless grin of an old drunk, heavy on the drunk.

Tomasetti had almost turned around and left. But despite its state of disrepair, there was something appealing about the place. His Realtor had twittered on about the 'astounding potential' and the 'opportunity for investment' and reminded him that the place was 'in foreclosure' and would go for a steal. Somehow, he'd persuaded Tomasetti to venture inside.

The house was small – by Ohio farmhouse standards, anyway – with just under three thousand square feet. The bedrooms and one of the two bathrooms were located on the second level; the living areas and second bath were downstairs. Not a bad floor plan considering the place had been built back when Woodrow Wilson was president and the Great War had yet to begin.

The age of the house was reflected in the interior, too, but the dilapidation was interspersed with unexpected flashes of character and the kind of architecture rarely seen in today's homes. Tall, narrow windows ensconced in woodwork adorned every external wall, ushering in a flourish of natural light. The ceilings were twelve feet high with intricate crown molding. A wide, arched doorway separated the formal dining room from the living area. The kitchen was 'all original' – a term Tomasetti deemed interchangeable with 'needs gutting and replacing.' A peek beneath the threadbare olive-green carpeting revealed a gold mine of gleaming oak that had never seen the light of day. Tomasetti didn't have an eye for design or color. The thing he did have an eye for was potential and the old house brimmed with it.

Never a pushover, he'd left his Realtor standing in the driveway looking decidedly depressed – perhaps due to the 'place is a dump' comment he'd uttered as they parted ways. He went back to his office in Richfield to immerse himself in work, which was an open case involving the unidentified remains of a Jane Doe found in Cortland, Ohio – and forget all about that dusty old farmhouse.

But he couldn't get it out of his head, which didn't make a whole lot of sense. Tomasetti was a city slicker from the word go. He preferred concrete over cornfields and the din of horns and gunned engines over the bawling of calves or spring peepers. He loved the hustle and bustle of downtown. The cultural centers and the bars and restaurants tucked away in unexpected places. He even liked the grittiness of the downtrodden neighborhoods and warehouse districts. So why the hell was he thinking about that shit-hole farmhouse out in the middle of fuck-all?

He might not want to admit it, but he knew why. And the notion that his life was about to change, especially by his own hand, scared the living hell out of him.

It had been a long time since he'd wanted anything with such ferocity, even longer since he thought he might actually have a chance of getting it. Or that he deserved something as ordinary as happiness or peace of mind or the opportunity for a fresh start. For the first time in four years, he was thinking about the future. A future that wasn't bleak.

Two days later Tomasetti called his Realtor and made a ridiculously low offer on the property. He assured himself even

a motivated seller would never accept that level of highway rob-
bery and a rejection would be fine by him. The last thing he
needed was a goddamn money pit. But the owner had surprised
him and accepted the price without a counter offer. Tomasetti
had surprised himself by handing over the cash. Three weeks
later, they closed the deal.

He'd figured the regret would sneak up on him any day
now. The knowledge that he'd screwed up and made a bad
investment. But a month had passed and he had yet to lament his
decision. He'd already resolved to do some work on the place.
Put in a new kitchen. Granite countertops. Cherry cabinets. Trav-
ertine flooring. The kitchen, after all, was the room in which you
garnered your best return. When the kitchen was finished, he'd
sand and stain the hardwoods. Repair and paint the siding. Slap
some paint on the interior. Then he'd sell the place to some
sucker who wanted to live out in the middle of nowhere so he
could listen to the frogs and get bitten up by mosquitoes. Hopefully, Tomasetti could make a little cash in the process.

His superiors at the Bureau of Criminal Identification and
Investigation had been urging him to take some time off for a
couple of years now – something Tomasetti had resisted because,
up until now, he'd *needed* to work. When he'd walked in to
Denny McNinch's office and announced he would be taking
the entirety of his vacation time, he'd thought Denny was going
to fall out of his chair. In fact, Denny had looked worried, like
maybe he thought Tomasetti was teetering on some precipice
with one foot already over the edge. Then he'd told Denny
about the house and his superior had seemed not only relieved,
but genuinely pleased.

The one person Tomasetti hadn't told was Kate. He wasn't
sure why; he knew she'd be happy for him. Hell, knowing Kate
she'd probably volunteer to drive up for the weekend to help
him paint. But Tomasetti knew why he hadn't told her and it

was those not-so-apparent motivations that scared him. This house wasn't just an investment or a place to live. It represented something much more important: the future.

Last summer, he and Kate had worked together on a string of missing persons cases in the northeastern part of the state. They spent some intense days together in the course of the case and one night he'd gotten caught up in the moment and asked her to move in with him. Tomasetti had never seen her look more uncertain – or terrified. He might have laughed if he hadn't been so damned disappointed.

Kate was independent to a fault. She could be closed off emotionally. Like him, she lugged around a good bit of baggage. She might be fearless when it came to her job, but she could be skittish when it came to their relationship.

Tomasetti got that, but he wanted her in his life. He wanted to share this with her. For the first time since he'd lost his wife and children, he wanted more. A lot more. The question was, did Kate?

He'd been making the forty-five-minute drive from Richfield to the farm for three days now and he'd fallen into a routine he liked, arriving at the crack of dawn, throwing open the windows, turning the old radio to a station in Dover. He spent twelve hours the first day demolishing the kitchen. Everything had gone: cabinets, countertops, sink, and pantry and most of the Sheetrock. He'd ripped up the linoleum to expose the subflooring, and hauled everything to the Dumpster he'd rented. The crew of painters had arrived the second day, repairing the exterior siding and porch, installing new shutters – black – and finally giving the wood a coat of fresh white paint. The house no longer looked like somebody's nightmare – at least on the outside.

Now, after three days, sunburned and sore, with a smashed index finger that was probably going to shed its nail, Tomasetti looked around and actually liked what he saw. He'd measured for cabinets, countertops, and flooring yesterday and ordered what he needed. When the materials arrived, he would begin installation. Tomorrow, a quick stop at the home improvement store in Wooster and he could start painting the interior.

It was nearly 10:00 P.M. when he walked to the cooler he kept in the hall off the kitchen. Digging inside, he pulled out a Killian's Irish Red and carried it to the back porch. Taking his usual place on the step, he uncapped it and drank. A three-quarter moon glinted off the tin roof of the barn and illuminated the hulking form of the silo beyond. Being away from the hustle and bustle of the city had bothered him at first; the quiet seemed unnatural and made him feel isolated and edgy. But by the end of the second day, he'd begun to hear the music inside the silence: The chatter of the squirrel that lived in the spruce tree outside the kitchen window that was none too happy about the new interloper. The family of red-winged blackbirds that swooped from the spruce to the weeping willow on the bank of the pond. At dusk, the peepers and bullfrogs took over, their night song floating through the windows like some ballad you never wanted to end.

Tomasetti drank the beer and listened to the land. He listened to the buzz of the fluorescent light overhead. The creaks as the old house settled around him. He thought about Kate and wondered what she was doing. He wondered what she'd think of this place. He missed her, he realized. He wanted her here, wanted to share this with her. He took another swig and thought about calling her, but something told him to wait. He'd get a few rooms painted tomorrow. Get the house one step closer to finished. And then he'd invite her up for dinner. Tomorrow, he thought.

Tomorrow.

*

Though it's nearly midnight and my shift is about to end, I won't be going home any time soon. The ambulances and fire trucks are gone, but the scene is lit up by the flashing emergency lights of law enforcement vehicles and crawling with cops. I count five vehicles, including one from the State Highway Patrol, two from the Holmes County Sheriff's office, and one from my department. The fifth vehicle is a news van from a television station out of Columbus. A pretty blond woman wearing a hot-pink jacket finger-combs her hair beneath the glare of lights and the glowing red eye of the camera.

She spots me as I'm climbing out of the Explorer, shouts an alert to her cameraman, and starts toward me at a fast clip. 'Chief Burkholder? Can we get a statement?'

I'm midway to the crime scene tape when she steps in front of me, effectively stopping me, and shoves the mike in my face. 'Can you confirm that this was a hit-and-run accident that killed this Amish family tonight, Chief?'

'The accident is still under investigation.' I step around her and keep going.

Holding the mike close to my face, she keeps pace with me. 'Can you tell us how many people were killed?'

'There were three fatalities. We're not releasing names pending notification of next of kin.'

'They were Amish?'

'That's correct.'

'Was the buggy affixed with a slow-moving-vehicle sign?'

Reflective signage has been in the news recently, and is an ongoing point of contention between law enforcement and some of the Old Order Amish, who believe any kind of signage is ornamental and, therefore, against the rules set forth by the *Ordnung*.

I stop and turn to her. She takes a quick step back, as if not quite trusting me not to pop her in the mouth, and lowers the mike to a more respectful distance. 'I can't confirm that at this time,' I tell her.

She tries to ask another question, but I turn away, bumping the mike with my shoulder as I start toward the scene.

Behind me, I hear her ask the cameraman, 'Did you get that?'

'Damn vultures,' comes a familiar voice.

Ahead, I see Sheriff Mike Rasmussen and a uniformed deputy striding toward me. I've known the sheriff for about a year now. Though I'm city and he's county, we've worked together on several cases, pooling the resources of our respective departments. We've butted heads on a couple of occasions, but he's a good cop and a quick study when it comes to the politicking side of his job. He's also one of the few in the local law enforcement community who knows about my relationship with John Tomasetti.

I extend my hand and we shake. 'You guys get traffic diverted?' I ask.

'Bunch of damn rubberneckers.' Rasmussen's expression is grim. 'Any news on the kid?'

'He was in surgery when I left the hospital.'

'I hate it when kids get hurt.'

I nod, trying not to think of Mattie, and turn my attention to the deputy. He's a burly man in his midthirties with a crew cut and the direct, probing eyes of a man who likes being in the thick of things. He's wearing a tan jacket with the Holmes County Sheriff's Department insignia on his left breast. Beneath the jacket, his uniform shirt stretches a tad too snugly across pecs the size of small hams.

'I'm Chief Burkholder,' I say, offering a handshake.

'Frank Maloney.' He looks at me with a little too much intensity and gives my hand a slightly too-hard squeeze.

'Frank's a certified accident reconstructionist,' Rasmussen says.

I nod, pleased he's on scene this early in the game. 'Any preliminary thoughts on what happened?'

Maloney's chest puffs out a little. He's proud of his certification and likes being the one in the know. 'Buggy was southbound on Delisle. The hit-skip was westbound on CR14 and broadsided the buggy.' He holds up an intricate-looking Bosch Laser Distance Measurer that in the last few years has replaced measuring wheels and tapes. 'This guy was hauling ass.'

'How fast?' I ask.

'I'd ballpark upwards of eighty miles per hour.'

'Jesus Christ,' Rasmussen mutters. 'The buggy didn't stand a chance.'

I glance toward the scene, trying not to imagine how that went down. The buggy hasn't yet been moved. Someone covered the dead horse with a tarp. The coroner has removed the dead, but left tarps over the bloodstained grass. I make a mental note to get the fire department out here with a tanker to flush away the biohazard.

'County Prosecutor been out here yet?' I ask.

'Came and left,' Rasmussen replies.

'I hope he's as pissed as I am.' I can tell by the men's expressions we're on the same page. They want this son of a bitch as badly as I do.

'We'll make sure everything's well documented,' Rasmussen assures me.

I nod. 'I put out an APB for an unidentified vehicle with a damaged front end.'

'I got my boys out looking,' the sheriff adds.

'Anything useful as far as debris?' I ask.

When a cop arrives on the scene of a traffic accident, his first priority is always the preservation of life. It takes precedence over everything else, including identifying and protecting evidence. Upon my arrival here earlier, I was so intent on locating the victims and rendering aid, I didn't get a good look at the buggy or debris. Any cop worth his salt will tell you that finding and identifying that debris – those pieces left behind by the vehicles involved – is the first step in identifying the vehicle and locating the driver.

Rasmussen sighs. 'We're going to be picking up pieces of that buggy for a while. We're going to load everything up and take it to impound for a closer look under some light.'

'Anything from the vehicle?' I ask.

'The only piece we've been able to identify is a side-view mirror,' the sheriff tells me.

As if by unspoken agreement, the three of us start toward the intersection. Someone has denoted the locations where the deceased victims came to rest with fluorescent orange marking paint. From where I stand I can see the blue tarp covering the horse. We stop a few yards from the point of impact and I take a moment to establish the debris field and for the first time I get a sense of the scope of the carnage.

'My God, this guy was fucking flying,' I say to no one in particular.

Maloney points to the place where Paul Borntrager had died just a few hours earlier. 'Adult male was thrown fifty-three feet.'

Rasmussen shakes his head. 'Youngsters were thrown even farther.'

'What about skid marks?' I ask. 'Or tire imprints?' Sometimes, if the skid marks are clean enough to get a measurement of the tire, we can use that information to help identify the offending vehicle. On rare occasions the tread is visible. Photos are scanned into a computer. From there, they can sometimes be matched to a manufacturer or retailer and, in some cases, if there is some identifiable mark on the tire – a cut or defect in the rubber, for example – a specific vehicle. Combined, those things can be invaluable to the identification process. Not to mention the trial.

Maloney and Rasmussen exchange looks that makes the back of my neck prickle.

'There are no skid marks,' Maloney says.

'Not a single one,' Rasmussen reiterates.

Something cold and sharp scrapes up my back. 'The driver made no attempt to stop?'

'Looks that way,' Maloney replies.

'The road surface was wet,' I tell him, thinking aloud. 'Is it possible he tried to stop, but couldn't due to conditions?'

'That son of a bitch didn't even tap the brake,' Rasmussen mutters.

'Could we be dealing with some kind of mechanical failure?' It's an optimistic offering, but I pose the question anyway.

Maloney shrugs. 'It's possible, I guess.'

'If someone's brakes fail and they slam into a fucking buggy, you'd think they'd stop and render aid,' Rasmussen growls.

Maloney nods. 'Even if they get scared and panic, they'd call 911.'

'Unless they've got something to hide.' I say what all of us are thinking. What we already know. 'We're probably dealing with a DUI.'

'That's my vote,' Rasmussen says.

'Or some idiot texting,' Maloney puts in.

I think of Paul Borntrager's last minutes. He'd been broken and bleeding and yet his only concern had been for his children. I think of Mattie, holding vigil at the hospital, waiting for word on the condition of her only surviving child. I think of David, an innocent little boy, hurting and frightened and fighting for his life. I think of the three lives lost and the countless others that will be destroyed by their passing. I think of the pain that has been brought down on a community that's seen more than its share of heartbreak in the last few years. And gnarly threads of rage burgeon again inside me.

I study the scene. My mind's eye shows me a horse and buggy approaching the intersection. I hear the clip-clop of shod hooves against the asphalt. The jingle of the harness. The creak of the buggy. The chatter of the children, oblivious to the impending tragedy. Dusk has fallen. It's drizzling. Visibility is low. The road surface is wet. Concerned about the coming darkness, Paul would have been pushing the horse, hurrying home. Around them, the symphony of crickets from the woods fills the air.

There would have been a flash of headlights. An instant of horror and disbelief as Paul Borntrager realizes the vehicle isn't going to stop. He plants his feet, hauls back on the reins. A firmly shouted, 'whoa!' Then the horrific violence of the impact. No time to scream. An explosion of wood and steel and debris. The horse is killed instantly, the harness rigging ripped from the buggy. The victims are ejected, their broken bodies violently impacting the earth.

'A lot of the Amish try to avoid the busier roads after dark,' I say.

Both men look at me as if I've inadvertently spoken the words in Pennsylvania Dutch. I add, 'They know it's dangerous.'

'We've all seen how impatient some of these damn drivers can be,' Rasmussen mutters.

'I cited some guy from Wheeling a couple of days ago for passing a buggy on a double yellow line,' Maloney says. 'I'd like to show him some photos from this scene.'

The three of us nod and then Rasmussen glances at his watch. 'It's too late to canvass.'

'I'll get someone out here first thing in the morning.' I think about that a moment. 'The driver might be looking for a body shop in the next few days.'

Rasmussen nods. 'We've got five or six body shops in Millersburg. I'll send a couple of my guys out first thing in the morning.'

'There are three in Painters Mill,' I tell him. 'We might include Wooster, too.'

'I'll notify Wayne County,' Rasmussen offers.

'Let's pull past DUIs, too,' I suggest.

'Can't hurt.' Rasmussen's eyes sharpen on mine. 'Any chance the kid saw something?'

'It's possible, but he was in critical condition and in surgery when I left the hospital.' I glance at my watch. 'I'll find out and keep you posted.'

But we know the majority of crash victims rarely remember the minutes preceding a crash, especially if they've sustained a head injury or lost consciousness.

'With this kid being Amish,' I begin, 'even if he saw the vehicle and remembers it, he may not be able to tell us the make or model.'

'Well that's just fucking peachy,' Rasmussen mutters. 'We need to find this son of a bitch, people.'

FOUR

Deputy Maloney, Sheriff Rasmussen, and I spend several hours walking the scene, photographing, video-recording, sketching, and surmising. At 2:00 A.M., Glock shows up with four large coffees from LaDonna's Diner, and we swarm him like zombies seeking flesh. It's hours before his shift starts, but he possesses a sort of sixth sense when it comes to showing up when he's needed. He never seems to mind putting in the extra time, even though he's got two babies and a wife at home. I'm invariably glad to have him on scene and unduly thankful for the caffeine.

I'm standing next to my Explorer when a Painters Mill volunteer fire department tanker pulls onto the shoulder. I watch the young firefighter disembark, link the hose, and begin to flush the blood from the road and grassy areas. A few yards away, local farmer and town councilman Ron Jackson arrives in his big John Deere to haul the dead horse to the landfill.

Glock wanders over and we watch a big Ford dually back a twenty-foot flatbed trailer to the debris field. A red-haired man from a local wrecker service contracted by the sheriff's department gets out. Maloney and Rasmussen don gloves and begin picking up pieces, dropping them into bags, and loading them onto the trailer.

For several minutes Glock and I stand there, sipping our coffees, watching.

'Hell of a way to start the day,' he says.

'Coffee helped.' I smile at him and he smiles back.

'You get anything from the vehicle?' he asks.

I tell him about the lack of debris and he shoots me a look. 'That's weird,' he says.

We stare at each other, our minds working that over. 'Maloney thinks this guy was going upwards of eighty miles an hour,' I say.

'There should have been debris.'

'A lot from the buggy,' I say.

'Maybe the debris from the vehicle got mixed in with it.'

Even as he says the words, something tugs at my brain, worrying me like a child yanking at his mother's dress to get her attention.

'Seems like the impact would have fucked up the grille of a vehicle,' Glock surmises. 'Or busted out a headlight or signal light or *something*.'

The feather touch of a chill brushes across the back of my neck, and I realize the lack of debris is the thing that's been bothering me all along. 'They're going to haul everything down to impound, take a closer look under some lights.'

Rasmussen approaches us. 'I think we've got everything loaded up.'

I address the sheriff. 'Did you find any more debris from the vehicle?'

'Just the side-view mirror so far,' Maloney replies.

I see a creeping suspicion enter the sheriff's eyes. 'If that son of a bitch was going as fast as you say, he should have left pieces scattered all the way to Cleveland.'

'Even with the work lights and generator, it's dark as a damn cave out here,' Maloney says. 'Maybe we missed something. Maybe it got tossed in with all those pieces from the buggy.'

'Driver might have had a brush guard on his front end,' Glock offers.

Rasmussen nods, but he doesn't look convinced. 'Even with a brush guard, he would have busted out a headlight or knocked off some plastic. Vehicles have a lot of plastic these days.'

'Maybe it's some kind of homemade job,' Glock offers.

Maloney tosses him an interested look and adds, 'All you need is a welder and some steel.' He turns to me. 'Any vehicles from around here come to mind?' he asks. 'Souped-up truck, maybe?'

'Or a fuckin' tank,' Glock mutters beneath his breath.

Images of a hundred vehicles scroll through my mind. Stops I've made. Citations I've issued. Recent DUIs.

'A lot of farm trucks,' I tell them. 'I'll see if I can come up with a list.'

'A lot of them farm boys got welders,' Maloney adds.

The sheriff makes a sound of frustration. 'We'll take a closer look at everything in the morning. In the interim, if you see something that fits the bill, make the stop.'

He tips his hat and the two men start toward their respective vehicles.

I glance at my watch, surprised to see it's almost 3:00 A.M. 'You want body shops or farms?' I ask Glock.

'Body shops.' He grins. 'Amish don't trust me for some reason.'

'That's because you cuss too much.'

He grins. 'Now that makes me feel misunderstood.'

'Hit every body shop or auto shop that does collision work, including anyone who works out of a home shop or keeps a can of Bondo on his workbench. If someone brings in a vehicle with a messed-up grille, I want to know about it.'

'I'm all over it.'

'I'll get Skid and Pickles to cover these farms in the morning.'

We saunter to the place where the accident happened and look in both directions. The grassy shoulder is trampled from all the traffic and muddy where the fire department flushed away the biohazard. The tractor that hauled away the dead horse left deep ruts. I think about the hit-and-run driver and something scratches at the back of my brain.

'Where was he going anyway?' I say, thinking aloud.

'If he was headed west,' Glock replies, 'he was on his way to Painters Mill. Millersburg, maybe.'

'If he was stinking drunk, where was he coming from?'

Our gazes meet. 'The Brass Rail,' we say in unison.

The Brass Rail Saloon is a couple of miles down the road; the scene of the accident is smack dab between that bar and Painters Mill. It's one of the area's more disreputable drinking establishments. If you want to get drunk, fight, buy dope, or get laid – and not necessarily in that order – the Brass Rail Saloon is one-stop shopping.

'Probably a long shot.' But I can't quite dispel the rise of dark anticipation that comes with the possibility of that all-important first lead.

'Unless the bartender remembers someone leaving in a souped-up truck five minutes before the accident.'

'Stranger things have happened.' I fish my keys out of my pocket. 'Let me know what you find out from the body shops, will you?'

'You bet.'

I leave him there, frowning and looking just a little bit worried.

I swing by the house for a shower and a few hours of sleep. I don't notice the blood on my shirt until I'm standing naked in the bathroom and look down at my uniform heaped on the floor. I'm usually pretty mindful of any kind of biohazard, but

I don't remember when I picked it up. I don't know whose it is.

I look down at my hands and see dried blood on my palms and beneath my nails and cuticles. That's when it strikes me this blood represents the death of a man I've known most of my life. The deaths of two innocent children. The injury of a third child. And the hell of grief for a woman who was once my best friend.

Unnerved, I turn to the sink, grab the bar of soap, and scrub my hands with the single-minded determination of a myso-phobe. When my flesh is pink, I twist on the shower taps as hot as I can bear and spend the next fifteen minutes trying to wash away the remnants of the accident, seen and unseen.

By the time I pull on a tee-shirt and sweat pants, I feel set-tled enough to call Tomasetti. I want to believe I'm calling him because he's a good investigator. Because he'll offer some gem of advice. Because he's great to bounce ideas with and he rarely fails to give me something I can use. But the truth of the matter is I need to hear his voice. I want to hear him laugh, hear him say my name. Or maybe I just need him to help me make sense of this.

I walk into the kitchen. The wall clock tells me it's three thirty in the morning; I shouldn't bother him at this hour. Like me, Tomasetti's an insomniac. Sleep is tough to come by some nights. For a moment, I sit there debating. In the end, my need to talk to him overrides decorum. I grab my cell phone off the counter where it's charging, pour myself a cup of cold coffee, and punch in his number.

He picks up on the second ring. 'I was just thinking about you.'

I can tell he was sleeping, and that he's withholding his usual upon-wakening grumpiness. His voice, so calm and deep, fills me with a sense of optimism and reminds me that the good things in life balance out the bad.

'You were asleep,' I tell him.

'This might come as a shock to you, but a man can actually think about a woman while he's sleeping.'

'So you were multitasking.'

He pauses. 'Is everything all right?'

He asks the question with the nonchalance of someone inquiring about the weather, but he knows something's wrong. I don't like it, but he worries about me. Because I'm a cop. A woman. Or maybe because he knows how easily those you care about can slip away.

I stick to cop-speak as I tell him about the hit-and-run, using terms like 'hit-skip' and 'juveniles.' I don't mention my past friendship with Mattie or that I'd known both of them since I was a kid. I don't tell him that when I close my eyes I see the faces of those dead children.

I don't have to; he already knows.

'How well did you know them, Kate?' he asks.

To my horror, tears sting my eyes. Though he can't see me, I wipe frantically at them, as if somehow he'll know.

'Mattie was my best friend,' I blurt. 'I mean, when we were kids. I knew Paul, too. Back when he was a skinny Amish boy with a bad haircut. We lost contact after I left, but those days were—' I fumble for the right word.

'Formative.' He finishes for me.

'I never had that kind of friend again.'

'Until I came along.'

I laugh and it feels good coming out. 'I knew you were going to make me feel better.'

'Is there anything I can do?'

'Not really. Holmes County is the primary agency.'

'You notified NOK?'

There are times when silence is louder than words. This is

one of those times. But I know if I speak, he'll know I'm an inch away from going to pieces.

'Are you okay?' There's nothing casual about the question this time. He knows I'm not okay and he's trying to figure out what to do about it.

'This is going to sound corny, but I think I needed to hear your voice.'

'My shrink would probably call that some kind of breakthrough.'

'For me or you?'

'Both of us.'

I laugh, but I can't think of a comeback.

'Kate, do you want me to drive down?'

'Do I sound that bad?'

'Maybe I just want to spend some time with my girl.'

'Is that what I am, Tomasetti?' I say the words in an offhand manner intended to lighten the conversation.

'You're my best friend.'

Somehow the exchange has turned too serious, too personal. I try to think of some flippant response that will make us laugh and move the conversation back on solid ground, but I'm too moved to speak. All I can think is that if I do and he hears the emotion in my voice, he'll know something about me I don't want to share.

'In case you're wondering,' he says easily, 'that was a favorable observation with regard to our relationship.'

'I know.'

'I thought you might want to say something reciprocal, like "you're my best friend, too."'

'You are. I hope you know that.'

'I do now.' He pauses. 'I'm taking some vacation time. I could drive down and we could hang out. Go on a picnic. Have sex. Not necessarily in that order.'

A laugh squeezes from my throat. 'Tomasetti, you are so full of shit.'

'Don't go all sentimental on me. I'm getting choked up.'

'I didn't know you were on vacation.'

'It was a take-it-or-lose-it situation.'

I think about that a moment. 'Let me tie up a few things here, and I'll let you know.'

'Don't wait too long.'

'I won't.'

'You sure you're all right?'

'I am now,' I tell him and disconnect.

Sleep is a fickle thing that has little to do with fatigue and everything to do with peace of mind. When I finally fall into a fitful slumber, I dream of Mattie and Paul, and two dead children who stare at me with accusing black eyes and rotting mouths that chant *schinnerhannes! schinnerhannes!*, which is the Pennsylvania Dutch word for a man who hauls away dead farm animals.

I jerk awake to the sound of tapping. I'm tangled in the sheets and slicked with sweat. I don't know the source of the sound, but I'm relieved to be free of the nightmare's grip. I sit up, listening. A glance at the alarm clock on my nightstand tells me it's almost 4:30 A.M. I'm trying to convince myself I only imagined the sound when it comes again and I realize someone's at the door.

Throwing the blankets aside, I get up, snag my revolver off the nightstand, and pad into the hall. *Tap. Tap. Tap.* Not the front door, I realize, and I move silently through the dark and into the kitchen. A few feet away from the back door, I recognize his silhouette against the curtains. Setting my weapon on the counter, I cross to the door and open it.

John Tomasetti stands on my back porch, frowning as if he's

got every right to be here despite the hour and I've kept him waiting too long. 'I'm sorry to wake you,' he begins.

I laugh at that because we both know he's not. I take a moment to process the picture of him, standing there, looking at me as if I'm the only person left in the world and he's ravenous for company, and I know this is one of those small slices of time that I'll never forget. Instead of his usual slacks and jacket, he's wearing faded blue jeans and a navy golf shirt. Shoes that look like a cross between a hiker and a work boot. His usual office pallor has been replaced by a tan.

'Vacation looks good on you,' I say.

'You look good on me.'

That makes me grin and I open the door wider. 'Is everything okay?'

'You mean aside from the slight paranoia that goes along with parking in the alley behind the police chief's house?'

'I thought that was part of the allure,' I say.

'Not even close.'

I catch a whiff of his aftershave as he steps past me, and my midsection flutters in a way that's now familiar: a powerful mix of attraction, affection, and excitement.

'You know we're probably not going to be able to keep this a secret too much longer,' I say, closing the door behind him.

'I'd hate to be the one to put a black mark on your reputation.'

'One more added to the collection isn't going to make a difference.'

Up until this point, we've sort of been dancing around each other. Not getting too close. Not touching. Neither of us wanting to make that first telling move. If it wasn't such an uncomfortable moment, I might have laughed at the absurdity of it.

I break the silence with, 'I've got a couple of Killian's in the fridge.'

'I thought you might.'

Before I can turn away, he reaches out and takes my arm, pulls me to him. Wrapping his fingers around both my biceps, he pushes me backward until my rump collides with the counter. I look into his eyes to find them dark and fixed on me, and my knees go weak. Then he bends to me and his mouth is on mine. I dive into the kiss with everything I have. His lips are firm and warm and move against mine with an urgency that sucks the breath from my lungs. My arms go around his neck. My body presses flush against his. I feel the hard ridge of him against my belly. His hands skim restlessly down the sides of my ribcage. Sensation courses through me with such power that I have to close my eyes against it, like some crazy ride at the county fair, the kind where you're dizzy and holding your breath but you never want it to end.

After a moment, he pulls back and smiles down at me. 'I've missed you.'

'I can tell.'

He laughs and then goes to the fridge and pulls out two beers. He hands one to me and, watching each other, we twist off the caps and sip.

'How's the investigation going on the hit-skip?' he asks.

'It hasn't changed in the last hour.' I'm still reeling from the effects of the kiss as I relay everything I know so far.

'You think it's someone local?' he asks.

I go to the fridge, find some grapes, cheese, and crackers, and toss them onto a plate. 'Probably. If not Painters Mill proper, then Holmes County or one of the surrounding counties. Vehicle was probably a truck.' I carry the plate to the table and sit.

Tomasetti takes the chair across from me, and for several moments we're caught up in our thoughts.

'How's your friend doing?' he asks.

'She's devastated. Camped out at the hospital waiting for word on her son.'

'He going to be okay?'

'Not sure yet.'

'Anything I can do?'

'In the coming days, we'll probably be using the lab. If things get jammed up, it would be a huge help if you could expedite.'

'I'll do what I can.'

We stare across the table at each other for a moment, then he says, 'Now that we've gotten the preliminaries out of the way, I've got something to tell you.'

A small thread of anxiety zips through me. Generally, I don't like surprises. I prefer to know what's coming so I can be prepared when it arrives. Tomasetti is a wild card. When I met him, he'd just lost his wife and children in a home invasion that left his life in tatters. Afterward, he fell to taking prescription drugs, mixing them with alcohol. I know he spent some time in an institution. He doesn't talk about it, so details are sketchy. I've never pressed him.

He's better now. Not fully healed, but I know he has happiness and hope in his life. I know I'm part of both of those things and that we've been good for each other.

'Do you remember that house in Wooster I told you about last summer?' he begins.

'The old farmhouse, on acreage?' An alarm begins to wail in the back of my head. A few months ago, I consulted on a case for the Bureau of Criminal Identification and Investigation. Several Amish teens had disappeared during their *rumspringas*. During that investigation he told me about a farmhouse he was thinking about buying, and then shocked the hell out of me by asking me to move in with him. I panicked and waffled and basically handled the situation badly, giving him a slew of mixed signals instead of the straightforward answer he deserved.

It was a cowardly response, but I'd felt waylaid and unprepared. He was astute enough to give me an out, but I knew the issue would resurface. He isn't the kind of man to give up, after all, especially when he wants something. I'm going to have to figure out how I feel about the prospect of moving in with him and give him a definitive answer, whether it's the one he wants to hear or not.

'I bought it,' he tells me. 'I closed last month.'

I stare at him, aware that I've broken a sweat. The bottle of beer feels like an icicle in my hand, the cold emanating up my arm and into my shoulder.

'Congratulations,' I manage.

'The place needs work, so I took some time off. New kitchen. Painting. Floors need refinishing.'

Discomfort climbs over me, a big, lumbering beast that presses down with the weight of a house. I don't know how to react to this. I'm not sure what to say or how to feel. I look away, take a long drink of beer.

'If you're game, I'd like to show it to you.'

I meet his gaze to find his eyes already on me. He's looking at me as if I'm a math problem that has unexpectedly perplexed him. 'Sure.'

'I promise not to tie you to a chair and keep you as my sex slave.'

I laugh outright and some of the discomfort sloughs off. 'Are you thinking about moving in?'

'When it's ready.'

'What about the commute?'

'It's a forty-five-minute drive from my office in Richfield.' His eyes burn into mine. 'Half an hour from Painters Mill.'

'Convenient.'

'You're afraid I'm going to ask you to move in with me

again.' Studying me, he takes a long pull of beer. 'I won't if you don't want me to.'

'I'm not sure what I want. I think that's part of the problem.' I set down my beer, look down at the tabletop. 'Tomasetti, you're the best thing that's ever happened to me.'

He laughs. It's not the response I expected. When I look at him I see something a little too close to sympathy reflecting back at me.

'I'm glad you find this so amusing,' I tell him.

'You don't want to commit and you're trying not to break my heart.'

'That's not exactly what's going on here.'

'Feel free to jump in and correct me at any time.'

'I'm still trying to figure this out, okay? I don't want to screw things up.'

'You can't.'

'Believe me. I can. Tomasetti, I could screw up a funeral.'

'Kate, I appreciate your handling me with kid gloves. But I'm a big boy. I can handle it.'

We stare at each other. My heart is pounding. I wish I could read him, wish I knew what he was thinking, what he was feeling, but his expression is inscrutable. 'Moving in with you would be a huge step for me. A big change. I need some time to think about it.'

'That's all I need to hear.' He contemplates me. 'Come by the farm for dinner tomorrow. I'll grill steaks if you bring the wine.'

'Steaks and wine.' I smile. 'That sounds serious.'

'As serious as you want it to be.'

He surprises me by scooting his chair back and rising. I feel my eyes widen as he steps toward me, takes my hands, and pulls me to my feet. 'Maybe we ought to sleep on it.' He pulls me to him.

My arms find their way around his neck. 'I have an early day,' I whisper, but there's no enthusiasm behind the words.

'Me, too.'

When he kisses me, the doubt falls away.

And thoughts of the case dissolve into the night.

FIVE

At 9:00 A.M. I'm back in the Explorer, on my way to Pomerene Hospital to check on Mattie and her son. Tomasetti was gone when I woke up, but I still feel his presence both on my body and in my heart. We talked until the wee hours of morning and made love until the eastern horizon turned pink. Shortly thereafter, I fell into a fitful slumber, but even in the afterglow, I couldn't shut down my mind. I couldn't stop thinking about Mattie or get the images of Paul and those two dead children out of my head.

I call Pickles to see how the canvassing of the farms near the accident is going. 'You guys have any luck?'

'Wish I had better news for you, Chief, but no one saw shit.'

The news isn't a surprise, but I'm disappointed nonetheless. 'You hit the Stutz place yet?'

'We're heading that way now.'

'Keep me posted, will you?'

'You got it.'

I dial Glock's number as I pull into the hospital parking lot. 'You have any luck at the body shops?'

'Struck out, Chief. No one's brought in a vehicle with a damaged front end, but they all agreed to let us know if something suspicious came in.'

I slide the Explorer into a No Parking zone near the front entrance and shut down the engine. 'Will you do me a favor and help Lois set up a tip hotline? Let her know there's a five-hundred-dollar reward for information that leads to an arrest and conviction. Tell her to get a press release out and send it to everyone she can think of.'

'Damn, Chief, how did you manage that reward?'

'I haven't.' I don't know where I'll get the money; I'm already over budget for the year and it's only September, but I know this is one expenditure the town council will support me on. If they balk, I'll write the damn check myself.

'You been to the Brass Rail?' he asks.

'I thought I'd wait until the same shift comes on.'

'Good idea. Let me know if you need backup.'

I snort. 'You just want to crack some heads.'

'Hey, a guy can hope.'

Disconnecting, I clip the phone to my belt, get out, and cross the parking lot at a brisk walk. In the back of my mind, I'm hoping the kid made it through surgery and is improving. I go through the double front doors and take the elevator to the second level. I'm expecting to find Mattie and the bishop in the surgical waiting area where I left them, but when I arrive they're nowhere in sight. The television is tuned to an infomercial no one's paying any attention to; a young couple sits in the corner talking quietly. For a moment, I'm afraid the boy passed away during the night. Feeling gut-punched, I stride to the nurses' station where I'm told David Borntrager is being moved to a regular room.

They give me directions and I take the elevator to the third floor and the patient rooms that were added during a recent renovation. I find room 308 and enter to find Mattie in a chair next to the hospital bed – which is vacant. She's leaning forward with her head against the mattress, her arms folded beneath her cheek, sleeping. In the corner, Bishop Troyer is lying in a recliner, snoring loud enough to rattle the windows.

Mattie startles awake and springs into an upright position. 'Oh. Katie. I thought you were the nurse.' She rises abruptly and looks toward the door. 'They're supposed to bring David.'

She sways as if she's not steady on her feet, and I wonder if she's had anything to eat. I step forward, set my hands on her shoulders to support her. 'Did you get any rest?'

'I'm not tired.' She makes a halfhearted attempt to shake off my hands and cranes her neck to see into the hall, her face twisted into a mask of worry. 'They should have brought him in by now. Where is he? Why isn't he here?'

'He's fine, Mattie. I just talked to the nurse. They'll bring him up soon.'

She looks at me as if she doesn't believe me. 'But they told me the same thing an hour ago. Do you think something's happened?'

'Why don't you sit down and catch your breath, and I'll check on him, okay?' Gently, I ease her backward toward the chair, but she refuses to sit.

She looks at me, blinking back tears. Her eyes are swollen and red rimmed from crying. The delicate area beneath them is the color of a bruise. Her complexion is so pale it's almost translucent; I see the blue strip of a vein at her temple. Her lips are nearly white beneath the fluorescent lighting of the room. But even sleep deprived and in the throes of a powerful grief, she's lovely.

'I keep expecting Paul to walk through the door,' she whispers. 'He always knew what to do.' Her legs give way as if they no longer have the strength to support her, and she collapses into the chair, leans forward, and puts her face in her hands. 'I need him. What am I going to do without him?'

'Everything's going to be okay.' But my words ring hollow

even to me. This is one of those times when everything isn't okay and may never be okay ever again.

Across the room, the bishop brings the recliner to an upright position, but he's having a difficult time getting to his feet. For the first time since I've known him, he looks fragile and old and utterly exhausted. I start toward him to help, but he raises a hand to stop me. 'No, Katie. I'm fine.'

Feeling useless, I step back. 'I'll check with the nurse to see what the holdup is.'

I'm midway to the nurses' station when I see an orderly and a nurse wheeling a gurney down the hall. There's an IV stand connected to it. Both bed rails are raised, and there's a small figure beneath the sheet. The nurse is wearing SpongeBob scrubs, with a pen behind her ear. Her name tag heralds her name as SUSAN M. The pin above it warns: I CAN BE DIFFICULT.

'Is that David Borntrager?' I ask as they approach.

The nurse looks up from the clipboard, gives my uniform a quick once over, and smiles. 'This little champ is ready for his room.'

Keeping pace with them, I glance down at David. He sleeps soundly, his mouth slightly open, head crooked to one side, completely unaware. His left arm is swathed in some kind of purple wrap, and he's got a raw-looking abrasion on his forehead. It's the first time I've seen him in decent light, and I can't help but notice the heavy brows and the down-slanted eyes, the too-small distance between his nose and upper lip, his obesity, and I remember hearing talk about Mattie and Paul having a special-needs child.

'How is he?' I ask.

'Doctor Reinhardt repaired a blood vessel in his abdomen and removed his spleen. He lost quite a bit of blood, so we gave him two units. It was touch and go for a bit, but his blood pressure is stable now. The only other trauma is the broken arm and a slight concussion.' Another smile. 'This little guy is going to be just fine.'

Relief shudders through me, and I release the breath I'd been holding. I follow alongside the gurney as they wheel him to room 308. We arrive to find Bishop Troyer standing at the door. His old face breaks into a grin when he spots the boy.

Mattie springs from her chair, one hand over her mouth, and rushes toward her son. 'Is he all right?' Her gaze goes to the nurse. 'Can I touch him?'

'He's going to be fine. And, yes, you can touch him all you like. Just don't jostle him or press on his tummy.' Unfazed by the fact that Mattie is Amish and there's a bishop standing a few feet away, the nurse smiles. 'I'm Susan, by the way. You must be Mom.'

Some of the desperation leaves Mattie's expression, but her eyes never leave her son. *'Ja.'*

'I'm David's nurse today.' Her voice is devoid of the phony cheeriness that grates in situations like this, and I find myself liking her.

The orderly, a big teddy bear of a man wearing blue scrubs with a long-sleeve tee-shirt beneath, maneuvers the gurney so that it's lined up with the bed. Mindful of the IV line and stand, the nurse peels down the blanket and sheet and fluffs the pillow. In tandem, they lift the boy and transfer him to the bed. The child stirs briefly, but doesn't wake. Once he's lying supine, the orderly covers him with a sheet and woven blanket, while the nurse hooks the IV bag to the portable stand next to the bed.

Mattie can't seem to take her eyes off her son. She's standing too close, getting in the way, but neither the nurse nor the orderly seems to mind.

The nurse picks up the clipboard and makes a note. 'The doctor will be in to talk to you later.'

'Thank you.' Mattie bends and presses her cheek against her son's, her eyes closed. 'My sweet little miracle,' she whispers.

Using an ear thermometer, the nurse takes the boy's temperature and scribbles something on the clipboard. 'If you folks need anything, just press the button over there.' She indicates a call button next to the bed, makes a quick adjustment to the IV drip, and leaves the room.

Mattie hovers over her son, caressing his forehead, rounding the bed and touching him through the sheets, looking down at him as if she's afraid to break contact lest he slip away.

I sidle over to Bishop Troyer. 'Do you need anything Bishop?'

'We are fine.'

'You should go home and get some rest.'

He gives me a stern look. 'If you're worried that I'm going to collapse from old age, I should tell you that Mattie's *mamm* is on her way.'

'I would have picked her up and brought her.'

'I know.'

'And it never crossed my mind that you're old.'

His mouth twitches, but he doesn't smile. That the boy is going to survive has eased the oppressive sense of doom from earlier. Still, we're mindful that we're in the midst of a monumental tragedy.

'Everything is taken care of at the house?' I ask, referring to Mattie's farm. 'Someone is there to feed the livestock?'

'Of course,' the Bishop replies. 'We are Amish.'

I'd known that would be the case, but I was compelled to ask. The Amish may not have phones in their homes, but the community has a healthy grapevine and news travels fast, especially in the face of tragedy. The instant word got out about Paul's death – probably with the help of the bishop's wife – Mattie's friends and neighbors converged with prayers and able hands.

'Katie?'

I look up to see Mattie approach. Though she's lost her husband and two of her children, the hopelessness is gone from her eyes. 'Thank you,' she whispers. 'For what you did. For being there. Thank you for everything. . . .'

The next thing I know her arms are around me, pulling me close and squeezing hard. Her mouth is close to my ear and I hear her sob quietly. Her body shakes against mine. As if of their own volition, my arms go around her. She smells of laundry detergent and sunshine and I find myself hugging her back with a fierceness that surprises me. 'I'm so sorry for your loss,' I say quietly.

'God called Paul and Norah and Little Sam home. It was His will and I accept that. But He decided this was not David's day to go to heaven. He answered my prayers and gave me back my boy. For that, I am thankful.'

There's more to say. At some point, I'll need to tell her the accident was a hit-and-run. If she asks about Paul's final moments, I'm obliged to tell her he was alive when I arrived on the scene. But for now, she has enough on her plate.

And I have a killer to find.

SIX

I'm on my way to the station when my cell phone erupts. I glance down, see Sheriff Rasmussen's name on the display, and snatch it up.

'Where you at, Chief?'

'Just left the hospital.'

'How's the kid?'

I give him the rundown on David. 'He's going to make it.'

'That's terrific news.' But I know that's not the reason he called. 'Look, we may have gotten a break on identifying the hit-skip vehicle. One of the deputies thinks the side-view mirror we found at the scene is from a Ford truck.'

'That *is* a nice break.' But a cynical little voice reminds me: *Nothing is ever that easy.* 'Now all we have to do is find the truck it belongs to.'

'I'm about to run it over to the Ford dealership. If they can confirm it, I'll add the make to the BOLO.' He pauses, gets to the point. 'Impound garage didn't have room for the buggy inside, and I didn't want to leave it outside, so I had it hauled down to the volunteer fire department garage. Prosecutor wants us to reconstruct it, so that once we get a positive ID on this guy, he'll be ready to file. If this case goes to trial, we need to have all our ducks in a row. What are the odds of your pulling some of your Amish strings and getting a buggy maker out here?'

'Pretty good.'

'I'm here with Maloney and we've been combing through this shit all morning.' He lowers his voice. 'We have two pieces from the vehicle. The mirror, and then this morning we found some kind of pin that's been sheared in half.'

'What kind of pin?'

'Not sure just yet. Almost looks like something you'd find on a tractor. To tell you the truth, we're not even sure it came from the hit-skip.'

My conversation with Glock floats uneasily through my mind. 'If this guy was going as fast as Maloney says, there should have been a lot of debris, Mike, even if there was a brush guard or something.'

'We thought maybe the driver stopped and picked it up.'

'It's possible.' Even as I say the words my gut tells me it's not probable. 'But it would have taken a lot of time and effort for someone to sift through all the debris and pick up only what he needed to cover his tracks. Think about it. It was dark. Drizzling. After an impact like that, the driver would have been shaken up. Maybe even injured.'

'Or drunk on his ass.'

'That's not to mention the emotional trauma of seeing the dead and knowing what he'd done. Even if he's some kind of sociopath, there's the fear of discovery. Who would have the wherewithal after a crash like that?'

'Maybe there was a passenger. Two of them.'

'Maybe.'

I hear frustration in his sigh and wonder if he got any sleep. 'I ran the sheared pin down to one of the body shops here in Millersburg earlier. The manager thought maybe it was from some kind of after-market part.'

'What does that mean?'

'It didn't come from the factory. It was added after the vehicle was purchased.'

'That could jibe with the brush guard theory.' Glancing in my rearview mirror I turn around in the parking lot of a Lutheran church and head back toward Millersburg. 'I'm going to swing by the buggy maker's place now, see if I can get him to ride down there with me.'

'Excellent. I should be back from the dealership in half an hour. Hopefully with some news.'

I've known Luke Miller since I was ten years old and we got into trouble for passing notes in the one-room schoolhouse where I received my early education. Blond-haired, blue eyed, and armed with a thousand-watt grin, he was one of the more interesting characters to grace my childhood. I'd had a huge crush on him. He was fun to be around because he was always breaking the rules and getting into trouble – a trait we shared – and he never hesitated to argue his position with the adults, a rarity among Amish children, since most are well behaved and respectful to the extreme. Together, we were a force to be reckoned with. I think the teacher was relieved when our eighth-grade education was complete and she was rid of us.

He's one of only a few Amish who no longer farms for a living. He resides in a small frame house in Painters Mill proper. He doesn't own a horse or buggy and gets around via an old Schwinn bicycle, or when necessary, he hires a driver.

I find him in the shop behind his house fitting a wheel to the axle of a finished carriage. When he hears me enter, he looks at me through the spokes of the wheel and offers a big grin.

'Katie Burkholder.' He rises to his full height, gives me an assessing once-over. 'What a pleasant surprise.'

He's wearing a straw hat, dark gray trousers with suspenders over a blue work shirt. As a kid, he'd been somewhat of a neatnik, and I notice immediately that quality has carried over into his adulthood. But then neat has always looked good on Luke.

It's odd to see an Amish man his age without a full beard. He's one of the few adults I know who never married, a feat that's almost unheard of, since family and children are touchstones of the culture.

'Nice man-cave you've got here, Luke.'

'Don't tell me you've decided to come back to the old ways and you're here to buy a buggy.'

'Not unless you can retrofit it with a V-8 and light kit.'

'Don't forget the sound system.' Laughing, he motions toward a well-worn wooden pew set against the wall. '*Sitz dich anne un bleib e weil.*'

I look at the bench, but I don't sit. 'I can't stay.'

Tugging a kerchief from his back pocket, he wipes his hands and starts toward me. 'How are you?' He extends his hand to mine and we shake.

'I need a favor,' I tell him.

'You're the one person I could never say no to.' He holds on to my gaze – and my hand – an instant too long and I find myself thinking about the time he took me behind the silo at Big Joe Bilar's farm when I was thirteen and kissed me.

'What can I help you with?' he asks.

Extracting my hand from his, I stroll over to the buggy. Even with my proletarian eye, I readily discern the exquisite workmanship and I know he's as good a buggy maker as his *datt* was.

'Paul Borntrager and two of his children were killed in a buggy accident last night,' I begin.

'I heard.' His face falls, a small sound of distress escaping his mouth. 'Damn.'

I outline some of the details of the accident. 'The driver fled the scene. We're trying to identify the vehicle.'

'I see.' He sighs. 'Paul was a good man. A good father and husband.' He looks down at his work boots. 'How's Mattie?'

'She's pretty broken up.' I pause. 'I was wondering if you could help with the reconstruction of the buggy.'

He looks at me as if I didn't even need to say the words. 'Of course I will.'

That's it. No questions. No dawdling. No excuses. No 'Let me finish what I'm doing' or 'I'll get back to you' or 'Will tomorrow do?' He doesn't even tell me he needs to wash his hands or change clothes first.

Because when you're Amish and one of your own is hurt or in trouble, you drop everything and you go to help them.

Half an hour later, Sheriff Rasmussen, Frank Maloney, and I are standing in a bay at the volunteer fire department, watching Luke Miller puzzle over hundreds of fragments from the buggy. Upon our arrival, Rasmussen informed me that the manager of the Ford dealership didn't recognize the sheared pin, but identified the side-view mirror found at the scene as belonging to a Ford truck built between 1996 and 2001. It isn't much, but when we have so little to go on, it's a start. Rasmussen updated the BOLO to include the make and year range. If any law enforcement agency makes a stop for any reason and the vehicle meets the criteria, we'll have the opportunity to take a closer look.

The main section of the carriage sits atop a large tarp with the right side axles propped on concrete blocks. The sheer number of pieces makes the task of reconstruction a mind-boggling endeavor. Progress is agonizingly slow. Beneath the hard fluorescent light, some of the parts are still recognizable. The seat. The floorboard. Two of the wheels are still attached to the frame, though the rims and spokes are broken. The other two wheels lie on the floor close to their respective axles. The cab and undercarriage sustained the brunt of the damage, especially the right side. Luke has begun rearranging segments, butting together shattered strips of wood and chunks of fiberglass, like the pieces of some grisly puzzle.

From my place near the door, I see dried blood on the seat. Dried spatter mars a slab of wood that looks like it might be part of the backrest. I wish someone had wiped it down before bringing it here. Luke doesn't seem to notice. Rasmussen gave him disposable gloves and shoe covers both to protect him from biohazard and to keep him from contaminating evidence. Luke walks the tarp, picking up one piece at a time and putting it where it belongs.

Maloney paces the perimeter of the tarp, asking the occasional question. I stand near the door, where the harness lies in a heap on the floor, so close I discern the smell of horse and leather and a trace of manure. Rasmussen stands next to me, looking dejected and cranky. Both of our cells have been ringing nonstop all morning, and now we're too tired to talk to each other.

'Katie.'

I look up to see Luke holding a two-foot length of wood that's jagged on one end. It's painted black on one side, naked on the flip side. 'I think I found something.'

The Amish man brings the wood over to us. 'This piece of wood is from the door on the right side of the buggy. The leading edge or forepart.'

Maloney, Rasmussen, and I form a circle around him and study the scrap of wood.

'My *datt* made this buggy,' Luke tells us. 'Probably ten or twelve years ago. Back then, we used more wood than fiberglass. Oak, I think. These are his initials, burned into the wood here.

See?' Smiling, he runs a calloused fingertip over small, black letters: JM. 'John Miller. He liked working with the hardwoods. Walnut, too.' Sobering, he indicates an irregularity in the surface. 'The wood is soft enough so that if something strikes it with force, it leaves an impression.'

The mark looks like someone took a hammer and struck a single hard blow against the wood. Only this was no hammer and I realize we're getting our first glimpse of something from the vehicle that killed Paul Borntrager and his children.

In tandem, Rasmussen, Maloney, and I lean forward for a closer look. I pull my mini Maglite from my belt and set the beam on the impression. Beneath the light, I discern that it's hexagonal in shape.

'That looks like a bolt head,' Rasmussen says.

Maloney nods. 'A big one.'

I look at the two men. 'On the front end of a Ford truck?'

Rasmussen shrugs. 'Maybe the driver had something bolted on.'

'Brush guard?' Maloney asks.

I glance at Luke. 'Do you have any idea what might have made that dent?'

Luke turns the wood over in his hands, runs his fingers over the impression. 'I agree that it looks like a bolt. No way to know what it attached.'

Rasmussen eases the board from Luke's hands. 'I'll run this out to the body shop, see if they can help us out.'

'Luke,' I begin, 'if the buggy were still intact and standing, how high off the ground would this piece be?'

The Amish man's brows knit. 'I would have to take a tape measure to it to be exact. Guessing, I would say thirty-six or thirty-eight inches.'

I look at Rasmussen. 'That's about the right height for a bumper.'

The sheriff frowns. 'So we may be looking at a Ford truck with a brush guard or some type of after-market bumper.'

My phone chooses that moment to vibrate against my hip. Turning away, I snatch it up and answer with a brusque, 'Burkholder.'

'Chief, I just took a call on the hotline I thought you ought to know about.'

It's Lois Monroe, my first shift dispatcher, and she's talking so fast I can barely understand her. 'Slow down.'

'The owner of a body shop in Wooster remembers a guy bringing in a truck to have the front end reinforced. He didn't think anything about it until he heard about the hit-and-run on the news this morning.'

'What kind of truck?'

Paper crinkles on the other end. 'Ford F-250.'

My interest surges. 'Which body shop?'

'Voss Brothers.' She rattles off the phone number and address. 'Guy's name is Bob Voss.'

I thank her and disconnect to find Rasmussen looking at me intently. 'You up to a trip to Wooster?' I ask.

'Tell me you just got a break,' he mutters.

Quickly, I recap my conversation with Lois. 'Could turn out to be nothing. Some guy who plays demolition derby on the weekend.'

'Or if you're a glass-half-full kind of guy like me, it could be our first break.'

Rasmussen, the eternal optimist.

SEVEN

The abandoned grain elevator sat at the edge of the woods like a ghost ship listing on a dark sea. The massive structure was slowly being devoured by a forest determined to reclaim its rightful domain. Trees embraced the backside, vines reaching into the broken windows and wrapping their spindly arms around the wood and concrete exterior, as if trying to pull the structure more deeply into the woods to consume it.

Jack Mott and his best friend, Leon, turned twelve last month, and they'd been coming here all summer. It was the perfect place to explore and play army. Once, Leon had brought his BB gun and they'd played cowboys and Indians. Leon had shot a bat that had been hanging from one of the rafters. It plopped down at their feet, a bloody hole in its side, dead as road kill. Jack thought it was a lucky shot, but Leon had spent the next week bragging about it to the girls at the pool where they were on the dive team. The girls had been impressed because word around town was that the old place was haunted. By whom, no one knew. Jack didn't care; the rumors made for some good stories, even if they weren't quite true.

Jack wheeled his bike up the gravel track and laid it on its side twenty yards from the yawning mouth. 'You bring smokes?'

'I got two off my dad.' Leon leaned his bike against a good-size sapling and hopped off.

'Just two?'

'My old man catches me smoking and I'm dead meat.'

The boys started toward the overhead door, which was rolled halfway up and off its track on one side. The afternoon air was humid, hot, and thick with end-of-summer bugs swarming in the rays of sun slanting down from the treetops. Jack ducked through the door first and stepped into the hazy shadows of the elevator. Even after coming here all summer, he couldn't get over how big the place was – or how creepy. The office was the scariest. There were papers and bird shit all over the place. Once, they'd found blood and feathers on the floor. They hadn't come back for almost a week. But this old place had been the most exciting part of their summer, and despite the creep-factor, neither boy had been able to stay away. They were explorers, after all, and danger was part of the allure.

School started on Monday, so this would be their last day to explore, before football practice and all those extracurricular activities crowded their schedules. Both boys would be in seventh grade. Jack wasn't looking forward to middle school. He liked being a sixth grader because that made him one of the oldest – and biggest – kids. He was king of the playground and no one messed with him. Seventh grade would put him back at the bottom of the totem pole and he'd have to start all over again. The good news was, once he got up the nerve, he planned to ask Lori Deardorf to go steady.

'Come on, you dip.'

Pulled from his daydreaming, Jack trotted up beside Leon. The murky interior smelled of dirt and mold and rotting wood. Jack liked the smells. He was going to miss this place when school started.

They walked along the cracked concrete slab where farm

trucks had once rolled in with loads of corn and soybeans. Ahead, the office with its broken windows and rusty file cabinets beckoned. There was an old chair inside. Some animal had ripped up the seat and pulled out the stuffing. Every time Jack walked in, he checked the office first because he was always afraid he'd find someone sitting on that old chair, watching them. Once when they'd come here on a windy day, they'd been in the office and the old overhead door where they entered fell down another foot. Aside from finding the blood, it was the creepiest thing that had ever happened.

Remembering, Jack quickened his pace. 'Gimme a cig.'

Leon reached into the pocket of his hoodie. 'Wish I'd brought the BB gun. We could have shot us some rats.'

Jack looked around uneasily. He didn't like the idea of rats. 'They only come out at night.'

'Still, it woulda been—'

Leon's words were cut off as he went down. One moment he was walking beside Jack, digging for his smokes. The next he was being sucked into the ground, like in the movie where the corpse grabs your ankle and yanks you into his casket. Jack looked down to see that his friend had stepped into some kind of hole and fallen in up to his waist.

'Crap!' Leon's hands scrabbled on the dirt as he tried to claw his way out. 'Help me!'

'Shit! Hang on!' Jack grabbed one of his arms and pulled as hard as he could.

Within seconds, Leon was back on his feet and both boys found themselves staring into a deep, dark pit. 'Holy cow!'

'That's a deep fuckin' hole!' Jack exclaimed.

'Gotta be ten feet down.'

'More like twelve.'

Leon brushed the dirt from his jeans. 'I ain't never seen that before. What the hell is it?'

Jack lived on a farm a few miles down the road. Just last week, he'd gone to the grain elevator in Painters Mill with his dad. He knew what the boot pit was and had a pretty good idea how it worked. 'It's where the farmers dump corn and shit.'

'I wonder why they didn't cover it up.'

'Looks like they did. Sort of.' Jack used the toe of his sneaker to uncover the edge of the steel grate. 'They just didn't cover it all the way.'

'Some old lady could walk in here and break her leg!'

Jack looked at Leon and they cracked up. 'Old ladies don't go into grain elevators, you moron.'

Leon felt around for the stolen cigarettes and his eyes widened. 'I dropped the smokes!'

'Hang on.' Jack had never had cause to use his new flashlight, and he was pleased he'd remembered to bring it along as he tugged it out of his back pocket. Leon watched as he dropped to his belly and shined the light into the pit. 'Whoa.'

Leon got down on his stomach beside him. 'Holy shit.'

'Man, that's creepy.'

'It's cool is what it is.' Leon thrust his finger toward the bottom of the pit. 'Lookit! There's the smokes!'

Jack shifted the beam. Sure enough, two tiny white cigarettes lay side by side atop a dust-covered two-by-six.

'Let's go down,' Leon said.

'I ain't going down there.'

'Come on! Man, this is the best! We can climb down—'

'We ain't got no way down.'

'I saw a rope in the office.' Leon jumped to his feet.

'It's probably rotten.' Jack rose as well. 'We get stuck down there and no one will ever find us.'

'Jack, you are such a puss! The rope's nylon and nylon don't rot. We're not going to get stuck.'

Realizing there was no way he could refuse the challenge

and save face, Jack sighed. The last thing he wanted to do was start seventh grade with Leon calling him chicken. 'Damn it, Leon.'

But the other boy was already running toward the office. Jack watched him disappear inside. Dread landed like a brick in his gut when he came back with a coil of dirty yellow rope.

'This is awesome!' Leon declared.

Jack didn't think so. 'We're going to have to tie it to something. Is it long enough?'

They looked around. 'That post over there,' Leon decided.

'We should probably tie some knots in it so we can climb out.'

'Good idea.' Leon took the rope over to a massive wood beam and tied one end around the base.

Jack reluctantly set to work on the rope, tying knots a foot apart so they'd have something to grip when they climbed out.

Within minutes, the rope was secure, knotted, and dangling into the pit. 'How're the batteries on that flashlight?' Leon asked.

'I just put 'em in.'

Leon looked at him, as if the gravity of what they were about to do was starting to sink in. 'You want me to go down first?'

Relief slipped through Jack, but he didn't let it show. Instead, he shrugged. 'I'll keep the light on you from up here.'

A grin spread across Leon's face. 'I can't wait to tell everyone about this.' He went to the opening, picked up the rope, and looked down. 'Wish I had some gloves.'

'Don't fall, you idiot.'

Leon gave a cavalier wave and started into the hole. 'Geronimo!' he cried, his voice echoing.

Jack held the flashlight steady and watched his friend descend. In less than a minute, Leon was standing at the base, looking up at him. 'Nothin' to it.'

'Here.' Jack tossed the flashlight at Leon, who caught it with one hand. Mr. Cool. 'I'm coming down.'

The descent was easier than Jack had imagined. The rope bit into his palms, but war wounds were a good thing when you were about to ask Lori Deardorf to go steady. He couldn't wait to brag about this.

When he reached the base of the pit, Leon was already lighting up. 'Jeez, you could have waited on me.'

Leon shoved a cigarette at him. 'Go for it, dude.'

Proud of himself for making it down without incident, Jack lit up, trying not to cough when the smoke hit the back of his throat. 'This place is cool.'

'A lot of crap down here.'

'Lookit all this old corn and shit.'

'Bet there are rats down here.'

'Probably as big as fuckin' groundhogs.'

The smoked in silence for a couple of minutes, and then Leon dropped his on the ground and crushed it beneath his foot.

Jack had just tossed his butt into the dirt and was about to step on it when something beneath a pile of wood caught his attention. 'Hey, Leon. What's that? Over there?'

His friend turned around, walked to the dusty heap. 'Looks like a rock.'

'I ain't never seen a rock like that.'

Leon squatted, reached for a splintered two-by-four, and tossed it aside. Dust motes swirled when it landed in the dirt behind him. Next came a rusty one-gallon paint can. A piece of rotted cloth.

Kneeling beside him, Jack reached for the rock, tugged it from its ancient nest. 'I got it.' It was smaller than a soccer ball, but too lightweight to be a rock.

'I bet it's a dog skull,' Leon said with a nervous giggle. 'Look at them eye holes.'

'Musta been a big dog.' Jack brought it to him, blew the dust off, and turned it over in his hands.

'Holy shit!' Leon sprang to his feet.

Jack Mott stared down at the human skull in his hands, and then he started to scream.

The Voss Brothers Body Shop sits at the edge of town next to a junkyard that's enclosed by a tall corrugated barrier fence. I pull into the pothole-laden lot, steering the Explorer around holes large enough to swallow a tire. A small frame house with a big stump in the yard serves as the office. Through the door I see a heavyset man in bib overalls behind the counter, watching us. Though the Explorer is clearly marked with the Painters Mill PD insignia, he makes no move to greet us.

The shop consists of a large metal building with two overhead doors in front. One of the doors stands open and I see a silver Toyota Camry on a hydraulic lift. A shop light dangles from the undercarriage and two men in coveralls squint up at the bottom side of the engine. Parked next to the building, an SUV that looks as if it's been run through an auto crusher waits its turn.

I park adjacent the office and Rasmussen and I get out. We're midway to the door when a man yells, 'Hey!'

We turn simultaneously to see a large, round-bodied man clad in denim bib overalls striding toward us. His gray hair and weatherworn face tell me he's well into his sixties. 'I'm Bob Voss.' From ten feet away, he sticks out his hand, leaves it extended as he closes the space between us.

Rasmussen and I identify ourselves. When we shake, Voss grins from ear to ear. 'I've never met a lady cop before.'

'There's a first time for everything,' I tell him.

'Thank goodness for that,' he says with a chuckle.

Rasmussen gets right down to business. 'You called the

hotline about a customer that had the front end of his truck reinforced.'

'Hope I ain't wasting your time. But when I saw the news about that hit-and-run kilt that Amish family, I remembered this guy bringing in a truck. I thought I should let someone know.'

'We're glad you did,' the sheriff says. 'What kind of work did he have done?'

'Well, that's the thing. He had the front end reinforced with a steel plate. We don't get requests like that every day so it kind of stuck out.'

'Did he say why?' I ask.

'Said he had this old stump he needed pushed out of the way.' He scratches his head. 'Anyone with a brain knows you don't use the front of your truck for that. You burn it or grind it or get a backhoe after it, but you don't use your damn bumper. To tell you the truth, he didn't look like the stump-pullin' type.'

'You get a name?' Rasmussen asks.

'I got everything.' Giving us some Groucho Marx eyebrow action, he motions toward the office. 'Pulled the invoice 'fore I called. Come on in and I'll show you.'

Rasmussen and I follow him to the house. He takes us up the steps, across the porch, and through the entrance, the old screen door banging shut behind us. The office is small with dirty linoleum floors, a ragtag sofa set against the wall, and a chest-high counter that looks as if it came from some highway roadhouse that got shut down by the health department. I glance at the man behind the counter and do a double take. He's an exact duplicate of Bob Voss, replete with a matching crew cut, bib overalls, and the SUV-size gut. He gives me a gotcha grin and I notice the only difference is that the man behind the counter is missing a lower tooth in the front.

The two men giggle like schoolgirls and I realize this is an entertaining moment for them. 'I'm Billy Voss,' the look-alike says, moving toward us, his hand outstretched.

'D'you see the look on her face?' Chuckling, Bob Voss wipes his eyes with a white kerchief.

'I guess your customers keep you two pretty amused,' Rasmussen says, and I realize his sense of humor is the first thing to go when he's sleep deprived.

'You guys are twins?' I ask.

'Born ten minutes apart,' Billy tells us as he slides a folder from the top of the file cabinet. 'I got the brains, he got the looks.'

Bob pours coffee into a nasty-looking mug. 'You guys want some lead?'

Rasmussen and I decline.

'What can you tell us about this customer?' I ask.

'Nice looking young fella.' Billy sets the folder on the counter and opens it.

Inside, I see a yellow sheet of paper from a legal pad that's scribbled with notes, and a generic-looking invoice that's filled out with blue ink.

Billy turns the invoice around, so we don't have to read it upside down and slides it toward us.

Date: August 25
Name: Howard Barnes
Address: 345 West Fourth St. Killbuck
Phone: 885-5452
Estimate for Repair Costs: Material: $92.00
    Labor: $300.00 Total = $392.00
Make and model of vehicle: Gry 1996 Ford F-250
    Plate # DHA3709
Description: Reinforce front end $1/4$ inch steel 18"×32"

For the span of several minutes, the only sound comes from an old Led Zeppelin song, 'When the Levee Breaks,' oozing from a sleek sound system set up on a TV tray behind the counter.

'Which one of you talked to this guy?' Rasmussen asks.

'I did,' says Bob.

Listening to the conversation with half an ear, I unclip my cell and hit the speed dial for dispatch. Lois picks up on the first ring. 'I need a ten twelve,' I say.

'Go ahead.'

'David, Henry, Adam, three, seven, zero, niner.' I hear keys clicking on the other end as she enters the tag number into the BMV database.

'That's weird,' Lois says. 'You sure that tag number is right, Chief?' She reads it back to me.

I glance at the invoice. 'That's it.'

'According to BMV, that number doesn't exist.'

'Well shit.' I get a prickly sensation on the back of my neck. 'Give me a ten twenty-nine on Howard Barnes.' I spell both the first and last names for her.

'Stand by.'

Computer keys click. While she checks for wanted and warrants, I turn my attention to Bob Voss. 'Did you happen to take a look at his driver's license?'

The old man stares at me, blinking, guilty. I feel Rasmussen's eyes on me, but I don't look at him.

'Well, no,' Bob says. 'We generally don't check.'

I say to Rasmussen, 'Tag number is bogus.'

The sheriff's eyes narrow. 'That's interesting as hell.'

I turn my attention to Bob. 'How did he pay?'

Bill pulls the invoice to him, lowers the cheaters from his crown, and points to a checkmarked box on the form. 'Cash.'

'That's a lot of cash for someone to carry around,' Rasmussen says.

'You sure about the make and model of the truck?' I ask.

Voss nods. 'That I am. I know trucks, and I saw it myself.'

'Short or long bed?'

He grimaces, shakes his head. 'I don't recall.'

'Chief?' comes Lois's voice over the phone.

I turn my attention back to the call. 'What do you have?'

'Nothing coming back on Howard Barnes.'

'You mean nothing as in he hasn't killed anyone lately? Or that he's not in the system?'

'Not in the system. You got a middle initial?'

'No.'

The prickling sensation augments into a creeping suspicion that drops into my gut like a stone. 'I've got a make and model to add to the APB. Gray Ford F-250, 1996.'

'I'll get it out ASAP.'

'I also need ROs for all '96 Ford F-250 trucks in the three-county area: Holmes, Coshocton, and Wayne.'

'I'm on it.'

'Thanks.' I disconnect to hear Billy saying, '. . . he was probably forty years old. I wish I remembered more, but it's been two weeks and we get quite a few customers in here.'

'How exactly did you modify the truck?' Rasmussen asks.

'That's the reason I remembered this guy,' Billy says. 'He had us remove the bumper and install a quarter-inch slab of steel and weld it to the frame with I-beams. When I asked him why, he mentioned the stump. Later, he said it was just for pushing things around. You know, kind of vague. I figured it was just a farm truck and he was going to let his kid drive it around or something.'

I look down at the invoice, spot the illegible scrawl at the bottom. 'Is that his signature?'

Billy tries to slide the invoice around for a better look, but I stop him. In the back of my mind I'm wondering if the lab will be able to raise some latents. 'Yes, ma'am.'

'Do you mind if we take this with us?' I ask, adding, 'I'll make sure you get it back.'

Both men stare at me as if they've just now realized this is serious and they're mentally working through all the dark possibilities.

'You think this guy killed them people down there in Painters Mill?' Bob asks.

'I don't know,' I say honestly. 'But I think it warrants looking into.'

'You got any other paper on this guy?' Rasmussen asks.

'No sir.' Billy shakes his head. 'That's it.'

Rasmussen reaches into his jacket and pulls out an evidence bag containing the sheared pin. 'This look familiar to either of you?'

Both men shake their heads.

Bob squints at the bag. 'Looks like a three-quarter-inch L pin.'

'Any idea what that kind of pin is used for?' I ask.

'Hard to say,' Billy says. 'One that size . . . could be from a tractor.'

'I seen 'em on farm implements,' Bob adds. 'Could be off a pivot bracket on a rototiller or mower. Honestly, since we don't know the length, could be for just about anything.'

Frowning, Rasmussen drops the bag back into his pocket. 'How exactly did you guys attach the steel plate?'

'We removed the bumper and welded it to the frame,' Billy explains.

'Did you use any type of pin or bolt?' I ask.

'No, ma'am.' Bob shakes his head. 'We welded it. Solid as a rock, too.'

Pinching the invoice between two fingers at its corner, the sheriff picks it up and slips it into the folder. 'We're going to need a description of the customer.'

'Do you guys have security cameras?' I ask.

Bob Voss nods. 'In the yard out back where we park the vehicles we're working on. We've had thieves come over the fence at night a couple times. Took some rims once and a fuel pump a few months back, so we had cameras installed.'

'Did this customer go into the yard?' I ask.

'Wish we could help you there,' Billy says, 'but he was only here in the office and the shop.'

It takes another ten minutes to wrangle a description from the two brothers. They disagree on the color of the guy's hair and the type of shirt he was wearing. But we walk away with height, eye color, and the general impression that he was a 'nice looking young fella' and 'dressed like a yuppie.'

As Rasmussen and I clamber into the Explorer, he turns to me and sighs. 'Not to throw a wrench into such a straight-forward case, but I'm pretty sure there is no Fourth Street in Killbuck.'

Nothing about the address had struck me as odd, but now that he mentioned it, I realize he's right. 'He gave a bogus address, too.'

'People who give false information usually have something to hide,' he says. 'And he didn't *just* have body work done. He had the front end of a big-ass truck with a big-ass engine re-inforced with a big-ass slab of steel.'

I pull onto the highway and glance at Rasmussen. 'He's our guy.'

'It would explain the lack of debris.'

'He had the work done two weeks ago. That shows premedi-tation.'

'Premeditated *what*?'

We look at each other for a moment, then he says, 'I can't see someone murdering an Amish man and two kids. I mean, the way this was done – with a vehicle – a lot of things could have gone wrong. He risked a witness seeing him. He risked the victims surviving to identify him. The impact could have disabled his truck and stranded him, gotten him caught. Hell, he could have killed himself.'

'Maybe what we're dealing with was more of a road rage situation,' I say.

Rasmussen nods. 'There's no shortage of meanness out there. We've seen it focused on the Amish before.'

I'm still turning over the road rage angle. 'Maybe it didn't have anything to do with this particular family. Maybe it was more about opportunity. It was dusk. They were alone on a little-used back road. Their paths crossed.' I'm tossing out ideas, trying to make sense of something that makes absolutely no sense.

'We did have that rash of hate crimes last year,' he says.

I think about the kids and shake my head, unable to wrap my brain around that kind of hatred. 'This takes hate to a whole new level of ugly.'

'I'll get that invoice to the lab, see what comes back.' He sighs. 'In the interim, I'd say we probably ought to keep our options open.'

I nod, but in the back of my mind I know we're no longer dealing with a simple DUI or hit-and-run or even a case of vehicular homicide.

We're now investigating three counts of premeditated murder.

EIGHT

I'm sitting in the conference room, working on my second cup of coffee, and going through my sparse collection of notes on the Borntrager case, as the rest of my team files in for an impromptu briefing. It's going to be a short meeting because we basically don't have shit in terms of information or suspects.

As usual, Pickles is the first to arrive and stakes his claim at the table adjacent me with a to-go cup from LaDonna's Diner in front of him. From where I sit, I can smell the cigarettes and English Leather. He's one of the few who actually enjoys these meetings. It's an added bonus if someone is getting their ass chewed.

Two chairs down, Glock has the case file open in front of him, various reports and photos spread out on the table, reading. On his left, Skid leans back in his chair, gobbling up the final remnants of a burrito. At the head of the table, T.J. thumbs some urgent message into his Droid. I can tell from the grin on his face it doesn't have anything to do with police business. Frank Maloney, the accident reconstructionist from the sheriff's office, stands at the whiteboard, his back to the rest of us, finishing a sketch of the scene in blue marker. Mona stands just inside the doorway, talking quietly to Lois, who's manning dispatch and listening for the phone. I put Mona in charge of overseeing the hotline, which has already given us our first lead. I'm hoping for more.

'You ready, Maloney?' I ask.

The deputy steps away from the sketch and sighs. 'I'm a damn good reconstructionist, but I suck at drawing.'

The sketch is a crude rendition of the accident scene, replete with intersection labels, a north-south directional symbol, the ditch, mile marker, and the location of the stop sign. He's indicated the final resting place of the buggy, the direction in which it was traveling, along with the point of impact. The victims and horse are depicted with stick figures.

Taking a final swig of coffee, I go to the half-podium at the head of the table and open the briefing with the only good news I've gotten since the accident. 'Before we begin, I wanted to let everyone know David Borntrager is going to be fine.'

Everyone gives a short round of applause along with an enthusiastic 'Fuckin' A' from Glock.

I motion toward Maloney. 'I think most of you have met Frank. He's going to give a short presentation on what we believe happened the night Paul Borntrager and his two kids were killed.'

'Emphasis on short,' Skid mutters.

I glance down at my notes. 'First, I wanted to run through everything we've got so far, give assignments, and get reports.'

I run through the list of information and evidence we've amassed so far. The as-of-yet unidentified pin and the side-view mirror. The hexagonal impression in the piece of wood buggy maker Luke Miller discovered. Then I face my team and tell them about Rasmussen's and my trip to the Voss Brother's Body Shop in Wooster.

'I made copies of the invoice for everyone. The original has been sent to BCI lab in London on the chance we can pick up some latents.' I scan the room. 'I believe it's relevant to the case that the work performed on the truck included having a quarter-inch-thick steel plate welded to the front end. If that vehicle is, indeed, the hit-skip, this adds premeditation and changes our case from vehicular homicide to murder one.'

'You get a description on this guy?' Glock asks.

I quote Bob Voss. 'Nice looking young man and dresses like a yuppie.'

'That narrows it down,' Skid says dryly.

'What about cameras?' Pickles asks. 'A lot of them body shops have security cameras.'

'They do,' I tell him, 'but only in the rear lot. Here's what we do know. The vehicle is a gray 1996 Ford F-250. BOLO is out, so other agencies including the SHP will be looking.' I don't need to tell them that vehicles can be altered, parked, or hidden indefinitely.

'I had Lois pull the ROs of Ford F-250 trucks built between 1995 and 2005 for the three-county area. We have a total of sixty-nine registered owners. Twelve of those individuals have had DUIs in the last five years.' I turn my attention to Pickles and Skid. 'I want you guys to get with Rasmussen and split everything up according to jurisdiction. Start talking to people, starting with those DUIs.'

Pickles nods. 'My pleasure.'

Skid, his mouth full of burrito, offers a two-finger salute.

I continue. 'There was an interesting piece of information from the buggy maker we brought in.' I pick up an enlarged photograph of the length of wood Luke Miller found. 'An imprint that may have been made by the hit-skip vehicle was found on this piece from the buggy. I sent it to the lab, but took a photo so everyone could take a look.' I pass out the photos.

I give everyone a few minutes to scrutinize, then my eyes land on Mona. This is her first official briefing. She's trying to hide her excitement, but she's not doing a very good job of it. She's been my dispatcher for about three years now. She attends college during the day and is close to earning a degree in criminal justice. Twice, she's approached me about an officer position. Both times I hedged, attributing my inability to promote her to my limited budget. The truth of the matter is that, despite her enthusiasm, she's not ready for police work. That doesn't mean that at some point I won't hire her; I think she'll make a fine cop one day. But she's not there yet.

'Reports,' I say. 'Mona, did you get anything off the hotline?'

She takes a deep breath, like a kid about to take her first dive off the high board. 'Hotline has been steady, but I've spent some time weeding out the crazy spaceship stuff.'

Skid interjects with, 'That fuckin' Mueller.'

Everyone laughs. Don Mueller has been calling in UFO sightings since he saw *E.T.* thirty years ago, at which point he became convinced extraterrestrials were out to kidnap him.

Mona continues. 'Mrs. Obermiller reported seeing a truck drive past her farm with its headlights off the evening of the incident. She couldn't give the color or model of the truck. Didn't get a plate number. Couldn't give a description of the driver. But she said it was moving fast, and she thought that was odd.'

Glock sits up straighter. 'She lives about four miles down the road from that intersection, Chief.'

I make eye contact with T.J. 'Will you go talk to her before you go home?'

'You bet.'

'What else, Mona?'

'Lots of people calling in wanting to know if Paul Borntrager and his kids were murdered. I guess word is getting around town. I'm telling them we're still investigating.'

'Good answer,' I tell her. 'Stick with it. Anything else?'

'That's all I got, Chief.'

'Nice job.' I don't miss the grin that spreads across her face before I turn my attention to Pickles and Skid. 'How'd the canvassing go?'

Pickles clears wet cobwebs from his throat. 'I hit the three farms off of CR 14. Amos Miller's place. Roy Stutz's farm. Don Jackson's place. No one saw shit.'

I look at Skid.

'I hit the Schlabach place, the Hertzler's farm, and that beat-up trailer home where Donnie Boyd lives.' He touches a button on his iPhone to check his notes. 'Everyone seemed to like Paul Borntrager, and the wife, too. Everyone I talked to had nothing but good things to say about both of them.' He squints at the small display. 'Schlabachs weren't very forthcoming, Chief.'

'Now there's a surprise.' The Schlabachs are a conservative Amish family and have about eight kids. I ticketed Amos Schlabach a few weeks back for refusing to display a slow-moving vehicle sign on his buggy. He reminded me I would be spending all of eternity burning in hell for having left the fold. 'Did you speak with Martha?'

'Tried to.' Skid shakes his head. 'She sent me packing.'

'I'll talk to them.' But I'm not too excited about the prospect of any helpful information. 'Anything else?'

'That's it, Chief.'

I motion toward Maloney. 'Take it away, Frank.'

He's removed his jacket and wears a short-sleeved uniform shirt beneath. I suspect he's trying to show off his biceps to Mona. That he doesn't realize she's more interested in his report than him makes me smile.

It takes Maloney twenty minutes to take us through the reconstruction. I'm impressed. Despite the poor quality of his sketching, he presents a credible rendition of the incident. He's good at what he does.

'In my estimation,' he tells us, 'the hit-skip broadsided that buggy at about 80 MPH.'

Because of the extent of the damage to the buggy and the location of the victims, all of us had known the truck was traveling at a high rate of speed. But to see the information in black and white, to hear the words spoken aloud, conjures images that draw a collective gasp from everyone in the room, including me.

Maloney continues. 'There were no skid marks. So we're either dealing with some kind of mechanical failure – brake failure, for example – or he was under the influence of alcohol or drugs and his reflexes were so slowed he didn't react to the situation.'

'Could have been texting,' T.J. offers.

Swearing beneath his breath, Pickles leans back in his chair and shakes his head. 'Or if he went to the trouble of having the front end of his truck reinforced, he planned this and carried it out.'

T.J. looks from Pickles to Maloney. 'Is that what you think?'

Maloney looks at me. 'If you combine the reconstruction with all the other data we've gathered . . .'

'If it quacks like a duck, it's a fuckin' duck,' Glock puts in.

'It sounds like it was premeditated,' Mona says from her place at the door. She blushes, but no one seems to notice. No one looks at her. No one argues.

'Kind of a messy way to knock off someone,' Skid says. 'I mean, a lot of variables involved. One miscalculation and he could have disabled his truck, gotten a flat tire, or stranded himself at the scene.'

'If that's what happened, this guy definitely took some risks,' Maloney puts in.

'He wanted it to look like an accident,' Glock says. 'That's the only explanation that makes sense. He planned it, carried it out, and covered his tracks.'

'That fits,' T.J. says.

Maloney looks down at his phone, frowns at the display. ''Scuse me, Chief. It's the boss. Gotta take this.'

I move to the podium. 'If we are dealing with premeditation,' I say, 'was it a crime of opportunity? An impulse thing? He planned to kill someone – *anyone* – and waited for the right set of circumstances? Or, for reasons unknown, did he target Paul Borntrager?'

'Why would someone want to kill an Amish man and his kids?' Mona asks. 'That's what doesn't make sense.'

T.J. chimes in. 'Good Amish family. Solid reputation. No enemies. I don't get it.'

A few feet away, the cadence of Maloney's voice changes. I glance over at him to find his eyes on me and I know he's got something. Everyone else has noticed, too, and the room falls silent, all eyes on the deputy. After another minute, he pockets his phone and crosses to where I'm standing and addresses me. 'Couple of kids playing in that old grain elevator down in Coshocton County found some human remains this afternoon.'

The words penetrate my brain like a bullet traveling in slow motion. They are words I've dreaded for seventeen years, but I always knew would come. Still, even after all this time, I'm not prepared. Shock echoes through my body. The floor tilts beneath my feet. I stare at Maloney, a thousand thoughts running through my head. They are not the thoughts of a cop, but of someone who knows something they shouldn't.

'Chief?'

I'm aware of Maloney looking at me oddly. The rest of my team silent and staring. I know someone spoke, but I have no idea what they said or if it was directed at me.

'Do you have any open missing person cases?' Maloney asks and I know he's repeating the question. 'Cold cases?'

'Nothing off the top of my head.' I'm operating on autopilot, going through the motions. Lying. 'How old are the remains?'

'All they got is bones, so probably months or years. They're waiting for the coroner to arrive now.'

I think of Tomasetti and something frighteningly close to panic leaps inside me. Aside from my sister and brother, he's the only person in the world who knows I shot and killed a man when I was fourteen years old. He knows my family covered it up and that the crime was never reported to the police.

'Are you talking natural causes?' Glock asks. 'Or foul play?'

'Considering the bones were hidden at the bottom of the boot pit, I'd venture to say we're looking at a homicide.'

NINE

The criminology texts will tell you that a murderer always returns to the scene of the crime. As I leave the city limits of Painters Mill and head south toward Coshocton County, I realize I'm no different. I wonder if other killers have an all-consuming need to know what the police are doing so they can plan their next move and stay one step ahead.

The grain elevator is the last place I want to be – the last place I should be, considering my involvement – especially when I'm in the midst of a difficult case that requires all of my time and energy. I tell myself I'm duty bound to make an appearance and offer up the resources of my department, even if the offer is token. The truth of the matter is, I can't stay away. I need to know what's happening with the investigation. I need to know which agency will be primary. I need to know if in the terror and panic of that night, my *datt* or brother left something behind that could lead the police back to me.

Caution whispers sweet warnings of impending disaster in my ear as I turn onto the desolate stretch of road where the elevator juts from the earth like some massive rock formation. I remind myself that I'm going to have to be careful. I know things about this scene, this case, this murder, that other people don't; it would be easy to let that knowledge slip. Many a killer has hung himself by revealing information he shouldn't have known.

The triple concrete silos of the old Wilbur Seed Company elevator loom into view as I make the turn into the gravel lot. The place had once been bustling with farm trucks and grain haulers loaded with corn or soybeans. Now, the lot is overgrown with weeds and saplings as tall as a man. Three cruisers from the Coshocton County Sheriff's office are parked haphazardly outside the overhead door. The coroner's van idles nearby, the rear doors standing open to welcome the dead. An ambulance from Coshocton County Memorial Hospital is parked a few feet away from the van. A fire truck from the volunteer fire department sits behind the ambulance, its diesel engine rumbling.

I wonder if the coroner's office has bagged and loaded the remains. I wonder if those remains are on their way to the crime lab in London, Ohio for identification. I have no idea if the bones still contain DNA or if Daniel Lapp's DNA is on file anywhere for a comparison analysis. I don't know if he ever had any dental work done or if there are records that could conceivably identify him. The one thing I do know is that people will remember Lapp's disappearance. Some thought he left to escape the Amish. But not his family. Lapp's parents are dead now, but his brother, Benjamin, will undoubtedly remember my parents' farm was the last place Daniel was seen alive. . . .

I experience a moment of déjà vu upon spotting a television news van from a station out of Columbus parked on the shoulder. A blond-haired woman wearing skinny jeans, stiletto heels, and a hot pink jacket finger-combs her hair. I wonder how much press the case will draw. Enough, I think. People love a good mystery, especially if it involves a dead body, and there's an Amish connection to boot.

I park well away from the other vehicles and start toward

the grain elevator. I've made this pilgrimage a thousand times in my nightmares, but never as a cop, never in an official capacity. Invariably, when I dream of this place, I'm either the victim, trying to save my life – or the killer, to cover my tracks. When it comes to murder, there is no in-between.

An appearance by me won't be deemed unusual. Cops generally tend to be a nosy bunch; we like to be in the thick of things. I try hard to slip into my chief-of-police persona, but for the first time in recent memory, it's not a good fit. I feel like a charlatan.

A flock of crows caw from the roof of the structure, mocking me as I approach. Yellow caution tape has been strung haphazardly around the area. I recognize a young deputy from the Coshocton County Sheriff's office. We worked together during a charity event a couple of years ago. The two of us spent a freezing cold afternoon sitting on the dunking tank chair to help raise funds for an animal rescue group after twenty-eight dogs were rescued from a puppy mill near Walnut Creek. It had been a multi-jurisdictional sting on an animal cruelty case, and I got to know some of local cops in the process.

The sheriff's deputy smiles when I reach him. 'How's it going, Chief?'

His name is Fowler Hodges, but everyone calls him Folly. We shake hands. 'I heard about the remains,' I begin. 'Thought I'd stop by and see if there's anything I can do to help.'

'Couple of kids playing in the boot pit found a skull a few hours ago. They called their parents. Parents called us. Sure enough, the bones are human.'

'Any idea who it is?'

He shakes his head. 'Coroner's down there now. We'll probably start checking cold cases.'

I nod. 'Kids okay?'

'They're fine. I suspect they're going to be talking about it for a while.'

'I would be.'

We laugh at that, then I say, 'Do you mind if I take a look?'

'Knock your socks off. Sheriff Redmon just got here a few minutes ago.' He lifts the tape. 'Watch your step.'

'Thanks.' I duck beneath the tape, walk through knee high weeds, and enter the structure through the overhead door.

The last time I was here was on a bitter January night two years ago. It was during the Slaughterhouse Murders case, and I drove over here in the dead of night to see if Daniel Lapp's remains were here – or if he'd somehow survived the shooting and returned to kill again. I found his bones that night. And John Tomasetti, who suspected I was hiding something and followed me, bore witness to my meltdown when I realized I had, indeed, killed Lapp in self defense all those years before.

The interior hasn't changed. Dust motes fly in the slant of light coming in from holes in the roof and walls. Cobwebs hang like Spanish moss from every visible surface. The smells of dirt and rotting wood and the tart stench of guano from the bats that have taken up residence taunt my olfactory nerves. Pigeons coo from the overhead rafters. Three Coshocton County sheriff's deputies, Chief Redmon, and a paramedic are standing around the boot pit. I recognize two of the deputies, but I don't recall their names.

I smile as I approach the sheriff. My heart pounds a hard tattoo in my chest when I extend my hand.

'Nice to see you again, Chief Burkholder.'

I've met Arnie Redmon on several occasions over the years. He's a charismatic man of about sixty and, from what I hear, a good sheriff – and even better politician. He's got a reputation for being tough – but fair, not only in terms of his job, but in the way he manages his department, which he runs like some elite military unit. His salt-and-pepper hair is shorn into a crew cut. He's sprouted a thin white mustache since the last time I saw him. It makes him look like someone's favorite grandpa. But I know better; this man is as harmless as a sniper. He's six feet tall and built like a prize bull – one that could feed a family of six for a year. Today he's wearing dress navy slacks with a crisp white shirt and patriotic tie. His badge is clipped to his belt like some hard-earned medal.

I shake hands with everyone in the group and then I ask the obvious question. 'Any idea who's down there?'

Redmon shakes his head. 'Techs are still gathering pieces. Bones scattered all over the place.'

Everyone looks into the pit, where a young African-American firefighter stacks old boards onto a polyurethane sheet. A second firefighter squats next to where a body bag has been unzipped, opened, and spread out on the floor. The technician from the coroner's office – a middle-aged man in full biohazard gear – squats next to the bag. From where I stand I can just make out the sphere of the skull and the dull white length of a femur.

'Male or female?' I ask after a moment.

'The technician thought the skull looked male. Something about a pronounced brow bone.'

'Maybe it's a Neanderthal,' one of the other deputies mutters.

The men laugh. I join in, but my voice grates like a rusty hinge.

'Maybe it's that chick you brought to the barbeque last weekend,' one of the deputies says. 'She had that female Neanderthal thing going on. What was she? Six one? Two fifty?'

'Don't forget the mustache,' says a paramedic.

'Sounds like your mom,' the other deputy shoots back.

The men break into laughter again. I smile as I watch the technician pick a bone from the dust and set it on the body bag. But the back and armpits of my uniform shirt are soaked with nervous sweat.

'You guys suspect foul play?' I ask.

The deputy standing next to me shakes his head. 'Hard to tell. The bones were kind of covered up with all that wood, so I don't think he just fell in. Looks like someone covered them up.'

The paramedic leans forward and looks at me. 'Firefighter said there're rats down there, too.'

'That'll fuck up a scene,' Redmon says absently.

'Anyone find a weapon?' I ask.

'Not yet.'

'What about an ID? Or clothes?'

The sheriff glances at me, curious about my questions. Sweat spreads to the back of my neck. 'There are some old clothes down there,' he says. 'Fabric's deteriorated.'

I nod, make eye contact with Sheriff Redmon. 'Let me know if there's anything my department can do for you.'

'Appreciate it.' The sheriff holds my gaze. 'You guys make an arrest on that hit-skip?'

'We're working on it.' I step back, hating it that my knees are shaking.

As I start toward the door, I feel the men's eyes burning into my back.

By the time I reach the Explorer, I'm in the throes of an all-out panic attack. I grip the wheel and suck in slow, deep breaths until it subsides. After a few minutes, I pull myself together, start the engine, and turn onto the road. A mile down I pull over and call Tomasetti.

He answers on the second ring with, 'I knew you couldn't stay away from me for long.'

'They found the bones,' I tell him.

A too-long pause ensues. 'Lapp?'

'Yeah.'

'Are you okay?'

'I'm scared.'

'We probably shouldn't discuss this on the phone. Do you want me to drive down?'

'I'm working this hit-skip. Give me a few hours to get some things done.'

'In the interim, will you do me a favor and stay the hell away from the scene?'

'Too late, Tomasetti.'

'Kate.' He growls my name.

My laugh is a frazzled, anxious sound. But knowing he cares, knowing I can count on him if the situation takes a turn for the worse, goes a long way toward calming me down.

'They don't know anything,' I tell him.

Tomasetti doesn't respond to that. Maybe because we both know that could change in a blink.

'Sit tight,' he tells me. 'And stay the hell away from that scene.'

He disconnects without saying good-bye.

TEN

I spend the afternoon at the station, poring over the list of names Pickles and Skid assembled on the registered owners of 1996 gray Ford F-250 trucks living in Holmes, Wayne, and Coshocton Counties. So far, everyone they've talked to has alibis for the time of the hit-and-run. None of the vehicles they've checked are damaged or have reinforced front ends. But I'm giving the task only a fraction of my attention. I can't stop thinking about the discovery of those remains in the grain elevator.

At 5:00 P.M., I head for the Brass Rail Saloon to talk to the bartender. The parking lot is jam packed with vehicles. I want to believe people stop in to wind down with a beer after work or maybe indulge in a burger-and-fries dinner before heading home for the day. It's an optimistic offering. The beer is watered down, the burgers are barely fit for human consumption, and about half of these vehicles have been here since noon. The truth of the matter is there's a faction of people in the county who'd rather drink their day away than earn an honest wage. The methamphetamine trade is at pandemic levels and rural areas have been hit particularly hard. While Amish country might be the poster child for wholesome living, it hasn't escaped the scourge.

I park next to a newish Toyota SUV that's been keyed from

headlight to taillight on the passenger side. I try not to notice the baby seat in the rear as I walk past. Ten yards from the door, the bass rumble of music vibrates the ground beneath my feet. By the time I step inside, I can feel it pulsing in my bone marrow.

The interior of the bar is dark as a cave and smells of cigarette smoke, cooking grease, and an unpleasant combination of aftershave and body odor. An old Talking Heads rocker blasts from dual speakers the size of caskets mounted on either side of a dance floor where a thin young man wearing a DeKalb cap humps a girl who's more interested in her beer than him.

Most of the patrons are young and male, an assemblage of tee-shirts and jeans, with the occasional leather jacket, which is good for secreting a weapon. Chances are I won't run into any problems; most of the people who frequent this bar aren't looking for trouble with the police. But I've been chief long enough to know even pretty, small towns have an underbelly, and that sometimes even the most benign of individuals can turn on you.

A pool game is in full swing at the rear. Cigarette smoke hovers like fog beneath the dim light of a stained-glass chandelier. A blond woman in snug yellow shorts leans across the table to make a difficult shot, drawing every male gaze within eyeshot. A couple of the pool players have noticed me. I stare back as I make my way to the bar, knowing it's never a good sign when a police uniform outstrips short shorts in a perfect size six.

I recognize the barkeep. Jimmie Baines is a small-time hood who keeps all the wrong company. He's in his mid thirties with the rangy build of a welterweight. Word around town is that he enjoys his meth. From the looks of him, a little too much. He's balding on top with a precision-cut goatee and a missing canine on the left side. He's wearing a black tee-shirt with the sleeves torn off. The tattoos on his biceps jump as he dries a shot glass with a moldy-looking towel. He's staring at me with the lazy nonchalance of an alligator sunning itself on a muddy bank while watching some fat rodent come down for a drink.

'How's it going, Jimmie?' I say.

'Fair to middlin'.' He doesn't look pleased to see me. Judging by the way his eyes are jumping around, I'd venture to say my presence is making him nervous. I'm not surprised. People like Jimmie are always up to no good. He leads a life of crime and spends most of his time trying to keep people like me from finding out about it.

'You're not going to ruin my day, are you?' he asks.

'That depends on you.' I smile. 'You got any coffee made?'

'Anything for you, Chief.' Turning his back to me, he snags a carafe from beneath the bar and slides it into an ancient-looking Bunn coffeemaker. 'What brings you out here this afternoon?' he asks, scooping grounds from a Sam's-size Folgers can.

I turn, set my elbows on the bar, and scan the room. The people at the rear have resumed their pool game, a few shifty gazes still flicking my way. The couple on the dance floor are swaying in time to Neil Young & Crazy Horse, oblivious to every-thing except the spot where skin meets skin. A young woman sits alone at a table, arguing with her iPhone.

'Did you hear about that accident out on Delisle last night?' I begin.

'You mean that buggy wreck?' He turns to the cabinet behind him and pulls down a white mug.

'There were three people killed.'

'Man, I hate to hear that.' He checks the mug to make sure it's clean and sets it on the bar in front of me. 'Them damn bug-gies is hard to see at night.'

I want to tell him they are particularly hard to see if you're knuckle-dragging drunk and doing eighty, but I hold my tongue. 'Did you work last night?'

'I'm here 'bout every night.' He doesn't meet my gaze as he pours coffee into the mug. 'You want creamer, Chief?'

'Black's fine.' I reach for my wallet, but he stops me.

'It's on the house.'

'Thanks.' I pick up the mug and sip. The coffee is weak, but it'll do. 'Jimmie, do you remember who was in here about this time yesterday?'

'Aw, we were so damn busy, I couldn't even get away to take a piss.' He picks up a glass that's already dry and starts wiping. I can tell by the way he's concentrating on the task that he knows where my line of questioning is going and he doesn't want any part of it.

'Anyone overly intoxicated?'

'Not that I noticed. Pretty mellow crowd out here most days.' He wipes the glass faster and harder. 'I cut off anyone gets out of line.'

'So you say.'

Jimmie sets down the glass, picks up another.

'The Brass Rail isn't too far from where that wreck happened,' I tell him.

'I wouldn't know anything about that, Chief.'

'We think the driver might have been intoxicated,' I say conversationally. 'If someone left here and headed toward Painters Mill, they would have had to cross that intersection.'

He dries faster, harder, and scrapes at a spot with a dirty thumbnail.

'Do any of your regulars drive a Ford F-250?' I ask.

'I dunno.'

'Jimmie.' I say his name sharply.

He looks up from the glass and meets my gaze. His mouth is slightly open and in that small space between his lips I see he's got a bad case of meth-mouth. 'What?' he says.

'There's a five-hundred-dollar reward for information.'

He tries not to look interested, but he doesn't quite manage. 'What's the catch?'

'No catch. Any information that leads to an arrest and conviction.'

'Can they stay anonymous?'

'Far as I know.'

He turns away, picks up another glass and runs his towel over it. 'Leland Dull was in here 'bout seven last night. Had some big fight with his old lady. He was all shit-faced and mean. You know how he gets. You didn't hear it from me, okay?'

I'm familiar with Dull. He and his wife live in Painters Mill, a small house by the railroad tracks. My officers have been called to their address several times in recent months. Leland has been arrested twice for domestic violence. Both times were alcohol related. If he was here last night, he would have had to pass the intersection where the accident occurred in order to get home.

'What time did he leave?' I ask.

''Bout seven-thirty, give or take.'

'What was he driving?'

'Don't know about that.'

I pull a ten-dollar bill from my wallet and lay it on the bar. 'Behave yourself, Jimmie.'

'Hey, don't forget about me if this pans out,' he says.

I don't look back as I start toward the exit.

Leland Dull and his wife, Gail, live on a tree-lined street of circa 1960 bungalows that might have been quaint if not for the tumbling-down chain-link fences and yards trampled to dirt. The neighborhood would have been redeemable if not for the railroad tracks fifty yards from their front doors and the freight trains that rattle by four times a day.

I asked my second shift dispatcher, Jodie, to run his name

for outstanding warrants. He comes back clean, but I discover a twelve-year-old conviction for vehicular manslaughter. According to police records, he was driving home late one night, missed a curve in the road, and drove through a house, killing the homeowner, a seventy-year-old woman. The county attorney dropped the charges down from vehicular homicide to vehicular manslaughter, and Dull pled guilty. He was sentenced to two years at the Mansfield Correctional Institution, but ended up doing nine months.

Chances are Leland Dull wasn't involved in this particular accident. But considering his history of drinking and driving, his proximity to the scene on the night in question – and the fact that he drives a truck – I'm obliged to check him out.

I find the house with no problem and park in the driveway, behind an old Dodge pickup. I can't see the front end of the truck from where I'm sitting. I hail dispatch, let them know I'm 10-23, get out and start toward the vehicle. A quick walk around reveals no damage.

'Ain't you going to kick the tires?'

I glance up to see Leland Dull standing a few feet away, glaring at me as if I'm about to steal his truck.

'Or maybe you ought to whip out one of them *CSI* Q-tips and swab the hood for blood. Hell, break out the shovel. Maybe I got a fuckin' body buried in the backyard.'

He's sixty years old with a full head of white hair that's gone yellow and hasn't seen a decent cut in a couple of decades. The stubble on his chin tells me he hasn't shaved for a few days, and I'm pretty sure the smell wafting over to me isn't from the aging mutt at his feet.

I pull out my badge and show it to him. 'You're not confessing to anything, are you, Leland?'

'What are you doing on my property?'

'I just want to ask you a few questions.'

He's looking at me as if he's thinking about traversing the space between us and slugging me in the mouth. Leland Dull is a vicious drunk and a woman-beating son of a bitch. There's a small, angry part of me that wishes he'd take his best shot.

I gesture toward the Dodge. 'That your truck?'

'It's parked in my driveway. Who the hell else would it belong to?'

'You got any other vehicles?'

'I got a Corolla. Wife drives it.'

'Any other trucks?'

'Nope.'

'Where were you last night?'

'Here.'

'You make any stops on your way home from work?'

'Nope.'

'Leland.' My lips curve, but the smile feels nasty on my face. 'You know it's against the law to lie to the police, don't you?'

'I swung by the Brass Rail after work.'

'What time was that?'

'A little after five.'

'What time did you leave the bar?'

'I ain't sure. Seven thirty or so.' His eyes narrow. 'What's this all about, anyway?'

'What route did you take home?'

'Same route I always—' He cuts the words short. 'Oh, for shit's sake. You don't think I'm the one killed them Amish, do you?'

'I'm asking you a simple question.'

'You're looking for an escape goat is what you're doing. Well, you're sniffing up the wrong ass.'

I puzzle over both of those statements a moment and make an effort not to laugh. 'I'd appreciate it if you just answered the question.'

'I took CR 14 to the highway, damn it.'

I walk to his truck, make a show of looking at the front end. 'Were you drunk?'

'On fuckin' apple juice.'

I turn my back and walk to the detached garage, peer through the window. The glass is grimy, but I can see there's no vehicle inside. Just an old washer and dryer. A table saw against the wall. A couple of fifty-gallon drums.

I hear him behind me. 'Why are you snooping around my garage, anyway?'

'The official term for it is taking a look around.' I turn, make eye contact with him. 'What's in those fifty gallon drums, Leland?'

I hear a sound like chalk against slate. It takes me a few seconds to realize he's grinding his teeth. I walk over to him, stop a scant foot away. I'm so close I can smell the dead-animal stench of his breath. The odors of filth and rage coming off him in waves. He's only a few inches taller than me, older and slower, but he's got eighty pounds on me. I suspect that beneath all that wrinkled, stinking skin is a reserve of muscle I'd be wise not to underestimate.

'Do you know anything about that hit-and-run?' I ask.

His lips curl, like two worms exposed to flame. 'I think it's time you hit the fuckin' road.'

I turn away and start toward the Explorer. 'Thanks for your cooperation,' I tell him and slide in without looking back.

ELEVEN

Ten minutes later I'm on my way to Pomerene Hospital to talk to Mattie, not as a friend this time, but a cop. I'm not convinced the deaths of Paul Borntrager and his two children were acts of premeditated murder, but with the evidence leaning in that direction, the possibility must be explored. That means I need to ask the hard questions I've been putting off, and delve more deeply into Paul's life. I need to know if he'd had any recent disagreements or disputes. If he had any enemies or if there'd been any threats against him or his family.

It's also my responsibility to keep Mattie apprised on how the case is progressing. That entails relaying some of the details I'd been withholding to spare her the pain of knowing the 'accident' was, in fact, something more sinister. None of it's going to be pleasant, especially when I'm tired and cranky and increasingly distracted by the discovery of Lapp's remains.

At the door to David's room, I knock quietly and step inside. The air smells of an odd combination of medicine, flowers, and cinnamon. On the windowsill, a little brown teddy bear is tucked into a bouquet of pink carnations. Next to it, several gas-filled balloons tug at the ribbons that bind them to the wicker handle.

David sleeps soundly in the bed. The bruises on his face are in full bloom, but his color is healthy. Mattie is curled on the chair with her head resting on her hands, asleep. In the recliner, a heavyset Amish woman lies on her back, snoring softly. Next to her, a partially eaten tin of homemade cinnamon rolls makes my mouth water.

I'm debating whether to come back later when David speaks from his bed. 'You want a cinnamon roll? They taste good.'

I glance over to see him sitting up, looking at me as if I'm some stray that's wandered into the room and needs feeding.

'Hey.' I feel a smile spread across my face as I go to the bed. 'How are you feeling?'

'My arm hurts and I miss my *datt* and Norah and Sam.' Using his uninjured arm, he brushes his hand over a cast that runs from wrist to elbow. 'It's broken.'

'I'm sorry about that.' I look down at the cast to see that someone by the name of Matthew drew a cat on it. 'I like the artwork.'

His face splits into a big smile. 'We have two cats at home. Whiskers and Frito. They're my favorites. I like it when they purr because it tickles my ear.'

'I like cats, too.'

'*Mamm* says *Datt* and Norah and Sam are with God.'

It hurts me to hear an innocent child make such a profound statement. I nod, not sure what to say to that.

His brows knit and I know he's trying to understand the incomprehensible: why three people he loved are gone from his life and won't be coming back. 'I think they miss me and *Mamm*, too. But heaven is the happiest place in the world, so we shouldn't be sad. One of these days, I'll be there, too, and I'm going to play hide-and-seek with Sammy and botch with Norah.'

I'm not much on touching, but this little boy is so sweet and vulnerable, I can't keep myself from reaching out and laying my hand over his. He looks up at me expectantly. I want badly to say something to comfort him, to reinforce and confirm what Mattie has already told him. But I find myself so moved I can't speak.

'Katie?'

I turn to see Mattie rise from the chair. She looks rested, and for the first time since the accident, she's not crying.

'I hope I didn't wake you,' I say.

'I must have drifted off.' She looks past me and smiles at her son.

The boy grins back, and she returns her attention to me. 'The doctor says he can go home tomorrow.'

For an instant, she almost looks like the girl I once knew. The one with the infectious laugh and mischievous expression. But grief returns quickly, making itself known in the hollows of her cheeks and the circles beneath her eyes. 'That's great news,' I tell her. 'How are you holding up?'

'These chairs aren't exactly made for sleeping.' Putting her hand to her back, as if in pain, she chokes out a laugh. 'I feel the way my brother must have felt the day he got tangled in the reins and the horse dragged him from the hayfield to the barn.'

I hadn't thought of the incident in years, but it rushes back with enough clarity to make me laugh. I'd been at Mattie's house, helping her and her older brother, John, spear tobacco. At some point her brother, who had a crush on me, decided he wanted to show off his horsemanship skills and hopped onto the back of a young plow horse. The animal bucked him off. John's wrist somehow became tangled in the reins and the horse dragged him all the way to the barn.

The recliner across the room creaks. I glance over to see the Amish woman who'd been snoozing rise, eyeing me with unconcealed suspicion. 'Hello,' she says.

I nod a greeting, then I turn my attention to Mattie. 'Can

I speak to you privately?' I motion toward the door. 'In the hall?'

'Of course.' She looks at the woman. 'Can you stay with David for a few minutes?' she asks in Pennsylvania Dutch.

'*Ja.*'

Mattie follows me into the hall. When we're out of earshot of the room and the nurse's station, I stop and turn to her. She's looking at me expectantly, a little perplexed, and I still don't know how to break the news. 'I need to let you know,' I begin, 'the driver that hit the buggy left the scene. It was a hit-and-run. We're trying to find him.'

'What?' She stares at me in disbelief. 'The person didn't stop?'

'They didn't stop. And they didn't call the police. Failure to render aid is against the law, so we're looking for the driver. I wanted to tell you because it's all over the news. I wanted you to hear it from me.'

'Paul and the children . . .' Her voice breaks. 'How could someone do such a thing?'

'I don't know. Maybe he got scared and panicked. Maybe he was drinking alcohol. Or texting. We don't know.'

She stares at me, her eyes wide, then her mouth tightens and she surprises me by saying, 'I will pray for him.'

I look away, not sure if I'm in awe of her capacity for forgiveness or annoyed because the son of a bitch doesn't deserve it. My own feelings aren't nearly as charitable.

'Is it unusual for Paul to be out so late with the children?' I ask.

'He'd taken them to the doctor in Painters Mill. He was on his way home. They had the last appointment of the day. Sometimes he bought them ice cream afterward.'

'Were the kids sick?'

Her eyes flick away and I realize the question hit a nerve.

'All three of my children have Cohen syndrome, Katie. We take them to the clinic every week.'

A wave of sympathy ripples through me. I've heard of Cohen syndrome, but I don't know much about it. It's a genetic disorder that causes mental and physical developmental problems in children. It's thought to be caused by the small gene pool of the Amish. And I realize that parenthood for Mattie and Paul had been challenging. 'I'm sorry.'

Her mouth curves, but the smile looks sad on her face. *'Sis Gottes wille.'*

I don't believe a lifetime of mental and physical difficulties is what God had in mind for her children, but since many of my opinions are unpopular among my former brethren, I keep it to myself. 'Mattie, I don't want you to read anything in to what I'm going to ask you next, but I need to know if Paul had been involved in any recent disputes or arguments.'

She blinks, wide gray eyes searching mine, and despite my request that she not read anything into the question, I see the wheels of her mind begin to spin. 'Katie, I don't understand. Why are you asking me that?'

'These are routine questions,' I tell her. 'Part of the investigation.'

It's a canned reply, and she's astute enough to know it's bullshit. I can tell by her expression that she knows I'm not being straightforward. But she's too well mannered to call me on the carpet. I wish I could tell her more, but experience has taught me to keep my cards close, sometimes even with those I trust. People talk, after all – even the good guys – and the last thing I need are more rumors of premeditated murder flying around.

She finally answers with a shake of her head. 'Everyone loved Paul. He was a good man. A friend to all.' Her face crumbles. 'A good father and husband.'

It hurts to see her in so much pain. I look away and give her a moment to compose herself before I continue. 'What about in the past? Did Paul have any enemies?'

'No. He was kind and generous. A good deacon. Always trying to help people.'

Amish deacons are highly respected members of the church district, helping with worship services and baptisms. If an Amish family falls on hard times and needs financial assistance, the deacon oversees the collection of cash. He is *Armen-Diener,* which means 'minister to the poor.' But not all of a deacon's responsibilities are benign; they also convey messages of excommunication.

'Have there been any recent excommunications?' I ask. 'Anything like that?'

'Katie . . .' She presses her hand to her breast as if she's run out of breath. 'Did someone do this thing on purpose? Because they were angry with Paul?'

'I don't know.'

'I may be Amish,' she snaps. 'But I'm not stupid. Please don't patronize me.'

'I'm sorry. I'm trying to spare you the—'

'It would be much kinder for you to tell me the truth.'

I nod. 'It's something we're looking at.' I say the words quietly, but it's not enough to temper the awful power behind them.

'*Mein Gott.*' She puts her hand over her mouth as if to smother a cry. 'Who would do such a thing? Who would want to hurt Paul or our children?'

'I don't know. But I'm going to do everything in my power to find out.' Reaching out, I take her hand and squeeze. 'I promise.'

Fresh tears glitter in her eyes. She stares at me as if she's barely able to process the information I've thrown at her.

'Mattie, have you talked to David about the accident?'

'What do you mean?' Her gaze turns wary.

'Have you asked him if he remembers anything that happened?'

'Oh, Katie.' She raises her hands and backs away from me. 'Please. He's been through so much. I don't want to upset him.'

'I wouldn't ask if it wasn't important,' I say gently. 'But I need to know if he saw anything. Or anyone. I'll do my best not to upset him.'

She doesn't respond for so long I think she's going to refuse my request. Then, looking resigned, she sighs. 'He's so fragile. Be kind to him. Please.'

'I'll be gentle, Mattie. I promise.'

She leads me back into the boy's room. David is lying on his side, looking out the window, rubbing absently at the cast on his arm. He looks at me when I approach the bed and smiles.

'Is that cast starting to get itchy already?' I ask.

'*Mamm* told me not to scratch, but I can't stop. It feels like that time I got poison ivy.'

I pull the chair closer to the bed and lower myself into it. 'Do you feel up to answering a couple of questions?'

He lifts his uninjured shoulder in a shrug, as if he doesn't know what information he could possibly have that would be valuable to me. 'Okay.'

'I was wondering if you remember anything about the buggy accident.'

His brows knit, his eyes skating away from mine, and he picks at the cast with a fingernail. 'Alls I remember is eating an ice cream cone and botching with Norah.'

'You know, I used to like to botch.'

'It's a girl game.'

'I bet Norah was good at it.'

'She was the best.'

'Were you botching when the accident happened?'

'We were singing the botching song. "All Around the Mulberry Bush."'

'I like that one.' I smile at him. 'Do you remember seeing a car or truck?'

'No.'

'What about people? Did you see anyone before or after the accident?'

Shaking his head, he sinks more deeply into the bed and pulls the covers up to his chin. 'I dunno.'

'Do you remember anything at all about the accident?'

'I remember lights.'

His voice is so soft, I have to lean forward to hear him. 'What kind of lights?'

'The kind on English cars.'

'You mean like headlights?'

'*Ja.*'

'What color were they?' I ask him to specify to make sure he's not confusing headlights with the emergency lights afterward.

'White.'

Many traffic accident victims that sustain head injuries don't recall the minutes, hours, or even days before or after the event. That David remembers seeing headlights could be significant.

'What else can you tell me about the lights?'

'There were two of them and they were bright.'

I smile. 'You have a good memory.'

'That's what *Datt* always says.' His expression is so sweet I want to pull him out of the bed and hug him to me.

'Did you see the vehicle that hit the buggy?' I ask gently.

He looks away from me to stare out the window, his

expression troubled. His fingers scratch absently at the cast. 'No. Just lights.'

'So you didn't notice the color? Or if it was a car or truck? Anything like that?'

'No.'

'Did you see any people?'

'No.' He glances at Mattie, and for a moment I'm afraid he's going to crawl out of the bed to get away from me and my questions. '*Mamm*, did I do something wrong?'

The words go right through me, as sharp and hurtful as any blade. 'No, honey. You did great.' I reach out and squeeze his hand. 'Thank you.'

Then Mattie is next to the bed, bending and pulling him to her. 'You didn't do anything wrong, sweetheart. Katie is a policeman and it's her job to ask questions.'

Feeling like an ogre, I rise and go to the window. I listen as Mattie coos to him, calming his fears. I try to remember if my own *mamm* ever did that for me and I can't.

A child's heart is a tender thing that never forgets. I can't imagine what it would have been like to lose a family member at such a formative age. When you're Amish, your family is the center of your universe. Jacob and Sarah had been my best friends, my confidantes – and partners in crime. I didn't have a perfect childhood, but I consider myself lucky to have had those few magical years.

I turn from the window and address Mattie. 'Will you let me know if you need anything?'

She pulls away from her son and crosses to me. 'Thank you, Katie, but we are fine.'

I feel myself stiffen when she embraces me. I close my eyes against the rush of emotion. For her. For the boy. For everything they've lost. For what I lost somewhere along the way.

I pull away first. Her hands slide down my arms and she

eases me to arm's length. Her gaze finds mine and for the span of several heartbeats our eyes hold.

'*Gott segen eich*,' she whispers. *God bless you.*

I turn away without responding.

TWELVE

I arrive home to a dark house that smells of coffee and stale air. I go directly to my bedroom, removing my holster as I go and dropping it along with my .38 on the night table. My shirt finds its place on the floor. I step out of my trousers, toss them on the bed. Boots are kicked into the closet. In the dresser, I find a pair of ratty sweatpants and an oversized tee-shirt and put them on.

The evening is cool, so I spend a few minutes walking the house, opening windows to let in some fresh air. I startle when I spot the orange tabby sitting on the brick sill outside the kitchen window, looking at me expectantly. He's a stray that's been coming around for months now. I'm no cat person, and this particular feline is neither pleasant to be around nor pleasing to the eye. But he's a survivor and he's loyal, two traits that usher me past the old battle scars and nasty personality.

When he mewls, I walk to the pantry and snag the bag of dry food I keep on the shelf in the back. I find his bowl in the sink strainer, fill it, and push open the screen. 'You know you eat better than I do, don't you?'

I hear him purring as I set the bowl on the sill.

I'm standing at the refrigerator with the door open, hoping I can find something edible inside, when a tap at the back door startles me. I spin, my hand going automatically to where my

.38 usually rests. Then I spot the familiar figure through the window and the stress of the day falls away.

I walk to the door, swing it open, and smile at Tomasetti. 'You know you're on the verge of becoming predictable, don't you?'

'What can I say, Kate? I've got an addictive personality, and at the moment you're at the top of my most-wanted list.'

'You're putting it out there this evening, aren't you?'

'Or piling it on, depending on your point of view.' His voice is light, but he's looking at me a little too closely. He's worried about how I'm reacting to the discovery of Daniel Lapp's remains, I realize, and what that discovery could mean if they're identified.

'You busy?' he asks.

I roll my eyes. 'Come in.'

He enters the kitchen and goes to the table. I feel silly because I was expecting . . . something else. Pretending I wasn't, I join him at the table.

'I thought you might want to talk about those remains,' he begins.

'You mean in addition to the possibility that I'm in deep shit?'

He scowls at me. 'Who's the investigating agency?'

'Coshocton County.'

'You know them?'

I shake my head. 'I've met the sheriff, but I don't know him. We're not friends.'

'We received a call from someone down there today,' he tells me. 'Bones are already at the lab. They want DNA.'

Of course I'd known that would happen. But hearing the words spoken aloud sends a quiver of anxiety through my gut. 'What are the odds that they'll get it?'

'Seventeen years is a long time for DNA to survive, but it's not out of the question.' He shrugs. 'It depends on how well the bones fared. The pit is dry, and that bodes well for the preservation of DNA. If it was a wet, muddy area, probably not. There might be DNA in the teeth.' He gives me a direct look. 'Since I've worked this area in the past, it won't be deemed unusual for me to stay on top of it.'

While it will be good to be kept abreast of any developments, forensic or otherwise, we both know there's nothing we can do about the outcome.

'Kate, do you think Lapp had dental records? I mean with him being Amish?'

'The Amish generally don't have a problem with going to the dentist if they're having problems, like a toothache or something. That said, they're not big on preventative tooth care. Daniel was young; I'm betting he hadn't yet been to the dentist.'

'That could work in our favor.'

'Even if they are able to extract DNA,' I say, 'don't they need something to compare it to? A hair root or something?'

'Or a close relative.'

'He's got a brother. Benjamin.'

'Keep in mind that because of the relatively small gene pool, that kind of analysis could be difficult to interpret,' he points out.

'Benjamin knows Daniel worked at my parents' farm that day,' I tell him.

'Are the parents still around?' he asks.

'They passed away a few years ago.'

He falls silent, thinking. 'Do you know if they filed a missing person report when Lapp disappeared?'

'They did, but waited almost forty-eight hours before going to the police.'

'Why did they wait so long?'

'Lapp was on *rumspringa*. I guess it wasn't unusual for him to stay out all night. By the end of the second day, they got worried and started looking, went to the police when they didn't find him.'

'Was he a drinker?'

'Sometimes.'

'Devout?'

'Not really.'

'So as far as anyone knows, *anything* could have happened to him. He could have fallen in with bad company. Gotten involved with drugs. Met with a bad end somewhere else.'

I nod, understanding. 'There was talk that he'd wanted to leave the Amish.'

He considers that for a moment. 'Do you have access to the file?'

'Yes.' I don't tell him I've pulled the file a hundred times over the years, that I've memorized every detail and if he asked, I could recite every word of it verbatim.

'Don't take this the wrong way, Kate, but you know you can't alter that file in any way, right?'

'I can't believe you felt the need to say that.'

'Just covering all our bases.'

I realize he's only trying to help me, that he's taking a certain risk himself by getting involved in this mess. But I need for him to know there are certain lines I wouldn't cross. Compromising my ethics is one of them.

'Tomasetti, for God's sake, I'm not a criminal.' I raise my hands to my temples and massage at the headache that's beginning to rage.

'I know what you are and what you aren't,' he says, unsympathetic.

'I killed a man. That makes me a murderer.'

'You defended yourself from a rapist. You give that to any court in the country and you'll be acquitted.'

I want those words and the vehemence with which he spoke them to make me feel better, but they don't. We both know the situation is more complicated than that. It isn't going to go away, and there's not a damn thing we can do to make it better. That's when I realize the sense of dread has less to do with the legal ramifications than with the thought of that piece of my past becoming public knowledge.

'I've lied by omission for seventeen years,' I tell him. 'The problem is made worse by the fact that I'm a cop. If this comes out, I'll probably be forced to resign. I can kiss any hope of ever working in law enforcement good-bye. And that's a best-case scenario.'

'You're getting a little ahead of yourself.'

'I can't stick my head in the sand. I've got to deal with it. I've got to be ready if—'

'Kate, you're not a suspect. You're not even on the radar.' He tries to temper his impatience with me, but he's not doing a very good job of it. 'We don't know if the lab will be able to extract DNA. Those remains may never be identified. Add those two probabilities to the fact that some people believe he left of his own accord, and you're off the hook.'

For the span of a full minute, the only sound comes from the hum of the refrigerator and the slow drip from the faucet. Then he asks, 'What kind of weapon was Lapp killed with?'

'Shotgun.'

'That means there's no slug. No striations. Nothing to match anything to. That's good.'

All I can think is that there's nothing good about any of this. Miserable, I look down at the tabletop. 'If there are pellets at the scene,' I say, 'or damage to the bone, they'll be able to determine the cause of death.'

'But there's no way to tie it to you,' he says. 'Where's the shotgun?'

'In my closet.'

He doesn't react, but he doesn't look happy about my attachment to the one item that could destroy my life.

Feeling stupid, I add, 'I almost got rid of it during the Slaughterhouse Murders case, but . . .'

'Why didn't you?'

'I don't have some overriding need to get caught, if that's what you're asking.'

He doesn't respond. I don't know if he doesn't believe me or if he's simply working through the myriad ways those bones could lead investigators back to me.

'Any paper on the shotgun?' he asks. 'Bill of sale. Repairs? Anything like that?'

'I don't think so. It's an antique. My grandfather used it for hunting and passed it down.'

'What about the shell casing? Do you know what happened to it?'

'I have no idea. It happened at our farm, so my *mamm* or *datt* probably threw it away.'

'So it went to the dump?'

I look at him, surprised that he would be so concerned about such a small detail after so many years. 'I don't know. We used to burn most of our trash.'

'Okay. That's good.' He thinks about that a moment. 'Would have been nice to have that casing.' His brows knit. 'Why was Lapp at your farm that day?'

'He was helping my brother bale hay.'

'Who knew he was there?'

'His parents. His brother.' I shrug. 'Benjamin is still around.'

'He's Amish?'

'I don't think that will keep him from going to the police when he hears about those bones. He never believed Daniel left of his own accord, so that's pretty much inevitable.'

'Nothing we can do about that,' he says. 'Who knows about all of this, Kate?'

'My brother, Jacob. My sister, Sarah.' I feel control of the situation slipping from my grasp, and I realize any semblance of influence I'd felt over the years was an illusion.

'The investigator will look into all cold missing-person cases right off the bat. He'll talk to Lapp's brother. If Lapp tells them Daniel was last seen at your parents' farm, they're going to talk to you and your siblings.' He gives me a hard look. 'You need to get with your sister and brother. Get your stories straight.'

'I don't know if I can count on my brother.'

'Why not?'

I go to the counter, open the cabinet, and snag a glass. I feel his eyes on my back as I turn on the tap and fill it. I'm not thirsty, but I drink half of it down. 'He blames me for what happened. At least in part.'

'What part?'

Setting the glass in the sink, I turn to him. My expression feels like that glass, but slowly being crushed and about to shatter. 'He saw me smile at Daniel earlier that day. He thinks . . . I mean, in the Amish culture . . .' I'm shocked to find my heart beating so fast I can barely speak. 'I guess there's a part of him that thinks I instigated the situation.'

He scrubs a hand over his jaw. 'You know it wasn't your fault, don't you?'

'I know that. I do. It's just that . . . Jacob and I used to be so close. This destroyed our relationship.'

'Will he cover for you?'

'I don't know. Probably.'

'If he helped dump the body, he's guilty, too,' Tomasetti points out. 'If you need leverage . . .'

I want to tell him it won't come to that. I suspect we both know I'd do it if I had to. I have that survivor mentality.

Sometimes I honestly don't know if that's good or bad. 'I hate this.'

'What about your sister?' he asks.

'I think she'll cooperate.'

We fall silent again and I sense the presence of fear in the room, a dark specter skimming cold fingertips across the back of my neck. 'I'm scared,' I say.

'I know.' After a moment, he scoots his chair back and rises. 'Get the shotgun.'

The word echoes, like some depraved statement uttered in the presence of children. 'It can't be traced. A lot of Amish have shotguns. For hunting.'

'I'd feel better if you didn't have possession of that particular shotgun. Go get it.'

I don't move. 'I'd rather you not get involved.'

'I think I can handle ditching a weapon.'

'Tomasetti, for God's sake. You're a state agent. Your past . . . If someone sees you—'

'It's late. It's dark. I'm parked in the goddamn alley.' He looks toward the window. 'Bring me the damn shotgun.'

I want to protect him from this, I realize. If word ever gets out that he helped me cover up a crime, my career wouldn't be the only one that goes down the drain. But I need his help, and it's that desperation that sends me to the bedroom closet where I retrieve the shotgun and carry it back to the kitchen. 'It's unloaded.'

He checks anyway. 'Do you have any shells?'

I shake my head. 'Where are you going to put it?'

He doesn't answer.

I've never considered myself an emotional woman. I'm relatively even-keel and not prone to crying jags. But I feel one coming on now, the tears hot and pressing at the backs of my eyes. If the situation wasn't so serious, I might have laughed at the absurdity of what we were about to do. That the most profound act of selflessness and kindness ever shown to me by a man I love involves a shotgun.

I dream of Mattie and the past, a tangled account of true events that are twisted and dark now because I see them through the eyes of the adult I've become. It's the summer of our sixteenth year and we've just begun our *rumspringas*. We're drunk on youth and innocence and the exciting new freedom bestowed us.

Amish girls are generally not granted the same level of freedom as boys for the simple reason that the Amish are a patriarchic society, a cultural foible as set in stone as our garb. But the teenaged mind is a determined thing and, despite our inexperience, Mattie and I were quick studies in all the ways of deception, especially when it came to our parents.

That afternoon we're lying in the sun on the grassy bank of Painters Creek. We've spread a couple of threadbare bath towels we stole from my *mamm*'s laundry basket on the ground. Earlier in the day, we'd met at Walmart and spent two hours in the dressing room, driving the attendant crazy and enjoying every minute of it. We walked away with the perfect swimsuits, identical sunglasses, and the sense that it was money well spent.

'I wish we could do this every day.' Mattie sits up and lights a cigarette, her third in the last hour.

It's not yet noon and we're sharing a can of Budweiser and smoking Marlboros. Mattie calls them 'cowboy killers,' which I think is hilarious. It's the most perfect day of the summer so far.

'Let's do it again tomorrow,' I say, reveling in the feel of the hot sun against my bare skin.

I light a cigarette and gaze at the creek twenty feet away. The water is murky and deep here. A big cottonwood tree grows at a forty-five-degree angle at the water's edge. Someone looped a rope around one of the branches that extends over the water. The vegetation at the base of the trunk has been compressed by the dozens of bare feet from teens swinging out over the water to drop into the murky depths. Secretly, we're hoping some boys will show up and catch us in our bathing suits.

'I wish we had a radio,' I say.

Mattie grins at me and breaks out into Sam Cooke's 'Wonderful World.' I take another swig of beer and join her. Swaying in time with our make-believe music, we sing off key, mangling the lyrics because we don't know the words, making up our own as we go, laughing at the silliness of them. After a minute of that, we fall back onto our towels, laughing so hard tears stream from our eyes.

A comfortable silence ensues and in that moment everything is right in the world. The sun warms my face. I'm lying next to my best friend. The whole summer stretches ahead of us. And there's no place else in the world I'd rather be.

I'm dozing off when Mattie speaks. 'Does your *datt* still hug you, Katie?'

It's such a strange and unexpected question that I raise up on an elbow and look at her. 'When I was little. Not much, though, even back then. I think I'm too old now.'

She doesn't open her eyes. 'My *datt* hugs me more now than when I was little.'

A strange and uncomfortable awareness creeps over me. 'Does he hug your brothers and sisters?'

'No. Just me.'

'Maybe he just loves you more.' I intended to say the words teasingly, but they come out sounding serious.

'Because I'm so loveable,' she retorts.

The odd exchange unsettles me, but I can't put my finger on why. Before I can think too hard about it, Mattie turns to me. 'The last one in the water is a rotten egg!'

She scrambles to her feet and sprints toward the muddy bank.

I watch her go, wondering why, in the instant before she turned away, I saw tears in her eyes.

THIRTEEN

Tomasetti left shortly after I gave him the shotgun. That particular type of firearm would be difficult, if not impossible, to trace. But he's a cautious man. I can only assume it ended up in some deep body of water between here and his place in Wooster. There are plenty of reservoirs and quarries in the area. He's probably right that I'm better off not knowing.

It's not yet 7:00 A.M. as I pull onto Main Street and head toward the police department. From the end of the block I spot the buggy parked in front of the building. The horse, a nice-looking bay, is tethered to a parking meter. The driver is nowhere in sight, so I assume he's inside, waiting for me.

I park in my usual spot, two spaces down from the buggy, and enter the reception area to find Mona Kurtz, my graveyard shift dispatcher, at her station, headset on, drumming her palms against her desktop to a funky dance tune on the radio, eating potato chips from a vending-machine-size bag. Mattie's father, Andy Erb, sits on the sofa, looking uncomfortable and out of place. Mona glances up when I enter, raises her hand to get my attention, and quickly swallows her food.

'Hey, Chief.' Rising, she snatches a stack of message slips from my slot and offers them to me. 'Mr. Erb was wondering if you have a few minutes to speak with him.'

I take the messages, trying not to notice her red miniskirt paired with a pink jacket over an orange tank. I think they call it color blocking. Somehow it works for her. 'Thanks, Mona.'

I turn to Andy and nod. *'Guder mariye.'*

He rises and crosses to me, holding his hat in one hand, a mug of coffee – at Mona's insistence, I'm sure – in the other. He bows his head slightly. *'Guder mariye.'*

'Would you like more coffee?'

He all but shudders. 'No.'

'I don't blame you,' I mutter as I start toward my office. 'Come in.'

I unlock the door, motion him into the visitor's chair, and slide behind my desk. 'I'm very sorry about your son-in-law and grandchildren,' I tell him.

He ducks his head, but not before I see the raw grief in his eyes. *'Sis Gottes wille.'*

'How is Mattie doing?'

'She is all right.'

I know she's not all right, but I didn't expect him to answer the question honestly. Andy Erb didn't much care for me back when I was a teenager and his daughter's best friend. The sentiment had been mutual. We haven't spoken in a decade, but even now I feel the rise of dislike inside me, and I realize some emotions aren't erased by time.

He picks at a loose straw on his hat. 'The funerals are this afternoon.'

'I'll be there.'

When he looks up from his hat, I'm surprised to see a flash of something ugly. It's so incongruous with everything I know about the Amish culture that I'm taken aback.

'Mattie told me the buggy accident wasn't an accident,' he says.

Only then do I identify the emotion I see in his eyes as rage.

131

He's entitled, but it's not a good fit. I choose my words carefully because the last thing I want to do is fan the flames. 'I don't know that for a fact, but it's something we're looking into.' I hold his gaze, trying to get a feel for his frame of mind. 'Do you know something about that, Mr. Erb?'

'Paul was a deacon,' he tells me.

'I'm aware of that.'

'Mattie sent me here. To speak with you. She reminded me that Enos Wengerd was excommunicated a few weeks ago. She thought I should let you know about it.'

I don't know Wengerd personally; our paths never crossed when I was Amish, and I've never had cause to speak to him since I've been back. But I keep my thumb on the Amish grapevine. I know he has a reputation for being Amish when it's convenient and breaking the rules when it suits him. He raises sheep on a small farm between Painters Mill and Millersburg.

I open my desk drawer and remove a pad of paper. 'Do you know why he was excommunicated?'

'He bought a truck. He attended *Mennischt* church services. *Er is en maulgrischt.*' *He is a pretend Christian.*

The mention of his buying a truck makes my antennae go up. 'Do you think his being excommunicated is somehow related to what happened to Paul and the children?'

Erb leans forward, his expression intensifying. 'When I went to the horse auction in Millersburg last weekend, I saw him arguing with Paul. *Der siffer hot zu viel geleppert.*' *The drunkard had sipped too much.*

'Wengerd was drinking alcohol?'

'*Ja.*'

'What were they arguing about?'

'I don't know, but Enos was in a state. He was angry about being placed under the *bann*. His family would no longer take meals with him. His parents refused to let him into their home. He blamed Paul when it was his own doing.'

'Do you know what kind of truck he purchased?'

He shakes his head. 'I don't know anything about English vehicles.'

'Did Enos threaten Paul?'

'I do not know.'

'Did the confrontation get physical?'

'Not that I saw.'

'Did anyone else witness the argument?' I ask.

'I don't know. They were out where they park the buggies.' He looks down at his hat. 'I wish I had done something. Talked to them.'

'I'll talk to Enos,' I tell him.

Andy rises with the arthritic slowness of a man twice his age and I know the anguish of the last two days has taken a toll.

'Thanks for bringing this to my attention, Mr. Erb.'

He leaves without responding.

It's too early for an official visit from the police department – even for the Amish, who rise early – so I decide to swing by my brother's farm before talking to Enos Wengerd. It's been months since I spoke to Jacob, and like so many visits in the past, I suspect it's going to be tense at best, unpleasant if I want to be honest about it. Jacob and I excel at both.

The old farm had once been owned by my parents and was passed down to Jacob – the eldest male child – after the death of our mother three years ago. I drive by the place several times a week when I'm on patrol. Every time, I envision myself stopping in to say hello to Jacob or sharing a cup of coffee with my sister-in-law, Irene. I envision myself getting to know my two young nephews, becoming part of their lives. But I always find an excuse to keep going.

When we were kids, Jacob, Sarah, and I were tight. We worked as much as we played and somehow we always managed to have fun. Jacob and I were particularly close. He was my big brother and I looked up to him the way only a little sister can. He could run faster, throw farther, and jump higher than anyone else in the world. If an Amish girl could have had a superhero, Jacob was mine. I could always count on him to watch my back, even if whatever trouble I'd found was my own doing, which was often the case. All of that changed when I was fourteen years old and Daniel Lapp came into our house and introduced me to the dark side of human nature. All of us lost our innocence that day.

I pull into the long gravel lane and speed toward the old farmhouse, white dust billowing in my wake. I steel myself against the familiarity of the place, but the memories encroach. To my right lies the apple orchard planted by my grandfather over fifty years ago, a place where Jacob, Sarah, and I spent many an afternoon picking McIntosh apples to sell at the fruit stand down the road. I see the cherry tree upon which Sarah and Jacob and I gorged ourselves every summer. The sapling maple tree I helped my *datt* plant is now tall enough to shade the house.

I pass by the house and the chicken coop looms into view. Jacob has replaced the wire and added a few concrete blocks at the base, probably to keep out the foxes and coyotes that roam the area at night. When I was a kid, caring for the chickens was my responsibility. I'd spend twenty minutes collecting eggs, changing the water, feeding, and raking the shit into an old dustpan for the compost pile. On a freezing January morning when I was eight years old, I came out to find feathers everywhere and all twenty chickens dead. It horrified me to realize I'd left the gate open and an animal had gotten into the coop during the night and torn them to shreds. It was a silly thing, but I'd become attached to the chickens. I had even named them. Frivolous, English names like Lulu and Bella and Madonna. When I saw what had been done to them I ran to the house, crying. My *datt* came out to assess the damage and quietly informed me, 'A lazy sheep thinks its wool is heavy.' I knew what that meant and the words devastated me. It was his way of telling me I was lazy and all of those pretty hens were dead because of me. He bought more chickens at the auction the following weekend, only this time he assigned their care to my sister. I wasn't allowed near the coop.

Jacob is married to a nice Amish woman by the name of Irene, who's little more than a stranger to me. She bore him two sons – Elam and James – who are six and seven years old, respectively. It pains me deeply that my nephews are strangers, too. I hate it that I don't know my sister-in-law. That I've never laughed with her or helped her in the kitchen or listened while she grumbled about her husband. What I hate most is the chasm that exists between me and my brother. Not for the first time, I think of all the things Daniel Lapp stole from me that day. What he stole from all of us. And I hate him for it.

I park near the sidewalk between the gravel parking area and the back of the house and shut down the engine. I don't want to go inside. I don't want to speak to Irene or even my brother, actually. I don't want to see my nephews because I know it will only remind me how much I've let slip by and how little I've done to rectify it.

'Katie?'

I turn to see Jacob coming up the sidewalk from the barn. For an instant, he looks like the brother I so admired all those years ago. A tall boy with a quick grin, a protective nature, and muscles I longed to possess myself. In that instant, I want to launch myself at him, throw my arms around him, tell him I've missed him, and beg him to love me the way he used to because I need him in my life.

Instead, I stand there and wait for him to reach me. Like all married Amish men, he wears a full beard. There's more gray threaded through it than the last time I saw him. He's wearing gray work trousers. A blue work shirt with black suspenders. Work boots. And a straw, flat-brimmed hat.

He stops a few feet away from me. 'What are you doing here?'

I had almost expected him to greet me with a smile or good morning or a how-are-you. Instead, his eyes are hard and he's looking at me as if I'm the tax man with my hand reaching for his mason jar.

'We have a problem,' I tell him. 'Do you have a few minutes?'

I hear a noise behind me and turn to see my sister-in-law, Irene, standing on the back porch, shaking the dust from a rug. She makes eye contact with me and nods, but she doesn't look happy to see me and makes no move to come over to greet me. I know my nephews won't be coming out to bid their *Englischer* auntie hello. It isn't the first time the Amish have let me know I'm a bad influence on their young.

'Has something happened?' he asks.

I didn't expect him to invite me inside for coffee and pie. I don't *want* to go inside, especially considering the conversation we're about to have. Still, it hurts.

'They found Daniel Lapp's bones,' I tell him. 'In the grain elevator down in Coshocton County.'

Jacob is a stoic man. Even as a boy he rarely displayed his emotions. But some responses are too powerful to contain, and I see a ripple of shock go through his body.

'Are you sure?' he asks.

'I'm sure.'

He looks toward the barn, then back at me. 'It's Daniel Lapp?'

I resist the urge to snap at him, ask him who else it could

be. 'The police haven't identified the remains. I don't know if they'll be able to. If they do, you can bet they'll come here to talk to you.'

The muscles in his jaws begin to work.

'Benjamin Lapp knows Daniel baled hay here the day he disappeared,' I add.

He looks down at the ground, but not before I see the extent of his concern. He may not have killed Lapp, but he was complicit. It was he, after all, who helped our father transport the body and dump it into the boot pit of that abandoned grain elevator.

'This is terrible news,' he says.

The statement doesn't require a response, so I say nothing. For the span of several minutes we stand there and watch the chickens scratch and peck the ground in the coop.

'Jacob, if the police come here, I want you to tell them Daniel left at the end of the day and you never saw him again. Just like you did seventeen years ago. Tell them he was fine when he left and you have no idea what happened to him.'

'Maybe they won't come here.'

'They will. We have to get our stories straight.' I hear myself say the words, hating the way it sounds, then push on. 'You have to be prepared.'

'I don't like this, Katie. The lying. The secrets.'

'Neither do I, but we have to deal with it. We can't change what happened.'

He looks away, studying something on the horizon. Or maybe he simply can't bring himself to look at me.

'There's a chance the police may not be able to identify the remains,' I tell him. 'There may not be DNA or dental records. If that's the case, you have nothing to worry about.'

'What happened that day . . . what we did . . . it has haunted me all these years.'

'It's haunted all of us, Jacob. But I'm the one who pulled the trigger. The sin was mine, not yours. Not Sarah's.'

His eyes find mine. 'It is our sin, Katie.'

I want to say something to remind him that Lapp was no innocent bystander. He'd still be alive today if he hadn't been a violent man to begin with. Even if I could find the words, I don't know if they would matter.

'I'm going to talk to Sarah,' I tell him.

He looks at me in a way I don't understand, then turns away and starts toward the house without saying good-bye.

I don't believe either of my siblings will divulge the truth about what happened the day Daniel Lapp was killed. Our *datt* swore us to silence, and for years none of us questioned his decision. We never discussed it after that day, and any emotional trauma we suffered was rebuffed or downplayed or both. But you never forget an ordeal like that, and I know, perhaps more than most, that injuries to the psyche run deep. Sometimes those scars break open and bleed.

The farm where my sister lives with her husband, William, sits at the end of a dead-end road. A razor-straight row of blue spruce trees whiz by my window as I zip up the lane. The barn and house loom into view. Like the Amish, both buildings are plain, without the ornamentation of shutters or even landscaping. In the side yard, trousers and dresses pinned to a clothesline flap in the breeze, reminding me of all the times Sarah and I helped our own mother with laundry.

The barn's sliding door stands open, telling me William is probably mucking stalls or feeding the livestock. I'm relieved. Like many of the Amish in my former church district, my brother-in-law believes I'll be spending all of eternity burning in hell. He thinks I'm a bad influence on my sister, as if some decayed part of me will rub off.

Most of the time, I'm able to overlook that kind of narrow-minded thinking because I understand the Amish mindset and I have great respect for the culture. Still, I was once close to my sister; I used to be part of this tight-knit community. While the pain of being unofficially excommunicated is no longer the agony it once was, I still feel the losses.

I park on a patch of threadbare grass where the driveway meets the backyard and kill the engine. I get my thoughts in order as I slide out and start toward the house. A glance behind me tells me William is still in the barn. He knows nothing of what happened all those years ago and I prefer to keep it that way.

I ascend the concrete steps to the porch. Before I can knock, the door swings open and I find myself face-to-face with Sarah. She's wearing a blue dress with a black apron. Her blond hair is pulled back and tucked into her *kapp*. She looks the same as the last time I saw her, pretty and plain, with an air of contentment I never seemed to find. Despite the reason for my visit, the sight of my niece in her arms makes me smile. The baby is swaddled in a blanket, a fat bundle of pink skin, colorless hair, and a bow mouth covered with spittle. Eyes the same color as mine stare back at me from within that round, perfect face.

'Katie! Hello!'

I look away from the baby. My sister seems genuinely pleased to see me. But I don't miss the exaggerated enthusiasm of her voice, or the way her eyes flick toward the barn as if she's concerned that William will notice my vehicle and come inside to scowl at me. While she may be happy to see me, she wants me in and out quickly, before he can pass judgment on both of us.

'*Sitz dich anne un bleib e weil.*' Sit down and stay a while. She speaks rapidly in Pennsylvania Dutch. '*Witt du wennich eppes zu ess?*' Would you like something to eat?

'*Nee, denki,*' I tell her. 'I can't stay.'

She feigns disappointment, but she can't hide the relief I see in the way her shoulders relax. I tell myself these games we play don't hurt. I know her husband is a large part of the reason she doesn't enjoy my company. But a keen sense of regret unfurls in my gut as I watch her flit around the kitchen with her child in her arms, trying desperately to find something to do so she doesn't have to sit down and talk to me.

'*Witt du wennich kaffi?*' she asks.

'Coffee would be great.'

'*Millich?* It's fresh from this morning.'

'Sure.'

I sit at the kitchen table and watch as she sets to work, pouring water from the tap into an old-fashioned percolator with one hand, holding the baby with the other. 'How old is she now?' I ask.

'Nineteen months.'

'Hard to believe that much time has passed.'

'You mean without a visit from her aunt?' She asks the question teasingly, but there's censure in her voice.

I sigh. 'Yeah. I'm sorry. I've been . . .' My response is lame, so I let the words trail.

She looks over her shoulder at me and smiles kindly. 'William doesn't help.'

When the coffee is made and milk added to my cup, she crosses to the table and sets a steaming mug in front of me. I sip while she takes the chair across from me, cooing to the baby. 'Is everything all right, Katie? You look . . . troubled.'

'The police found Daniel Lapp's remains,' I tell her.

Sarah goes still. '*What?*' Her eyes fly to mine. 'You mean . . . in the grain elevator?'

I nod.

'But . . . how? I thought . . . I mean, *Datt* and Jacob buried . . . everything.'

'Two kids playing in the boot pit found the bones. The parents called the police.'

'Oh no.' For a moment she looks physically ill. I see her trying to digest the information, work her way through the repercussions. 'What does this mean, Katie? Are we going to get into trouble?'

'You didn't do anything wrong,' I tell her.

'What about you?'

'I don't think the police will be able to identify the remains.' I pause. 'Someone from the sheriff's office will probably come and talk to you.'

'Me?' Her eyes widen. 'But why?'

I tell her the same thing I told Jacob. 'Daniel's brother, Benjamin, will tell them the last place Daniel was seen was our farm. That he'd come over to bale hay that morning.'

She looks down at her baby, but her mind is no longer on the child. 'What do I tell them?'

'Same thing you told them when he initially disappeared. You were in town, selling bread, remember?' That much, at least, is true. 'Tell them you *think* Daniel was helping bale hay, but you don't remember seeing him. That's all you have to say.'

'Katie, I don't want to speak with anyone. I don't want to lie to the police.'

'You don't have a choice. If they come, you have to talk to them. You have to be consistent. You can't tell them what happened.'

'How will I explain all of this to William?' she whispers furiously, as if her husband is standing at the back door, listening. 'He knows nothing of this.'

'Tell him the same thing you tell the police. Keep it simple. Stick to your story.' I feel like a hypocrite – or worse, a crooked cop – saying those words. How many criminals, in an effort to conceal their crimes, have said the very same thing?

'I don't like all of this lying, Katie.'

'None of us do,' I say, meaning it. 'But the alternative is worse.'

She says nothing. That worries me because I know a decent number of cases are solved not because of solid police work, but because someone with intimate knowledge of the crime talks about it to the wrong person or says the wrong thing to the police.

'What about Jacob?' she asks.

'Don't worry about Jacob. I've already talked to him.' When she says nothing, I add, '*Datt* made a decision that day, Sarah. We were children; we didn't have a choice but to go along with it.'

'He was trying to protect you.'

I don't have anything to say about that, so I remain silent.

She looks down at the baby, but there's no joy in her eyes now. It's as if she's no longer seeing the child because of this massive black cloud I've brought with me and laid at her feet. Kate, always the bearer of something dark.

'Sarah.' I say her name with an urgency I hadn't intended. My sister is not a liar; it doesn't come naturally to her. There's a part of me that's terrified she won't keep her mouth shut. During the Slaughterhouse Murders, she sent a note to the bishop, telling him I knew something about Daniel Lapp. The bishop went to the mayor, who passed the note on to Tomasetti. He held on to the note, protecting me in doing so, but my sister's actions put me in a precarious position. What if she does something like that again?

'I'm the chief of police,' I remind her. 'If word of this gets out – if you tell anyone what happened that day – I'll lose my job. I'll never work in law enforcement again. Sarah, I could be charged with a crime. All of us could be charged.'

'It wasn't your fault.'

'That doesn't matter. I killed a man. My guilt or innocence

won't be determined by you, but by a jury. If it goes that far, it's over for me. At least in terms of my career.'

'Fine.' She snaps the word without looking at me. 'I'll do it. But I don't like it.'

Leaving my coffee unfinished, my little niece unacknowledged, I rise and start toward the door without thanking her.

FOURTEEN

I'm still worrying over the exchange with my sister when I pull onto the dirt track of the Wengerd farm fifteen minutes later. There's no doubt in my mind that the sheriff's investigators will be taking a hard look at the disappearance of Daniel Lapp – if they haven't already. Even without DNA or dental records, they'll be able to match height, age, and sex. They'll look at the timing and start connecting the dots – right back to me.

The Explorer bounces over deep potholes. To my left, a pasture with the grass shorn down to bare earth accommodates a dozen or more pygmy goats. On my right is a cornfield with slightly crooked rows of yellow stalks fluttering in a stiff breeze. The lane swerves and I see a mobile home with a nice wood deck tucked into a stand of trees. Beyond, a red metal building surrounded by a wood pen holds a dozen more goats with kids. Twenty yards away, Enos Wengerd stands next to a pile of burning brush, poking at it with a good-size stick, looking at me.

The breeze carries gossamer fingers of smoke my way as I get out of the Explorer. Somewhere nearby, a dog begins to bark. I hit my radio, 'Six two three. I'm ten twenty-three.'

'Ten four.'

I slam the driver's side door and start toward Wengerd. 'Enos Wengerd?'

He stabs at the brush pile with the stick. 'That's me.'

'Do you have a few minutes, sir? I'd like to ask you a few questions.'

'There's no burn ban,' he says. 'I checked.'

I'm midway to him when I notice the truck parked at the side of the metal building. 'Not too windy yet,' I comment.

'It'll do.'

The truck is blue, but I can't discern the make or model. I stop ten feet from Wengerd. 'Is that your truck over there?'

He leans on the stick, takes his time answering. 'Yup.'

He wears a straw, flat-brimmed hat, a faded work shirt, and gray trousers with suspenders. I guess him to be in his mid-twenties. Six feet tall. Two hundred pounds. I can tell from the breadth of his shoulders he partakes in a good bit of physical labor.

'I hear it caused you some trouble with the deacon,' I say conversationally.

'That's not against the law, is it?'

'No,' I tell him. 'Unless you have an argument with the deacon and then he turns up dead.'

'*Wer lauert an der Wand, Heert sie eegni Schand.*' It's an old Amish sobriquet about gossip. *If you listen through the wall, you will hear others recite your faults.* 'Andy Erb gossips like an old woman,' Wengerd says, but he doesn't look quite as cocky now that he knows why I'm here.

'Did you have an argument with Paul Borntrager?' I ask.

He stares at me for a long time before answering. 'We had a disagreement.'

'What about?'

'Paul and the bishop put me under the *bann*.' The muscle in his jaw begins to work and I realize the bad attitude is by design, perhaps to conceal just how much the excommunication has upset him.

'Why?'

'Because I bought a truck. It's against the *Ordnung*.' He doesn't mention attending Mennonite services. 'But then you know all about breaking the rules, don't you, Kate Burkholder?'

I ignore the question. 'Did you get angry?'

Instead of replying, he stabs at the smoldering brush, sending a scatter of sparks into the air.

'Where did the argument happen?' I ask.

'At the auction. In Millersburg. You already knew that, though, or you wouldn't be here.' He pokes harder, watching as new flames lick at the dry kindling. He's got large, strong hands and forearms turned brown from the sun. He wraps his fingers around the length of wood so tightly his knuckles go white. 'I didn't run him over, if that's what you're going to ask me next.'

'Where were you two nights ago?'

'Here. Clearing brush.'

'Was there anyone with you?'

He sighs. 'It was just me and all these goats.'

'Do you mind if I take a quick look at your truck, Mr. Wengerd?' I say amicably. 'Then I'll get out of your hair and let you get back to work.'

'It's right there.' He motions toward the vehicle, but his attention stays riveted on me.

'Thanks.' I start toward the truck, aware that he's right behind me, stick in hand. Not for the first time, I wish I had eyes in the back of my head.

'It run okay?' I glance over my shoulder. He's less than three feet away. So close I can smell the smoke and sweat coming off his clothes.

'Good enough to get me under the *bann*,' he grumbles.

The truck is an old blue F-150. Not the model I'm looking for. I'm no expert, but it also looks older. 'What year?'

'Nineteen ninety-two.'

I look at him over the hood as I round the front of the truck. There's no damage. No recent body work. It's not the right color, either, though I'm well aware how easily paint can be changed. But it doesn't look freshly painted. The driver's side door is covered with patches of primer. There's no brush guard. No evidence the front end has been altered in any way. Both headlights are intact and covered with dried-on insects. Aside from a small crease and a few areas of rust, the bumper is undamaged. This truck was not involved in any recent accident, certainly not the kind that took out that buggy.

'Do you own any other vehicles?' I ask.

He gives me an are-you-kidding look and shakes his head.

I make two complete circles around the vehicle and then turn to him, extend my hand. 'Thanks for your time, Mr. Wengerd.'

He looks surprised by the gesture, but quickly reciprocates the handshake. It makes me wonder if it's the only gesture of kindness he's received since his Amish brethren excommunicated him.

The people I'm closest to have told me I have an obsessive personality, particularly when it comes to my job. I argue the point, but my defense is usually halfhearted, because they're right. When I'm in the midst of an investigation – especially a horrific and baffling one like the Borntrager case – I think of little else. I have difficulty focusing on other things that are going on in my life. I've been known to brood.

I've always chalked up my obsessive behavior to my work ethic, my black-and-white stance on right and wrong, or maybe my intolerance of people who hurt others. It wasn't until I worked the Plank case last October – the murders of an entire family – that I was forced to take a hard look at myself and examine my shortcomings. I stepped over a line in the course of that investigation. I did some things I shouldn't have. But I hate injustice. Even more, I hate the thought of someone getting away with murder.

I'm on my way back to the station when I drive by the Hope Clinic for the Amish. It's the medical facility where Paul had taken his children the afternoon of the accident. On impulse, I pull into the lot and park opposite a shedrow designed to shelter the buggy horses. A single black buggy is parked inside, the sorrel horse standing with its rear leg cocked, swatting flies with its tail. Six parking spaces are marked not only with the buggy symbol, but a handicapped sign as well, and I'm reminded the clinic deals mainly with children afflicted with some of the genetic disorders plaguing the Amish. It opened a few years ago to study several rare genetic diseases that apparently aren't so rare among the Amish.

The facility is housed in a small farmhouse that's been completely refashioned to look like an Amish home, with hanging planters, a porch swing, and even an old-fashioned clothesline in the side yard. The owner of the original property, Ronald Hope, passed away four years ago. His son, Ronald Jr., rather than sell the entire farm, donated the house and outbuildings to the clinic while maintaining ownership of the land for farming. People still talk about the appropriateness of the donor's last name.

I park adjacent the shedrow, cross the parking lot to the house, and ascend the steps to the porch. The facility is wheelchair friendly with a ramp stenciled with horseshoe prints. A sign in Pennsylvania Dutch written in an Olde English font proclaims Welcome to All.

A bell jingles merrily when I enter the homey reception area. The receptionist is a fifty-something woman with curly brown hair and blue eyes. She's wearing pink scrubs with a tag telling me her name is NATALIE. Beneath her name are the words THERE'S ALWAYS HOPE.

'Hi! May I help you?'

I show her my badge and introduce myself. 'I'm working on a case and was wondering if someone can talk to me about Paul Borntrager.'

'Oh my goodness.' She presses her hand against her matronly bosom. 'That was *awful* about Paul and those sweet little children. Just horrible. I cried my eyes out when I heard what happened. All of us here at the clinic were just crushed.'

A door that presumably leads to the interior of the clinic opens. A young blond woman, also clad in pink scrubs, steps out and then holds open the door for an Amish woman pushing a wheelchair. A boy of about eight or nine sits in the chair, playing with a stuffed bear. He's wearing trousers and suspenders and a white shirt. Through the thick lenses of his eyeglasses, I see that he suffers with what used to be referred to as lazy eye.

I offer both of them a smile. The Amish woman takes in the sight of my uniform, gives me an obligatory smile, and continues on. The boy, however, hits me with a huge, lopsided grin that's so infectious I find myself grinning back.

'Chief Burkholder, Doctor Armitage has a few minutes until his next appointment,' the receptionist tells me. 'He can speak with you now if you'd like.'

'That would be great.'

She stands and calls out to the Amish boy. 'See you next week, Jonas! Bye, Sweetie!'

The boy turns in his chair and waves vigorously. 'Bye!'

Still smiling, the receptionist motions me through the door. 'Third door on the right, Chief.'

My boots thud dully against the hardwood floors as I make my way down the hall. I pass three examination rooms with paper-covered exam tables, laminate counters, and sinks. But all semblance of clinical ends there. Framed photos of farm animals – horses and pigs and ducks – cover the walls. An oil winterscape of Amish children frolicking on a snowy hillside. A second painting depicts a horse and sleigh and a group of children ice skating on a frozen pond.

The last door on the right is partially open, and a brass nameplate reads: DOCTOR MIKE IS IN! I push open the door and find myself looking into a large office with a double set of French doors that open to a small deck. Judging from the size of the room, I suspect it was originally a master bedroom. It has gleaming hardwood floors and plenty of natural light. An old-fashioned banker's lamp sits atop a lovingly distressed cherrywood desk, the surface of which is littered with papers and forms and files. On the wall, a dozen or more tastefully framed diplomas and certificates are prominently displayed.

Through the French doors, I see red-stained Adirondack furniture. Two chairs, a lounger, and a table. Beyond, in a small patch of manicured grass, is an old-fashioned rocking horse and a sandbox filled with plastic shovels and colorful buckets. A man in a white lab coat and blue jeans sits on one of the wooden chairs, thumbing something into his phone.

I cross to the French door and push it open. 'Dr. Armitage?'

The man startles, and only then do I realize he's smoking a cigarette. I almost laugh when he makes a feeble attempt to conceal it. He stands and drops the cigarette, sets his foot over it. 'Oh, hello.' Hand extended, he starts toward me. 'You must be Chief Burkholder.' He glances down at the butt. 'I guess I'm busted.'

'It's not against the law to smoke,' I say.

'Well, it should be. I'm a doctor, for God's sake. You'd think I'd know better.' He chuckles. 'Stupidest damn habit I ever started.'

We shake. His grip is firm, but not too tight. The lack of callouses tells me he doesn't do much in the way of manual labor.

He maintains eye contact with me, his expression intelligent and full of good humor.

'Never too late to quit,' I tell him.

'I plan to.' He gives a self-deprecating laugh. 'As soon as the divorce is final. Which should be any day now.'

I nod. 'Sorry.'

'Ah, it was my own doing. All work and no play made me a pretty bad husband.' Shrugging, he motions toward the door. 'I've got about five minutes before my next appointment. Would you like to sit out here or would you be more comfortable inside?'

'Outside is fine.'

'It *is* a nice day, isn't it?' He settles back into his Adirondack chair.

I sit opposite him and take a moment to look around. The yard is small and fenced with white pickets. A big maple tree shades the corner where an old-fashioned swing set sits. A basketball hoop and backboard has been installed in a gravel area, the mesh net swaying in the breeze. It's the perfect retreat for kids and stressed-out parents. 'This is a nice facility,' I tell him.

'I love this clinic. I love the people – the Amish in particular. I love this part of Ohio.' He grins. 'Even the long winters. For the first time in my life I can honestly say the work I do is important – and not only to me.'

'It must be very gratifying.'

'It is. Immensely.'

'I remember reading about the grand opening of the clinic,' I tell him. 'I understand most of your work involves genetic disorders.'

'Almost exclusively.' He smiles. 'Though I've been known to treat a sore throat when indicated. Through the work done here, we've identified some genetic disorders that are almost unheard of elsewhere in the world.' That he uses 'we' instead of

'I' tells me he's a modest person, content to share his achievements with his colleagues, the mark of a man who loves his work and whose mind enables him to see not only the big picture, but the end goal.

'The Amish are unique in that the gene pool is relatively small,' he adds, leaning forward and gesturing. 'Most of our patients are special-needs children. We're talking quality of life disorders. Cohen Syndrome. Ellis-van Creveld syndrome. Dwarfism. Founder effect inheritable diseases mostly.'

'Founder effect?'

'Disorders that can be attributed to a limited gene pool,' he replies. 'We're working with community leaders on a way to broaden the scope of that pool, and I think we've had some success. My colleagues have been in touch with the bishops of church districts in other states. Colorado and upstate New York, mainly. To a lesser degree, Indiana and Illinois. We're trying to get a relocation-and-exchange program up and running, which is difficult because the Amish are so family oriented. And, of course, the church districts have different rules.' He leans closer to me. 'But, if we can overcome those things, if we can get young men and women of marrying age to emigrate to out-of-state Amish communities, marry, and have children in their new locale, we could broaden the gene pool and, in effect, eliminate some of these genetic disorders. Of course, only time will tell if—' He stops himself short. 'Sorry. Once I start talking about my work here, it's hard to shut me up. Used to bore my wife to tears.'

'Sounds fascinating.'

'Or maybe you're just too polite to tell me I'm boring you to death.'

I smile, find myself liking him. 'It's good to be passionate about your work.'

'Some might argue that I'm a little *too* passionate.'

It's obvious he's married to his career – and that his soon-to-be ex-wife had had to compete. I see him as a hopeless workaholic, always coming home late, working weekends, sequestered behind his computer when he's home at all. Hence the pending divorce. 'How long have you been in Painters Mill?'

'Going on eight months now. I came down from Cleveland. Different world up there. I needed a change after my wife filed. I'll never go back to the big city. This area, this clinic, has been my salvation, so to speak. It's exciting work, and I couldn't ask for a better group of people to work with.'

'The Borntrager children were patients here?'

'They were.' His lips twist as if he's bitten into something rotten. 'I couldn't believe it when I heard what happened to them. I still can't. Those poor kids. And Paul. My God, I can't imagine what Mattie must be going through.' He gives me a direct look, and I see a layer of thinly veiled outrage in his eyes. 'I heard it was a hit-and-run.'

'It was.'

'Any leads?'

'We're working on it.'

'I meant to get up to the hospital to see David, but I've been putting in long hours here and never made it. How's he doing?'

'He's going to be fine.'

'Great. I hear they've got an excellent trauma team at Pomerene.'

'I'm wondering, Dr. Armitage—'

'Call me Mike, please.'

'Mike,' I say. 'Can you tell me what the children were being treated for?'

'All three were afflicted with Cohen syndrome, to differing degrees.'

'What is Cohen syndrome, exactly?'

'Like most of the disorders we treat here, it's genetic in

nature. Rare, but not so much among the Amish. It causes a delay in mental and physical development. Neutropenia, or low white blood cell count. Hypotonia, which basically means low muscle tone. A whole array of symptoms that can impact a kid's life in a negative way.' He shakes his head. 'Mattie and Paul were good with those kids. It never seemed to bother them that they were special-needs. Hell, they barely noticed. Never complained or felt sorry for themselves or their children. Paul and Mattie loved those kids and raised them the best they could.'

'How well did you know them? Paul and Mattie, I mean.'

'Well, they'd been coming to the clinic since I arrived. It was a professional relationship, you know, just to talk about the kids enough for me to ascertain how they're doing and gauge improvements or changes, if any.' Looking inward, he smiles. 'First month or so we pretty much talked about the weather. Mattie and Paul were wary of me. You know, the whole outsider thing. Until I began working here in Painters Mill, I hadn't had much contact with the Amish or their culture, so I was clueless. All of us had to open our minds, so to speak. Once that happened, they began to trust me. I think they realized I care, and they knew I'd do my utmost to help their children. They're good people, Chief Burkholder. Nice family. Kids are well behaved and sweet. I hope to God you get justice for them.'

The urge to tell him I plan to do just that is strong, but I don't because I know better than to make some emotion-driven promise I may not be able to keep. 'How well did you know Paul?'

'He was a great guy. Quiet. Religious. To tell you the truth, he had a pretty wicked sense of humor for an Amish guy.' He chuckles as if remembering. 'I only met him a handful of times, but he was terrific.'

Something pings in the back of my brain. 'I was under the impression that he had a standing appointment here at the clinic.'

'Mattie was the one who usually brought in the kids. Every week like clockwork. For bloodwork, mostly. The children were on medication offered for free as part of a clinical trial. I like to keep a handle on the levels in the bloodstream. And the neutrophils, of course. We also discussed nutritional needs. Every month or so, I had a psychologist come down from Wooster and we did some problem solving and IQ testing.' He gives a nod. 'Mattie was great with them. Attentive. Gentle with discipline. Good instincts. Patient.'

'How well do you know her?'

'Well enough to know those kids were her life. "Gifts from God" is the way she referred to them. I can't imagine what this did to her.'

We fall silent, and for a moment the only sound comes from the chatter of sparrows from the canopy of the maple tree. 'Did either of them mention any disagreements or problems? With other family members or neighbors? Friends or acquaintances?'

'Neither of them ever mentioned any conflicts of any kind. They were the type of folks who seemed to get along with everyone.'

'Is there anything else you can tell me about the family, Dr. Armitage? Any insights you can offer? Or general observations you can share?'

He takes a moment to consider the question, then shakes his head. 'Not that I recall. But they were very private people. Not the type to confide. Our relationship was of a doctor-patient nature. When they were here, it was all about the children.' Then he gives me a candid look. 'I'm reading between the lines, Chief Burkholder, but it sounds as if there's something going on here that I haven't read about.'

'I hate to leave you in the dark, Dr. Armitage, but since it's an open investigation, I'm not at liberty to discuss the details just yet.'

'I understand.' He sits back in his chair and huffs out a sigh. 'It's such a senseless, unimaginable tragedy. Frankly, it pisses me off.'

My smile feels wan on my face as I rise. 'I appreciate your taking the time to talk to me, Dr. Armitage.'

'I wish I could do more.' He gets to his feet and we shake hands again. 'If you need anything else, Chief, please come see me.' His mouth twists into an ironic smile. 'I'm usually here working until ten or eleven p.m.'

I'm midway to the door when he calls out my name.

I stop and turn to see him striding toward me, his expression troubled. 'One more thing,' he says, and stops a few feet away. 'This may or may not be relevant to the case, Chief Burkholder, but you asked, so I'm going to skate uncomfortably close to stepping over the physician-patient privilege line and tell you about an observation I made early in my relationship with the Borntragers.'

I feel myself go still inside, silencing my thoughts and the clutter in my brain, the way you do when you know you're about to hear something important and you don't want to miss a single word or gesture or the manner in which it's delivered.

'Let me preface by saying that Paul and Mattie are good and loving parents. Of that, I'm certain.' He sighs, looks down at the floor as if he's debating how to broach the subject at all. 'The first time I examined David, I found a handprint on his behind. A red welt in the shape of a hand with some bruising beneath the skin. It was evident someone had spanked bare skin with a good bit of vigor. When I asked David about it, he said his *datt* smacked him for stealing a pie and then lying about eating it. As you know, David is overweight, which is typical of children suffering with Cohen syndrome. I must admit, I was a little taken aback. I know corporal punishment is an acceptable form of discipline in many households. But the fact that this spanking left a bruise gave me pause. I'm sure you know that, as a physician, I'm mandated by state law to report any indication of child abuse.'

'I'm aware of the statute,' I say.

'I debated whether to file an official report. In the end, however, I elected not to. After much personal deliberation, I drew the conclusion that the discipline was administered in a manner consistent with the Amish culture. In addition, I surmised the bruising was probably a result of the neutropenia, that's a common attribute of Cohen syndrome.' He offers a grim smile. 'You're not going to tell me I did the wrong thing, are you? Because let me tell you, I lost sleep over it.'

'My gut tells me your judgment didn't steer you wrong.'

'You sound pretty sure of that.'

'I used to be Amish,' I say.

He doesn't quite manage to hide his surprise. 'Wow. I didn't know. That's quite fascinating, actually.'

'I don't know if fascinating is exactly the right word.' I give him a smile. 'But I received my fair share of "smackings" as a kid. You're correct in that in many Amish households, spanking is a common form of discipline. Some of the stricter parents have been known to use a belt or even the old-fashioned willow switch.'

'If it had been welts or bruising from either of those things, I probably would have filed the report.'

Knowing it's time for me to move on, I extend my hand again and we shake. 'I'll let you get back to your patients.'

'Good luck with the case, Chief Burkholder.'

I start toward the door.

*

Back in the Explorer, I call Glock and recap my conversation with Armitage.

'So what's your take on the bruising?' he asks.

'It's troubling,' I tell him. 'Whether you approve or disapprove of spanking as a form of punishment – and most Amish fall into the former category – this particular situation is unfortunate because he's special needs.'

'Did the doc say which parent did the spanking?'

'Paul Borntrager.'

'Do you think it's relevant?' he asks. 'I mean, to the case?'

'No.'

'It's interesting that Mattie's the one who had the standing appointment,' he says.

'I think that's the bigger issue.'

'If this hit-and-run was planned, do you think *she* might have been a target? Or do you think this was random? What?'

'I don't know. None of it makes any sense.'

Another stretch of silence, then he says, 'You don't think this has anything to do with those special-needs kids, do you?'

The words creep over me like a stench and linger. 'That paints a pretty ugly picture. I can't fathom a motive.'

'Me, either. Something to consider, though.'

I pause, the possibilities running through my head. 'I'd feel better if we could keep an eye on things out there until we get a handle on this.'

'You mean around the clock?'

'Ideally.'

'Going to require some O.T.' He whistles. 'Or a miracle.'

'Never underestimate the power of groveling.'

He guffaws. 'There is that.'

'If Rasmussen can spare a deputy, we might be able to cover it between our two departments.'

'Rasmussen can't spare the toilet paper to wipe his ass.'

But the words have already passed between us. I know if my request is denied, we'll find another way. I know I'll be able to count on Glock.

'I'm on my way to the funerals,' I tell him. 'Will you let the rest of the team know about all of this?'

'You bet.'

I'd wanted to arrive at the Borntrager farm to speak with Mattie well before the funerals. I'd wanted to accompany her to the *graabhof* – not as the chief of police, but as her friend – to bury her husband and children. Instead, I got caught behind a procession of buggies and ended up issuing a citation to an impatient tourist for passing on a double yellow line. He let me know in no uncertain terms that he wasn't happy about the ticket. I told him no one driving to the cemetery was particularly happy either, so he's in good company. Have a nice day.

By the time I arrive, dozens of black buggies, each numbered with white chalk so they know the order in which they belong in the convoy, are parked in the gravel lot. The smells of horses and leather and fresh-cut grass float on a light breeze. The lot is filled to capacity and many of the remaining buggy drivers have begun to park alongside the road. Using my emergency lights to alert traffic to the slow-moving and stopped vehicles, I park on the shoulder well out of the way, grab a few flares and toss them onto the road to make sure passing drivers slow down.

The graveyard exists as the Amish have existed for over two centuries: plainly. Hundreds of small, uniform headstones form razor-straight rows in a field that had once flourished with soybeans and corn. Unlike English cemeteries where the headstones vary from massive works of sculpted granite to tiny crosses, the Amish *graabhof* is an ocean of white markers etched with a simple cross, the name of the deceased, their birth date and the date of their death.

The cemetery is a somber yet peaceful place and pretty in its own way. My *mamm* and *datt* are buried fifty yards from where I stand. The reality of that sends a wash of guilt over me. I haven't been here since I worked the Plank case last fall and attended the funerals of five members of an Amish family slain in their farmhouse. I tell myself I'm too busy to spend my time mingling with the dead. The truth of the matter is that, despite its bucolic beauty, this is the one place in Painters Mill that scares me.

I pass through the gate and start toward the gravesite. Dozens of families, young couples, the elderly, scads of children, and mothers with babies stand in the cool afternoon air. As is usually the case, the Amish community has come out in force to mourn the Borntrager family and support Mattie and young David. Grief hovers in the air like a pall.

Because I'm no longer Amish – and not necessarily welcome here – I hang back from the mourners, an outsider even in death. Once everyone is in place, the crowd falls silent. Bishop Troyer reads a hymn in Pennsylvania Dutch as the pallbearers lower each of the three plain pine coffins into hand-dug graves. When he finishes, heads are bowed, and I know the mourners are silently reciting the Lord's Prayer. Instead of fighting the words that come with such ease, I lower my head and join them, something I haven't done in a very long time.

When the ceremony is over and the Amish start toward their buggies to return to their farms, I thread my way through the crowd toward the gravesites. I nod my respect to everyone who makes eye contact with me. Some nod back. A few offer grim smiles. Some of the older Amish, the ones who know I left the fold, give me a wide berth.

It takes me a few minutes to find Mattie. She's standing next to Bishop Troyer, David, and her parents while several young men shovel dirt into the graves. Her face is red and wet from crying. But she doesn't make a sound. Her *datt*, Andy Erb, looks nearly as shaken as his daughter and grips her hand so tightly his knuckles are white. Her *mamm*, stoic-faced and tense, holds David's hand just as tightly.

This isn't the time or place to speak with Mattie about the information I learned from Armitage earlier; I can tell from her expression she's barely holding it together. But I can't delay much longer, because if someone tried to kill her and failed, the possibility exists they'll try again.

FIFTEEN

Anyone who's ever worked in law enforcement – or watched crime TV – knows the first forty-eight hours after a crime is committed are the most important in terms of solving it. Most cops work around the clock those first vital days, when the clock is ticking and their chances of achieving a solve diminish with every minute that passes. My tactic on this case is no different. I've been chasing the clock all day, and despite my best efforts, there's no way I'm going to make dinner with Tomasetti. A law enforcement veteran himself, he'll understand. That doesn't mean he won't be disappointed. It won't alleviate my own disappointment. It will, however, give me a little more time to decide how to respond if he pushes the issue of my moving in with him.

I call him on my way to the Borntrager farm and break the news.

He takes it like a man. 'I guess I'm going to have to drink this bottle of wine all by myself.'

I chuckle. 'Don't get too close to the pond. I'd hate to find the empty bottle on the bank and you floating facedown in all that moss.'

'Anyone ever accuse you of having a dark sense of humor?'

'You're the only one who appreciates it.'

He pauses. 'Any luck on the case?'

I tell him about my meeting with Armitage and we cover the same ground Glock and I covered earlier. 'Will you do me a favor?' I ask.

'You know I will.'

'Will you pull arrest records for hate crimes in the two-county area?'

'I'm all over it.' In the background I hear a dull popping sound.

'What was that?' I ask.

'Breaking the seal. Going to let this breathe for a few minutes.'

'I'm sorry I didn't make it.'

'Me, too.'

I turn onto the dead-end road that will take me to the Borntrager farm. I can just make out the silhouettes of two buggies moving down the lane toward the house.

'If you can get away tomorrow,' Tomasetti begins, 'I've got a nice cabernet from California in the pantry.'

'I'll be there,' I tell him. 'Come hell or high water.'

'Hopefully it won't come to that.'

I'm smiling when I disconnect.

The Borntrager farm seems hushed as I park off the sidewalk at the rear of the house. The two buggies sit adjacent the barn. The barn door is open and I presume her neighbors have arrived to take care of the chores. Bishop Troyer is gone, probably home to rest and take care of his own affairs. Another family or neighbor will be looking after Mattie and David tonight.

I take the sidewalk to the back door and knock. A young woman wearing a gray dress with a white apron and prayer *kapp* answers. Her eyes widen when she spots my uniform. 'May I help you?'

'Hi, I'm Kate Burkholder.' I show her my badge. 'I'm here to see Mattie.'

Her mouth tightens with disapproval, and I wonder if people still talk about my abandoning my roots, or maybe someone has recently mentioned me in an unflattering light. 'Mattie was very distraught after the funerals and is lying down upstairs.'

She's trying to find a way to deny my request without being openly rude. 'I wouldn't ask to see her at a time like this if it wasn't important.'

'Maybe you could come back later?'

I look beyond her to see a stout older woman with a dish towel draped over her shoulder marching toward us, her practical shoes like jackhammers against the floor. Recognition flickers and I realize I knew her back when I was a preteen; she was an assistant teacher at the school I attended. Mattie used to call her *Leih*, the Pennsylvania Dutch word for cow, mainly because even though she was only a few years older than us, she was already a large woman and enjoyed bullying anyone smaller or younger or weaker.

'Mattie is sleeping and asked not to be disturbed,' she informs me in Pennsylvania Dutch.

'Hello, Miriam,' I begin. 'Nice to see you.'

She doesn't smile. 'Come back in the morning like a decent person.'

I push open the door. Both women move back to avoid me when I step inside. The younger woman's eyes widen as I brush past her. Miriam isn't deterred and blocks my path. 'You just hold your horses right there, Katie Burkholder.'

'This is official police business,' I tell her. 'I'm not leaving until I speak with Mattie.'

'In that case I'll bring you a pillow and you can sleep on the porch.'

In the back of my mind, I know this is funny. Especially

because she's serious and I'm getting pissed. Under different circumstances I might have laughed, or at least enjoyed the comedy of it. But my sense of humor has shriveled to the size of a pea in the last couple of days and I'm tired of people making my job difficult. 'Get out of my way or I will arrest you. Do you understand?'

'Where's your sense of decency?' Miriam asks crossly. 'Can't you see the poor girl's mourning?'

'*Katie?*'

I glance through the kitchen to see Mattie standing in the doorway, looking as pale as a ghost, as inanimate as a mannequin. She appears physically ill, depressed, and utterly lifeless.

Miriam casts me an I-told-you-so look. Her eyes don't soften when they fall on Mattie and I wonder if she remembers the name calling from when we were teenagers. 'Back upstairs with you,' she says none-too-gently. 'Go on now. You need your rest.'

'It's okay, Miriam.' A tremulous smile touches Mattie's lips. 'Katie and I are friends.'

The woman shoots me a disapproving look, her eyes lingering on my uniform. '*Sie hot net der glaawe.*' *She doesn't keep the faith.* Catching the eye of the younger woman, she motions toward the kitchen and then they leave us.

For several seconds, Mattie and I contemplate each other. She looks too raw to partake in a long question-and-answer session, especially when none of it's going to be pleasant. I don't have the luxury of sparing her.

'*Leih,*' I whisper. *Cow.*

Mattie chokes out a laugh, but tears fill her eyes. 'She's only trying to help.'

I nod, my temper fading. 'I'm sorry to bother you so late and so soon after the funerals.'

'It's okay. I know you're only doing your job.' She tilts her head. 'Has something happened?'

'I talked to Dr. Armitage at the Hope Clinic today. He told me you're the one who usually takes the children to their appointments.'

She seems confused by the statement, as if she doesn't comprehend its significance. '*Ja.* That's true.'

'Is there a reason why you didn't mention it?'

'I guess I didn't think of it. I didn't know it was important.'

'Mattie, the crash that killed Paul and your children wasn't an accident. Someone did it on purpose. We thought Paul might have been targeted. That's why we were looking at people who might've had a falling-out with him.'

'But I told you, Katie. He didn't have any enemies.'

'Mattie.' I step closer to her, reach out, and take both of her hands in mine. Her fingers are cold and clammy; it's like touching a dead person. 'If you're the one who drives the children to the clinic every week, *you* may have been the target.'

'But . . . I don't understand. I'm a nobody. An Amish woman and her *children*? Why would someone do such a thing?'

'I don't know.' I study her face, but all I see is the weight of grief in her eyes, fatigue, and the sharp edges of a burgeoning realization.

'Mattie, I need to ask you all the same questions I asked about Paul. Do you have any enemies? Have you been involved in any disputes or arguments? Anything you can think of that might have led to this?'

'No, of course not.'

'Any problems related to the children? Or money perhaps?' I think of her beauty and add, 'Any jealousy?'

'No, Katie. None of those things.'

'What about strangers? Have you seen any strange vehicles or buggies in the area? Driving by too often? Anyone watching you or the house or the children?'

'No. That's just crazy.'

Out of the corner of my eye I see Miriam peek at us from the kitchen, casting a reproachful look my way. I stare at her until she turns away. 'What about in town?'

'Nothing like that has happened.'

I stare at her for a second, noticing the pale, dry lips. Flesh the color of a bruise beneath her eyes. The part of me that was once her best friend wants to spare her these questions. I want to protect her from the likelihood that someone wishes her harm. But the part of me that is a cop knows I can't. 'Is it possible Paul was being unfaithful? Maybe there was a jealous husband?'

I know she's going down an instant before her eyes roll back. Her knees buckle. Her head lolls back. I lunge forward, catch her beneath her arms just in time to keep her from hitting the floor. But she's too heavy for me; her body is slack, dead weight in my arms. Though she's small framed, the best I can do is break her fall.

'Mattie. *Mattie!*'

The two Amish women rush into the mudroom.

I position her on the floor so that she's lying on her back. Miriam kneels beside her. 'You and your *Englischer* ways.' She snaps the words without looking at me. 'What did you do to her?'

'She collapsed,' I tell her.

'You are bad for her,' she says nastily. 'You were always bad for her and you still are.'

I know better than to let the words affect me, but they hit some obscure bull's-eye, that small part of me that, even after all these years, still longs to belong despite the fact that I'm not wanted. 'Shut up, Miriam.' I pull out my cell to call for an ambulance.

She hisses at me, bats my phone away with her hand. 'She

is fine.' Miriam looks over her shoulder at the younger woman. 'Bring me a wet towel and a pillow.'

Leaning over Mattie, Miriam slips her hand beneath Mattie's head and lifts it slightly. 'Everything's going to be all right,' she whispers.

Dispatch responds to my call. 'Ten fifty two,' I say, giving the code for requesting an ambulance.

'She'll be fine as soon as you stop badgering her with questions and scaring the daylights out of her,' Miriam snaps.

Ignoring her, I give the dispatcher the address.

I'm in the process of clipping my phone to my belt when Mattie's eyes flutter open. For an instant, she stares at me as if she doesn't recognize me. Then she startles, gets her elbows beneath her, and tries to rise. 'What . . .'

'You had a spell is all,' Miriam coos.

'You fainted,' I tell her.

'I'm . . . fine,' Mattie says quickly. 'I just . . . got a little dizzy.'

The younger Amish woman arrives with a damp kitchen towel and an embroidered pillow from the sofa.

'You just lie still for a moment.' Miriam sets the towel on Mattie's forehead and then slides the pillow beneath her head. 'Catch your breath.' She orders the younger Amish woman to fetch a glass of water, then addresses me: 'We don't need an ambulance. What she needs is some peace and quiet, two things that don't happen whenever you're around, Katie Burkholder.'

I direct my words to Mattie. 'You should get yourself checked out at the hospital.'

'It was just a dizzy spell, Katie. I'm okay . . . just tired from everything that's happened.'

'We'll take care of her,' Miriam tells me. 'She'll be fine once you and your questions go away.'

The words make me sigh. I shake my head, knowing that

when the ambulance arrives, Mattie will probably refuse treatment. Still, I don't cancel the call.

I glance down at her and offer a smile. She looks embarrassed, not only because she fainted, but because her caregiver is being rude to me. 'I'll let you get some rest,' I tell her.

She raises her hand to mine. I take it and squeeze. 'I'm fine,' she says, offering a tentative smile. 'Don't worry. Miriam will take good care of me.'

I get the impression Miriam doesn't much care for either of us, but I don't say the words. 'Will you do me a favor?' I ask.

'Of course I will.'

'Keep your doors locked. Watch your back.'

Miriam makes a sound of annoyance.

Mattie holds on to her smile, but for the first time I see an uneasiness that wasn't there before. I know she doesn't need anything more to deal with, but I also know there are times when fear is a healthy thing, when a look over your shoulder might be the only thing that saves your life.

While I'm sitting in the Explorer, waiting for the ambulance to arrive, I pull out my cell and call T.J. 'You in the mood for some O.T.?' I begin.

'I'm game. What do you have in mind?'

'I want you to camp out at the Borntrager farm tonight.'

'Sure.' He falls silent. 'You think someone's going to go after the wife, too?'

'I don't know. I'd just feel better if we could keep an eye on things out here.'

'Damn, Chief. That's bizarre. Why would someone want an Amish lady dead? I mean, an Amish *mother* with three little kids to take care of?'

'That's the sixty-four-thousand-dollar question.'

The ambulance arrives, the red and blue lights flashing, no siren. I watch as the paramedics are turned away at the door and I sigh.

'Let me know if you figure it out.'

It's a dangerous thing when a cop knows too much about a crime, especially if said cop possesses information that would be helpful to the investigating agency and doesn't speak up. I don't know if the bones found in the grain elevator will ever be positively identified. Seventeen years have passed. Investigators are reliant upon DNA or dental records, neither of which may exist. That doesn't mean I'm home free. Not even close.

Rural areas have long memories when it comes to any kind of major crime, an inescapable fact that doesn't bode well in terms of my avoiding getting sucked into the case. It was big news when Daniel Lapp went missing. Many believed he'd left town to escape the heavy hand of the Amish. But not everyone. Not his parents. Certainly not his brother, Benjamin.

By virtue of the timing alone, the police will question Benjamin. Once they learn Daniel was last seen at my parents' farm, they'll be knocking on my door, Sarah's door, and Jacob's door, asking questions none of us want to answer, just like they did seventeen years ago. This time, however, they'll be wondering why I didn't come to them first. I wonder if it would be beneficial for me to call Sheriff Redmon and start lying now, instead of waiting and letting them come to me.

I burn through an hour, stuck behind my desk, returning calls and e-mails and putting out fires. After receiving a slew of media inquiries earlier in the day, I ask Jodie to write a press release, a generic piece that basically rehashes the things everyone already knows. For now, it's going to have to be enough. Best case, it will buy me some time, because this story has all the hallmarks of a sensational headline in the making. It's Amish focused, includes a father and two dead children, and a mystery that expands with every new piece of information tossed our way.

At seven o'clock, Rasmussen returns my call. 'Around-the-clock protection?' He laughs. 'Are you kidding?'

'Not protection, exactly.' I hedge, knowing my request is so far out there, he's well within his bounds to laugh at me. 'Mattie might've been the target. I'd feel better knowing someone was out there, keeping an eye on things.'

'In a perfect world, we could do that. As you know, we don't live in a perfect world.'

'*Mike.*'

'Look, I can have my guys drive by every so often,' he offers. 'Round-the-clock is out of the question.'

'Can't you spare one deputy?' I ask. 'One shift?'

'Wish I could, Kate. I just don't have the budget for O.T. We're already operating on a skeleton crew here. I wish I could help, but I can't.'

I sigh, only slightly peeved because I know he'd do it if he could. 'I'll figure something out.'

'Look, while I have you on the phone . . . I heard from the lab on that piece of wood Luke Miller found,' he tells me. 'The indentation is, indeed, from a bolt. And it's recent.'

'How recent?'

'Days or maybe even hours.'

'Is it from the sheared pin we found at the scene?'

'That's the kicker. It's not the same.'

'Do the lab guys have any idea what that pin is for?'

'They're running some comps, but it's going to take a while.'

'We're relatively certain we're dealing with a Ford F-250. I wonder if we should take the piece of wood with the indentation to the local Ford dealership?'

'Since it was an after-market part, a Ford guy probably isn't going to be much help.'

'Shit, Mike, you're just full of positive offerings this evening.'

'Yeah, well, I try.'

For the span of several seconds, neither of us speaks, but I sense our minds working over everything we know about the case so far and how little we have to work with in terms of solid facts. 'Will you do me a favor?' I ask.

'Well, since I owe you now . . .'

'Will you have one of your guys take that bolt to someone who knows about after-market parts? Someone who might recognize it? Maybe that custom hot-rod shop in Millersburg?'

'Worth a shot.'

I thank him and disconnect, then sit there for a moment, the exchange running through my head like a bad script. My stomach growls, reminding me the most nutritious substance I've put in it all day is coffee.

'Damn it,' I mutter and look down at the phone.

I want to call Tomasetti and run all of this past him, but I hesitate. Only then do I realize that, while I *have* been busy with the case, my reasons for avoiding him are a lot more complex than I'm admitting, even to myself. The truth of the matter is, I'm afraid he's going to ask me to move in with him again – and I don't know how to answer. I hate it that I haven't been honest. Not with him – or myself. I need to sort out my feelings and make a decision. He deserves an answer, and I owe it to myself to give it to him, no matter where we go from here.

SIXTEEN

I make a stop at the grocery and buy a bottle of my favorite cabernet, a bunch of grapes, some crusty French bread, cheese, and a corkscrew bottle opener. I tuck everything into a grocery bag and makes tracks toward Wooster. It takes me twenty minutes to find Tomasetti's new place. I get lost twice and end up having to call my dispatcher for a quick Google map search. I could have called Tomasetti, but somewhere along the way realized I wanted to surprise him.

Dusk falls in Impressionist hues of lavender and gray. I'm so intent on the peaceful beauty of the countryside, I nearly miss my turn and have to make a hard stop. The rust-bucket mailbox has been bashed in, but the number is still legible, so I turn in. The canopies of the massive elm trees arc over the lane, lending the illusion of driving through a lush, green cave.

Despite my earlier hesitancy, a sense of anticipation keeps pace with me as I barrel toward the house. I think about the man waiting for me and I suddenly can't wait to see him. I want to hear his voice. I want him to make me laugh at something I shouldn't. For a little while I want to forget about this case. I want to forget about the discovery of Lapp's remains.

The old Victorian sits at the end of the lane looking lost and out of place, like some B-movie actor who knows, no matter how hard he tries, he'll never master the part to which he's been cast. In an instant, I take in the wraparound porch, the tall, narrow windows, and the crisp white paint. Huge shade trees hulk on every side of the house. Behind it, a rusty silo that had once been painted silver and a tumbling-down barn watch over the place with mournful, longing eyes.

Tomasetti's Tahoe is parked adjacent a one-car detached garage. I can tell by the way the overhead door lists that it's not functional. I get out of the Explorer and I'm met by a dissonance of birdsong: blue jays and cardinals and the occasional caw of a crow. The breeze smells of cut grass and the honeysuckle that grows wild on the barbed wire fence behind a small chicken coop. I stand there, taking in the disarray, and all I can think is that this world I've stepped into is completely incongruous with the man I've come to know.

I take the crumbling sidewalk to the back porch. The door stands ajar, but the screen door is closed. I hear the crackle of a radio beyond. The smells of fresh paint and new wood waft through the screen. Using my knuckles, I rap on the door and wait, incredulous because my heart is pounding and there's a small, insecure part of me that's terrified he won't come.

A full minute passes. Thinking he might be upstairs, I use my key chain and knock harder. 'Tomasetti?'

When that doesn't draw his attention, I push open the door. The hinges squeak as I step inside. The kitchen has been gutted down to the drywall and subflooring. A radio is set up on a five-gallon bucket and The Wallflowers blare 'One Headlight.' A wide doorway to my right beckons, so I take it to a good-size living room. Three of the walls are painted an attractive dark tan. A stepladder stands next to a tall window. Plastic drop cloths cover hardwood floors the color of semisweet chocolate. I turn in a slow circle, spot the massive hearth behind me, and find myself smiling.

'Tomasetti?'

The only reply is the birdsong coming in through the open window and sound of the breeze rattling the drop cloth on the floor.

I take the stairs to the second level. There are three large bedrooms and an art-deco-style bathroom with teal-colored tile and a claw-foot tub. More evidence of work up here, too. There are two sawhorses set up with a sheet of plywood stretched across them. A power saw sits on the floor atop a layer of saw-dust, an orange extension cord coils like a snake against the wall.

'Tomasetti!' I call out.

No answer.

'Well, shit.' Still lugging the grocery bag, I go down the steps, through the kitchen, and back outside. The doors of the barn and silo are closed, telling me he's not there. I stroll to the Explorer and look out over the pasture beyond. I'm about to reach through the window and lay on the horn when I spot the pond. It's a good-size body of water – at least half an acre. A big cottonwood tree demarks the north side. A stand of weeping willows flourish near the shore to the west. I see some type of dock from where I stand and I'm pretty sure the person sitting on that dock is Tomasetti.

Hefting the grocery bag, I start toward the nearest gate, careful to close it behind me in case he inherited cattle with the place, and I follow a dirt two-track to the pond. From fifty feet away, I see Tomasetti slumped in a lawn chair with his feet stretched out in front of him. He's wearing blue jeans, navy golf shirt, and sneakers – a far cry from his usual custom-made suits and Hermès ties. Next to him, a bottle of Killian's Irish Red sweats atop a good-size cooler.

I make it to within twenty feet of him before he hears my approach and glances my way. His usual inscrutable expression shifts, and it delights me to see surprise on his face. He's not an easy man to surprise. Smiling, he rises and faces me. For the span of several heartbeats, we stare at each other, contemplating, finding our feet, and the rest of the world falls away. After a moment, I look around and spot the fishing pole lying on the dock, the clear nylon line running into the water.

'Tomasetti, are you *fishing*?' I ask.

He bends and opens the cooler. I'm expecting him to hand me a Killian's Red. Instead, the cooler is filled with water and three good-size fish, which are swimming around. 'I'm catching dinner, actually.'

'Are those largemouth bass?' I ask.

'You know your fish. I'm impressed.'

'My *datt* used to take me fishing when I was a kid.'

'Who knew? I could have used some pointers early on.'

'Looks like you figured things out.'

He replaces the cover and straightens.

'I'm sorry I didn't make it last night,' I say a little too abruptly.

'You're here now.' He unfolds a second lawn chair and sets it next to his. 'How's the case coming along?'

'Still looking for the driver.'

'Anything new on those bones?'

That's when I realize one of the reasons I'm here is to escape the pressures of my job. I know it's shortsighted; not only does Tomasetti usually offer pretty good insight and advice, but I'm well aware that the weight of both cases will drop back onto my shoulders when I leave. But I don't want tonight to be about work. I want it to be about us and this short stretch of time between us.

'Let's not talk about work,' I tell him.

He tilts his head, puzzled, and then shrugs. 'We could just sit here and fish.'

I look down at the bag I'm holding. 'I brought wine.'

He takes the bag, peeks into it. 'You want to go inside?'

From where I'm standing, I can smell the foliage and the water on the breeze. I can hear the buzz of insects and the coo of a mourning dove. 'I kind of like it out here, Tomasetti. If you don't mind.'

'I don't mind.' He sets the bag atop the cooler and proceeds to set out the things I bought. Wine. Grapes. The cheese and bread. On the other side of the pond, a family of red-winged blackbirds swoop across the water's surface and chatter from within the branches of the cottonwood tree.

Kneeling at the cooler, Tomasetti raises his brow at the plastic wine glasses. 'You came prepared.'

That couldn't be farther from the truth; I'm not prepared for any of this. Being here with him is like stepping into deep water when I've barely learned to swim. I don't want to choke, but I desperately want to explore the depths of this man and the relationship we're building.

He uses the corkscrew to open the bottle. 'We'll just let that breathe.'

'I like your new place,' I tell him.

'A little different from the loft in Cleveland.'

'More wildlife.'

'Or less, depending on your definition of wildlife.'

He's got paint on his shirt. A smear of white on the front of his jeans. It makes me smile. 'I like the new look.'

He grins. 'That's what all the female chiefs of police say.'

'You look happy,' I say. 'I like it.'

He's staring at me, assessing, weighing, as if he knows something's different about me, too, and he's trying to figure out what it is. The air between us is charged, and I'm left with the sense that we're dancing around some white elephant I should see, but can't. So much of our relationship has taken place during the hardship and stress of whatever case we're working on. Our pasts are always in the backs of our minds. So much of where we are now is derived from dark times. Being here with him, like this, is new ground that feels crumbly and uncertain beneath my feet.

I suppose I've always used my job – our work – as a buffer between us. I've used it as an excuse to see him. To spend time with him. Tonight, I can't fall back on that comfortable old ground, and there's a part of me that's terrified he'll know I'm here because I couldn't stay away.

'You're thinking way too hard about something,' he says.

I laugh self-consciously. 'I probably am.'

'Well, cut it out.' He shoves the lawn chair toward me. 'We need one more bass, Chief. Then we'll go inside and fry them up.'

'I didn't see a stove in that kitchen.'

'I've got a Coleman and cast-iron skillet in the Tahoe.'

I don't take the chair. I stand there like an idiot, staring at him, trying to put my thoughts and the things that I'm feeling into some kind of meaningful order.

'Kate . . .'

Before realizing I'm going to move, I'm crossing the distance between us. I hear my boots scuff against the wood planks. The red-winged blackbirds calling. The next thing I know my body is flush against his. He's lean and solid and warm against me. Somehow my arms find their way around his neck and then I'm pulling his mouth down to mine.

The force of the kiss sinks into me and goes deep. His lips are firm and moist. I take in the sweetness of his breath. When I open my mouth he's ready. His tongue intertwines with mine and for a moment I can't get enough. Vaguely, I'm aware of his essence surrounding me. His hands restless on my back. His breaths in my ear.

The sound of something scraping across the wood surface of the dock draws me from my fugue. I glance down to see his fishing pole clatter across the planks. It takes me a moment to realize what's happening.

'I think you've got a bite,' I whisper.

'Shit.' Tomasetti lunges away from me, snatches the pole off the dock, and begins to reel. 'I think this might be the big one,' he says.

'That's what all you guys say.'

He casts me a look, but I see the grin in his eyes. For several minutes he pulls back on the pole and reels in the slack. I watch the line skim through the water as the fish on the other end fights.

'Gotta be a bass,' he tells me. 'They usually put up a pretty good fight.'

I see a flash of silver beneath the water's surface, then the fish is out. Tomasetti was right; it's a bass, probably weighing in at six or seven pounds.

He kneels, grasps the fish in his right hand, and works the barbed hook from its mouth with the other. 'I almost hate to eat this guy.'

'Toss him back.' When he frowns at me, I add, 'He'll spawn. Breed more fighters.'

Holding the fish in both hands, he bends close to the water's surface and lets it go. 'We're going to have to make do with the three I've caught, and they're kind of scrawny.'

'We have grapes and cheese,' I tell him.

'And wine.' He wipes his hands on his jeans and turns his attention to me. 'Where were we?' he asks.

'I think I was in the process of putting my tongue down your throat.'

He leans in to me and kisses me on the mouth. It's just a peck, a soft brushing of his lips against mine, but it moves me, makes me want more.

I laugh. 'So are you going to show me around, or what?'

'How much time do you have?' he murmurs.

'I can't stay,' I tell him. 'A few hours.'

'In that case, let's go inside and get started.'

It's odd that after being with Tomasetti I would dream of Mattie. Prior to the hit-and-run, I hadn't thought of her in any meaningful way in years. Since, I haven't been able to get her off my mind. She was a huge part of my formative years. She taught me many things, about myself, about boys, about the way life worked. Only now, as an adult, do I realize not all of the things I learned were good.

If you were a teenager and living in Painters Mill, the Round Barn Creamery was *the* place to go in the summertime. The owners, a husband and wife team I always fancied as former hippies from the 1970s, boasted fifty-three flavors of ice cream, sherbet, and gelato and ran their business out of a historical German-style round barn that had once been a dairy operation. The real draw, however, was the patio in the rear. Nestled beneath the shade of a massive maple tree, the area was paved with flagstones and dozens of potted tropical plants. An old rococo fountain spurted water that trickled over river rock and made the most amazing sound. A smattering of antique ice-cream tables and chairs were scattered about. Best of all, the owners piped alternative rock through massive walnut speakers, which drew teens by the drove and guaranteed a full house all summer.

My *mamm* and *datt* didn't know about the music – or the boys – both of which would have ended my new favorite pastime. I made sure they never found out. As long as my chores were finished, they didn't mind my going with Mattie for ice cream. We'd meet on the dirt road in front of my house and ride our bicycles into town. Friday afternoons at the Round Barn Creamery became part of our summer routine.

When you're fourteen years old and Amish, being away from the farm with your best friend was the epitome of independence. I drank in that newfound sense of freedom until I was drunk on it and giddy for more. Still, walking into an 'English-owned' establishment – even a place as teenager friendly as the Round Barn Creamery – wasn't easy. I was ever aware that because of the way I dressed, some people would stare as if I were some kind of oddity.

One hot July afternoon, Mattie and I parked our bikes outside the shop. We'd been in such a hurry to get there and pedaled so fast, we arrived drenched with sweat. The bell on the front door jingled merrily when we walked inside. A wash of air-conditioned air sent gooseflesh down my arms as I made my way to the counter. I wanted to order my usual: a chocolate shake with a single dip of coffee ice cream, but we were both short on cash that day so we settled for small iced teas instead and carried them to our favorite table on the patio, where Kurt Cobain belted out a song about teen spirit.

I was so embroiled in the music and this special time with my best friend, I didn't notice the group that came in behind us. Two boys and two girls. English teenagers about the same age as Mattie and me. The boys wore cut off shorts with T-shirts depicting different rock bands. The girls were pretty. One wore blue jeans with a white tank top. The other wore shorts that displayed long, slender legs. I stole looks at them as they walked onto the patio, and I couldn't help but wonder what it would be like to dress like that. To have jewelry and wear makeup and be surrounded by boys.

'They're fat cows.' Mattie whispered the words in Pennsylvania Dutch.

I couldn't help it; I laughed. That was one of the things I loved most about Mattie. Her unapologetic audacity. She was bold and brave and completely unstoppable.

When the group received their ice cream orders – big sundaes stacked high with whipped cream and slivered almonds – they strolled onto the patio. I could tell by the way their eyes swept toward us that they were curious. I wondered if they were tourists, if they'd ever seen an Amish person before. I wondered what that would be like, too.

'We ought to put on a show, give them a reason to stare,' Mattie said, watching them unabashedly.

The group wandered to the table next to ours and sat down. I turned my attention back to my iced tea, hoping they left us alone. Mattie had no such ambitions. She was completely unperturbed by their not-so-covert ogling and the whispers they didn't bother to conceal.

But I felt the burn of their stares like fire against my skin, and I wanted to kick her under the table. After a few minutes, the two boys sauntered over to us. The first boy had brown hair that was nearly as long as mine. The second was blond with a slightly feminine air. I suspected he might have been confused for a girl if it hadn't been for the tuft of peach fuzz sticking out of his chin.

Mattie cast me a quick smile and winked. I couldn't believe she thought they were going to be nice. Even at the tender age of fourteen, I had developed a sixth sense when it came to spotting troublemakers. These two boys had it written all over their too-pretty faces. I sucked hard on my straw, uncomfortable because all of them were watching us expectantly, looking bored and mean and a little too anxious to focus those things on us.

'Do you ladies come here often?' the brown-haired boy asked.

A round of snickers erupted from the girls sitting at the table next to ours. I didn't look up from my drink. But I was quickly running out of tea. That was a problem because once that happened, I'd have nothing to do.

'We're regulars,' Mattie said breezily. 'Haven't seen you around, though.'

He grinned, pleased to have received a response, and shot the girls a this-is-going-to-be-fun look. 'Do you mind if my friend and I ask you a few questions? We're working on a report for school. You know, about Amish people.'

More snickers.

Mattie sucked on her straw, studying him from beneath long lashes. 'What's in it for us?'

'I don't know.' He shrugged. 'What do you want?'

'Buy us a couple of chocolate shakes and we'll tell you everything you ever wanted to know.' She smiled sweetly. 'Won't we, Katie?'

I kicked her, annoyed because I was certain she was about to get us involved in something that would surely backfire.

The two boys exchanged looks, then the brown-haired boy nodded. 'Sure.' Rising, he fished his wallet from his pocket and walked to the counter.

'What are you doing?' I whispered in Pennsylvania Dutch.

'You wanted ice cream, didn't you?' she shot back.

I shook my head, dread building in my chest. This wasn't going to be fun and it wasn't the way I'd wanted to spend my afternoon.

I risked a glance at the table next to us. Only then did I notice the girls sitting there by themselves, looking irritated, and it struck me that they didn't appreciate their boyfriends buying ice cream for us. I experienced a moment of triumph because I realized it was part of Mattie's plan.

A few minutes later, the brown-haired boy set two chocolate shakes in front of us, and they joined us at our table.

Mattie wrapped her lips around the straw. '*Danki.*'

For the first time, the brown-haired boy's smile was genuine. He liked the Pennsylvania Dutch. Almost as much as he liked the way she was sucking on that straw. 'What's your name, anyway?' he asked.

'Mattie. What's yours?'

'Hunter.' He motioned to his friend. 'This is Patrick.'

Patrick leaned forward. 'No offense, but what's up with the old lady getup? You know, the granny dresses? You two are pretty hot-looking and that shit you're wearing isn't exactly sexy.'

The girls giggled.

Cruelty glinted within his smile, telling me he was out to impress his friends and that was going to happen at Mattie's and my expense.

'Ask her if they shave their legs,' one of the girls blurted out.

'Better yet, why don't you *show* us your legs?' Patrick said.

The girl wearing the blue jeans cackled. 'I bet their legs are hairier than yours, Hunter!'

Hunter shook his head. 'As you can see, my friends have no manners.' He spread his hands, trying for innocuous. 'But we'd really like to know. Do you ladies shave your legs?'

To my utter shock, Mattie swiveled from her chair, hiked up her dress and exposed a slender, beautiful, *shaved* leg.

The other girl slapped her hand over her mouth and hooted around red-tipped fingers.

'Wow.' But Hunter couldn't take his eyes off that long stretch of milky flesh. 'I'll never think of an Amish woman in the same light ever again.'

A moment of silence ensued as the teens took a good, long look. Out of the corner of my eye, I saw the blue-jean-clad girl staring, her eyes alight with jealousy.

'What about your armpits?' she blurted.

'Do you trim up those Amish snatches of yours?' Patrick asked.

'Oh my *Gawd!*' one of the girls chirped.

I nudged Mattie with my foot, letting her know I'd had enough and wanted to leave. When her eyes flicked to mine, I was surprised to see that she wasn't the least bit upset by any of this. In fact, she seemed to be enjoying herself. I didn't understand how she could remain so cool while I was embarrassed and humiliated. Worse, I was angry because they'd ruined my big afternoon out with my best friend.

'You girls want to go smoke a joint?' asked Hunter. 'We promise not to bite.'

'I hear the Amish have the best shit,' one of the girls added.

I stood abruptly, my shake forgotten. All four sets of eyes burned into me, their expressions alight with the anticipation of fireworks. The blue-jean-clad girl looked me up and down, her eyes lingering on my feet. 'Oh my God, look at her shoes!'

'That takes practical to a whole new level,' muttered the girl sitting next to her.

'That takes *ugly* to a whole new level,' she amended.

'I'm leaving,' I said to Mattie in Pennsylvania Dutch.

Taking her time, Mattie picked up her shake and scooted away from the table. 'Don't forget your ice cream,' she said, picking up my glass.

Ignoring her, I started toward the door without looking back. My face was burning, my heart pounding. I'd been taught to be forgiving, and that included forgiving people for ignorance and cruelty. But I was a teenager; I hadn't yet learned to curb my emotions. I wanted to put these cruel *Englischers* in their place. I wasn't proud of the fact that I didn't have the guts.

Before I could make my escape, one of the boys stuck out his leg and lifted the hem of my dress with the toe of his sneaker. My hand whipped out, brushed my dress back down. I didn't look at him. Didn't stop walking. I didn't voice the words running through my head.

'D'you see those fuckin' bloomers!' he screeched. 'My granny wears those! Holy shit!'

Laughter exploded from the table. Praying I'd find Mattie right behind me, I glanced back to see that she'd paused next to the boy who'd lifted my dress. All I could think was: *Oh, Mattie what are you going to do?* I almost couldn't believe my eyes when she raised both of our cups and dumped the shakes onto his lap.

SEVENTEEN

It's 2:00 A.M. when I leave Tomasetti's farm. I didn't want to go. Tonight was probably the closest thing to a perfect evening I'd ever had in my life. Sometimes it's hard for me to believe I've arrived at this place. That two people as damaged as us have been granted this small slice of happiness by the same God who took so much from us in the past. When we're together, yesterday doesn't matter. The future is without limit and ours for the taking. I don't have to play the tired role in which I'd been cast. The one with the hackneyed script and rehashed lines. My new role is fresh, and I like the character I've become.

We spent the evening cooking on a camp stove set atop a card table Tomasetti brought from his loft in Cleveland. I scaled and deboned the fish while he showered. He fried the mangled filets while I washed the grapes and sliced cheese. We sat on the stoop out back and ate fresh bass from paper plates and drank cabernet from plastic glasses.

We didn't talk about the Borntrager case. He didn't ask me about Lapp. We didn't discuss the past. We didn't even talk about the future or where all of this might lead. For the first time since I've known him, we simply lived in the moment. It came as a shock when I realized there was no place else in the world I wanted to be.

Earlier, during the drive over, I'd feared he would bring up my moving in with him again. By the end of the evening, I almost wished he would because I realized that being with him like this makes me happy. It makes me want more.

After dinner, he gave me a tour of the house and outbuildings. We walked the pasture and he told me about all the things he had planned for the property. The amount of work to be done is mind-boggling, but to my surprise, Tomasetti is handy and plans to do most of it himself.

Later, as we stood on the front porch, looking out over the land, he kissed me. I lost half of my clothes before we made it through the door and onto the cot he'd rented, laughing because it was too small for two people. We made love twice, somehow ending up on the floor, tangled in his sleeping bag. Afterward, I lay against him, my head on his shoulder, my leg thrown over his, and we dozed.

I should be tired, but I'm not. I've never partaken in illicit drugs, but I feel high, a warm and pleasant buzz that hums through my body and mind like music. I know it's stupid, but I'm only twenty minutes from the farm and already I miss him. I miss him so much my chest hurts and I want to turn around and go back. I know at some point I'll have to come back to earth. Back to the realities of the Borntrager case and the secrets of my past that have returned to haunt me. I know it will probably be a hard landing when I do.

I'm ten minutes out of Painters Mill, doing fifty-five miles per hour with my window down and humming along to an old Sting tune when the truth of what I've let happen hits me. Abruptly, all the breath leaches from my lungs. I've never been prone to anxiety attacks, but I'm pretty sure another one has me in its grip. Tugging at the collar of my uniform, feeling as if I can't get enough air into my lungs, I pull off the road and onto the shoulder, braking so hard the tires skid in the gravel and the

Explorer goes sideways. Then I'm out the door, cool air on my face. I stumble to the front of the Explorer, breaths ripping from my throat. I set my hand against the hood, concentrate on the warm steel against my palm.

I've always fancied myself immune to the craziness that sometimes accompanies intense emotional entanglements. The kind that makes smart people lose perspective and do foolish things. I was always above it and too cautious to give up too much of myself to someone else. Love was some intangible frailty to which I was not predisposed. Now, standing on a deserted road in the middle of the night and in the throes of a panic attack, it shocks me to realize I was wrong.

The problem is, I like my life the way it is: even keel. I own my emotions. I call the shots. I don't have to rely on anyone else or, God forbid, be responsible for someone else's happiness. All I have to worry about is me – and I'm an easy keeper.

For a full minute, I concentrate on getting oxygen into my lungs. Slowly, my surroundings come back into focus. The trill of the crickets from the woods. The hoot of an owl from the abandoned barn across the road. A dog barking in the distance. When I can breathe again, I push away from the Explorer and stand there, trying to figure out how to handle this new and uneasy situation. And I realize I've been lying to myself all along. I can no longer deny what I've allowed to happen. I'm going to have to face it. Deal with it. I'm going to have to decide where I stand and if I want to move forward. Because I'm pretty sure I've let myself fall in love with John Tomasetti and I haven't a clue what I'm going to do about it.

At 2:30 A.M., I radio T.J., who's on graveyard, and let him know I'm on my way to relieve him from surveillance duty at the Borntrager farm.

'Didn't mean to wake you,' I begin.

'I wasn't—' Realizing I'm ribbing him, he laughs. 'You're up late tonight, Chief.'

'I got some rest earlier,' I tell him. 'I just wanted to let you know I'm on my way to the Borntrager farm. You can head out, finish your shift. Thanks for covering.'

'No problem,' he says. 'Place was quiet all evening.'

'That's the way we like it.'

He pauses. 'You expecting trouble?'

'I'm probably being overly cautious.'

'Let me know if you need anything.'

Our vehicles pass where the dirt road Ts at the highway, and we flash our headlights in greeting. A minute later, I park the Explorer on the gravel turnaround fifty yards from the mouth of the Borntrager farm.

I open the window a few inches, punch off the headlights, and kill the engine. A chorus of crickets, frogs, and peepers from the swampy area at the edge of the woods encroaches. It's a clear, crisp night; I can see the Big Dipper through the treetops to the west. My police radio is quiet, which is normal for Holmes County this time of night. Sliding my seat back for some extra legroom, I settle in for a wait.

In the pasture, a small herd of cattle works its way toward me, watching me as they graze, curious. I can just make out the darkened silhouette of Mattie's farmhouse two hundred yards away. When the quiet begins to annoy me, I tune my radio to an FM station out of Wooster. The same station Tomasetti and I listened to earlier. When I find my thoughts sliding in that direction, I force them back to Mattie and David and the killer who still walks free in my town.

I've worked some mind-boggling cases in the years I've been in law enforcement; I'm no stranger to all of those dark crevices of the criminal mind. Still, the things people do to each other never ceases to disturb and confound me. Usually, I can get a handle on motive relatively quickly. From there, I can develop a theory, even when information is sketchy. This case is so far out there, so utterly senseless, I can't get my mind around it.

The evidence indicates premeditation and an effort to conceal the crime. Someone conceived the idea, anticipated the details and what the execution of it would entail, and then carried it out. But who would want to murder a well-liked Amish deacon and two children? What could he possibly stand to gain? If Mattie was the intended victim, the scenario is even more baffling. Why would anyone want an Amish wife and mother dead? What am I missing?

By 4:00 A.M. frustration and fatigue are starting to take a toll. Worse, I'm beginning to feel foolish for sitting out here in the middle of nowhere when the only things moving are the cattle. I'm about to call it a night when movement in the pasture between the house and the woods snags my gaze. I squint through the windshield, wishing I'd taken the time to clean off the bugs when I filled the gas tank.

At first I think it's a deer that's wandered into the pasture for some illicit grazing. But in the weak moonlight filtering through the clouds, I recognize the silhouette of a man. Six feet tall. One hundred eighty pounds. Dark clothing. Wishing for binoculars – or a night-vision scope – I watch him cross the pasture.

'What the hell are you doing?' I whisper.

Curiosity edges into alarm when he scales the rail fence. Then he's in the side yard and walking toward the house. I've got my hand on the door handle when I realize the dome light could alert him to my presence. Never taking my eyes off the intruder, I lower the driver's side window and slither out.

Once I'm standing on the shoulder, I hit my lapel mike and whisper, 'T.J., I've got ten eighty-eight at the Borntrager farm. Can you ten twenty-five?'

'I'm ten seventy-six.'

'What's your ten seventy-seven?'

'Ten minutes, Chief.'

'Expedite. No lights or siren.'

'Roger that.'

The figure disappears behind an old outhouse and lilac bush, and I lose sight of him. When he reappears, he's twenty yards from the house and making a beeline for the back door. I have no idea who it is or what his intentions are. I don't know if he's armed or lost or some drunken idiot trying to find his way home. The one thing I do know is that I've got to confront him.

'Shit.' Setting my hand over my .38, I jog through the ditch and duck between the rails of the fence. Then I'm in the pasture. Wet grass beneath my boots. Staying low, I run full out toward the house. Twenty yards in, I squeeze between the rails of the fence and then I'm in the front yard. I ascend a small hill that puts me scant feet from the porch. I go left toward the rear of the house to intercept him at the back door.

Thumbing the leather strap off my holster, I sidle along the side of the house, my senses honed on my surroundings. Every sound seems exaggerated. Something jingles my equipment belt. My boots crunch against the gravel that's gathered at the drip line from the roof. Knowing surprise is my best tool, I slow down.

Unlike the suburbs and cities, Amish country is extraordinarily dark at night. There are no street lamps or porch lights or even light from windows. There's not much in the way of moonlight tonight, either, so I'm working blind, relying as much on my hearing as my sight.

I reach the back of the house. From where I'm standing I can just make out the silhouettes of the barn and outbuildings. Pressing my back against the siding, I peer around the corner. At first, all I see are the hulking forms of the maples in the side yard. The pampas grass nearer the porch. The outline of a picnic table. Then I discern movement. Adrenaline jolts me when I realize the man is standing on the porch, thirty feet away.

I slide my revolver from its nest, ease my mini Maglite from my belt. The hammer clicks when I thumb it back. I cringe at the sound, but he doesn't seem to hear. I step around the corner, bring up my .38 and shine the flashlight beam in his eyes. 'Police!' I call out. 'Stop right there! Keep your hands where I can see them!'

He spins toward me, hands flying up to obscure his face, and steps back. For an instant it's as if we're suspended in a world without gravity, floating, two fish in an aquarium gaping at each other. I break the spell by stepping closer. 'Identify yourself!' I shout.

He bolts.

'Shit.' Then I'm running full out. Past the porch, around the pampas grass, and into the side yard.

For an instant I consider firing off a shot. But it's dark and I have no idea who I'm pursuing. A teenager. A neighbor I've spooked. *Or a killer,* a little voice adds. While I'm always cognizant of my personal safety, the last thing I want to do is hurt an innocent bystander. I jam my weapon into its holster. 'Stop!' I shout. 'Stop right there!'

We've only gone ten yards when I realize he's faster than me. Unless he somehow screws up – or runs into a tree – he's going to outrun me and get away. I hit my lapel mike. 'Ten eighty! Ten seven eight!'

'Ten seven six.'

In the periphery of my thoughts, I hear my radio light up as the call goes out to Holmes County. But I'm so intent on following my quarry, I give it only half an ear.

He takes me across the side yard, beneath a clothesline, past several trees, and down a hill. He's forty feet ahead and pulling away. 'Stop!' I scream. *'Now!'*

He doesn't look back, doesn't even pause. He vaults the rail fence as if it's not there, stumbles on the other side, but quickly regains his footing, and then he's sprinting across the pasture toward the woods fifty yards beyond.

'Son of a bitch.' I reach the fence, set my right hand on the top rail, and hurl myself over the top. Too much momentum sends me to my knees on the other side. Mud soaks through the material of my trousers. Then I'm back on my feet and running as fast as I can toward the woods.

'Halt!' I shout. 'Stop right there or I will shoot you!'

Mud sucks at my boots as I streak across the pasture. I'm aware of the cattle scattering to my right. The black shadows of the trees ahead. The impenetrable darkness of the forest. If he makes it to the woods, I'll lose him.

I'm no slouch when it comes to running. In college, I could do four hundred meters in sixty-seven seconds. But I'm older now and no longer in top physical condition. My suspect, on the other hand, runs like a goddamn cheetah and disappears into the woods like some prey animal running for its life. Training my gaze on the spot where he entered, I plunge into the forest.

It's like entering a cave. The smells of wet foliage and rotting leaves rise. I'm running blind, but I don't slow down. Vegetation slaps wetly at my arms and face. Only then do I realize I'm on some kind of trail.

I've lost sight of my suspect. I stop and listen. Footfalls thud ahead, so I pick up the pace, let the sound guide me. He's following the trail, I realize. *He knew it was here,* a little voice whispers. I know there's a creek ahead. Some areas are shallow enough to cross, but there are deep holes, too. I know this because Mattie and I swam in this creek as kids. If this guy tries to cross and runs into deep water, it'll stop him.

Slowing to a jog, I hit my mike. 'Suspect is in woods,' I pant, 'heading south toward the creek.'

'Ten four.'

I yank the mini Maglite off my belt. The path curves left. I hear the rush of water ahead. No footsteps, but I'm winded and it's difficult to hear over the rasp of my breaths. I stop and listen, scanning the woods around me. There's no movement. No sound, other than the water. Even the night animals have gone silent, as if knowing their domain has been invaded. I point my beam ahead. The cone of light reveals a dirt path, wet earth covered with leaves and trampled grass. Thick brush on either side.

'Where are you?' I mutter.

Something shifts to my right. I spin, bring up the flashlight. I catch a glimpse of a man. Dark hoodie. Pale face. Something in his hand. I hear a *whoosh!* Before I can bring up my .38, something cracks across my left cheekbone. White light explodes behind my eyes. Pain zings up my sinuses and slams into my brain.

The next thing I know I'm laid out on the ground. Wet soaking through the back of my shirt. Cold mud against my scalp. The salty tang of blood in my mouth. I roll onto my side and get to my hands and knees. Knowing I'm done if he hits me again, I shake off the dizziness and look around. My attacker is nowhere in sight.

I spit blood, run my tongue over my teeth, and I'm relieved to find them intact. I don't trust my balance so I twist and push myself to a sitting position, my legs splayed in front of me. That's when I hear him splash through water several yards away. I'm in no condition to pursue him, and I curse myself for letting him get away.

'That hurt, you fuck!' I call out to him.

After a minute or so, I get to my feet. But I'm woozy. A headache creeps up the left side of my face toward my temple. I speak into my lapel mike. 'Suspect crossed the creek. Heading south toward Hog Path.'

'I'm eastbound on Hog Path, approaching the bridge,' comes T.J.'s voice. 'No one in sight, Chief.'

'Vehicle?'

'Negative.'

'Damn it.'

Kicking a half-buried log, I look around for my flashlight and spot the beam in a pile of leaves. I bend, my cheek pounding, and snatch it up. I shine the light toward the creek. The trail curves, but through the trees, I see the glint of water. I lower the beam to the ground and see footprints in the soft earth. I squat for a better look and realize the tread is visible. He was wearing sneakers.

Straightening, I look around, trying to get a sense of why he'd stopped to ambush me when he could have continued on and gotten away without a confrontation. I find a two-foot-long branch lying in the path. It looks out of place, so I toe it aside, realizing that's what he hit me with.

I follow the footprints to the creek bank where they disappear. The water is shallow and fast-moving, so he likely crossed without a problem. I run my beam along the opposite bank, but it's too rocky to see any prints. To my left, reeds as tall as a man grow from a rocky shoal. Right, the huge stump of a dead tree leans out over a deep pool.

Aggravated because I can feel my cheekbone beginning to swell, I turn around and start back toward the house. I've only gone a few yards when I hear someone on the path ahead of me. I thrust my beam forward and find Glock standing on the trail, flashlight pointed down at the ground. He's staring at me, his expression concerned.

'Shit, Chief, you okay?' he asks.

I lower my beam. 'Peachy.'

He crosses to me, his expression concerned. 'You're bleeding pretty good.'

I raise my hand to check and my fingers come away red. 'Great.'

'You want me to call an ambulance?'

'I'm fine.'

He doesn't look convinced. 'You're going to have a hell of a shiner.'

'Good thing I look good in purple.'

His gaze follows the trail toward the water's edge. 'You get a look at him?'

'White male. Six feet. One eighty. Wearing a hoodie. Fast as hell.' I blow out a sigh of frustration. 'Anybody else see him?'

He shakes his head. 'T.J.'s out on Hog Path Road. Holmes County set up a perimeter. If this guy's around, we'll find him.'

'Unless he had a vehicle parked somewhere.'

'Or he lives nearby.'

I see him trying to get a better look at my cheek and I frown. 'Any idea who it was?' he asks.

'Not a clue.'

'What happened?'

'He got ahead of me. Waited for me. Ambushed me.' I motion toward the path behind us. 'Hit me with that branch.'

'Motherfucker.'

I laugh despite the pain in my cheek. Glock always seems to say the right thing at the right time. 'I think he knew about the path. He knew it was here. Seemed to know where he was going.'

'So he's used it before.'

'Or he's been watching the place.'

His eyes sharpen on mine. 'You think this is related to the hit-skip?'

'I think it's a damn good possibility.'

'You think he was after Mattie Borntrager? Or the boy?'

'He was standing on the back porch when I stopped him. If

I hadn't shown up when I did, there's no doubt in my mind he'd have gained entry.'

His brows furrow. 'Maybe he thinks the kid saw something and can identify him or his vehicle.'

'I don't know, Glock. All of this seems so . . . excessive. I've been wracking my brain and I can't figure motive. An Amish deacon? Two kids? That's not even to mention the premeditation factor. Who would go to those kinds of lengths?'

'Someone desperate enough to clean your clock to stop you.' His eyes catch mine and hold them. I see something in their depths that sends an uneasy prickling up the back of my neck.

'Chief, this is going to sound strange with Mrs. Borntrager being Amish and all, but she's an extremely attractive woman.'

I shouldn't be surprised. But while I've always been cognizant of Mattie's beauty, it never crossed my mind that it could have anything to do with the case.

'Do you think this is some kind of stalking situation?' I ask.

'I don't know. She's . . . I don't know . . . she's got that sexy librarian shit going on, you know?' Looking uncomfortable, which is unusual for Glock, he shrugs. 'If she's caught the attention of some nutcase . . . that kind of obsession can be a powerful motivator.'

It's an angle worth looking into. 'I'll talk to her.' I motion toward the place on the path where I found the footprints. 'Will you keep an eye on the scene until I can get a CSU out here?'

'I'm on it.'

'And tell him to bag that damn branch, will you?'

EIGHTEEN

Glock's take on Mattie troubles me all the way back to the house. I arrive to find a sheriff's cruiser parked in the driveway, lights flashing. I cross through the yard where I chased the prowler just minutes before and take the sidewalk to the back porch. I'm reaching for the knob when I notice the broken pane. Pulling my mini Maglite from my belt, I shine the beam on the door to find that the pane nearest the knob has been shattered. Most of the glass fell inward, telling me it was smashed from the outside. There's no blood, which means we won't be able to collect DNA. If we're lucky, we might be able to pick up some latents.

Pulling a single glove from a compartment on my belt, I use it to open the door and enter. I find Mattie and a young deputy sheriff in the kitchen. An overhead natural gas fixture pours light over the table where a loaf of bread is wrapped in foil. The deputy stands at the doorway between the kitchen and living room. I nod at him, then turn my attention to Mattie. She's standing at the sink, looking shaken and disheveled. She's thrown a black sweater over her nightshirt, probably due to modesty rather than the chilly night. Even in the thin light, I see her hands shaking.

'Is everyone all right?' I ask.

The deputy nods. 'Everyone's fine.'

'David, too,' Mattie says. 'I checked him first thing. He's still sleeping.'

'Good.' I turn my attention to the deputy. 'Was that glass broken when you arrived?'

He nods. 'The door was standing open, too,' he tells me. 'He hadn't gotten inside yet, though.'

I look at Mattie. 'Did you see him?'

'No.'

'What happened?' I ask.

'Something woke me,' she says. 'The glass breaking, I think. I ran downstairs and found the door open. But there was no one there.'

'Was the door locked?'

'Yes. Since . . . all of this happened, I took your advice and began locking up at night.' She wraps her arms around herself. 'I must have scared him off.'

'I did,' I tell her.

She tosses me a quizzical look.

'I was outside, keeping an eye on things. He came out of the woods, crossed the pasture, and went right to the back door. I confronted him on the back porch and he ran.' Even as I say the words, my imagination takes me through all the things that might have happened if I hadn't decided to watch the place tonight. . . .

'Do you use the path in the woods?' I ask.

She nods. 'Paul and the children used it sometimes when they would walk back there to fish or swim.'

'Does anyone else know about it?'

'We're the only ones who use the path, Katie. It's on our property. No one else even knows about it.'

'Someone does,' I tell her.

Craning her head, she moves closer as if to get a better

look at my face. She puts her hand over her mouth. 'Oh, Katie. You're hurt.'

'Looks like you took one for the team,' the deputy says. 'Do you want me to call an ambulance or drop you at the hospital?'

'I'm okay,' I tell him. 'Looks worse than it is, I think.'

Mattie turns to the kerosene-powered refrigerator. 'Let me make you a cold pack at least.'

'It's okay,' I tell her.

'It's not okay. None of this is okay.' She opens the freezer door and begins rummaging around inside. 'You could have been seriously injured.'

The deputy catches my gaze. 'I'm going to take a look around, Chief. You okay in here?'

I give him a nod and he leaves the room.

For several seconds it's so quiet I can hear the tick of the clock on the wall. The hiss of the gas in the light fixture overhead. Mattie turns to me, a frozen bag of peas in her hand.

'You sure you're all right?' I ask.

'Silly of you to ask me that when you're standing there bleeding.' She wraps the bag in a dish towel and shoves it at me.

Obediently, I press it to my cheek. 'Thanks.'

'Katie, I don't understand what's happening.' When she raises her hand to tuck a strand of hair behind her ear, I see it shaking. 'Why would someone try to break into our home? What does he want?'

I motion to the table. 'Let's sit, Mattie.'

For a moment, she looks like she's going to refuse. She's frustrated and wants answers. I wish I could give them to her; I wish I could offer her peace of mind. But I don't have either of those things. Not even for myself.

She goes to the table, pulls out a chair, and lowers herself into it. 'What if he'd gotten in?' she asks. 'What if he'd hurt David? Katie, he's all I have left. What if—'

'He didn't,' I cut in as I slide into the chair across from her. 'Mattie, I want you to tell me everything that happened. From start to end. Don't leave anything out, even if it seems unimportant.'

'I already—'

'Tell me again,' I snap.

Tightening her lips, she takes me through everything that transpired. 'By the time I got to the kitchen, he was gone. The door was standing open and there was glass everywhere. I ran to David's room, but he was still sleeping.'

'Did you get a look at him?'

'I told you. No.'

'Not even as he ran away? An impression?'

'I didn't even see him. It was dark.' She frowns as if she's angry with herself. 'Katie, why did he come here? What does he want?'

'Do you keep valuables in the house?'

'A little cash.' She motions toward a cookie jar on the counter. 'Paul kept it there. A couple hundred dollars.'

'Can you think of any other reason someone would try to break in?'

She sets her hand over her mouth, as if to smother a cry, and looks at me over the top of her fingers, tears glittering in her eyes. 'What if he's after David? Katie, I've heard of children being kidnapped and their parents never seeing them again. There've been stories of children being taken for terrible reasons—'

'No one's going to take David,' I tell her.

'I know God will take care of us. But I'm frightened for my son. He's all I have left.' She stands abruptly, looking around as if she's expecting some masked gunman to come through the door to mow us down. 'I'm going to move him into my room. Tonight. We'll sleep in the same bed until the man is—'

'I'm not going to let anything happen to either of you.' I know better than to make those kinds of open-ended promises. I can't guarantee her absolute safety; I don't have the manpower or budget for twenty-four-hour protection. Despite the fact that I mean those words, I know all too well that good intentions aren't enough.

She offers a sad smile. 'That's my Katie. You were always so brave. You still are.'

'I'm doing my job, Mattie.'

I see admiration in her eyes and I realize she's counting on me to keep them safe. The weight of that responsibility is crushing because I don't think I could bear it if something happened to them.

My cheek is numb from the frozen peas, so I remove the bag and set it on the table. Never taking her eyes from mine, she rounds the table and lowers herself into the chair to my left.

'Mattie,' I begin, 'have you had any unusual encounters or confrontations with anyone in the last months?'

'No.' Guileless eyes. No hesitation.

'What about your daily routine? Has anything unusual happened in the course of your day? Maybe a stranger came to your door? Someone selling something? Someone looking for work? Any strangers approach you while you were in town?'

'None of those things.'

'Maybe Paul hired someone to do some work around the house or help in the fields? Anything like that?'

'Paul never hired out help. He did all the work himself to save money.'

'What about while you were in town? Has anyone bothered you recently? Or said something inappropriate? Paid too much attention to you?'

Her brows knit as if she's thinking back, trying to remember. 'No.'

'Maybe it was something that didn't seem unusual at the time,' I prod. 'An odd look as someone passed you on the street.'

'I'm sorry, but I don't remember any such thing.'

I recall the way the suspect scaled the fence. He's in good physical condition. Athletic. 'What about teenagers, Mattie? Any teenage boys misbehaving around you? Saying things they shouldn't?'

'I don't even know any teenaged boys.' She raises her gaze to mine. 'I think it must be someone I don't know.'

I don't respond, because I'm familiar with the statistics. If someone has become fixated on Mattie, chances are she has at least met him at some point.

'What about your children?' I ask. 'Has anyone approached them? Said or done anything inappropriate?'

'No.'

'What about Paul? Did he mention anyone approaching him or causing problems?'

'Just Enos Wengerd.' We fall silent. Mattie looks down at her hands, her expression anxious and upset. 'Katie, I'm scared. If he'd gotten into the house, he could have killed us both.'

I choose my next words carefully. I don't want to frighten her any more than she already is, but I know that in cases like this one, ignorance is never bliss. 'I want you to talk to your *datt* and see if he'll stay here with you for a while. At least until we figure out what's going on. Or maybe you could pack a few things and stay with your parents.'

'I'll check with *Datt*.'

'You need to be proactive about your personal safety. That means be aware of your surroundings at all times, Mattie. Keep your doors locked, day and night. Let me know if you need to go into town and I'll either go with you or have someone accompany you. I'm going to get you a cell phone, too.'

'No cell phone, Katie. You know the *Ordnung* forbids—'

I silence her by raising my hand. 'Don't argue, Mattie. This is a serious situation. No one needs to know.'

Her mouth tightens, but she's either too smart – or too scared – to argue.

'I'll do my best to keep an officer here at the farm, too, but I can't guarantee it.'

'I understand.'

I sigh. 'Do you keep a firearm here at the house?'

'Paul keeps a shotgun in our closet. For hunting.'

'Do you know how to use it?'

'Katie, I haven't fired a shotgun since I was ten years old and my *datt* took me quail—'

'That's not what I asked.'

'Yes. I know how to use it.'

'What about shells?'

'There's a box on the shelf, I think.'

'I want you to load it. Keep it out of David's reach. But keep it loaded and handy. Do you understand?'

'Of course I understand.'

I stare at her, hating it that she looks more frightened now than when I arrived.

It's nearly dawn by the time the CSU arrives. I leave him with instructions to capture any footwear imprints from the path in the woods and the perimeter of the house, and to dust the back door for fingerprints. Twice, Glock suggested I swing by the hospital to have the cut on my cheek checked out. Twice, I tell him I'm fine. But by the time I climb into the Explorer and start the engine, my head is pounding.

At 6:00 A.M., I park in my driveway and let myself into the house. I barely notice the clutter that has accumulated over recent days or the stuffy air as I lock the door behind me. I'm hungry so I go directly to the kitchen. I find some mushy grapes and old cheese in the fridge. I'm in the process of cutting away the mold when I hear a scratch at the window. The orange tabby peers at me from his place on the sill.

Smiling despite the headache, I go to the pantry for the bag of cat food and fill his bowl. Back at the sink, I open the window and push open the screen. 'Sorry I'm late, buddy.'

He ignores me and hunkers down to eat.

I shed my clothes on the way to the bathroom. I know better than to look in the mirror; somehow seeing the damage done to my face is only going to make it hurt more. I look anyway. The cut isn't too bad, but the lump beneath is a hard blue knot. The area under my left eye is filled with fluid, and I suspect in the coming hours I'll have a full-blown black eye.

Snagging a bottle of ibuprofen that expired two months ago from the medicine cabinet, I down four of them with a full glass of tap water and drag myself into the shower.

Ask for a lot, get a little.

That's been my mantra when dealing with Painters Mill's governing body, the town council. In the three years I've been chief, that philosophy has served me well. At 9:00 A.M. I'm standing before the six council members and Mayor Auggie Brock, ten minutes into my pitch for the allocation of funds so I can hire a new police officer. I've given them a summary of the Borntrager investigation, ending with my encounter in the woods last night. It took them less than a minute to shoot down my request, so I moved on to Plan B, which is additional budgeting for overtime.

Anyone who knows me will tell you I'm not above using whatever tool I have at my disposal to get what I want. That includes brandishing the hen's-egg-size bruise on my cheek and my burgeoning black eye, both of which are in full bloom this morning. My wounds are drawing plenty of attention, and I make sure everyone gets a damn good look, because they are the biggest bullet in my box of ammo.

'Three members of the Borntrager family were killed,' I explain. 'The incident is still under investigation, but the evidence gathered by the Holmes County sheriff's office and my own department suggests this was no ordinary hit-and-run accident, but a deliberate act of homicide.'

Auggie gasps with the appropriate level of shock. 'I've heard the rumors, but *murder*? My God, Kate, are you sure?'

I give him my full attention and decide to put my neck on the chopping block. 'I'm reasonably certain Paul Borntrager and his two children were murdered.'

'Do you know who did it?' he blurts.

'Not yet, but the investigation is ongoing.'

Town councilwoman Janine Fourman speaks up. 'Chief Burkholder, with all due respect to you and your department, murdering a family of Amish people with a truck seems rather far-fetched and, frankly, an odd way to kill someone.'

She's in her midfifties, with dyed black hair, shifty brown eyes, and a body as short and round as a milk-fed heifer. We've butted heads a dozen times in the years I've been chief. Still, I give her points for making it this far in a town that still has a boy's-club mentality. I suspect she's got her sights set on the mayor's office, an ambition that would be detrimental to not only me, but my department.

'She's got a point, Kate,' Auggie says. 'A hit-and-run seems like a roundabout way to go about it. And what would the motive be?'

I bullet-point everything we've uncovered so far, beginning with the lack of debris at the scene and the bogus invoice, and ending with the attempted break-in, the foot chase, and ensuing struggle last night.

Councilman Stubblefield grimaces. 'Is that how you got the tattoo there on your face?'

I nod, let him take a good, long look at it. 'I believe the suspect I chased is the same person who killed Paul Borntrager and those kids. I believe Mattie Borntrager was his target. If I hadn't been there last night, he might have killed her and her young son.' I pause to let that sink in and look from member to member. 'I think he'll try again.' I make eye contact with Auggie. 'I need eyes on that house twenty-four-seven, Auggie. That means a budget for overtime.'

The mayor's expression twists as if he's in the grip of a stomach cramp that's going to end badly. 'Kate, I know you're stretched thin—'

'I've been stretched thin for three years,' I cut in.

'Painters Mill isn't exactly New York City.' Bruce Jackson pipes up for the first time.

I don't look at him, don't let my annoyance alter my expression.

Auggie spreads his hands, a generous king who's run out of bread for his starving peasants. 'You're already over budget.'

'The budget allotted the police department wasn't adequate to begin with,' I point out.

'You signed off on it,' Janine interjects.

I ignore her, knowing that if I speak I'll overstep the boundaries of civility, which won't help. 'My officers can't even take a vacation day without my having to call someone in to cover. This woman and her son, and the community as a whole, deserve better than that. They deserve protection.'

I can't tell if they're moved by my argument or if this is just another business-as-usual meeting. They are, after all, politicians. Best case scenario, they'll sanction additional budget for overtime. Worse case, they'll send me off with a pat on the hand and a warning to get my labor cost under control.

I look at Auggie, but he glances down at the notepad in front of him, pretends to jot something. I let my eyes rest on each member of the council. Dick Blankenship. Ron Zelinski. Bruce Jackson. Norm Johnston. Janine Fourman. They are citizens, like me, doing their best with the resources they have. At least that's what I tell myself as I wrap it up.

'We appreciate what you're up against here, Chief Burkholder,' Zelinski says earnestly.

'But if the funds aren't there, they're not there,' Norm Johnston puts in.

'We simply don't have the money,' Janine adds.

'Hold on.' Auggie steps in, taking control, aware that this is his show and he's the star. 'Kate, let me get with the bean counters, see if there's anything they can do, okay? I'll get back to you in a couple of days.'

Everyone at the table nods, looking pleased with themselves, and for an instant I struggle not to laugh, because they look very much like bobbleheads.

On the short drive from the council meeting to the police station, I can't help but think of all the pet projects to which monies were allocated as a result of political back-scratching, and I kick myself for not pointing them out. But I know it wouldn't have mattered; it definitely wouldn't have helped my cause. The last time I took on the council, I was accused of not being a team player. The fact of the matter is, they were right; I'm not a team player. If I can do something better on my own, without having to rely on someone else – especially if there's a life at stake – fuck the team. If I want to keep Mattie and David safe, I'm going to have to do it myself.

I'm still angry when I walk into the station. Mona looks up from her place at the switchboard. Her mouth falls open when she notices my black eye. 'Whoa.'

'Whatever you do,' I mutter as I head toward the coffee station, 'don't tell me I look like shit.'

'Actually, Chief, I was just thinking you look kind of good roughed up. I mean, in a badass kind of way.'

I can't help it; I laugh. 'I love you, Mona.'

Lois emerges from the hall with a box of office supplies in her arms. She nearly drops a ream of copy paper when she notices my face. 'Janine Fourman didn't do that, did she?'

I'm in the process of pouring coffee and laugh so hard I slosh some over the side of my cup. 'She would not survive the attempt.'

Lois reaches the desk and sets the supplies next to the switchboard. 'Judging from the look on your face, I'm assuming the council meeting didn't go well.'

'That would be an understatement.'

Passing the headset to her counterpart, Mona meets me at the coffee station. I try not to notice that she's looking at me with a little bit of awe in her eyes. 'There's ice in the fridge in the back, Chief, do you want me to make you an ice pack?'

'If you don't mind, that's probably not a bad idea.' Armed with coffee, I head toward my office.

My computer has gone through the lengthy process of booting up, and I've just opened my e-mail software when I hear a tap on the door. I look up to see Mona standing outside my doorway, ice pack in hand.

I motion her in. 'Thanks.'

Waving off my gratitude, she hands me the pack and takes the chair opposite my desk.

Gingerly, I set the pack against my cheek. 'Your shift ended an hour and a half ago,' I point out.

'I stayed late to work on tip-line stuff.' She shrugs. 'I guess I lost track of time.'

'You know I can't pay you overtime.'

'I know it's not for lack of trying, Chief.' Blushing, she looks away. 'We know you go to bat for us.'

My chest swells with unexpected force. 'Thanks for saying that. I needed to hear it.'

Shrugging off my thanks, she shoves two sheets of paper at me. 'I put the tip-line stuff into a spreadsheet. Twenty-two calls so far. I thought you might want a peek.'

I take the papers and find myself looking at a table with column headings for the date and time, the name and contact information of the caller, and the particulars of the tip. I'm impressed by the level of organization and attention to detail, and I feel a little guilty because she's good at what she does and I haven't done much to recognize it. I'm reminded of her interest in becoming a police officer and I realize should the budget ever materialize, I'll consider her as a candidate.

'Most of the callers didn't leave contact info?' I ask.

'They wanted to remain anonymous.'

'Damn Amish,' I mutter.

She snickers.

'I'm surprised we didn't get any alien calls.'

'We did,' she tells me. 'I didn't put them on the list.'

I flip the page and my eyes are drawn to the final call, which came in late yesterday. An Amish woman, who refused to give her name, claims one of her children saw Mattie Borntrager on the road in front of her farm late at night, arguing with an unknown male.

'Do you have anything else on this anonymous Amish woman?' I ask.

Mona shakes her head. 'She wouldn't leave her name.'

'Huh.' But the simple fact that the caller saw or heard the argument is telling. If the incident took place late at night on the road in front of Mattie's farm – a dead-end road no less – the caller would have had to be walking or driving by, or else she lives nearby. Considering the late-night hour, I'm betting on the latter.

'This is good work, Mona. Thank you.'

She beams. 'You want me to follow up on any of these?'

I don't believe any of the other calls are viable, but I say, 'Why don't you give Mr. Oren a call and get an alibi?'

'Sure.'

'Then why don't you go home and get some sleep?'

She grins. 'I'll do it, Chief. Let me know if you need anything else.'

I return her smile. 'I'll let you know when the number crunchers get the hell out of the way.'

NINETEEN

I've just pulled into the gravel lane of Mattie's neighbors to speak with Martha Schlabach and, hopefully, get the details on the alleged argument between Mattie and an unidentified male, when my cell phone vibrates against my hip. I glance down, recognize the number as the Amish pay phone on the edge of town, and I pick up on the third ring.

'Katie?'

Something in my sister's voice makes the muscles at the back of my neck go taut. 'What is it?' I ask.

'Two policemen just left,' she tells me. 'They were asking all sorts of questions about Daniel Lapp.'

My foot hits the brake even before I realize I'm going to stop. All the while my sister's words echo in my ears.

They were asking all sorts of questions about Daniel Lapp.

'Which policemen?' I ask. 'When?'

'Twenty minutes ago. I hitched the buggy and drove right to the phone to call you. Katie, I told them what you told me to say, but I was nervous. I don't think they believed me. They kept looking at me as if they thought I was lying.'

You were, I think. 'Which policemen were there? Did you get their names?'

'The sheriff from Coshocton County. Redmon was his name, I think. There was a deputy, too. I don't remember his name.'

The information flies through my mind like shrapnel tearing through skin and muscle and bone. I force myself to calm down and think. 'What did they say exactly?'

'They asked me about that day. You know, the day . . . it happened. I told them I was in town. I didn't actually see Daniel. But I thought I remembered my brother saying something about him coming over to help bale hay.'

'Okay,' I tell her. 'That's good. What else?'

'Katie, they asked about you. I didn't know what to tell them. My words got all jumbled up. I told them you were in the house that day and the boys stayed in the field.'

'Have they talked to Jacob?' I ask.

'I don't know. They didn't say and I didn't ask. I didn't want them to think I was concerned.'

Or getting our stories straight . . . 'It's okay, Sarah. Don't worry. You did good.'

But none of this is good. It means the police have identified Daniel Lapp's remains. It means they've questioned his brother, Benjamin, and they know Daniel was last seen at my parents' farm. They know I was there the day he disappeared. Even more disturbing is the fact that Redmon questioned my sister without giving me a heads up. He's not obligated, but it would have been a courtesy, since it involved a family member of a fellow law-enforcement official. The usual rationale for leaving a cop out of the loop is if said cop is suspected of wrongdoing.

I tell myself that's not the case in this instance. I'm being paranoid; there's no way the police could know what happened that day. That doesn't prevent the wash of panic that rises in my chest. My siblings are wild cards; neither has experience dealing with cops. They're probably not very good liars. I want to know if Redmon talked to Jacob. Did my brother stick to the story we discussed? Why didn't the sheriff's office inform me that they would be talking to my family? Will they be talking to me next?

Redmon is probably wondering why I didn't mention Lapp's disappearance upon discovery of those remains. In hindsight, I wish I had because my silence, and my lack of action, could be considered unusual behavior. But I'd been hoping the remains wouldn't be identified, and now it's too late.

I wish I could call Jacob. But like most Amish, my brother doesn't have a phone. I resolve to swing by his farm when I finish here. Realizing my hands are wrapped around the steering wheel so tightly my knuckles ache, I force myself to relax them and proceed up the driveway toward the house.

I find Martha Schlabach and two children in the side yard, hanging clothes on a clothesline. I don't miss the quiver of surprise that runs through her body when she spots me walking toward them or the smugness of her expression when she notices my black eye. She probably thinks I deserve it.

Martha is a few years older than me, but we went to school together for a couple of years as kids. She's got a tanned face with patches of rosacea on both cheeks. I see a slightly receding hairline beneath her *kapp* and blond hair that's gone curly and gray at her temples.

Two wicker baskets filled with wet laundry sit on the ground at her feet. A bag of wooden clothespins have fallen over and spilled onto the grass. She's got a clothespin clamped between her teeth and peers at me over the trousers in her hands. She doesn't greet me, but then she'd never liked me. I never took it personally, because I knew it had more to do with my relationship with Mattie than me personally. When we were teenagers, Martha had her eye on Paul Borntrager, going so far as to tell some of her Amish girlfriends that she was going to marry him. I remember feeling sorry for her, because everyone knew Paul had eyes only for Mattie.

'*Guder mariya,*' I begin, wishing her a good morning.

My usage of Pennsylvania Dutch doesn't impress her. 'It's almost afternoon now.'

'Good day for laundry,' I say.

'The breeze is nice.'

I turn my attention to the two children. The boy is about three years old and blond with blunt cut bangs and a scab on his nose. He's too little to help, but he's trying, mimicking his *mamm* and handing her clothespins. The girl is about four and wears a light blue dress. Her feet are bare and dirty, and with a keen sense of nostalgia I remember a time when my own feet looked much the same way. I was lucky because my childhood was carefree. Up until my fourteenth year, it was unblemished, filled with wholesome living, of work and play, faith and family. The world has become a lot more complicated since then, and I can't help but wonder if that's true even here among the Amish.

'Looks like you've got some good helpers,' I say.

'They do what they can.' She bends to pick up another pair of trousers, snaps out the wrinkles, and hangs it on the line.

'I need to ask you some questions about the Borntragers,' I say.

'I don't know much about them. Don't know how I can help.'

'How long have you been neighbors?'

'Since Amos and I were married. Ten years now.' She removes a pin from her mouth, uses it to fasten a blue work shirt to the line.

'Are they good neighbors?'

'Of course. They're Amish.' She cuts me a direct look, the meaning of which doesn't elude me. *You are not one of us.* 'Mattie helped me with the babies once or twice. Paul mucked stalls for us when Amos broke his leg last year. He was a good man.'

I hear laughter and look past her to see a young girl running toward us, a black lab-mix puppy running alongside her, nipping at the hem of her dress. The sight warms me unexpectedly. I smile when I notice the torn fabric.

The woman looks over her shoulder and frowns. 'Sarah, your dress.'

'He won't stop.' The girl is laughing uncontrollably now, and the puppy is attached to the hem. '*Mamm!*'

'You'll be taking a needle and thread to that hem this evening,' the woman scolds, but her lips twitch.

The girl collapses onto the grass a few feet from her mother and begins to play with the puppy, lifting its face to hers and giggling as it licks her cheeks.

I cross to them and kneel. 'What's his name?'

'Sammy. Ouch! He bites.'

'He's teething, like babies do,' I tell her. 'He needs something to chew on. An old doll might keep those little teeth busy.'

Martha Schlabach continues with her chore, but I feel her eyes on me as I reach for the puppy and bring its snout to mine. I get a whiff of puppy breath an instant before he bites the end of my nose and I'm reminded that my face is still sore. 'He's a feisty one.'

'*Datt* says he's going to be a good hunting dog some day.'

'And a good friend, too.' I pass the puppy back to her and rise. Brushing the grass from my knees, I make my way back to Martha. I'm wary now of saying something inappropriate in front of the children, but I need to know if she called the tip line. If she did, I need to know exactly who saw what.

Martha is a no-nonsense woman, a busy mother of seven whose days are filled with work from the crack of dawn until her head hits the pillow at night. Neither of us has the time or the patience for a polite Q & A session so I decide to take the direct approach.

217

'I know you called the tip line,' I say quietly.

She doesn't look at me as she pins an apron to the line. 'My husband wouldn't approve of such a thing. My getting involved in someone else's affairs.'

'All information that comes in is confidential,' I tell her.

'As if you can be trusted, Katie Burkholder.' Her laugh grinds from her throat like a sludged-up engine on a cold morning. 'I don't partake in idle gossip about my neighbors.'

I resist the urge to roll my eyes. Martha didn't have a problem blathering about Mattie or me when we were teen-agers. Not only was she a gossipmonger, but half of what she passed along came from her own imagination. For an instant I'm tempted to remind her of that. Instead, I move closer to her and lower my voice. 'If there was an argument or confrontation between Mattie Borntrager and someone else, I need to know about it.'

She turns her attention back to her laundry, snapping open a work shirt, pinning it to the line, biting down on another clothespin.

'The buggy accident that killed Paul wasn't an accident,' I tell her.

The Amish woman's hands go still on the trousers she's holding. 'I don't want to get involved.'

'You already are.'

Sighing, she looks down at the trousers and lets them drop into the basket, as if what she's about to tell me requires all of her concentration. 'I called,' she admits.

'Thank you.'

'I know it was God's will, but my heart is broken about what happened to Paul and those precious children. If someone did this thing . . .'

'Someone did,' I say. 'If you know something, you need to tell me about it.'

The woman stares at me, assessing me, trying to decide if I'm worthy of whatever information she's safeguarding. I hold her gaze, willing her to open up.

In Pennsylvania Dutch, she orders the youngsters to the house to wash their hands. When the girl with the puppy rises to go with the others, Martha stops her. 'Sarah, put that puppy down and come here.'

Reluctantly, the girl sets the puppy on the grass and starts toward us. Big hazel eyes go from her *mamm* to me and back to her *mamm*. The puppy continues to bite at the hem of her dress, but she doesn't seem to notice now. She's looking at us as if she's done something wrong. I want to reassure her, but I defer to her mother and wait.

When the younger children are out of earshot, Martha turns her attention to the girl. 'Sarah, do you remember when Sally had that bay colt?'

'*Ja*. I got to stay up past my bedtime to help *Datt*.'

The woman smiles. 'That colt is almost as much trouble as that puppy of yours.'

'*Datt* says he's going to be a good trotter.' The girl looks down at the puppy growling and tugging at the hem of her dress and giggles.

Martha glances toward the house, watching the children, and addresses me. 'Sarah and I have discussed gossip and we know it's wrong to speak badly of our neighbors, don't we, Sarah?'

'Yes, ma'am.'

'I'm going to ask you to make an exception, Sarah, and tell Chief Burkholder what you saw that night you went out to the pasture to get Sally and bring her in.'

The girl looks down at her bare feet, drags her toes through grass and dandelions. '*Datt* sent me to the pasture with the halter to get Sally while he put straw in her stall. He knew she was going to have her colt and it was time to bring her in.'

Sarah looks nervous about retelling the story to me, an out-sider, so I do my best to put her at ease. 'What did you name your colt?'

'Jim.'

'How old is he?'

'Six months now.'

I nod. 'So this happened six months ago?'

The girl nods. 'When I walked into the pasture, Sally was grazing by the road, where the grass is thick and there's lots of clover. I walked over to her and when I was putting the halter on her, I saw Mattie Borntrager standing on the road, talking to a stranger.'

'Was the stranger a man or woman?'

'Man.'

'Did you recognize him?'

Sarah shakes her head.

'Was it Mr. Borntrager maybe?' I ask.

'No. He was a lot taller than Mr. Borntrager.'

'Was he Amish or English?'

'Amish, I think. He was wearing a hat. And he had a beard.'

If the man was Amish, the beard indicates he was married. 'Do you remember what time it was?' I ask.

'I don't know. The middle of the night, I think.' The girl looks at her mother.

'The horse began her labor at about two A.M.,' Martha tells me.

I turn my attention back to Sarah. 'What were they doing on the road?'

'Arguing, I think.'

'Their voices were raised?'

'Well, just the man. He sounded all mad and mean.'

'Do you know what they were arguing about?'

'I'm not supposed to listen to grown-up talk, so I just put the halter on Sally and took her to the barn.'

'Did the man touch Mrs. Borntrager?'

'I don't think so, but it was pretty dark. Mrs. Borntrager was all upset.'

'How do you know?'

'She was crying.'

By and large, Amish children's lives are more sheltered than their English counterparts. They're not exposed to movies or pop culture. There's no sex education or social media or Internet. Most of the things kids learn come from within their own family circle. As they enter their teen years and make friends outside of their family, they begin to see other perspectives and, perhaps, learn things their parents may not want them to learn.

I suspect Sarah's witnessing an argument between two adults in the dead of night was discomfiting. 'Did you see anything else unusual?' I ask.

The girl shakes her head. 'That's it.'

I put my hand on her shoulder. 'Thank you for telling me, Sarah.'

She looks at her mother. 'Is Mrs. Borntrager in trouble?'

The Amish woman shakes her head. 'Chief Burkholder is just investigating that terrible buggy accident.'

'Oh.' The girl nods solemnly. 'I miss seeing Sam and Norah. I used to wave to them. They were sweet.'

Martha licks her thumb and uses it to clean a smudge of dirt from her daughter's chin. 'Now you just forget all about Mrs. Borntrager, you hear? It's time for the midday meal. Go make sure your brothers and sisters washed their hands. I'll be inside in a few minutes.'

Snatching up the puppy, the girl hightails it toward the house.

I snag Martha's gaze. 'Do you have any idea who Sarah saw that night?'

'No.'

I try something open ended. 'Is there anything else you'd like to add?'

She waits so long before answering that I think she's not going to respond. Then she bends and picks up the trousers and pins them to the clothesline. 'I think the men like looking at Mattie Borntrager a little too much. Even Amish men. But that's men for you.'

'What do you mean?'

'Don't play dumb with me, Katie. You know how it was with her when she was a girl. Well, it hasn't changed all that much.'

I think about the rivalry between Martha and Mattie and the fact that, in the end, Paul Borntrager chose Mattie. I know it's cynical, but I can't help but wonder if that's what this is about, at least in part. Back when we were teens, Martha tolerated me and my antics. But she had no tolerance for Mattie. I wonder if her indictment of Mattie is the result of some long-standing jealousy that's festered into something ugly over the years. I wonder if this woman has an axe to grind.

'You mean with her being pretty?' I ask.

'Pretty. And she knows it, too, doesn't she?' She huffs, a sound of disgust that broadcasts something stronger than dislike for Mattie. 'All I'm saying is that her being married in the eyes of God didn't change the way men look at her.'

'And that's Mattie's fault somehow?' The question comes out sounding defensive, so I reel in the part of me that wants to defend her.

'That's not for me to say now, is it?'

'Are you talking about a particular man?'

'Take your pick. They all look at her with their tongues

hanging out like a bunch of panting dogs. Fall all over themselves helping her when she doesn't need any help.' The Amish woman grimaces as if she's bitten into the bitter pith of a lemon. 'But then she's got that way about her.'

'What way is that?'

She looks at me as if I'm dense. 'One look from her and she's got them eating out of her hand, pecking like a bunch of chickens, that's what way.'

'Are you saying this is something Mattie does on purpose, Martha?'

'I wouldn't know.'

'Do you think Mattie and Paul were having marital problems?'

'Look, Katie, none of us is perfect. But when Sarah told me what she'd seen, I wasn't surprised.'

'Was Paul aware of any of this?'

'The man was blind to it. Mattie could do no wrong in his eyes.' She shakes her head, and for the first time I see pity in her expression. 'She uses those children, too. For attention, you know. Always putting other people out to save herself some trouble, if you ask me.'

I don't know what to say to that. I don't know what to think or feel about any of what's been said. The weight of the words that have passed between us settle onto my shoulders like a boulder.

'You were always partial to her, though, weren't you?' Martha's lips curl, but her smile is cruel. 'I've said my piece, Katie Burkholder. You do with it what you will and God will take care of the rest.'

I hand her my card. 'If you think of anything else, will you get in touch with me?'

She refuses the card and glances toward the house. 'You'd best go. I've got children to feed.'

She leaves me standing next to her empty laundry basket with the wet clothes flapping in the breeze and the turmoil of my thoughts.

TWENTY

In the course of an investigation, a cop receives all kinds of information. A fair amount of that information is based on fact. Some is based on lies or half-truths that have been put forth to further someone's agenda. A large percentage of information is pure bullshit. It's my job to sort through it and separate fact from fiction, even if I don't like the direction it's taking me.

There's no doubt in my mind that young Sarah Schlabach was telling the truth about seeing a man and a woman that night on the road in front of her house. Martha might have an axe to grind when it comes to Mattie, but I don't think she'd ask her eight-year-old daughter to fabricate a story to further some fifteen-year-old grudge. I didn't get the sense that the girl was lying.

Who was Mattie arguing with and why? More importantly, why didn't she mention it to me? As with any witness, the possibility exists that Sarah misinterpreted what she saw. Could the man have been Paul Borntrager? Had Mattie and her husband had a spat and decided to take it outside so they wouldn't wake the children? Or is there another possibility I'm not seeing?

One vital piece of the puzzle that's been missing from the start of this case is motive. I've been leaning toward the possibility of a stalking situation. Mattie is, after all, a stunningly beautiful woman. The kind of beauty that draws attention, perhaps even unwanted attention. I know from experience that a high percentage of stalking victims know their stalker. Does Mattie know him? Did she confront him? Did they have words that night? Is it possible that she's oblivious to the dangers and protecting him for the simple reason that he's Amish? That she doesn't want any of this to come to light to protect her own reputation?

When Mattie and I were teenagers, the boys were drawn to her with the mindless glee of children to chocolate. Several times, there had been more than one boy courting her at the same time. Petty jealousies and, once, a fight had erupted. Unlike Martha, I didn't begrudge Mattie the attention. I was content to sit back and watch. Mattie had seemed oblivious to her charms. But even with my limited view of the world, there was a part of me that was cognizant of these things called jealousy and lust, and the lengths to which people would go to get what they want.

I'm sitting at my desk in my office, troubled and brooding, when my phone buzzes. Absently, I hit the speaker button. 'What's up, Lois?'

'Sheriff Redmon's here to see you, Chief. You want me to send him in?'

The visit isn't unexpected but my nerves jump anyway. 'Sure. Thanks.'

I end the call, look down at my hands to see them shaking. 'Goddammit.' I press them against my desktop, order myself to stay calm.

A moment later, Sheriff Arnold Redmon and the young deputy I spoke to at the grain elevator, Fowler Hodges, appear at the door. 'Afternoon, Chief Burkholder,' the sheriff drawls.

'Sheriff Redmon.' Standing, I round my desk, a smile pasted to my face, and extend my hand to the sheriff.

He steps into my office and reciprocates the handshake, giving me a quick once-over. His grip is firm, his palm meaty and calloused. His eyes are the color of tarnished coins. He's got a powerful presence and the kind of stare that goes right through you.

'I heard about that tussle you got into out at the Borntrager place,' he says, studying my face. 'Hate to see bruises on any cop, but it always seems worse on a female.'

'We'll get him.'

I turn my attention to the deputy, hoping my nervousness doesn't show, and we shake. 'Good to see you again, Folly.'

'You guys have any luck on that hit-skip?' he asks.

I give him the highlights of the investigation so far. 'We're basically looking at everyone at this point.'

By the time I turn my attention back to Redmon, I've decided how to handle this. 'My sister tells me you identified those remains as Daniel Lapp,' I begin.

'ID isn't official yet, but his brother, Benjamin, remembered him having a chipped front tooth, and sure enough we found a chipped tooth in that mess of bones. We think it's him.'

'I always figured he left to get away from the Amish,' I tell him.

'He tell you that?'

'Just an assumption.'

'Benjamin told us Daniel helped your brother bale hay the day he disappeared. Your sister verified it. She told us Daniel was at your folks' farm that day.' He holds my gaze, waits for me to elaborate.

'He was,' I say simply. 'All this came up after he went missing. It's in the file.'

'I know it was a long time ago, Chief Burkholder, but do you recall actually seeing him that day? Did you talk to him?'

I shake my head. 'I don't remember seeing him. I was in

the house most of the day. Daniel and Jacob were in the field, behind the barn.'

'He didn't come in for a drink of water? Anything like that?'

'I don't think so.' I smile. 'The hose is usually good enough for Amish kids.'

Redmon watches me closely, hanging on to each syllable, as if he's memorizing every detail so he can take them apart later. 'Did Lapp's parents talk to your parents when he didn't come home?'

'It seems logical that they would have, but I don't recall them visiting our farm,' I say. 'If they did, my parents didn't mention it to me.'

'Did Daniel help your brother bale on more than one occasion that summer?'

'It's possible,' I tell him. 'Amish kids are always looking for work. It was a long time ago and those memories kind of run together.'

'Were Jacob and Daniel friends?'

'More like friendly acquaintances.'

'So they didn't hang out? Spend time together?'

'I don't think so.'

'Do you mind my asking how old you were that summer?'

'I was fourteen.'

He grins as if imagining me at that age. 'You probably had better things to do than pay attention to a bunch of sweaty boys.'

I smile, but it's so forced I feel a tick in my lip.

'Benjamin Lapp thinks something happened to his brother that day,' Redmon tells me.

'Like what?'

'He thinks Daniel might've had some kind of accident while he was working in the field.'

'That's the first time I've heard that.' I shrug, but my heart is pounding so hard I can barely hear my own voice. I wonder if Redmon can see the vein pulsing at my throat.

'You know how these things go,' the sheriff says. 'Something happens to a loved one, they go missing or whatever, and the family starts looking for someone to blame. People's imaginations get to running when someone disappears.'

'If anything had happened to Daniel that day, if he'd been hurt while working on our farm, I'm sure my *datt* would have taken him to the hospital.' I tilt my head, make eye contact with Redmon. 'In case you're wondering, the Amish have no problem utilizing doctors or the ER when necessary. There are no rules against that.'

'To tell you the truth, Chief, I wasn't sure what the belief system was in that area,' he drawls. 'Did you ever wonder what happened to Daniel? I mean, since he'd been at your parents' farm that day and no one saw him again?'

'Sure,' I tell him. 'Everybody wondered.'

He waits, watching me.

I don't believe the sheriff suspects me or anyone in my family of wrongdoing. But he hasn't ruled us out and he's not above using law enforcement interview techniques to trip me up. In this case, it's the give-someone-enough-rope-and-they'll-hang-themselves tactic. I don't bite. 'Like I said, I always thought Daniel took the money he was paid that day and left.'

'Benjamin was adamant that Daniel wouldn't do that. Said he was looking forward to getting baptized.'

I shrug. 'No offense to Benjamin, but sometimes the family is the last to know. The Amish don't want to believe there are others living among them who no longer want to be Amish.'

'I guess you got a point there.' He chuckles, a grand-fatherly sound designed to disarm. I don't buy it for a second. The sheriff is about as grandfatherly as Charles Manson. 'So you think Daniel Lapp, an eighteen-year-old Amish kid, just up and left town without so much as a good-bye to his brother and parents?'

'It wouldn't be the first time.'

When neither man responds, I look from Redmon to Fowler and back to Redmon. 'Do you have any idea how he got down in that pit?'

'We're not sure,' Redmon tells me.

'Do you suspect foul play?'

'Coroner says someone shot him with a shotgun.'

I tamp down a quick rise of alarm. 'So you got results on the autopsy?'

'Autopsy isn't complete, it's all preliminary at this point. Coroner didn't have much to work with.' He makes a sound of distaste. 'We're talking bones and a few strands of rotted fabric, as you can imagine. While they were gathering samples for the lab, one of the technicians took a metal detector to the scene and found shotgun pellets in the soil. They're pretty sure the pellets were inside Lapp's body.'

'So we're talking homicide.'

'Looks like.' He scratches his head. 'I just can't figure who'd want an Amish kid dead.'

The phone on my desk buzzes; the sound echoes in my ears as if I'm standing in a cave. I let it go to voicemail. 'Wasn't that grain elevator closed down back then?' I ask.

'Wilbur Seed Company closed down back in 1976,' Redmon tells me. 'I checked.'

'Perfect place to hide a body,' Fowler adds.

Redmon's gaze burns into mine. 'Anyone in your family ever have any kind of dispute with Lapp? You know, over money or pay? Anything like that?'

I've lived this moment a thousand times in the last seventeen years. I've coached myself on how to respond right down to my body language and the tone of my voice. Now that the time is here and there are two cops looking at me as if I know more than I'm letting on, all the words I had so diligently rehearsed fly out the window, leaving me alone with my conscience and the lie I've been living with half of my life.

'Nothing that I know of,' I say. 'My father was an honest man and fair with wages.' I put on a face of disappointment and look from man to man. 'Whatever happened to Daniel Lapp didn't happen at our farm.'

'Well, I appreciate your answering my questions, Chief, especially when you're occupied with that nasty hit-skip.' Redmon pulls his card from his shirt pocket and hands it to me. 'We had to do our due diligence. You know how it is.'

'No problem.' I set the card on my desk. 'If I remember anything else, I'll call you.'

I stand and watch the men shuffle to the door. Tension runs like hot wires up and down the back of my neck. At the doorway to the hall, the sheriff stops and turns. 'Oh, one more thing, Chief, before I forget. Did your father own a shotgun?'

I stare at him, aware that my knees are shaking, my hands are shaking, so I lower myself into my chair and press them against the desktop. 'My father kept a twenty-two. For hunting.'

'Thanks.' He ducks his head slightly. 'We'll get out of your hair now.'

The men trundle out, leaving me with a knot in my gut, an old, familiar fear in my heart, and the disturbing suspicion that while this visit is over, the case remains open.

My encounter with Redmon leaves me restless and edgy. Despite my best efforts, I can't get my focus back on the Borntrager case. I can't stop thinking about the secrets and the questions and an investigation that could mean the end of my career.

I arrive at Mattie's farm to find two buggies parked near

the barn, the horses standing with their back legs cocked, their heads down. Two Amish men, one of whom is smoking a pipe, stand at the open barn door, talking. They stare at me as I get out of the Explorer. I raise my hand in greeting, but neither man reciprocates. I take the sidewalk to the back porch. I don't bother knocking this time and go directly to the kitchen.

I find Mary Miller at the sink. She's a tall, angular woman with skinny legs and feet that look too big for her body. I've known her since my days at school, where she taught for a while. She worked hard to make sure I knew my multiplication tables and smacked my hand with the ruler on more than one occasion to ensure she had my undivided attention. She's married to the Amish man I saw near the barn when I arrived. They're a nice couple, with eight children, and live on small farm south of Painters Mill.

'Is Mattie here?' I ask. 'I need to speak with her.'

'She's resting.' She turns her back to me and goes back to her dishwashing. 'I see your manners haven't improved with age.'

'Where is she?' I walk past her, half expecting her to snap the dish towel at my back.

The smells of mock turtle soup and lye soap follow me into the living room. I make my way to the stairs and take them two at a time to the top. Four doors stand open. The first is a bathroom with robin's-egg-blue walls and a claw-foot tub. I'm midway to the second door when Mattie appears in the doorway ahead.

'Katie?'

I can tell by the soft paleness of her complexion that I roused her from sleep. A crease mark from her pillow mars her right cheek. She's wearing a black dress and is in the process of tying her head covering as she steps into the hall. 'I didn't know you were here.'

'We need to talk,' I tell her.

Her expression goes wary. 'Has something happened? If I'd known you were coming, I would have made coffee.'

'I don't want coffee. What I want is for you to level with me.'

'About what?' Her eyes go into sharp focus on mine. 'Have you found out something about the accident?'

'It wasn't an accident, Mattie. Someone mowed them down. There's a difference.'

'I know that, but . . .' Her voice trails and she looks down at the floor. 'I don't know what else to call it.'

'Try triple murder.'

She steps back, sets her hand on the jamb as if she needs the support to remain upright. 'Why are you angry with me?'

I cross to her so that I'm less than a foot away. Her skin is as pale and flawless as a baby's. Her eyes are deep and clear. She's magnetic and, even as a female, I can understand why men are drawn to her. She smells of baby powder and laundry detergent and summer sun.

'Let me spell it out for you.' My voice feels like a steel zipper being ripped from my throat. 'I asked you if you'd had any recent disagreements or arguments with anyone. It's a straightforward question, Mattie. Then I hear about you and an unidentified man arguing on the road in front of your house in the middle of the night. What am I supposed to make of that?'

She chokes out a sound that's part laugh, part incredulity. 'I don't know who you've been speaking with or what they said to you, but no such thing ever happened.'

In the years we've been friends, Mattie has shocked me, infuriated me, and made me laugh. The one thing she's never done is lie. But I see the quicksilver flash of conscience in her eyes, and the truth of it hurts a hell of a lot more than I thought it would. 'You're keeping something from me. I suggest you start talking and, if it's not too much trouble, focus on the truth.'

She takes a step back, presses her hand to her breast. I steel myself against the hurt in her eyes, remind myself that a man and two children are dead and I have a job to do.

'You're being purposefully cruel,' she says quietly.

'I'm asking a question I want answered. Who was the man?'

'Katie, I am a Plain woman. I don't speak with strange men in the—'

'There's nothing Plain about you,' I cut in, and the words make me sound like a petty, jealous shrew.

She looks away as if the words shame her.

'I have a witness, Mattie. They saw you. They saw him. I know he's Amish—'

'*Sell is nix as baeffzes.*' *That is nothing but trifling talk.* Looking shaken, she sputters the words in Pennsylvania Dutch.

'Is it?' I tilt my head and lean closer, invading her space, getting in her face. '*Wu schmoke is, is aa feier.*' *Where there's smoke there's fire.*

'Please stop.'

'Someone ran down that buggy and killed your husband and children. I've been beating my head against the wall trying to figure out who and why.' I slam the heel of my hand against the jamb next to her head. 'And you're playing games with me!'

'I'm not . . .' Her breaths come short and fast, as if she's in the throes of a panic attack. 'I would never . . .'

I don't know if I'm right about any of this. The one thing I do know is that she's keeping something from me, so I don't give her a respite. I'm truly angry, but part of my display is calculated. I want her shaken. Even better if she's furious with me. Because I know Mattie. Pressure is the only way I'm going to get anything out of her.

'I want the truth and I want it now!' I shout.

'Please. Leave me alone!' She lowers her head and puts her

face in her hands. The cry that follows is so wrenching I feel the hairs on my arms prickle, the threat of tears at the backs of my own eyes. I shake off both.

I give her a moment to regain her composure, then ask, 'Who is he?'

Her shoulders shake as she sobs uncontrollably into her hands. I wait, letting her hurt, resisting the urge to set my hand on her shoulder. All the while doubt and guilt poke a pointy finger at my back, laughing at me because I'm wrong about this. I'm wrong about her and I've destroyed one of my oldest friendships on a hunch I wasn't sure about to begin with.

After a moment, she raises her gaze to mine. Her nose is red, her cheeks mottled and streaked with tears. 'Please don't tell,' she whispers. 'Please, Katie, I couldn't bear it if anyone knew.'

'Knew what?' I snap.

'Wayne Kuhns. He tried to . . . He wanted to . . .'

I know most of the Amish in and around Painters Mill, but that name isn't familiar. 'What did he do to you?'

'He didn't do anything. But he . . . he wanted to . . . be with me. He tried to . . . you know, the way men do sometimes.'

Surprise is like the slash of claws across my face. I break a sweat beneath my uniform. I'm aware of my heart thrumming against my ribs. I stare, knowing I shouldn't be shocked, but I am.

'Mattie, did he hurt you? Did he force you to do something you didn't want to do?'

'No. I . . . pushed him away.'

'Did you have an affair with him?'

'No! Of course not. Katie, I'm married in the eyes of God. I would never forsake my vows. I wouldn't do that to Paul or to myself.' Her mouth quivers. 'I can't believe you would think that about me. Now please, I just want to forget it ever happened.'

'Are you kidding me?' I choke out a laugh, incredulity ringing hard in my voice. 'What were you arguing about?'

'He wanted to . . . be with me, and I told him it would never happen. He became upset and began shouting. It was upsetting and very uncomfortable.'

'Where was Paul?'

He was at his parents' house up in Fredericktown. His *mamm* had just had a stroke.'

I nod, recalling that Paul's mother recently passed. 'What were you doing outside that time of night?'

'It wasn't that late. Still light, in fact. I saw Wayne coming down the lane in his buggy.

'That's not what I heard.'

'I don't know where you're getting your information, Katie, but I know exactly what time it was. I'd just put the children to bed.' Mattie cocks her head. 'You've been talking to that Schlabach girl, haven't you?'

'I'm not going to get into that with you.'

'I don't want to speak ill of a child, especially a troubled child. But Sarah is known for telling tall tales.'

I say nothing.

'Sarah Schlabach makes up stories, just like her *mamm* used to. You remember how Martha was. She never liked me.' She looks down, presses her hand against her abdomen. 'Sarah may have a sweet little face, but she's a troubled child, Katie. In fact, she was mean to Norah once. They were playing and my sweet little girl came in with a black eye.'

That wasn't my impression of the Schlabach girl, not even close, but I keep the thought to myself. The time discrepancy bothers me, but I can get to the bottom of that later. For now, I need to know about Wayne Kuhns.

'You need to tell me about Kuhns, Mattie. And I mean all of it. Right now.'

She looks down at her hands. 'Let's sit.' But I know she doesn't want to risk the woman downstairs overhearing us.

I nod, and she takes me into her bedroom. Closing the door behind us, she motions toward a rocking chair at the window. She sits on the edge of the bed and puts her hands in her lap. 'He started coming over about eight months ago.' She says the words so quietly I have to lean forward to hear. 'At first it was innocent. The kind of thing a neighbor does. He would drop by on his way to the market and ask if we needed anything. Sometimes he would bring squash or eggs or bread. Once he helped Paul dig some postholes.'

She stops speaking and takes a moment to gather herself. 'After a while, I knew it wasn't innocent.' Shame seems to emanate from her pores, like greasy, nervous sweat. 'I could tell by the way he looked at me. Nothing I could put my finger on. But his eyes were too bold. I knew it wasn't right. I knew he wasn't coming over to just to be a good neighbor.'

'He was coming to see you.'

'I think he was lonely and sad. I think he was having problems in his life. His faith.'

I stare at her, wondering how she could be so naïve. 'Did you tell Paul?'

'No.'

'Why not?'

'I didn't want to upset him or turn it into some big issue. I know it may not make sense to you, Katie, but you're not Amish anymore. You're not married.' She struggles to find the right words. 'I felt . . . ashamed. I mean, I know it wasn't my fault; I hadn't done anything wrong. But still . . . I know this sounds dense, but I didn't want to get Wayne into trouble. His wife had just found out she was expecting. I thought it was a passing thing.'

I stare at her, sensing I'm not getting the full story. She's leaving something out, so I push. 'What aren't you telling me?'

She picks at a hangnail that's already picked down to the quick. 'You know how the Amish are. Sometimes they talk.'

'You mean about you?'

'About the way I look. Some of the women . . . they don't like me. Sometimes they're all too willing to lay blame where there is none.'

'So you didn't mention it to Paul or anyone else because you thought the women would gossip about you? Blame you?'

'Come on, Katie. You know how they are. Look at how they treated you.' Grimacing as if the memory of my leaving still pains her, she lowers her head, rubs at her forehead with her fingertips. 'The women would think I'd somehow tempted him. That it was my fault.'

'Tell me the rest of it.'

'Things got bad when Wayne started coming over when Paul wasn't home. That was when I knew the problem wasn't going to go away on its own.'

'Did he ever touch you inappropriately, Mattie? Did he ever try to do something you didn't want him to do?'

Before she looks away, I see misery and shame in the depths of her eyes and, despite everything, I'm moved. I want to put my arms around her and tell her everything's going to be all right. That she didn't do anything wrong. But I don't.

'He tried to, you know, kiss me. Once. He'd brought eggs and we were in the kitchen. He just sort of tried to put his mouth on mine. You know, all awkward-like, and I pushed him away.'

'Did he get the message?'

She averts her eyes again. 'That last night, the night Sarah told you about, I threatened to go to his wife and tell her what he was doing. He stopped coming after that.'

'You never told Paul?'

'No.' Fresh tears pour from her eyes, but she makes no move to wipe them away. 'Now I feel as if I betrayed him. As if I've done something wrong. I know I didn't, but he's gone and I'll never have the chance to make it right.'

I look away. Even though the door is closed, I can hear the clanging of pots and pans being washed and dried in the kitchen. 'How did Kuhns take it when you threatened to go to his wife?'

'He was angry. I mean, at first. But he is Amish, Katie. Aside from his weakness for the women, he's a good man. He knew what he was doing was wrong. He loves his wife. In the end, he agreed to stay away.'

'Did he ever lose his temper or threaten you in any way?'

'Oh, no, Katie. He knew it was the devil's thoughts running through his mind. He fought them and in the end he won.'

'Is he a jealous man? Did he ever show any anger toward you or Paul?'

'Never.'

'When's the last time you had contact with Kuhns?'

'That night on the road six months ago. I've prayed for him every day since.'

'Has he tried to contact you?'

'No.'

'Did he ever stalk you?'

'No,' she says.

'Have you seen him at all? Or run into him anywhere? Even by accident?'

'I see him at worship on occasion. He never even looks my way.'

'What about in town? Or when you're out running errands?'

'No.'

'Have you seen him hanging around the farm?'

'Never.'

I stare hard at her. 'Is there anything else you want to tell me about Kuhns? Is there anything you left out?'

'He didn't do this thing, Katie. He would never hurt Paul or the children. He is a husband and soon to be a father. More importantly, he is Amish. He wouldn't hurt a fly. Of that, I'm certain.'

As I rise and make my way to the door, all I can think is that she has a hell of a lot more faith in human nature than I do.

When you're Amish – even formerly Amish, like me – some things are so ingrained you can't escape them. Harsh judgment is one of them. I haven't been Amish for almost eighteen years – more than half of my life – but as I turn onto the highway I feel all of those tattered morals rising to the surface. I don't consider myself a religious woman. I don't attend church or pray before meals. But I do believe in fidelity.

I'm well aware that the Amish are held to higher moral standards than their English counterparts. Because of their strict belief system, they have farther to fall from that perch of righteousness. It's hypocritical of me to stand in judgment of another soul. My own résumé isn't exactly squeaky clean, and you sure don't have to dig too deep to find dirt. I'm a sinner just like everyone else. Perhaps more so because of the nature of my crimes. But old habits die hard.

I find myself chomping at the bit to speak with Wayne Kuhns. Finally, I have a possible motive. It wouldn't be the first time a stalker had acted on some dark impulse. One of the first objectives of the stalker is to isolate his victim. Eliminate their support system in the hope they will turn to him. In Mattie's case, he would have also eliminated his competition: her husband.

I call Lois on my way to the station and ask her to run Wayne Kuhns through LEADS. I'm not surprised when he comes back clean. But even seemingly decent, God-loving people can have a hidden dark side, especially when it comes to lust.

Normally, when dealing with the Amish, I prefer to do it alone, for the simple reason that they're more apt to speak openly to me, if only because of my background. But because of my past friendship with Mattie, I want an objective opinion, so I swing by the station and pick up Glock. I give him the details of my conversation with Mattie on the way to Kuhns's house.

'You think Kuhns was stalking her?' he asks.

'I thought we might ask him.'

'Damn.' He whistles. 'The kids. That's cold blooded.'

'Wouldn't be the first time some obsessive narcissist took out his competition.'

'Takes a sick son of a bitch to do something like that.' He motions right. 'There's the street.'

I make a hard right and park at the curb in front of a nondescript frame house with white siding and small concrete porch in the front. From where I'm sitting, I see a one-car detached garage off the alley. The overhead door stands open and yellow lantern light spills into the backyard.

Most Amish in the area live on farms. But with a limited amount of land, and the cost of owning it increasing, some have adapted their lifestyle to keep up with the times. Glock and I take the sidewalk to the front porch. The sound of hammering draws my attention and I realize someone is in the garage off the alley. Instead of going to the front door, we take the sidewalk around the side of the house toward the rear. An old chain-link fence stops us, but there's no dog in sight, so I open the gate and we continue toward the garage.

I'm a few yards from the door when the sound of sawing reaches me. Through the window, I see Kuhns hunched over whatever project he's working on. The smells of sawdust and kerosene greet me when I enter. The shop is organized and well lit. A lantern burns from atop the workbench behind him. A second lantern hangs from an exposed beam overhead. Kuhns glances up from his sawing, but takes the time to finish his cut. He's wearing typical Amish garb: gray trousers with suspenders, a blue work shirt, and a straw hat. I guess him to be in his midthirties. Physically fit. Attractive.

He doesn't look surprised to see us as he straightens and sets the saw on the workbench. He's building a doghouse, I realize. A nice one with stained trim, faux shutters, and a roof that opens for easy cleaning. Indoor/outdoor carpet lines the interior.

'Looks like that's going to be a nice doghouse,' I begin.

He glances at his creation and I see a quick flash of pride in his eyes. 'It's a custom order for one of Mrs. Steinkruger's customers.'

'Are you Wayne Kuhns?' I ask.

'Yes.' His eyes sweep to Glock and back to me. 'What's this about?'

I show him my badge and identify myself, then we shake hands. Glock hangs back, unobtrusive, but I know he's watching the other man closely.

'I'm working on the Borntrager case,' I tell him. 'If you have a few minutes, I'd like to ask you some questions.'

He physically recoils when I mention the Borntragers, and I know instantly that while Wayne Kuhns is either a wannabe adulterer or a stalker, he's not proud of it, and he's not very good at hiding his emotions.

'Did you know Paul?' I ask.

He nods. 'I met him several times. At worship. The horse auction. Helped him a few times at the farm.'

'What about Mattie?'

He looks down at the floor. I give him a moment, but he doesn't answer. I'm aware of Glock moving around, looking at the workbench, peering into the trash container.

'Mr. Kuhns?' I say.

'I know Mattie.'

'How do you know her?'

No reply. I don't know if he doesn't want to answer or if he's so upset he can't.

'How do you know Mattie, Mr. Kuhns?'

'I haven't seen her for a long time.'

'How long?'

'Six months or so.'

'What was the nature of your relationship?'

His gaze flicks toward the door and I wonder if his wife is inside. I wonder if she knows he'd recently had his sights set on another woman. His silence is telling.

'I know you approached her about a relationship,' I tell him.

He winces as if I slashed him with a blade. 'I wasn't . . . I mean I didn't . . . we didn't . . .' He lets the words trail as if he's not sure how to finish the sentence. 'I figured that's why you're here.' He doesn't meet my gaze.

'Were you stalking her?'

'Is that what she told you?'

'I'd appreciate it if you would just answer the question.'

'No. I would never do such a thing.'

I glance over at Glock to see him shake his head. 'Do you own a vehicle, Mr. Kuhns?'

'I don't drive. I have no use for a vehicle. If I need to travel, I hire the Mennonite down the street.'

'Where were you three nights ago?'

His eyes widen as if he's suddenly realized why we're here. 'I was here. Working.'

'Can anyone substantiate that?'

'My wife.'

'Anyone else?'

'No.'

I stare hard at him. 'Tell me about your relationship with Mattie.'

'That is in the past, Chief Burkholder. I do not wish to speak of it.'

'Mr. Kuhns, this is a police investigation. You don't have a choice.'

A flash of anger crosses his features. 'Who are you to ask me such a thing?' he snaps. 'Who are you to judge me?'

He's referring to my being ex-Amish, but I let the condemnation behind his words roll off me. 'I'm the chief of police, and I'm conducting a murder investigation.' I step toward him, put my finger in his face. 'If I were you, I'd answer the question. If you don't, I'll get a warrant and we'll finish this at the police station. Do you understand?'

His face goes crimson. Sweat beads on his forehead and upper lip. I can't tell if it's temper or humiliation, but if a man can look like a volcano about to blow, Wayne Kuhns is Mount Pinatubo. 'She and I . . .' he stammers. 'We were . . . friends.'

'Did you have a sexual relationship with her?'

A flush of embarrassment deepens his color. His eyes skate away from mine. 'No.'

'Did you *want* a sexual relationship with her?'

He looks everywhere except at me.

'Shall I interpret that as a yes?' I ask.

'I did nothing wrong.'

'Who broke it off?'

'She did.' He sighs. 'What happened . . . is in the past. I've prayed for forgiveness and made peace with the Lord. And myself.'

'Were you angry when she told you she wanted to be left alone?'

His eyes narrow and I know he's trying to figure out just what she told me, how much I know. 'No.'

'Were you angry when she threatened to tell your wife you were bothering her?'

Another, deeper flush. 'I didn't get angry. I respected her wishes.'

'Did Paul know?'

'I don't know.'

'Did you ever have words with him?'

'Never.'

'Does your wife know?'

'No.' He fastens his gaze on the floor at his feet and shakes his head. 'I'd like to keep it that way.'

'Does anyone else know about it?'

'No.'

I take him through some of the same questions I asked Mattie earlier to see if their answers correspond. He replies mechanically, without looking at me. Hating me, I think. Hating the questions and realizing the consequences of his actions are going to adversely affect his life.

'Is your wife inside, Mr. Kuhns? I need to speak with her.'

'No.'

'No, she's not inside? Or no, you don't want me to speak with her?'

Splotches appear on the skin at his collar and climb up his throat like a rash. He blots sweat from his forehead, looks from me to Glock and back to me. 'She knows nothing of this.'

'Mr. Kuhns, I'm not trying to make this difficult or uncomfortable for you,' I tell him. 'But this is a homicide investigation and I need to speak with your wife.'

He makes no move to accommodate my request. 'You do not have my permission to speak with her.'

Behind me, I hear Glock laugh.

'I don't need your permission,' I tell him.

'She is with child,' he hisses.

'If I were you, I'd start figuring out how to fill her in because she's obviously going to have some questions for you when we're finished.' I look at Glock. 'Let's go.' I make eye contact with Kuhns and motion toward the door.

'You are going to burn in hell, Kate Burkholder.'

'I have a feeling I won't be alone,' I mutter and start toward the door.

The interior of the house smells of candle wax and sweet rosemary from a meal that had been cooked earlier in the evening. Kuhns takes Glock and me through the dimly lit mud room and into a kitchen filled with the bright light of an overhead gas-powered fixture.

'Wayne?' A lilting female voice calls out from somewhere in the house. 'I just swept the floor so you'd better brush off all that sawdust—' A young Amish woman wearing a gray dress with an apron appears in the doorway. Her words trail when she spots Glock and me. 'Oh. Hello.'

'Mrs. Kuhns?' I say.

'Yes?' She sends a questioning look to her husband. 'What's going on?'

'I'm Chief Burkholder and I'm looking into the deaths of Paul Borntrager and his children. I'm sorry to bother you this evening, but I'd like to ask you a few questions.'

'I don't see how I can help you.' Looking baffled, she enters the kitchen, and for the first time I notice her bulging midsection and I realize she's nearly to term. 'We barely know the Borntragers.'

Wayne rounds the table, pulls out a chair, and slumps into it, saying nothing. I offer my hand to the Amish woman and we shake.

'I'm Hannah,' she tells me, her gaze flicking to Glock. 'Would you like coffee? I think I've got lemonade, too.'

'No thank you, ma'am,' I say. 'Just a few questions and then we'll leave you to the rest of your evening.'

She nods, her expression turning grim. 'I couldn't believe it when I heard about Paul and the children. It's one of the saddest things I've ever heard. I took a pie over to Mattie yesterday. Poor thing is all broken up.'

'How well do you know the Borntragers?' I begin.

'Just to say hello, really.' Her eyes narrow and I know she's still wondering why we're here. Why we're asking questions about a family she had little or no contact with. 'I spoke to Mattie briefly a couple of weeks ago at worship. I ran into her at the grocery store last month.'

'Would you mind telling me where you were three nights ago?'

'*What?*' She casts a did-you-hear-that look at her husband. 'I was here. Why are you—'

'Alone?'

'I was with Wayne.' Her brows knit. 'Why are you asking me that?'

'Both of you were here? All night?'

'Yes.'

'Mrs. Kuhns, did you ever have any kind of disagreement or dispute with Mattie or Paul?'

'Of course not. I told you. I barely knew them. How can you have a dispute with someone you don't even know?'

'What about your husband? Did he ever have any kind of argument or disagreement with them?'

'No.' She looks from me to her husband, as if she's the only one in the room who didn't get the punch line of some joke. 'What's going on here?'

'These questions are just routine. We're exploring all sources of information. Thank you for your time,' I tell her. 'We'll see ourselves out.' Glock and I start toward the front door. I feel her eyes on my back as we traverse the living area.

'You think he's going to come clean?' Glock asks when we're outside.

'I don't think he has a choice.'

TWENTY-ONE

Solving a case is akin to putting a puzzle together. The kind that has a thousand infinitesimal pieces, some of which are missing, damaged, or false. Initially, none of those pieces seem to have a place in the big picture. They're the wrong color or shape or size. It's my job to persevere and figure out which ones to toss aside, which ones to keep. One excruciating piece at a time, an image will emerge.

After leaving the Kuhns' place, I drop Glock at the station and start for home to grab a shower and then head to Wooster to see Tomasetti. Somewhere between the station and my house, I change my mind. I blame the case, of course. Work is an acceptable excuse – especially when you're a cop – and one he's obliged to understand. The problem is, it's a lie.

John Tomasetti is probably the best thing that's ever happened to me. I know I'm risking this thing we've created between us. But some small, self-destructive part of me won't let me reach out. Perhaps the same part that won't let me partake in the happiness that's within my grasp for the first time in my adult life.

It's 10:00 P.M. and once again I'm behind the wheel of my Explorer, camped out at the dead-end turnaround fifty yards from the mouth of the Borntrager lane. The light inside the house went dark half an hour ago. Nothing has moved since. Not a single vehicle or buggy has been on the road, not even to turn around. I don't think anyone is going to show up, but sitting here is better than going home to face an empty house and my own uneasy thoughts.

My mind is on Mattie tonight. Oddly, the things I'm dwelling on have little to do with the case and everything to do with the past that built us into the women we are today. I wonder where her thoughts have taken her tonight. Is she agonizing over the deaths of her husband and children? Is she thinking about the words between us? Wondering if Wayne Kuhns did something unforgivable? Blaming herself for not handling the situation differently? Is she as troubled as me?

At ten-thirty, I call Tomasetti.

'I take it you're not going to make it,' he says without preamble.

'I'm sorry.'

'Don't apologize. You're exactly where you want to be and that's the way it should be.'

Something in his voice scrapes at my conscience. Makes me feel callous and self-centered. I tell him about Wayne Kuhns.

'Are you watching her place now?' he asks.

'I thought I'd camp out for a couple of hours.'

'You sure you're not hiding out?' he asks after a moment. 'From me?' *From us?*

He doesn't have to say the words; we're both thinking them. 'I could be.'

'You know, Kate, sooner or later we're going to have to deal with this white elephant that's been hanging out with us for the last few months.'

My initial impulse is to tell him I don't know what he means, but the response would be disingenuous. I'm well acquainted with the white elephant he's referring to, and while it's the one subject I don't want to broach, I owe it to him – to myself – to be honest. If only that weren't so damn hard.

'Do you want me to spell it out for you?' he asks. 'Clear the air?'

His tone reveals no anger. But his frustration with me comes through the line as clearly as if he'd shouted the words. 'You don't have to spell it out.'

'One of us has to, or things are going to stay the same until one of us gets sick of it.'

I bite back the urge to snap at him for bringing up our personal relationship when I'm in the midst of a difficult case. But this discussion has been building for quite some time. Sooner or later – whether I want to or not – we're going to have to deal with it. *Just not tonight.*

'Let's set it aside for now,' I tell him.

'Because of the case? Or because I'm asking for something you can't give?'

'Because I need more time. I don't understand why that's so difficult for you to grasp.'

I know the instant the words are out that they're a mistake. Tomasetti won't be placated by snarky phrases or bullshit. 'Is that lover-speak for we're good as long as things don't get too complicated for you?'

His tone is challenging and cool. I sit there, mute, not sure how to reply. It's as if I'm frozen on the outside, unable to speak my mind. Inside, my emotions are a jumble of molten rock, hot and churning and fusing into something unwieldy and volatile.

'I didn't mean to make you angry,' I say.

'I'd like to know where I stand, Kate. Where *we* stand. I don't think my asking for a little clarification is unreasonable at this point.'

'It's not,' I concede.

He waits, putting me on the spot.

A hundred responses scroll through my mind. *I'm sorry. I like things the way they are. I don't want to ruin what we have.* But I've said it all before. None of them are the answer he's looking for. They won't solve the problem we face now.

'I've given you your space,' he says after a moment. 'I haven't pushed.'

'I know.'

When I don't elaborate, he lowers his voice. 'You're brushing me off. I don't like it.'

'I'm sorry I can't give you what you want.'

'Kate, what the hell does that mean?'

'That means I need some time to figure this out.'

'If you haven't figured this out by now, we're in trouble.'

'Tomasetti, I can't discuss this right now. I have to go.'

He laughs. I don't know if he's genuinely amused by this perplexing impasse, or if he's trying to anger me. 'Of course you do. That's your MO. When things get complicated or difficult, you cut and run.'

'That's not fair.'

'I'm not a fair man. You should know that by now.'

I wait a beat and say, 'Tomasetti, what the hell are we doing here?'

'Arguing, apparently.'

Silence falls between us. I discern his elevated breathing coming through the line and I wonder if he's as upset as I am.

After a moment, he sighs. 'For chrissake.'

The line goes dead.

I know he's gone, but before I can stop myself, I say his name. 'Tomasetti?'

I hate the uncertainty, the need, the hurt I hear in my voice. The hiss of the dead line mocks me. I look down at the phone in my hand, rap it hard against the steering wheel. 'Nice going, Burkholder.'

I start to call him back, but change my mind and end the call before it dials. I get out of the Explorer and slam the door hard enough to rattle the window. The impulse to succumb to the supremely adolescent urge to throw my phone into the ditch is strong, but I resist. Barely. Instead, I opt for the more mature route, stride to the front of the vehicle, and kick the tire as hard as I can.

Feeling like an idiot, more pissed than I have a right to be, I stand there shaking my head at my own stupidity. I'm in the process of clipping my phone to my belt when it vibrates. Mentally, I count to ten, determined to keep a handle on my temper this time. But instead of Tomasetti's number on the display, I'm surprised to see CORONER.

I hit the TALK button. 'You're working late tonight.'

'I have a feeling I'm not the only one.'

Dr. Ludwig Coblentz and I have worked together on several cases in the last few years. He's a respected pediatrician with a busy private practice – and part-time coroner for Holmes County.

'Kate, I'm finalizing the autopsy reports for the Borntrager children, and I wanted you to know about an irregularity I found on the body of the female victim. The six-year-old female, Norah Borntrager.'

Thoughts of Tomasetti fall away. I find myself pressing the phone more tightly against my ear. 'What do you have?'

'In the course of the autopsy, in addition to the physical trauma from the accident itself, I found older bruising. On her buttocks. The backs of her legs.'

'What kind of bruising?' Even as I pose the question, I already know.

'I believe the bruises were put there by a long, narrow instrument, such as a switch or leather crop.'

The thought of those kids being disciplined with a switch

disturbs me deeply. I want to think Mattie is a gentle soul and would never discipline her children in such a harsh manner. But I know that's my own bias talking. Even if she didn't partake in the spanking herself, she looked the other way while her husband did.

'Doc, are you saying she was abused?'

He sighs. 'Look, Kate, I know some parents paddle their kids. I know it's an accepted practice in many homes – and many Amish homes. *I* was spanked as a child and, admittedly, I occasionally spanked my own boys when I thought they needed it. This is different because the vigorous use of a switch is not an acceptable form of discipline for any kid, much less a child with special needs.'

I tell him about my conversation with Dr. Armitage at the Hope Clinic. 'The surviving child, David, told the doctor his father had spanked him for stealing a pie and eating it.'

'So we have a pattern.' He pauses, thoughtful. 'Even though Paul Borntrager – the likely perpetrator of the discipline – is deceased, I'm bound to notify Children Services. As you know, that will prompt an investigation. A social worker will likely perform an in-home evaluation.'

'As much as I don't like the idea of putting David through any more emotional trauma, I think that's our best route. Our only choice at this point.'

'Now that I know about Armitage's findings, I'll direct Children Services to the clinic as well. They'll want to talk to him, of course. They'll want to know if he has documentation. Some physicians maintain photo or video records.'

'You know they're going to remove David from the home, don't you?'

'Temporarily, I'm sure.'

I fall silent, trying to get my head around all of this and how it will affect the case. How it will affect David. And Mattie.

'Kate.' Doc Coblentz says my name gently, as if he already knows the direction of my thoughts. 'I know you were close to this family. I just want to say this is not an indictment against the mother. If she's innocent in all of this, and by all indications she is, Children Services will conduct a psychological evaluation and see to it that she gets some parenting classes or counseling. It's a win for her and the boy.'

I sigh, unhappily. 'I'll make the call to Children Services,' I tell him. 'Tonight.'

'I know it's not an easy thing, but it's the right thing to do. The only way either of us will have any peace of mind.'

When I end the call, I'm still ruminating the 'peace of mind' comment.

Ten minutes later, I'm back in the Explorer, heading toward the station. Doc Coblentz's words dog me, running through my head like a ticker tape repeating the same bad news over and over again. . . . *the vigorous use of a switch is not an acceptable form of discipline for any kid, much less a child with special needs . . .*

I never would have thought of Paul or Mattie as abusive parents. The notion is a weight on my chest I can't dislodge. I rap my hand against the steering wheel. 'Damn you, Mattie. How could you do that to those kids?' I mutter.

I wish I hadn't pissed off Tomasetti earlier. I'd like to run this by him, get his take on it. I'm thinking about biting the bullet and making the call when I pass by the Hope Clinic. A light in the front window snags my attention, telling me Armitage is still there, working late. I make a quick turn into the lot. There's no vehicle in front, so I drive slowly to the rear of the building. Sure enough, there's a silver Lexus parked at the side. I resolve to talk to the doctor first and then make the call to Children Services.

I park head-in against a row of scraggly bushes, walk around to the front of the building, and take the steps to the porch. I knock. Moths and other insects circle the light as I wait. After a moment, I try the door. Surprise ripples through me when the knob turns. Pushing open the door, I step inside. The place is so quiet I can hear the bugs striking the window.

'Hello?' I call out. 'Dr. Armitage? It's Kate Burkholder.'

I walk past the reception desk, peer over the counter. The phones are quiet, the desktop tidy. I go to the door that leads to the rear and push it open. Three of the four exam room doors are closed. The fourth, Armitage's office, stands open, the light from his banker's lamp bleeding into the hall. I call out again, but no one responds. I'm midway to his office when I hear the French door open. Smoke break, I think, and continue toward his office.

Armitage startles upon spotting me, nearly dropping the ashtray in his hand, a distinctly feminine yelp escaping him. 'Shit, Chief!'

'I didn't mean to startle you.' I raise my hands. 'I was making my rounds and saw the light.'

He lets out a belly laugh. 'Just don't tell anyone I screamed like a girl.'

'Your secret's safe with me.' If I knew him better, I might have razzed him. Since I don't, I keep it professional.

'You're not going to scold me for leaving the door unlocked, are you?' he asks.

'I was thinking about it.'

'You know, when I was working at the clinic in Cleveland, I'd never dream of leaving the front door unlocked, especially at night. Here . . .' He shakes his head. 'I guess I'm getting lax.'

'Well, clinics have become targets of drug thieves in the last few months.' I tell him about a local veterinary hospital that was recently burglarized.

'I do keep some drugs on hand here at the clinic. Sleeping aids. Antianxiety drugs. Samples I've received from my pharmaceutical reps.' He shrugs. 'Living in a town like Painters Mill . . . you don't think about crime like that.'

'Look, Dr. Armitage, I stopped by to follow up on our earlier conversation about the Borntragers.'

'You mean about the children?'

I tell him about the coroner's discovery of bruises on Norah. 'I'm bound to notify Children Services now.'

'I see.' His expression turns troubled. 'That's going to be difficult for Mattie.'

I nod. 'Dr. Armitage, do you think Mattie had anything to do with any of those bruises?'

'I talked to both Paul and Mattie during the months I've been treating the children. I can tell you right now she isn't the one who spanked those kids, Chief Burkholder. Paul was the disciplinarian in the family. He doled out the punishment when it came to the kids.'

'The social worker will probably want to talk with you.'

'You know I'll help in any way I can.' He shakes his head. 'I just hate to see this happen to Mattie, especially now that she's lost Paul.'

'Me, too,' I tell him, meaning it. 'But we have to think of David.'

He nods, but his mouth is pulled into a grimace.

'I appreciate your time, Dr. Armitage, especially so late.'

'No problem.' He motions toward the hall. 'I'll walk you to the door.'

He takes me down the hall and through the reception area. At the front door I extend my hand and we shake. 'Don't work too late, Doc.'

'Twenty minutes and I'm out of here.'

I hear the door close as I descend the steps. Flipping on my Maglite, I traverse the lot to where I parked the Explorer. I'm rounding the front end when something metallic glints in the beam of my flashlight. I glance down to see part of a large steel pin lying in the gravel beneath the bushes. I kneel for a closer look. I almost can't believe my eyes when I see that the pin has been sheared in half.

A tingle of recognition moves through me. 'What the hell?'

I've seen the other half of that pin. I've held it in my hand. Pondered its existence. It's the missing half of the pin found at the scene of the hit and run. How did it get here?

Tugging an evidence bag from a compartment on my belt, I use it to pick it up. It's L-shaped, with a cotter pin intact and still in place. I stare at it, trying to make sense of it. But my heart is pounding because my brain has already made the connection. I don't want to give voice to the thoughts running through my head. Once I unleash that beast I won't be able to contain it. The last thing I want to do is overreact and make an accusation that can't be taken back.

But I don't have the luxury of sticking my head in the sand. It's possible the driver of the truck that hit the Borntrager buggy, for whatever reason, pulled into this lot the night of the murders, perhaps to hide. It's possible that the pin, having been somehow loosened during the impact, fell out and landed here in the gravel.

I look around, my eyes gravitating to the old barn and detached garage. Both buildings were originally part of the farm before the house was donated to the clinic. I don't know if Ronald Hope retained ownership, intending to use them to park his tractor and farm implements or if they're now part of the clinic. The one thing I do know is that either building would be the perfect place to stash a vehicle you didn't want found.

I glance right to see the slant of light coming from the

French doors of Armitage's office. He told me he would be working another twenty minutes. Enough time for me to move the Explorer and have a quick look-see in those outbuildings.

Tossing the evidence bag onto the passenger seat, I start the engine, back out of my parking space, and make a right onto the street. Twenty yards down I find a two-track entrance to a hay field that's shrouded by trees. I pull in and cut the engine. Grabbing my Maglite, I slide out and, sticking to the shadows cast by the trees that grow alongside the road, I backtrack to the clinic.

Once again in the rear lot, keeping an eye on the French doors, I jog to the nearest outbuilding, which is a dilapidated two-car garage. The area is overgrown with weeds and scraggly young trees that have sprouted through the gravel. I stop at the window, set my Maglite against the glass, and peer inside. I see two rusty fifty-gallon drums. An old rotary push mower. A workbench that runs along the wall to my right. Rotting pegboard that hangs at a cockeyed angle. No vehicle in sight, so I start toward the barn.

The massive wood structure was once painted red, but the years and elements have faded it to the color of old blood. Much of the siding has rotted and fallen away. The window glass is long gone. To the right of the barn, an old wood gate has fallen onto its side. I can see where a horse once cribbed at the top rail and gnawed it nearly through. I'm surprised to see evidence that a vehicle has been back here, the grass crushed beneath tires, and I wonder who would be driving around here and why.

It takes a good bit of effort to shove open the massive sliding door, but I take the time to close it behind me. Inside, I flick on my Maglite. Dust motes fly in the beam. The interior smells of dust, moldy hay, and rotting wood. Part of the loft has caved in and boards are scattered about the dirt floor. Above me a startled pigeon takes flight, sending a shower of dried bird shit to the ground. I look up, see the stars through the hit-or-miss boards of the roof. I can hear bats squeaking from the rafters.

I step over a pile of wood, bent nails sticking out like rusty claws. My beam illuminates falling-down stalls, the wooden rails broken and lying on the floor in heaps. Cobwebs cover every surface. I fan the beam in a three-hundred-sixty-degree circle. That's when I spot the newish-looking silver tarp in the corner. Threading my way around the fallen boards and other debris, I make my way toward it.

I suspect there's an antique vehicle under the tarp. Maybe a vintage car or farming implement. After my *mamm* passed away, my siblings and I sold an antique manure spreader for five hundred dollars to one of the tourist shops in town. It sits on the front lawn of the shop to this day.

From ten feet away, I see newish rubber tires peeking out from beneath the tarp. I reach for the corner and pull it off. Dust billows in the beam of my flashlight. I barely notice as the gray Ford F-250 looms into view.

TWENTY-TWO

I'm so stunned by the sight of the truck, I take a step back. I run my beam along the side of the vehicle. It's an older model, but not vintage. Late nineties, maybe. Then I'm around the hood, my eyes seeking out the grille. Something twists in my chest when I spot the snow blade affixed to the front end. The slab of steel where the bumper should be.

'Oh my God.' In the silence of the barn, my voice is wispy and high.

I kneel for a closer look. A sound escapes me when I see black paint on the blade. *Buggy paint*. There's no doubt in my mind that this is the vehicle that hit the Borntrager buggy.

'Son of a bitch.' I hit my lapel mike. 'Six two three.'

'Go ahead,' comes Mona's voice on the other end.

I hear a sound behind me. I spin and catch a glimpse of someone standing there. A burst of adrenaline sends me scrambling back. Simultaneously, I reach for my revolver, yank it out. Before I can bring it up, something slams into the left side of my head.

White light explodes behind my eyes. Pain streaks from my temple to my chin. I careen sideways, lose my balance. My shoulder hits the floor. My head bounces against the hard-packed dirt. Stars fly in the periphery of my vision, but I don't

261

let go of my weapon. Disoriented, I roll, blink to clear my vision, bring up the .38.

The second blow comes down on the crown of my head. The impact snaps my teeth together. I hear my scalp tear. My vision dims. The next thing I know I'm laid out on the floor, looking up at the rafters. I don't know how much time has passed. I have no idea if I'm injured. The one thing I do know is that I screwed up and it's probably going to cost me my life.

Dr. Michael Armitage stands over me, my .38 in his right hand, my flashlight in his left. He's red-faced and sweating profusely. His hair is mussed and pasted to his forehead. But a cold calm resides in his eyes. The transformation from mild-mannered doctor to violent thug stands in such stark contrast that I almost can't believe my eyes.

I taste blood, feel it pooling in the back of my throat, and turn my head to spit. I start to sit up, but he jabs the gun at me. 'Stay down. Don't get up.'

I lie on my back, look up at him. 'What the hell are you doing?'

'Everything I swore I wouldn't.' He uses the muzzle of the gun to tap on his temple, one side of his mouth curving into a smile. 'That happens when we don't exercise our best judgment, doesn't it?'

'I'm a cop.' I intended the words as a reminder that he can't do this to a police officer and get away with it. But my voice is little more than the chirp of a baby bird.

'I know what you are.'

'You can't do this. You won't get away with it.'

'I guess we'll see about that, won't we?'

I can tell by the way he's holding my weapon that he's not proficient with a firearm. He's high on adrenaline. His hands are shaking. But his finger is inside the guard, snug against the trigger. That's the thing about revolvers; they're idiot proof.

Proficient or not, he's close enough so that he could easily get off a lucky shot.

There's still a chance I can regain control of the situation and end it before anyone gets hurt. But it's not going to be easy.

'It's not too late to stop this right now,' I say quietly.

'So if I let you up, we can just shake hands and forget about all of this and be best friends again?' He barks out a laugh. 'Please. You insult my intelligence.'

'A good lawyer could get this knocked down to a lesser charge. You could get off with probation. You can afford the best.'

'Here's a news flash for you, Chief Burkholder: I'm not going to prison because of you.'

I fall silent, use the time to take a quick inventory of my injuries. My left ear is ringing. Pain thuds at the top of my head. Something warm runs down my cheek. I touch my temple with my fingertips and they come away red.

'It wasn't supposed to be like this, you know,' he says.

When I look at him, he's frowning at me. 'Come on, Mike. This isn't you. You're a doctor, for God's sake. Look at all the good you've done. For the kids. Don't throw it away.'

'Word of this gets out and I'll never practice medicine again,' he tells me.

'Probably not.' I glance down at my belt, but my phone and radio are gone. 'There are other things you can do. Research, like what you're doing here. Come on. Let's go inside. Talk things over. You haven't done anything that can't be undone.'

His mouth twists into a parody of a smile. 'You can't undo murder.'

Images of Paul Borntrager's bloody and broken body flash in my mind's eye. I see the dead children, their pale and tender faces upturned to me. They'd wanted to live; they'd deserved the opportunity to live their lives. This man took that away from them.

I envision myself rushing him, grabbing my weapon from his shaking, sweating hands, jamming the muzzle against his chest, and putting a bullet through his heart. If anyone deserves to die, it's this man. This chameleon. This child-killing son of a bitch.

'Did you kill them?' I hear the words as if someone else spoke them. Someone whose hands aren't shaking, whose heart isn't beating out of control. All the things I am not at this moment.

'Perhaps we'll save this discussion for another day. Unfortunately for you, we've run out of time here.' He gives me that strange half smile again. 'Roll over for me.'

I barely hear the command over the thunder beat of my heart. 'How could you?' I ask. 'How could you murder those innocent children?'

'Shut up and turn over. Facedown. Now.'

When I don't obey, he kneels beside me, drops the Maglite to the ground with the beam on me. Then is hand is on my bicep, forcing me onto my stomach.

I keep my head raised, maintain eye contact. He's still holding my .38, the muzzle leveled at my face. 'What are you going to do?' I ask.

'I'm going to fix this situation we've found ourselves in.' He pulls a scrap of fabric or scarf from the waistband of his slacks. 'Put your hands behind your back for me.'

I try to get my hands under me to rise, but he sets the muzzle of the .38 against my back and pushes me back down. 'I will kill you where you lie if you don't do as I say,' he snarls. 'Am I clear?'

When I don't obey, he reaches for my left wrist. There's no way I can allow him to tie me up. He's already killed three people. There's no doubt in my mind he'll do it again to cover his tracks. I twist, make a grab for the .38. My fingers close around his hand, but he yanks it away. I bring up my knees, get them beneath me. I ram his midsection with my shoulder. He reels backward. I reach for the gun with my right hand. I know he's going to hit me with the Maglite an instant before it slams down on my forearm. Pain zings up my arm with such intensity that I cry out. He swings again. I try to get out of the way, but I'm not fast enough and the blow glances off my collarbone.

His hand snakes out, clamps around the back of my neck. Grunting with effort, he shoves my face to the ground, grinds my cheek into the dirt. 'Bitch.'

I try to twist around, lash out at him with my feet, but he's stronger than me and I only manage to graze his thigh with my heel. He climbs on top of me and yanks my hands behind my back. I feel something soft being wrapped around my wrists and drawn tight.

He gives the tether a final yank and then slides off me. 'There. That wasn't so bad now, was it?' Rising, he brushes at his slacks. 'Get up.'

I spit dirt from my mouth. As inconspicuously as possible, I test the binds at my wrists, but they're tight enough to cut off my circulation. When I raise my gaze to his, I find the .38 pointed at my chest. He holds the Maglite in his left hand. I glance around for my radio and cell but he shines the beam in my eyes, blinding me. 'Get up. I won't ask nicely again.'

I get my knees under me and struggle to my feet. 'What are you going to do?'

'We're going to go inside and figure this out.' He motions with the gun toward a side door. 'Walk.'

Up until this point, I'd been operating under the assumption that I could talk my way out of this. That at some point, rationality would intervene and he'd give himself up. Or maybe make a mistake that would cost him the upper hand. Looking at him now, I realize I'd underestimated him.

I start toward the door. 'Let me go, and I'll do what I can to keep you out of prison.'

'What? You'll put in a good word for me? Tell them I'm a good boy who's been misunderstood?' He laughs, but his expression falls abruptly. 'Go through that door or I will drag you.'

Pain thrums in my arm where he hit me with the Maglite earlier. I don't let it keep me from working at the binds on my wrists. I take small steps, keenly aware of Armitage behind me. My mind scrambles for a resolution to this that won't get me killed. Spin and kick the weapon from his hand? Break away from him and run?

I reach the door. He steps around me and pushes it open. I step into the night. 'Is that your truck?' I ask. 'Are you involved with what happened to Paul and the children?'

He doesn't respond. I glance at him out of the corner of my eye. In the glow of the flashlight, I discern the blankness of his expression. It's as if he's gone someplace inside himself. A place where he's no longer hindered by fear or conscience. A dangerous place I can't reach.

We cross the lot and enter the house via the deck. He opens the French door and then we're in his office. I stop, thinking we've reached our destination, but he sets his hand between my shoulder blades and shoves me toward the hall. 'Keep going.'

I start toward the reception area. In the back of my mind I wonder if my dispatcher has tried to raise me on the radio after my abrupt disconnect earlier. I wonder if she became concerned when I didn't respond. I wonder if she notified T.J. and he's out looking for me. That's a best-case scenario, because no one in my department knows I'm here. I parked the Explorer out of sight from the street. Armitage isn't a suspect; he's not even on the radar. No, I think darkly. No one's going to come. If I want to survive, I'm going to have to get my hands on the gun.

Keys jingle and I glance over to see Armitage unlock one of the exam rooms. He opens the door and then steps back. 'Inside.'

'You can't—'

He grabs my arm and manhandles me into the room. The light flicks on. It's a small space, about twelve feet square, with a colorful mural on the wall depicting an Amish boy playing with a Labrador. To my left, there's a sink and counter. A glass canister of tongue depressors. Another filled with cotton-tipped swabs. A Dr. Seuss calendar hangs on the wall. Wood cabinets painted country white. A single window covered with blinds. A frilly valance at the top.

Armitage goes to the counter, pulls a key chain from his pocket, and unlocks an upper cabinet. He's holding my .38 in his right hand and uses his left to remove a small plastic medical kit from a shelf. Glancing at me, he sets it on the counter and begins rummaging inside.

I concentrate on loosening the scarf at my wrists, but I'm not making much headway. There's no phone in the room, but I recall seeing one in the reception area. I wonder if I can reach it before he shoots me in the back.

Armitage is still standing at the counter, pulling items from the kit and setting them next to the sink. Rubber tubing. Packages of needles. A glass vial, the label of which is too small for me to read. A prepackaged syringe. I get a sick feeling in the pit of my stomach.

'What are you doing?' I ask.

'I think I've landed upon a solution to the problem. A little ingenuity and some luck and I might just pull it off.'

I visualize myself rushing him, knocking him off balance, grabbing the gun with my bound hands, turning and firing blind. Emptying the cylinder into him, his body jerking with every slug. But while I'm proficient with a firearm, hitting a target with my hands bound behind my back isn't a realistic scenario.

He turns to me, motions toward the exam table. 'Why don't you slide up on the table for me?'

Behind him on the counter, I see a syringe affixed with a small-gauge intravenous needle. I have no idea what's in it. The one thing I'm certain of is that he plans to harm me.

'I'm not going to let you use that,' I say.

'We'll see.'

I move toward the exam table as if I'm going to obey, then I lunge at him. Bending, I go in low and ram his abdomen with my shoulder, putting the full force of my body weight behind it. He grunts and careens backward, striking the counter. Snarling an expletive, he raises the gun. I kick it from his hand and the weapon clatters to the floor. I scramble toward it, kick it toward the door. It skitters into the hall like a hockey puck.

Armitage dives at the gun. Knowing I don't stand a chance of wresting it from him, I sprint in the opposite direction toward the window. Ducking my head to protect my face and neck, I launch myself at it, shoulder first. The wood blinds crack. Glass shatters. But the blinds keep me from going through. I'm trying to elbow past them when hands slam down on the back of my shirt. A scream rips from my throat as he yanks me back and slings me to the floor.

With my hands bound, I can't break my fall. My head strikes the tile and darkness falls like a curtain.

TWENTY-THREE

The first thing I become aware of is bright light raining down on me from above. I'm lying on the exam table with my arms pinned beneath me. I try to shift, but someone presses me back. A headache pounds at my brain hard enough to make me nauseous, and for a moment I think I'm going to throw up.

'That was a foolish thing to do.'

I try to focus on the face above me. Armitage stands over me, but I'm seeing him as if through waves of heat. I blink, try to clear my vision, but it doesn't help. Snatches of memory trickle into my consciousness. I remember going to the clinic. Finding the truck in the barn. The struggle with Armitage . . .

'You're going to have a bump on your head. That's unfortunate.' He looks at me the way an emergency room physician might look at a patient who's been brought in due to some ridiculous, avoidable accident, which adds a weird twist to an already bizarre situation. 'How are you feeling?'

I raise my head and look around. The room spins. I feel lightheaded and sick to my stomach. I wonder if I sustained a concussion in the fall. Then I remember the syringe and terrible realization dawns.

'What the hell did you do?' My voice is phlegmy, my words slurred.

'Word around town is that you've had some problems with alcohol, Chief Burkholder.' He's wearing studious-looking glasses and peers down at me through the bifocals. 'Do you know how patients with acute alcoholism are treated when they enter rehab and go into detox? It's quite fascinating, actually. I wrote a thesis on the subject when I was in college, before I decided to go into pediatric genetics.'

I stare at him, trying to make sense of his words, the situation. Beneath me, the exam table dips as if I'm on a raft that's careening down some wild, white-water river.

'The abrupt cessation of alcohol can send a patient's body into severe physical withdrawal, which can be very unpleasant. As a preventative measure, the attending physician may administer an IV infusion of grain alcohol.' A faint smile traces his lips. 'The college kids call it Everclear, I believe, though I've never indulged in any of that brain-cell-killing behavior myself.'

'What did you do?' My words are garbled. When I try to rise, he pushes me back down. *What the hell did you do!* But I recognize the effects. I feel the alcohol flowing through my veins, attacking my coordination and balance, affecting my reflexes and thought processes. 'You son of a bitch.'

He tsks. 'I administered the injection while you were unconscious. Directly into your bloodstream with a small-gauge hypodermic at the groin, where no one will find the site.' Gently, he pats my left thigh an inch or so from my crotch. 'Sorry.'

I can't bring his face into focus. My eyes keep trying to roll back. I know the table isn't moving, but the rocking sensation is so real, I feel as if I'm going to be flung into space. In the back of my mind, I wonder if he gave me a fatal dose. If he's waiting for me to take my last breath.

'Why would you do that?' I twist and try to slide off the table. *Why?*

He grasps my throat, pushes me back. For the first time I

notice the latex gloves on his hands. 'We're going to take a little ride.'

'I'm not going anywhere with you.'

The corners of his mouth curve. 'Do you know that old stone quarry a mile or so down the road? The one off that dirt track by the Shilt farm? I'm told the kids swim there in summer.'

I'm so overwhelmed by the bizarreness of what's happening that it takes me a moment to recall the place he's referring to. It's an abandoned quarry known for its deep, cold water.

'You're out of your mind,' I slur.

'I'm afraid you're about to exercise some extraordinarily poor judgment this evening, Chief Burkholder. Being a peace officer, you should know better than to drink and drive.' He brandishes a small bottle of vodka. 'Your drink of choice, no?'

'Nobody will believe that.'

'People *always* believe the worst. Especially if it's juicy.' His smile is cruel. 'You see, you're going to have an unfortunate accident this evening.'

'You can't do that.' My thoughts are so muddled I can barely speak. 'You're insane.'

'I assure you, I'm quite sane.' Bending, he puts his mouth next to my ear and whispers, 'You're going to drive your Explorer into the quarry. You'll be belted in, drunk out of your mind and, unfortunately for you, unable to escape. The weight of the engine will carry your vehicle to the bottom some sixty feet down. It's a tragic accident and the perfect murder rolled into one.'

The cigarette stench of his breath repulses me. 'There's no such thing as the perfect murder.'

'Oh, there might be a few questions. An autopsy will be conducted.' His eyes narrow on mine. 'They won't find the injection site. And any bruises you've sustained tonight can be explained away in your struggle to escape the sinking vehicle. With so much alcohol in your system and this bottle of vodka as evidence . . .' He shrugs. 'On the bright side, the alcohol will act as a sort of anesthesia and ease your discomfort. Drowning isn't such a bad way to go, is it? No blood, anyway.'

I roll, swing my feet to the floor, but my balance is skewed. I stagger and go to my knees. My head spins and I fall onto my side and end up flopping around like a fish.

I'm aware of Armitage coming around the table and pulling me to my feet. I try to curse him, but my words are unintelligible. 'Sonva bitch.'

The room dips and I lean against the exam table. Somewhere in the periphery of my thoughts I'm aware that my face and hands have gone numb. I can barely hold my head upright. My mouth is so dry I can't lick my lips. Unconsciousness beckons, a dark, safe cave I could crawl into, curl up, and sleep until this nightmare is over . . .

My knees wobble and I almost go down again. Holding me upright, Armitage drags me into the hall. I hear my boots against the floor, but I can't seem to keep my feet under me. He takes me to his office and through the French doors and then we're outside, heading toward the gravel area behind the clinic.

'I took the liberty of moving your vehicle while you were out. I hope you don't mind.' He chuckles, and all I can think is that this man has descended into the deepest depths of lunacy.

We reach the Explorer. He props me against the quarter panel, yanks open the passenger door. The instant his hands are off me, I lunge away and totter toward the road. There's not much traffic this time of night, but if a car happens by, I'll flag it down. I only manage to run a few feet when Armitage catches me. I try to twist away from his grasp and end up going to my knees.

'Get off me!' I try to get my feet under me, dig in with my heels, but he drags me back to the Explorer.

'Get in,' he snarls.

When I don't move, he shoves me onto the seat. I lash out with my feet, send him backward with my foot. Twisting, I grapple for the door latch with my bound hands, manage to slam it closed. I hit the lock with my elbow. Hampered by my bound hands and the alcohol in my bloodstream, I scramble over the console, twist, hit the door locks with the heel of my hand. I look for the keys in the ignition, but they're not there.

Then I hear the locks disengage. Through the window I see the keys dangling from Armitage's hand. He opens the driver's side door. Grinding his teeth, he pushes me back over the console and into the passenger seat. Even through the haze of alcohol, I feel the pain of having my arms pinned behind me as he leans close and buckles me in.

A sense of doom envelops me as he starts the engine and pulls onto the road. The gravity of my situation hits home with paralyzing clarity. There's no doubt in my mind he's going to kill me. For the first time I'm afraid I won't be able to stop him.

I can just make out his profile in the dim light from the dash. He's muttering to himself. Nonsensical words only he can understand. It's as if he's in his own world and I'm not there. My eyes fall on my police radio mounted below the dash.

I test the seat belt, but the straps are tight against me. I yank against the fabric binding my wrists, hoping to leave bruises or chafing so that, if I die tonight, the police will know it wasn't by my own hand. It's a desperate, terrifying thought.

Armitage turns onto a gravel road. Tree branches scrape both sides of the vehicle. Dust whirls in the glow of the headlights. He drives too fast, as if he's in a hurry to get this over with and an overwhelming sense of despair grips me. I think of Tomasetti, how we left things, and I realize how desperately I want to live. I'm not going to let this son of a bitch end my life. Hunkering down in the seat, I lift my leg and ram my boot against the shifter.

Gears grind. The Explorer lurches to a stop. Armitage screams, 'You bitch!'

I ram the heel of my boot against the ignition key. The engine dies. Armitage tries to backhand me, but I shrink away and he misses. I twist around and try to get my hands on the seat belt buckle. Simultaneously, I ram my knee against the door handle, hoping to open it. Once. Twice. If I can get out and run, I might be able to lose him in the woods. . . .

Armitage punches the back of my head. My forehead strikes the passenger window hard enough to crack the glass, but I barely feel the pain.

His nails scrape my scalp as he slaps his hand down on the top of my head and grabs a handful of hair. Fire streaks across my scalp when he yanks me toward him. All I can think is that he's leaving evidence. Even if he takes my life, he won't get away with it.

I lean against the seat, breathing hard, my head spinning.

'Don't do that again.' Glaring at me, he starts the engine and puts the Explorer in gear. There's sweat on his temple. A tuft of hair hanging low on his forehead. A crazy light in his eyes.

'The cops are going to appreciate all the evidence you're leaving behind, you son of a bitch,' I tell him.

He sneers. 'I think all the little fishes and turtles down there in that quarry will take care of any so-called evidence.'

Armitage turns onto another dirt road that will take us to the quarry. Tall grass whispers against the floorboards. Tree branches scrape the doors as we bump over ruts and rocks. Then the headlights play over the black surface of the water.

He stops the Explorer scant feet from the bank and engages the emergency brake. I look out over the water, black and glimmering, and fear sweeps through me. Panic threatens, but I fend it off. I know that if I want to live, I've got to keep my head and think my way out of this.

Beside me, Armitage grips the wheel and gazes out over the water. 'I don't know if you can believe this, but before . . . this mess with Paul, I'd never hurt anyone in my life. I'd never broken the law.' He says the words without looking at me. 'I love her, you know.'

He doesn't have to say her name; I know he's talking about Mattie. 'She'll never forgive you for this. She'll never forgive you for what you did to her husband and children.'

He shoots me a look I don't understand. 'Loyal to the end. That's admirable. Really. Unfortunately, it's not going to save your life.'

I look into his eyes, seeking some shred of humanity, but there's nothing there. 'Don't do this, Mike. I'm a cop. If you kill me, you'll get the death penalty. They'll fucking fry you. Let me go and you'll be out of prison in twenty years.'

Without speaking, he gets out and comes around to the passenger side. I hit the lock with my elbow, but he uses the remote key and gains entry. Leaning close, he reaches in and unfastens my seat belt.

'Let's get this over with,' he says.

I stare at him, fear and adrenaline pounding through me even through the effects of the alcohol. 'If the police find my body in the passenger seat, they'll know this wasn't an accident.'

'Nice try. But if you read up on the Chappaquiddick incident, you'd know Mary Jo Kopechne's body was found in the back seat. You see, when cars become submerged, the people inside sort of scramble around, trying to find their way out. It'll be fine.'

Horrific images fly in my mind's eye, but I shove them back, refusing to believe my life will end this way. That's when I realize the effects of the alcohol are starting to wane. I'm still impaired, but my head is clearer. I'm able to think. My coordination is beginning to return.

Gripping the back of my neck, he forces me to lean forward, pressing my forehead against the dashboard. He clips my cell phone to my belt then tosses my radio onto the seat. I'm surprised when he cuts the binds at my wrists. The instant my hands are free, I lunge at him, wrap my arms around his hips, drive him backward. He tries to keep me in the car, but I brace my feet against the rocker panel and shove off. He reels backward. I go with him and we land in the weeds with me on top. An animalistic sound erupts from his throat and the next thing I know he punches me below my ribs. The air leaves my lungs in a rush. I double over, retching, fighting for air. I mentally grab for consciousness, drag it back. But I know I'm done. Better to save my energy for what comes next.

Vaguely, I'm aware of him rising, lifting me, and carrying me back to the vehicle. He shoves me into the passenger seat. Wheezing, I reach for him, grasp his shirt with my fists. But he disentangles himself, slams the door, and locks it.

I'm not claustrophobic, but I feel the dark cloak of it descend. I'm trying to unclip my cell phone from my belt when the driver's side door opens. Armitage leans in, releases the emergency brake and puts the Explorer in gear. The transmission engages. The Explorer rolls forward.

Terror rips through me. 'Help me!' I try to open the door, but it's locked. When I start to scramble over the console, he thrusts the bottle of vodka at me, splashing the alcohol in my eyes. I'm too frightened to feel the burn. I claw at his arm, but he shoves me back. He tosses the bottle and my .38 onto the driver's side floor. I make a wild grab for the gun, but miss.

'Safe travels.' Armitage slams the door and lurches back.

'Fuck you!' I scream.

The Explorer rolls down the bank and plunges into the water.

TWENTY-FOUR

The quarry bank is a sheer drop-off, like that first big plunge of some monster roller coaster. The Explorer jolts as the front tires roll off the rocky ledge. Steam sizzles and shoots out from under the hood. Through the windshield, I see the dual slash of headlights through tea-colored water. The sight of that water washing over the hood induces a moment of mindless panic.

On instinct, I press my hand against the dash, as if I can somehow prevent the vehicle from the inevitable nosedive. Water pours in around my feet and climbs up my legs at an alarming rate. The smells of moss and fish and mud fill my nostrils. Panic slashes me, a heavy blade busting through bone. I fight to stay calm, but some fears are so ingrained they can't be overcome by logic or reason.

Water rises over the dash. The Explorer noses down at a steep angle. Gravity throws me face down in the water. I come up sputtering, suck in a breath, and then I thrust my body across the console. Arms outstretched, I plunge into the water and feel around for my .38. Past the steering wheel. The front of the seat. I touch the floor mat. The brake pedal. *Where the hell is my gun?* All the while the vehicle fills and begins to sink.

I jam my hands into the space between the door and the seat.

My fingertips brush against steel. I make a wild, blind grab, and my hand finds the barrel. Twisting, I feel my way through the darkness to the driver's side door. Lungs bursting, I fumble for the latch, yank it hard, but the door doesn't budge. The pressure of the water, I realize.

Gripping the .38, I push off the seat with my feet to find air. My face smashes into the cage that separates the backseat from the front. There's air beyond, but I can't get to it. I kick the driver's side window with both feet. Once. Twice. I can't get enough thrust to break the glass.

I touch the window with my hand to orient myself. Then I bring up the .38 and fire twice. A muffled *plunk!* sounds. The concussion brushes against my face. I can't see; I don't know if I hit my target. Twisting, I bring up my feet and mule kick the glass. Relief crashes over me when I feel it give beneath my boots. I thrash, snake through the window, and kick clear of the vehicle. For an instant, I don't know up from down. Then I catch a glimpse of the headlights below me, and I swim in the opposite direction.

The cold and darkness crush me. My need for air is an agony. Ears bursting, I claw toward the surface. My lungs convulse, and I suck in water. Coughing wracks my body. Water in my mouth. In my eyes and ears. And I know this is what it's like to die.

I break the surface, choking and retching. Drowning is not a silent thing and terrible sounds tear from my throat as I struggle to breathe. I'm aware of the vast emptiness of deep water beneath me, my boots and clothing tugging me down. Treading water, I look around, try to get my bearings. I'm a strong swimmer and dog-paddle toward shore. Five feet from land, my feet make purchase on a rocky ledge. I reach out, feel moss-slick rocks. I crawl through a stand of cattails. When I'm clear of the water, I collapse in the weeds and throw up twice.

For several minutes, I lay there, gasping and shivering and nauseous. When I can move, I reach for my phone, but it's dead.

That's when it strikes me that Armitage could be standing on the bank, waiting to finish me off. Sitting up, I scan the shore, but there's no sign of him. I suspect he's already hoofing it back to the clinic, which is a mile or so down the road, to hide any evidence that I was there. With no radio or phone, my only option is to walk to the nearest house.

My boots are filled with water so I toe them off, dump the water, and put them back on. I struggle to my feet, but stagger, nearly go to my knees. My clothes are waterlogged. I'm lightheaded and seriously cold, shaking uncontrollably. I don't care about any of it because I'm alive.

Waist-high weeds crackle beneath my feet as I stumble up the bank. At the brink, I stop and listen, but the night is silent. I skirt the north side of the quarry and then follow the path back to the road. I've gone only a few feet when I spot Armitage thirty yards ahead, running along the shoulder.

Sticking to the shadows of the trees that grow alongside the road, I follow him. When he reaches the clinic, he cuts through the parking lot and bypasses the front door, going around the right side of the building. I hang back, out of sight, and watch him disappear. I wait until I see a light in the window and then walk along the tree line toward the rear.

I reach the deck. I see Armitage through the French doors. He's disheveled and pacing his office. He looks panicked and scared, his hands going repeatedly to his head and clenching his hair as if he's going to pull it out. After a several minutes of that, he goes to his desk, collapses into the chair, and puts his face in his hands.

Holding my .38 at the ready, I step onto the deck. My feet are silent as I sidle to the French doors, one of which stands open a few inches. Four feet away, Armitage sits at his desk with his back to me, his phone to his ear. I wonder who he's calling and why. I ease open the door. The hinge creaks. Armitage jumps to his feet, spins to face me, makes a sound like the growl of some startled animal. The phone falls to the floor at his feet.

I step inside, level the .38, center mass. 'Get your hands up. *Get them up now!*'

He blinks at me as if emerging from a fugue. His face goes corpse white. His mouth opens, his jaws working, but he doesn't make a sound. He doesn't obey my command.

'Get your hands up or I will shoot you!' I shout. 'Get them up! Get on your knees! *Now!*'

His hands fly up. His eyes go wild. I see the fight or flight instinct kick in and I know he's not going to go down easy.

'On your knees!' I shout. 'Get your hands behind your head! Do it now or I will put a bullet in you!'

My pulse skitters wildly, a high-octane mix of adrenaline and rage and fear that's powerful enough to make me shake. But my gun arm is steady, my finger snug against the trigger. I have no compunction about using deadly force if I have to.

'This is not my fault!' he chokes out as he lowers himself to his knees.

'Get on the floor, you sick fuck. Facedown.'

He goes to his hands and knees and then lays flat. 'I tried to get to you. After the vehicle went into the water. I tried, but it went down too fast.'

I glance down at his feet. His slacks are wet only to his knees. His shoes are covered with mud. 'I guess that's why your clothes are wet,' I say nastily.

'I swear! I—'

'Put your hands behind your back.'

He obeys, keeping his head turned toward me. 'I didn't want to do this. I'm no killer.'

Blocking his voice lest I lose control and ram my fist into his face, I pull the handcuffs from the compartment on my belt and walk toward him. 'Do not fucking move or I swear to God I'll put a bullet in your heart. Do you understand?' I kneel and set my knee in the small of his back. Holding my gun with my right hand, I snap the cuffs onto his wrists with my left and crank them down tight.

'You son of a bitch.' Relief is a sigh against my nerves as I holster the .38. Rising, I look around for a phone, spot the wireless on the floor. Keeping an eye on him, I snatch it up and dial the station. Mona answers on the first ring. 'Painters Mill PD!'

I identify myself and tell her, 'Ten twenty-six.'

'Chief! My God, I've been trying to get you on the radio for an hour. T.J.'s looking—'

'I'm at the Hope Clinic. Tell T.J. to get out here as fast as he can.'

'Roger that.' In the stunned silence that follows, I hear the click of computer keys. 'He's seven minutes out.'

'Ten thirty-nine.'

'Ten four.'

I toss the phone onto the desk and look at Armitage. I feel like kicking him after what he did to me. He's watching me, his expression telling me he might try to talk his way out of this, so I put my temper aside and recite to him his Miranda rights. 'Do you understand those rights?'

He nods, then sighs, puts his forehead against the floor as if he's considering pounding it against the wood. 'It wasn't supposed to happen this way.'

'What way is that?'

'No one was supposed to get hurt.'

I hear my molars grinding. 'What the hell did you expect when you rammed that buggy with your truck?'

'It wasn't like that. It was an accident. I was frightened. I hit my head and I suspect I was in shock. I panicked.'

'You killed an Amish man and two children. You devastated a family.'

He chokes out a sound of indefinable emotion. 'I know what happened. Like I told you, it was an accident. Once I came to and realized what had happened, I felt . . . it was the worst feeling I've ever experienced in my life.'

'I guess that's why you stopped to render aid while that man and two innocent children were lying on the shoulder dying. That's why you called nine one one. And that must be the reason why you tried to kill me tonight. Because it was an *accident*, right? Because you *care*?'

He shakes his head as if disbelieving I could be so callous. 'You don't understand.'

'I don't want to understand.' Disgusted, I glance toward the hall, watching for the flash of police lights through the front window. 'Is that your truck I found in the barn?'

The look he gives me is so cold, so devoid of anything human, that I feel the hairs on my arms prickle. 'I'm not going to answer any more questions until I have an attorney.'

'That's your right.' I force a smile that feels like broken glass on my face. 'You know we've got you dead to rights, don't you? No matter what you say or do, you're going down.'

Closing his eyes, he sets his forehead against the floor.

Movement outside the French doors draws my attention. I glance over, expecting T.J., wondering why he's come around the rear. Shock jolts me when I discern the slender figure in the black dress and apron. The pale face and white *kapp*. I catch a glimpse of the shotgun an instant before the blast shatters the door.

Glass and fragments of wood pelt me. I drop to a crouch, but not before something hot tears through my right hand, knocking the .38 from my grasp. I watch in horror as the weapon clatters away. I start to retrieve it, but shock freezes me in place when

Mattie steps through the destroyed French door, a shotgun in her hands, the muzzle leveled at me.

The room falls silent. Papers from Armitage's desk flutter down. Pain thrums in my hand and shoots like a hot wire to my elbow. I glance down to see blood dripping on the floor next to my foot. A sliver of wood the size of my thumb sticks out of the top of my hand and through the palm.

My .38 lies on the floor to my right four feet away. 'Mattie.' My voice is so low and rough I barely recognize it. 'What are you doing?'

Her expression chills me. There's no shock. No emotion. Her demeanor is calm, her eyes filled with purpose and deadly intent. Armitage wriggles toward the gun, uses his foot to slide it closer to him. 'Give me the key to these handcuffs, Burkholder.'

I can't tear my eyes away from Mattie; I can't make sense of her being here. Disbelief is a bullwhip snapping at my back, laughing at me, flaying my flesh, drawing blood, slicing me open so that some vital part of me pours onto the floor like entrails.

'Mattie,' I say, 'put the gun down.'

'Shoot her,' Armitage says. 'Kill her. Do it!'

'For God's sake, don't.' I look at him, motion toward Mattie with my eyes. 'Backup is on the way. Stop this or you're going to get her killed.'

'The key.' His lips peel back in an animalistic snarl, and for an instant he looks as if he's going to pounce and tear me to shreds with his teeth. 'Give it to me. Now.'

I turn my attention to Mattie, try to break through the shell of whatever she's surrounded herself with to get to the warm and caring person beneath. The woman I've known for half of my life. The girl I'd once loved more than my own sister.

'Mattie,' I whisper. 'Honey, don't do this. Think about David. He'll be alone without you. Please. He needs you.'

She looks at me, but her eyes skim over me as if I'm not there. 'David doesn't matter anymore.'

Something sick and ugly moves through me. 'What do you mean?' I ask.

'He saw us.'

'Saw what?'

'He's the only one who knew,' she tells me. 'He was going to ruin everything.'

'What did you do?' Panic and urgency and cold, hard fear echo in my voice. 'Mattie, for God's sake what did you do? Where's David?'

My words have no effect. When she looks at me, her eyes are devoid of everything that had once made her a human being, a mother capable of love and compassion. Her mind has fractured and something evil has crawled out of the crevice. I'm no longer her friend, but an impediment to her goal. And I know that no matter what I say or do, this is going to end badly. It's only a question of who will die and at whose hand.

The shotgun is an old break-action, double barrel, probably handed down to her from her father. A deadly weapon to be sure. But there's only one shot left. . . .

I try to flex my injured hand. Fresh pain sends red streaks across my vision. I don't think any bones are broken, but it's badly damaged. Even if I can reach my .38, I'm not sure I can grip it or pull the trigger.

Armitage gets to his knees, his eyes on me. 'I'll happily take that key off your dead body. Give it to me!'

Ever aware that Mattie is less than ten feet away with a shotgun, I ignore him, try instead to engage her. Get her talking, bring her back to a place where I can reach some small part of her. 'Do you want me to give him the key?'

She looks at me, and for an instant she looks like her old self. As if she's going to lower the weapon and burst into laughter.

She'll tell me this is a big joke and we'll spend the next ten minutes laughing our asses off.

But there's an icy glint in her eyes. A sheen I've seen before in the course of my career. She has the dead eyes of a killer. And I can't help but think: *Please don't make me kill you.*

Armitage is staring at Mattie, his eyes narrowed, his expression anxious and sharp. 'Everything's going to be all right, Matt,' he tells her. 'Just get the key from her and take these cuffs off me. We'll take care of her and then we can go. Just you and me. Like we planned.'

Like we planned.

Until this moment, I've been able to keep a handle on all those gnarly suspicions trying to claw their way into my brain. Keep my emotions at bay. I'm in cop mode and focused on staying alive, stopping this by whatever means necessary. But the realization that Mattie knew, that she was a willing participant in the murders of her husband and children, knocks me off kilter.

A thousand memories of her rush my brain. Mattie, my big sister and best friend rolled into one. Mattie, the instigator of mischief. The girl who could make me laugh until I cried and ease my hurt with a single word. She was the one person in this world I'd trusted and admired. Looking at her, I know that girl, the person she'd once been, is gone, replaced by a stranger I've never really known at all.

'Mattie, I'll do whatever you want.' I raise my hands, making sure she gets a good look at my injured hand. 'I'm going to give him the key, okay?'

With my left hand I reach for the compartment on my belt. Next to me, the banker's lamp atop the desk casts soft light onto the blotter where slivers of glass glint like diamonds. No one turned on the overhead lights so it's the only source of light in the room. The lamp's electrical cord dangles less than a foot from where I stand.

Snapping open the handcuff compartment, I make a show digging out the key. 'Everything's going to be all right.' But my focus is on my .38, which is on the floor, next to Armitage.

'Hurry up.' The doctor glances at Mattie. 'Matt, honey, get the key from her. Quickly, before the police arrive. Take these cuffs off—'

I kick the power cord. The lamp flies off the desk. Light plays crazily on the ceiling and then the lamp crashes to the floor. The room goes black. I drop and dive toward the .38.

Armitage shouts, 'Kill her! Shoot her!'

On my hands and knees, I scramble for the gun. Armitage kicks at me, but his foot just grazes my shoulder. My right hand brushes the gun. I grapple for it, grip it hard, ignoring the pain. Armitage lashes out again, so I bring the gun around and fire blind.

He howls like a dog on fire. I hear him rolling around, feel him moving against me. Too close. Still dangerous. No time to do anything about it. I glance toward the French door. In the faint light, I can just make out Mattie's silhouette, shotgun raised to her shoulder.

'Mattie! *Don't!*' I scream the words as I raise the .38, take aim.

Time stops. My eyes meet hers. For the first time in the course of my career, I freeze. I see her finger on the trigger. I know she's going to kill me if I don't stop her. I see intent on her face. I brace for the inevitable blast.

Suddenly I can move. I drop and roll toward the desk, my only cover. The blast deafens me. Tiny missiles of wood and pellets and debris pelt me. But I feel no pain. All I know is I'm alive.

Somehow I get my hands and knees under me. Pieces of wood and glass fall from my hair and shoulders as I struggle to my feet.

The shotgun clatters to the floor.

'*Mattie!*' Armitage screams her name, but I barely hear him.

I stare at the dark shadow of her standing motionless just inside the French door. Not trusting my legs, I lean heavily against the desk, holster my .38.

'Nobody move.' I'd intended the words as a command, but they're little more than a whisper. 'Don't move.'

On the wall next to the ruined door, I see a wash of headlights and the flashing red and blue strobes from T.J.'s cruiser. I choke out a sound; I don't know if it's a sob or a laugh of irony because even though no one was killed here tonight, he's too late to save any of us.

In the dim light I see Armitage lying on the floor, looking at me, his hands still secure behind his back. 'I've been shot,' he croaks.

I see blood on his shirt, but I don't know where it's coming from. I don't go to help him. I'm not sure I can move, even if I wanted to. My arms and legs are shaking violently. I can feel my heart pulsing in my throat. The pound of it making me dizzy. I stumble to the light switch by the door, flip it on. Stark light rains down. Glass and bits of wood from the French doors cover the floor. The shattered lamp lies in pieces next to the desk. Drops of blood from my injured hand glitter like tar against the hardwood floor. The shotgun lies just inside the French doors. I see Mattie standing on the deck outside, unmoving, looking like the dazed survivor of some natural disaster.

Using the desktop for support, I start toward her. Glass crunches beneath my boots as I cross to the door. I open it, step onto the deck. 'Mattie.'

Slowly, she turns to me. Her face is pale. Eyes that had once been so lovely and full of mischief are cruel and level on me.

I know better than to feel anything at this moment, especially for a woman who doesn't deserve compassion, least of all mine. But some emotions are so powerful, some losses so profound, that they can't be stubbed out by logic or will. My brain orders me to go through the motions and do my job. Cuff her. Make the arrest. Be done with it.

Since I used my cuffs to secure Armitage's hands, I tug the zip ties from my belt. 'Turn around and give me your wrists,' I tell her.

When she doesn't move, I reach out, turn her around, and slip the ties around her wrists, pull them tight. It doesn't elude me that while my hands are shaking, hers are rock steady.

Once the ties are in place, I turn her to me. 'Where's David?' I ask.

She looks at me, but there's nothing behind her eyes. It's like looking into the face of a mannequin and expecting to see life. 'I had to do it,' she says. 'He wasn't supposed to live, you know. He was the only one left who knew.'

Using my forearm, I push her against the wall, hold her in place. *'What did you do?'*

'Chief?'

The sound of T.J.'s voice spins me around. He's standing at the door, his .38 in his hand. 'You okay?' He starts toward me, his eyes flicking from me to Armitage to Mattie. 'What happened?'

'Get someone out to the Borntrager farm,' I tell him. 'Fast. I think she hurt the boy. Ambulance, too. *Hurry.*'

Never taking his eyes from mine, he hits his lapel mike and puts out the call. When he's finished, he crosses to me. 'What the hell happened?'

Somehow I get the words out. It's as if someone else is speaking them. Someone stronger than me. Someone who isn't coming apart on the inside.

The radio cracks to life as the call goes out and I know every cop on duty within a ten-mile radius is making tracks to the Borntrager farm.

'I need to get out there. Check on the boy.' I start toward the door only to realize I don't have a vehicle.

'No offense, Chief, but you're looking a little shaky on your feet.'

He's right. I don't know if it's from my ordeal in the water, the alcohol that was injected into my bloodstream, or the shock of learning my childhood friend is a monster, but I'm shaken and dizzy. That's not to mention the shard of wood sticking out of my hand, which is starting to hurt in earnest now that my adrenaline has ebbed. But I'm worried about David. I can't help but think of all the terrible things that could have happened to him.

T.J. squats next to Armitage and begins checking him for weapons. I turn toward Mattie. She's looking at me, as if trying to figure out how to work the situation to her advantage, how to play me. Never taking my gaze from hers, I place her under arrest. She remains silent as I Mirandize her. 'Do you understand your rights?'

Before she can reply, a communiqué crackles over T.J.'s radio. The Borntrager farmhouse is in flames. I listen, horrified and outraged, on the verge of a panic I can barely contain. I wait, expecting the worse.

I turn back to Mattie. I feel my eyes crawling over her, and I understand how a police officer could step over the line. 'How could you do that to your own child?'

She regards me with a cool resolve. 'David saw us together. Michael and I. At the clinic. I told him it would be our little secret, but I knew eventually he'd tell someone. He was a stupid, stupid child.'

'What in the name of God happened to you?' I ask.

'You think you know what it's like.' Her voice is so cold I feel the rise of gooseflesh on my arms. 'Being Amish. Having three special-needs children. A weak, ignorant husband who was so afraid of God he could barely bring himself to touch me. They were a burden. They relied on me for everything. *Everything*. I was a slave to them. To the Amish and all of their self-righteous morals. I wanted more. I *deserved* more.'

'You could have left.'

'That's so easy for you to say.' Venom leaches into her voice. 'You got out. You found your life. I stayed and they were killing me. I hated them for it.'

Sirens wail in the distance. Somewhere in the periphery of my consciousness I hear T.J. moving around. His boots grinding broken glass against the floor. The hiss and chatter of his radio.

I glance over my shoulder to find him looking at me expectantly. I don't know what he sees in my eyes, but I'm compelled to say, 'I'm okay.'

'I know you are,' he replies.

He's barely gotten the words out when a Holmes County Sheriff's deputy's voice comes over the radio to report that he's found David Borntrager unharmed.

Casting a final look at Mattie, I walk away.

TWENTY-FIVE

The next hours pass in a flurry of activity of which I don't seem to be a part of because I'm not participating. I'm not in shock, but as I answer a barrage of questions from T.J. and two deputies from the Holmes County Sheriff's department, I feel as if I'm operating from inside an airtight jar. I hear my voice, I see their responses, hear their words. But somehow we're not quite connecting.

Within minutes of T.J.'s initial call, Glock and a young social worker with Children Services were sent to the Borntrager farm. A second deputy was dispatched to the quarry where my vehicle sits in sixty feet of water. I'm standing on the sidewalk in front of the clinic with a blanket over my shoulders when Mattie is taken into custody. Time slows to a crawl when her eyes meet mine. I don't know what she sees on my face, but she can't seem to stop looking at me. I'd wanted a few minutes alone with her. I want to know how much she knew. When she knew it. I need to know if she's as guilty as Armitage. But I let the moment pass and then she's gone.

I was given an obligatory physical exam by an EMT at the scene. I balked, of course, but because of my ordeal in the water, the injury to my hand, and the injection administered earlier by Armitage, I was taken by ambulance to the ER at Pomerene Hospital, where a young resident took two vials of blood, removed a four-inch sliver of wood from my hand, and spent an hour bandaging, prodding, and making jokes that weren't quite funny. I appreciated the attempt at humor nonetheless.

Sheriff Mike Rasmussen showed up shortly after my arrival and stuck by me like a two-year-old to his mommy. I don't know if he was there in a law enforcement capacity or if he was there to support me. It didn't matter; I was glad for the company. Once I was given a clean bill of health, he whisked me to his cruiser and did a decent job of making small talk during the drive to the Sheriff's Department in Millersburg. Once there, I was given coffee, offered a cigarette – which I accepted despite the fact that the office is a smoke-free environment. I was taken into the largest and most comfortable interview room and spent the next hour going over every detail, from the moment I found the pin in the gravel behind the clinic to when T.J. arrived on scene. I answered every question posed, laughed when appropriate, and basically played the role to which I'd been cast. By the time we're finished, I'm exhausted and numb and want badly to go home, shower, and fall into bed.

I don't know who called Tomasetti, but he's waiting for me when I walk out of the sheriff's office. My stride falters when I spot him, leaning against the Tahoe, his cell phone against his ear. He watches me approach, mutters something into the phone, and hangs up, all the while his eyes never leaving me.

I greet him with, 'Who are you talking to at two o'clock in the morning?'

'My mom.'

The sound that escapes me sounds nothing like the laugh I intended. His mother passed away some ten years ago. I suspect he was getting a quick update from Rasmussen.

He rounds the front of the SUV and opens the passenger door for me. 'Everything go okay in there?'

'I'm probably off the case.' I slide onto the seat and fasten my belt.

'You're too close to it. Might be a good thing.'

'I wanted to finish this.'

'Imagine that.' His voice is teasing, but a thread of gravity comes through. 'Just so you know, Kate, I'm not going to let you go home and lay into that bottle of vodka.'

'The thought never crossed my mind.'

He gives me a knowing look before slamming the door.

We don't speak on the drive to my house. He doesn't bother parking in the alley this time, but I don't remind him about small towns and gossip. The truth of the matter is, I don't care. I'm like a zombie as he guides me to the front door and takes my key to open it.

It's strange, but my own house feels alien to me. After the last hours, it seems too normal and homey, as if I don't belong in such a place after everything that transpired tonight. Tomasetti takes me to the bathroom off the hall, shoves open the shower curtain, and turns on the water.

'I'll get you some clothes and a plastic bag for that hand,' he tells me.

My uniform smells of lake water and sweat. When I look down at the front of my shirt and slacks, I'm shocked by the sight of blood. I don't know if it's mine or Armitage's. Tomasetti returns with a plastic bag, which he places around my bandaged hand and secures with a rubber band at my wrist. Then he's gone and I'm alone again. I try to avoid the mirror as I undress, but it's a small room and I catch a glimpse of myself as I peel off my shirt. I see a pale, bruised face and haunted eyes and all I can think is that I don't know this woman. She can't be me because she looks like a victim and that's the one thing I swore I'd never be again.

Turning away, I drop my clothes on the floor and step into

the shower. I turn the water on as hot as I can stand and spend ten minutes scrubbing my skin pink. I don't let myself think as I go through the motions. My mind flatlines. When I'm finished, I emerge to find sweatpants, underwear, and a tee-shirt on the counter.

I find Tomasetti sitting at the kitchen table, texting. He looks up when I enter and puts away his cell. He's got a good poker face, but I don't miss the quick flash of concern at the sight of me – or the wariness that follows.

'Texting your mom?' I ask.

He withholds a smile. 'How's the hand?'

'Hurts.'

'Are you hungry?'

I shake my head. 'Any word on David Borntrager?'

'I talked to Glock while you were in the shower. David's fine. He's going to spend the night with a foster family. It's still early in the game, but the social worker thought they'd eventually place him with his grandparents.'

'He's only eight years old. In the last week, he's lost his entire family. His *datt*. His siblings.' I can't bring myself to say Mattie's name. 'Have they taken Armitage's statement?'

'He's asking for his attorney.'

'We've got him dead to rights.'

'I think you're right.'

'Did they find the pin?' I ask. 'The piece I found?'

'Rasmussen didn't say.'

'They're still processing the scene?'

'Probably going to be there all night.'

'What about the quarry?'

'Highway patrol and a couple of your guys are out there now. First light, they'll send in a couple of divers, get a wrecker out there to pull out your Explorer.'

For an instant I'm back in the vehicle. Black water closing

over my face. Like ice against my skin. The stink of mud in my nostrils. The need for a breath an agony in my chest . . .

The sound of my name snaps me back. I think about the Explorer sitting at the bottom of the quarry, and I choke out a laugh that sounds slightly hysterical. 'The town council is going to have to buy me a new vehicle.'

Tomasetti smiles, but it's a polite gesture. He's worried about me and trying to get a handle on my frame of mind. Good luck with that.

We fall silent again. To my right, the faucet drips into the sink. The vent at the bottom of the refrigerator rattles when the motor kicks on. 'Did Rasmussen find the truck parked in the barn behind the clinic?'

Tomasetti nods. 'It's already been towed to impound for processing.'

'It's the vehicle Armitage used to killed Paul Borntrager and his two children. Tomasetti, there was a snow blade attached . . .' I lose my breath and can't finish the sentence.

'I know,' he says gently.

'That son of a bitch murdered those two sweet children,' I tell him. 'How could someone do that? How could Mattie allow it?'

He stares at me. 'I don't know.'

For the span of several minutes neither of us speaks. We contemplate each other. I can only imagine how I must look to him. Emotionally shaky. Too involved. Slightly off. I feel like glass that's been blown too thin and will shatter at the slightest touch.

'She almost killed me.' I try to swallow, but I don't have enough moisture in my mouth. 'I loved her like my own sister. What in the name of God happened to her?' It hurts to say the words, and for the first time tears threaten.

Tomasetti looks away, sighs. 'I don't know, Kate.'

'Have her parents been told?'

'I don't know.' He glances at his watch. 'Probably by now.'

'I should have done it. I should have been the one to tell them.'

'You're the last person who should be talking to them about their daughter. You're exactly where you need to be.' He walks to the refrigerator, pulls two bottles of Killian's Irish Red from the shelf, turns back to me, and holds them up. 'In lieu of the Absolut.' He sets the bottle on the table and pulls out my chair. 'Sit down.'

I lower myself into the chair and pick up the beer, but I don't drink. 'Mattie and Armitage . . . I think they were having an affair.'

'That makes sense.'

'The night there was an intruder at her farm. It was Armitage.' I think about that a moment, feeling foolish and inept. 'He couldn't stay away from her. He didn't know I was watching the place. It was Mattie who broke the glass. To cover for him. I was too blind to see any of it.' I look up from the table-top and meet his gaze. 'He killed Paul and the children so he could have her for himself.' I take a drink of the beer, but I don't taste it. 'I think she knew. About all of it.'

'The truth will come out.'

'Tomasetti, I *knew* her. Inside and out. Her thoughts. Her dreams. Her heart. I can't believe I didn't see something. I should have—'

'Some people lie to their last breath.'

'She was my best friend.'

'I'm your best friend.'

The words, the kindness, and the truth behind them triggers something inside me, like the shattering of glass. Setting down the beer, I lower my face into my hands and begin to cry.

*

It took me two days to catch the cat. It's not that he doesn't like me. He does. But he's feral. Like me, he's been kicked around a little and sometimes it shows, usually to his own detriment. He doesn't easily trust. Sometimes he scratches the people who care for him most. I finally nab him using his favorite food. He's not a happy camper when I put him in the carrier.

'It's for your own good,' I tell him as I lug the carrier to my rental car and place it on the passenger seat.

He responds by hissing at me.

Ten minutes later, I take the Toyota Corolla down the lane of Mattie's parents' farm. I pass by an old barn with a fresh coat of white paint, and then the lane curls right, taking me toward the house.

It's been seventeen years since I've been here, but so little has changed I feel as if I'm fifteen years old again as the house looms into view. The kitchen window where Mattie and I used to wash dishes while we whispered about boys still looks out over a cornfield that never seems to produce enough corn. The big maple tree still stands sentinel outside the window that had once been Mattie's bedroom. The same tree she climbed down the night we went to see the midnight screening of *Basic Instinct*. Even the clothesline post still leans slightly toward the barn. I wonder how a place can remain the same for so many years when the rest of the world barrels on with such astounding speed.

It's been two days since my ordeal at the clinic with Mattie and Michael Armitage. I've been put on administrative leave, though I've been told I'll be back on the job by tomorrow afternoon. I haven't slept since that night. Strangely, I'm not tired. I haven't been able to eat, but I'm not hungry. I'm hurting, but it's a silent pain because, after that first morning with Tomasetti, I haven't been able to cry.

Being here today is one of the most difficult things I've ever done in my life. Tomasetti tried to talk me out of it. It's not the first time I didn't heed his good advice. Avoiding Mattie's parents made me feel like a coward. I'm a lot of things – and not all of those things are good. But I'm not a coward.

Ten yards away, the door to the milk barn stands open, so I pick up the cat carrier and the brown paper bag that contains his kibble and head that way. I hear the generator that powers the milk machine rumbling from inside the small building next to the barn. I find Andy Erb in the aisle, sanitizing the udders of the cows he's just brought in from the field. The rest of the cattle are in stanchions and David is pouring feed into the long feeder.

Man and boy look up from their work when I approach. 'Guder mariya,' I say.

Andy Erb stiffens. His expression doesn't change as he straightens and looks at me. He reaches for his grandson, but young David is already running toward me, grinning. 'We're getting ready to milk the cows. Do you wanna watch? I know how to do it.'

I muss his hair, amazed at how resilient he is. That life goes on for him, even without his mother, father, and siblings. 'It looks like fun, sweetheart, but I can't stay.'

He's already eyeing the pet carrier. 'What's inside the little box?' he asks.

Andy approaches us, sets his hand on the boy's shoulder, and eases him away from me. When the Amish man's eyes meet mine, I feel an instant of guilt. I spent half of my life wondering if he'd abused his daughter, never doubting Mattie's insinuation that he had. I'd hated him; I'd hated his wife for looking the other way. If Mattie had asked for my help, I would have done anything to protect her from them. Now, as an adult – and a police officer – I'm relieved she hadn't, because we would have destroyed this man's life and torn his family apart in the process.

Andy's eyes flick to the house, telling me Mattie's mother, Lizzie, is inside and I'm not to go there. 'She doesn't want to see you.'

'Mr. Erb . . .' I say his name, but all the words I so diligently rehearsed on the way over tangle in my throat. Instead, I shove the cat carrier at him. 'I brought this,' I blurt. 'For David.'

'What is it? I want to see!' The boy disentangles himself from his grandfather's hands and bends to peer inside. '*Grossdaddi! Sis kot!* An orange one! Can I keep him?'

To the cat's credit, he doesn't hiss.

Erb stares at the cat as if he's never seen one before. After a moment, he pulls a white kerchief from the pocket of his trousers and wipes his eyes. 'Is he a good mouser?' he asks.

'He's the laziest cat I've ever owned,' I tell him. 'He's got an unpleasant personality. A mean streak, actually. He hisses. A lot. Sometimes he scratches. But he's never bitten me. I suspect he never forgave me for having him neutered.'

The Amish man nods. 'He sounds like a good cat.'

David lets out a squeal. 'What's his name?'

'I've been calling him Custer, but you can rename him if you like.'

'Hi there, Custer. *Wei bischt du heit?*' David peers into the carrier. 'You have a nice pink nose.'

I kneel next to the boy. Setting both hands on his shoulders, I turn him to face me. 'You promise to take good care of him? Make sure he has plenty of food and water at all times, right? Make sure he has shade in the summer and a warm place to curl up in winter?'

'*Ja!* We're going to be best friends. I won't be lonely anymore.'

I offer him the carrier, trying not to look at the cat. I'm not attached to him. Sure, he's gotten me through some tough times; I'll miss him. But I work too many hours to be a good owner to him. Besides, David needs him more than I do.

'Offer him some milk, David,' Mr. Erb says.

'Okay, *Grossdaddi*.' The boy looks into the carrier and eyes the cat. 'You're going to like the milk here, Custer.'

He starts to walk away, but I stop him with, 'Hey.'

He grins at me and I bend to give him a quick, awkward hug. 'Take care, sweetie.'

'I will.' But his attention is on the cat. 'Come on, Custer.'

We watch him walk away. The silence that follows is thoughtful and somehow rings with a sense of finality. After a moment, Erb looks through the open door at the field beyond and sighs with the weariness of a beaten man. 'We knew something was wrong with her.'

He says the words without looking at me, uncomfortably, and the pain I see on his face profound, as if he, as a parent, somehow failed.

I let the silence ride until he meets my gaze. 'I didn't,' I tell him. 'I loved her. I spent a lot of time with her. And I didn't know.'

The sound of a door slamming draws our attention. I turn to see Mattie's mother coming down the steps of the back porch of the house, wiping her hands on a dish towel, looking our way.

Mr. Erb motions for me to leave. *'Die zeit fer is nau.'* Time to go now.

I want to embrace him, but I'm not sure it will be welcomed, so I don't. Instead, I turn away and leave the barn. As I'm walking toward the Toyota, I glance over at Mattie's mother. She's standing at the foot of the steps, clutching the towel, her eyes on me, crying.

The sight of her crushes something inside me. I fight tears as I get into the car and I drive away without looking back.

TWENTY-SIX

It's pouring rain by the time I arrive at Tomasetti's farm. I'd hoped to do some fishing with him on the dock – catch dinner, maybe – drink a couple of beers, listen to the arrival of dusk. But I can't complain about the rain since it's been dry most of the summer and it matches my mood to a T.

I park behind his Tahoe and punch off the headlights. Grabbing the grocery bag off the passenger seat, I swing open the door and hightail it to the back porch. I'm soaked by the time I enter the kitchen, but I don't mind. The rain feels good against my skin. Cleansing somehow. A new start. I keep a change of clothes in the bedroom closet, anyway. Jeans and a tee-shirt I'd brought for an overnight stay, but didn't use.

The house smells of paint and freshly sawed wood. I'd expected to find Tomasetti in the kitchen, finishing up the cabinets that had been delivered the day before, but he's not there. The radio sitting on the five-gallon bucket in the corner is on, the newscaster announcing flash flood warnings for all of Holmes, Warren, and Coshocton Counties until midnight. It crosses my mind that I should get back to Painters Mill in case Painters Creek floods and some dummy decides to drive through the water that sometimes rushes over Dog Leg Road. Then I remember I'm off duty and I put it out of my mind.

'Tomasetti?'

No answer.

I wander into the living room. An aluminum stepladder is set up near the window. A five-gallon bucket of paint sits atop a plastic drop cloth on the floor. Tomasetti is nowhere in sight, so I take the stairs to the second level.

I find him in the largest of the three bedrooms, using a roller with an extension bar as he rolls paint onto the ceiling. He's painted the walls butter yellow. The woodwork and crown molding are still the original stained mahogany. It's a nice look that reminds me of red-winged blackbirds and misty summer mornings.

He glances at me over his shoulder when I enter the room and his eyes linger. He's wearing faded blue jeans that are speckled with paint and worn through at one knee. A gray tee-shirt with the logo from the Cleveland Division of Police. I'm moved by the sight of him. This man who's looking at me so intently, as if he's glad to see me. I don't see how anyone could be glad to see me these days; I haven't exactly been pleasant.

'Forget your umbrella?' he asks.

I glance down at my wet clothes. 'Sorry,' I tell him. 'I'm dripping all over your floor.'

'You can drip all over my floor any time, Chief.' He finishes the section he'd been painting and sets the roller in the paint tray. 'How did it go?'

The question needs no explanation. 'All right, I think. They're pretty broken up, but . . .' Unsure how to finish the sentence, I let my words trail.

He waits, as if knowing there's more I need to say. 'Rasmussen talked to Wayne Kuhns,' I tell him. 'He thinks that at one point Mattie tried to use Kuhns's obsession with her to manipulate him. She told Kuhns that Paul was abusive and Kuhns believed her. She didn't come right out and say it, but she tried to persuade him to do away with Paul. She used the promise of sex as a lure. Once she realized he didn't have what it took, she turned to Armitage.'

'That's classic sociopath behavior.'

'Initially, I thought Kuhns was a viable suspect. But he wasn't. It was her. Kuhns was in love with her. Nothing more than an errant husband. That's why he was so worried about us talking to his wife.'

Tomasetti crosses the distance between us and stops a foot away from me. 'What about the boy?'

I see David's face in my mind's eye. The way he looked at me when I handed him the carrier. The simple joy in his eyes at the sight of the cat. The protective way his grandfather set his gnarled hand on his shoulder. 'I think he's going to be okay.'

He tilts his head, as if trying to get a better look at my face. 'What about you?'

'You know me.' I smile, but it feels tremulous on my face. 'I always land on my feet.'

He nods, but I see something in his eyes that belies the gesture. 'I hate to bring this up, but I thought you should know. Sheriff Redmon has requested a forensic anthropologist from BCI. They've already identified those pellets as number six lead shot.'

The words impact me like a sucker punch to the solar plexus. The kind that takes your breath and makes you sick to your stomach. I look away, trying to absorb the enormity of them. I should have been prepared; I'd known all of this would come. But there are some things no one can ever prepare for. The reemergence of a past that wields the power to destroy your life is one of them.

'I wasn't expecting that,' I tell him.

'I know. I'm sorry to be the bearer of bad news.'

'So what's next? I mean, in terms of the case?' Even as I ask the question, I already know.

'They're trying to extract DNA from the teeth.'

I nod, grappling for a calm I don't feel. 'This hits kind of close to home for you, doesn't it?'

Tomasetti ignores the statement. 'The FA is going to take a look at everything. Soil. Whatever's left of the clothing. Whatever was in the pockets. The bones are probably going to be the most important in terms of cause and manner of death.'

'I thought . . . I mean, I'd hoped . . . there would be some deterioration.'

'I'm sure there is, but to what extent, we don't know.'

I can actually feel the blood stalling and going cold in my veins as the reality of the situation sinks in.

'I'm sorry,' he says. 'I know you've been carrying this around inside you for a long time. I know you want it to be over.'

'How long do you think the investigation will take?'

'You know nothing ever happens quickly in these kinds of situations. Everything has to be looked at. Labs get backed up. Reports have to be written.' He shrugs. 'A few months.'

I've borne the knowledge of what happened that terrible day for half of my life. I learned to live with what I did. I learned to cohabitate, however uneasily, with the knowledge that I took a man's life, that my family covered it up. I learned to deal with the ever-present fear of discovery and the possibility that if the truth is revealed, my life as I know it would end.

As if reading my thoughts, he adds, 'They're not going to be able to tie you to the case, Kate. I've looked at every angle. There's nothing there. No evidence.'

'I have to be prepared either way. So do you.'

He bends, picks up a five-gallon can of paint, and dumps some into the pan. Straightening, he saturates the roller and goes to work on another section of the ceiling.

'Look, Kate, I know you've already tried and convicted yourself, but those bones are too deteriorated to reveal any meaningful evidence. Coroner's going to rule cause and manner of death undetermined.'

'What if you're wrong?' I ask. 'What if by some fluke we haven't conceived, they link Lapp's death to me? Tomasetti, that could pose a problem for you, especially if we're living together. It could put you in a precarious position. It could affect your career.'

He stops painting, lowers the roller to his side, and turns to stare at me, his expression perplexed. 'You like to keep a guy on his toes, don't you?'

'Sometimes it just works out that way.' I try to smile, but don't quite manage. 'I think it's something you need to consider.'

'I've considered everything I need to consider.' He sets down the roller and crosses to me. He stops a scant foot away, so close I can feel the heat coming off him, discern the smells of aftershave and sawdust and man. 'I've worked a lot of cases that hinged on DNA,' he says. 'Even if the lab is able to extract DNA from the teeth, all that does is confirm the identity of the victim. They won't be able to ascertain how or where he died. And there's no evidence whatsoever that could lead them to you. You're safe, Kate. It's over. I promise.'

We stand frozen for the span of several heartbeats. Not touching. Barely breathing. The magnitude of what's been said shaking the air between us.

'I know this isn't an ideal set of circumstances. I mean, for us.' His voice is low and thick. 'I don't know where this will lead. But I love you, Kate. I want you in my life. I don't know what else to say.'

I know this is one of those life-altering slices of time. A moment that will take me down a certain road. There's no way for me to know if it's the right direction or if I'll slam into some dead end or freefall off a cliff. But everything inside me tells me to take that first step. Sometimes life is about taking chances, about putting yourself out there even when you don't know what's going to come back at you. John Tomasetti is a chance I want to take.

'No one's ever said that to me before,' I tell him.

'So we're breaking new ground.'

'In a lot of different ways.'

'I hope that's okay.'

'Better than okay.'

Raising up on my tiptoes, I brush my mouth across his. 'I don't think you're going to get much painting done tonight.'

'It'll keep until morning,' he whispers.

extracts reading groups
competitions books new
discounts extracts
competitions extracts
books new reading groups
new extracts events discounts
events books extracts events
reading groups new reading groups
books new reading groups
interviews extracts
events extracts new books
discounts events
new books events interviews
events new new
discounts extracts discounts
www.panmacmillan.com
extracts events reading groups
competitions books extracts new